Legacy of a Warrior Queen

Legacy of a Warrior Queen

Maria Herring

TOP HAT BOOKS

Winchester, UK
Washington, USA

First published by Top Hat Books, 2014
Top Hat Books is an imprint of John Hunt Publishing Ltd., Laurel House, Station Approach,
Alresford, Hants, SO24 9JH, UK
office1@jhpbooks.net
www.johnhuntpublishing.com

For distributor details and how to order please visit the 'Ordering' section on our website.

ISBN: 978 1 78279 733 3

A CIP catalogue record for this book is available from the British Library.

Design: Stuart Davies

Printed in the USA by Edwards Brothers Malloy

This book is dedicated to my beloved sisters and brother,
Elizabeth, Catherine, Lucy and James.
Also for my cousin, Lulu,
The strongest woman of all time.

The moon of Elembiuos (Claim-time), 60 C.E.
Coed Celidon, Atrebates tribal lands, Brython

Boudica, in her chariot with her daughters in front of her, rode up to tribe after tribe ...

"But now it is not as a woman descended from illustrious ancestry, but as one of the people that I am avenging my lost freedom, my lashed body, the outraged honour of my daughters. Roman greed has developed to such an extent that not even our persons, nor even our age or our virginity are left unpolluted. But heaven is on the side of just vengeance: one legion which dared to fight has been destroyed; the rest are cowering in their camps or anxiously seeking a means of escape. They will not stand even the din and shout of so many thousands, let alone our attack and our weapons. If you balance the strength of our armies and the reasons for this war, then you must conquer or die. This is a woman's decision: as for men, they can live and become slaves."

(Tacitus: Annals, XIV. 35)

– 1 –

The moon of Samonios (Seed-fall), 332 C.E.
Kaer Gradawc, near the Stone Circle, Atrebates tribal lands, Brython

Two of the clay bricks cracked when they hit the ground, scattering salt. Arawn stooped to collect it, knowing he'd never finish before his father came home but needing to take his mind off his sister, who was giggling and skipping towards the roundhouse. This was his home during the dark season. How much better it would be without her and her scurrilous deeds.

"You useless pile of dung! Why can't you watch what you're doing?"

"I'm sorry, Papa," he said, looking up into the time-worn face. "It was Ffraid. She—"

A clout to the head. "You say nothing of your sister. Clean this up before your mother comes out here demanding to know what all the noise is about."

Arawn nodded, pulling his lips tight between his teeth so his father wouldn't see them tremble. He'd passed his sixteenth summer only a few moons back; it wouldn't do to let anyone see him cry.

Misery settling around him like a winter fog, he watched his father stomp towards the roundhouse, heaving his shoulders every now and then under the weight of the tack he'd had mended at the smith's. He watched him until he disappeared through the hide door, nothing but a black hole now the dying sun was setting. He imagined the blast of heat that would blanket him as he stepped into their home, and shivered in the cold.

The first tear fell and he scrubbed at it with a callused fist. Even the pain of knuckles on his face didn't unravel the boiling knot of shame that burned his throat and chest. But his father was right; if Mother deigned to look outside and saw the waste of precious salt, not only would the cursing continue through the rising and setting of the moon, he would be forced to pass another night without any supper.

Squatting, he gathered as much as he could, taking care to pick out any detritus, and put it back in the clay bricks. He placed the broken halves together, wrapping them with hide, then stowed them upright in the pits he'd dug earlier. More hides he packed in around them, as his father had taught him, then covered it all with earth.

A conspicuous amount of salt littered the ground still, and Arawn sought for a solution, rocking back and forth on his haunches while he thought; what should he do? His darting eyes finally landed on a bucket next to the water urn. Soon the Samhain frosts would come to freeze it, but for now there was plenty to flow. His hide shoes made barely a sound when he ran to it, but his heart sped as fast as the water decanting into the bucket from the unstopped tap. Hoping he wouldn't trip and cause a racket, he dashed back to the spilt salt and doused it with water. Still clutching the bucket he scuffed at the ground, ensuring no evidence was left for Mother to see in the morning. The ground looked wet from where he stood, but at least if she poked her head out now she'd see nothing.

His breath rushed out in a steaming cloud and he felt light-headed at the thought of another punishment averted. He turned and walked towards the roundhouse where the rest of his family gathered in the warmth. With only two more steps to go, the heavy hide door whipped aside, filling his vision with the figure of Mother.

"What are you smirking at, boy?"

He shook his head, tongue-tied. Light from the hearth-fire behind her cast insidious shadows on her face and he stepped back. In the sunlight, women still considered Mother handsome despite her thirty years, though Arawn suspected they only said such because she took every opportunity to demonstrate her skill with spear and sword.

"And why are you lurking in the gloam?" She looked down at his hands. "Holding an empty bucket."

He willed his mind to think of something but it quailed before her. Every settlement they visited, local women exclaimed surprise that she became a merchant and a wife instead of a warrior. This always made her smile, though it degraded into a sneer when she looked at her husband.

"Water," he said finally. "I was going to bring in some water, in case it were needed."

"Dinner's cooked, you fool, that useless Pict's already done it. Half a moment later and you'd've missed out."

The door slapped shut in his face. Gingerly he pulled it back and peered inside. This caused no outcry so he stepped in, grateful to be in the warmth at long last. The Pict boy had just finished serving the meal—deer stew again, by its aroma. Mother and Ffraid received brimming silver bowls and two loaves of barley bread to feast on. A shallow wooden bowl of stew and half a loaf to share was considered ample for Arawn and his father, though the boy gazed at them as though they held a great treasure. His stomach growled, causing the two women to sneer, but still the boy waited patiently like the runt of a litter who couldn't feed until until the rest of his pack had had their fill. Arawn stuffed his share of bread up his sleeve; the boy would at least get something in his belly this night.

"And Gwynfor told me he's conducting the Samhain ritual," Ffraid said with her mouth full.

"Good," said Mother. "Then it is ready."

"What's ready, Mother?" said Arawn, but all he received for his attempt at conversation was a bruise where his wooden cup struck his head and a sopping shirt from his wasted ale. Nothing now for him to drink this even.

Smirking, his sister recounted for Mother the day's lessons under Gwynfor. No lesser Druid than he for the daughter of Gwladus Salt-merchant.

"You eating that, or just waiting for it to congeal?"

Arawn started. "Sorry, Papa."

"It's only good while it's hot, you know," he said, nudging his son and murmuring so the women weren't disturbed. "Say what you like about the Picts, but they can't cook for shit."

* * *

"I'll not waste my own food on that Cantiaci whore."

Arawn placed another log on the hearth-fire and closed his ears to Mother's morning rant.

"Bringing her and her whore mother here on Samhain eve is insult enough," she continued. "We should be praising the goddess Boudica and begging her protection from evil spirits, not playing host to treacherous tribes. And then to demand we all bring meat to the bonding feast? Pah!" She knocked the wooden cup of ale that Arawn had poured for himself off the table with a swipe of her fist.

"I don't think we've got any choice, Gwladus," murmured his father. "Inside this house your word is law, but outside—"

"Pah! Epona shames the memory of Boudica with her appeasement of the traitor tribes." She turned and spat three times into the fire to avert evil. "And so do you, Emlyn, with your submission. Her curse of bearing naught but sons doesn't mean she can invite stray bitches in from outside to breed with them. And that bitch will be superior to Epona's dog son, and when our warrior-queen dies, what happens then?"

"I don't doubt your wisdom, my goddess wife," he said. "But we can't disobey the warrior-queen."

Gwladus narrowed her eyes and peered at her husband. "*You* can't," she said. "But there are many here who won't be ruled by the traitors who suckled at Rome's tits."

"Gwladus, my goddess; more than three hundred summers have passed—"

"Fast-breaking is over."

Arawn ground his teeth so that his jaw ached, then refilled silver goblets with Gaulish wine and handed one to Mother, one to his sister. He'd heard this argument innumerable times and it always ended with her cursing the day she weakened enough to take Papa as a husband, then he'd scrape and beg for forgiveness. He'd asked his father, once, why he allowed Mother to speak to him so and he'd simply whispered, "It's the life we're born to, son."

"Emlyn, take Arawn and the boy to the market with half our salt and make people believe that's the last of our stock. I want as much coin as I can get for it."

"Of course, Gwladus, whatever you wish. And how does my goddess see fit to spend her time today?"

"As I see fit." She rammed a handful of nuts into her mouth and crunched them.

"Well then," said his father eventually, rising to get his cloak, striped the red and black of Atrebates. "No doubt we'll see you at the bonfire this even."

"Indeed you will," she said with a strange little smile. "With the coming of that whore, I don't doubt this will be a Samhain to remember." Father looked at her for several heartbeats, but her attention was solely fixed on her platter of dried meat, berries and nuts. He nodded once then left the roundhouse.

"What do you suppose that meant?" said Arawn, watching the slave boy unearth the salt bricks he had buried yesterday.

"I don't suppose it meant anything."

"But only moments before she was angry about the warrior-princess joining our tribe, and just now she seemed ... pleased, perhaps."

"I said, I don't suppose it meant anything."

The boy loaded a sixth clay brick of salt on the cart and looked at Arawn's father, who nodded at him. With the same expressionless face, the boy plodded around to the front of the cart and lifted the two handles either side of it, waiting for the command to start pulling.

"Can we not use the ox today, Papa? Just this once."

"A working boy eats far less than a working ox."

"But he barely ate—"

"Let's go, boy."

Obediently, the boy started forward, the screeching of the frost-cold wheels startling a murder of crows into flight from their roost in the thatched roof. Arawn wondered what omen the women would read from that, but only briefly for they were soon embroiled in the bustle of the lower settlement, and he decided to sell the salt as fast as possible so the boy could go back and steal some rest.

Rising up from the surrounding hills like a gentle mountain was the kaer, the old fortress that gave the settlement its name, Kaer Gradawc: fortress by the gentle river. Generations ago the entire tribe lived up there, but now it was solely the province of the warrior-queen and her family, warriors, and Druids. As the settlement grew so it began encircling the kaer, and Arawn saw slaves still dragging bundles of wood up the spiralling path to its zenith, except now they were joined by menfolk hauling the spoils of their hunts. Every year, Epona Warrior-Queen of Atrebates hosted a magnificent feast and bonfire to bid farewell to the light half of the old year and welcome the dark half of the new one; starting with the festival of Samhain. The new moon heralding Samonios, seed-fall, would be black in the sky; but the plains would be ablaze with the bonfires of all the families in the tribe, all watching the kaer's beacon so they could light their own, as though passing on an urgent message. And to some extent they were; for wasn't it this night when the spirits were free to pass from their world into his? It was a time of great joy, but also of great fear. And for Arawn the excitement was almost too much to bear.

"I don't see what's so shameful about Rosmerta Warrior-Princess coming this night."

His father looked at him and frowned.

"It's an important night. Your mother is concerned that Samhain will be diminished by the oath to bond our tribes. Our ancestors could well be angered if we ignore them."

"But," said Arawn, "a new oath at the start of the new year seems fitting."

"Son, we are but humble men. Our place is to carry the burden, serve our purpose, earn the coin, not to question the wisdom of our betters."

Several young men staggered past, each carrying a deer carcass on his back. Their antlers would be removed to make tools or carved into weaving combs to untangle wool for the looms, their skins tanned to make hides. But their meat would be roasted to serve at the feast tonight and all would be carried out under the watchful eye of the women-folk.

"Is that what you truly believe?"

Emlyn cuffed him on the side of his head, stinging his cold ear. "A loyal man wouldn't dare think that question let alone ask it."

"But—"

The blow was harder this time. "Enough. It is what it is. Be grateful you're the son of a merchant and not the son of slave. At least you'll have the possibility of bonding into a respectable family. Then your only concern will be fathering enough daughters to continue your goddess-wife's line. And may Boudica protect you if you fail in that task."

Arawn would swear an oath that he saw a flicker of regret pass across his father's features, but it was too fleeting for him to be sure. "I think," he said, an image of his sister bursting into his mind, "that I will be just as proud to father a useful son. Like you have."

His papa chuckled, though not with mirth. "I failed your mother, and she knows that well. So let's see if we can lessen the sting a little today, eh? You run along and tell everyone the last of the salt's on its way to market. There's plenty who'll want to start preserving meat for the dark season. And if we're very fortunate there'll be some of Epona's slaves around to hear you. Off you go now. We haven't got all day to waste."

Lining the walkways were women of all ages, some standing in groups or sitting on stools, threading rosemary, thyme and sage into fragrant garlands. Men were bloody up to their elbows; skinning and disembowelling the beasts for tonight's feast. A particularly gnarled old woman with no front teeth and an opaque eye whispered something to her cronies which set them looking and laughing at the menfolk. Arawn didn't want her attention ensnaring him so he sidled over to the nearest young woman decorating venison with herbs and brought up the subject of Mother's salt.

In many ways, their day at market was profitable. Arawn and Emlyn learned of the imminent arrival of Rosmerta and her warrior-queen mother, Sulis. She was famed throughout the southern tribes for her skill at chariot-dancing, and many of the women wagered that she would put on a spectacular show to celebrate the oath-bonding of her daughter to Dewydd, the son of Epona. There would also be chariot racing amongst the spear-women of Cantiaci and Atrebates, not to mention the feasting that was to take place. It added an entirely new dimension to the celebration of Samhain, one that Arawn had never experienced before, and he found it exhilarating. As well as that, people were willing to spend a lot of coin on salt. Nothing was too good, it seemed, for the feast of the two tribes.

"Shall we go back and get the rest of it?" he whispered to his father when the last customer left.

Emlyn shook his head. "Samhain is only just seeping underneath the door. I think it wise to wait until it's reached our hearth-fire before exchanging all our commodities."

On their return, they found the roundhouse empty. The boy, having been sent back from the market with the cart earlier, was outside scraping the skin of a culled cow, stretching out the hide ready to hang and dry next to the curing meat in the roundhouse rafters, for use in repairing cloaks or tunics or leggings. He barely acknowledged their presence when they walked past.

"I expect Ffraid's off with her Druid," said Arawn. "But where's Mother?" It wasn't often she left the men of the household with no one to give them orders.

"Her friends and family are here and they've not seen her for many moons," said his father. "Or it may be she's already at the kaer."

Arawn raised his eyebrows. "You think she'll witness the oaths?"

"Not if she can help it," said Emlyn with a shrug. "But she'll want to witness the lighting of the Samhain bonfires. Nothing would keep her from that."

"And I should think she'd want to make a point of not bringing meat to the feast."

Emlyn clasped his son's shoulder firmly but had no time to reprimand him, for the ground trembled beneath their feet and a great wave of cheering washed over the lower settlement.

"Does that sound like horses and chariots to you, Papa?"

He looked over with crooked smile. "I'd say the Cantiaci have arrived."

* * *

The spear-women arrived first. Glorious and terrible they looked in their armour of leather and bronze upon their chariots of wood and iron. Crowned with a figure of a fighting boar, their bronze helmets glinted in the seed-fall sun; their green, blue and silver-striped cloaks flailed behind them like beastly wings. Brandishing their spears and swords, they screeched as they whipped their horses into a faster gallop. Hooves pounded the winter-bound earth, tackle clashed, and chariot wheels thundered. The spectacle terrified Arawn—it was no wonder the Romans had fled from them in fear and been defeated.

Then came the acrobatics. Spear-women leapt from chariots racing at full speed, running up the harnesses that coupled the chariot to the horse, only to leap across to the next horse, and the next and the next, all the while screaming their battle song and brandishing their weapons ready for the kill. Muscles in their arms bulged under sun-browned skin, glistening now from the sweat of their exertions, might pouring from them as heat from a hearth-fire. They were beautiful demons, leaping and chasing the souls of the living, eager to feast on them in the depths of Otherworld.

Behind them and all about the walkways people hailed and called for more, goading the spear-women into ever more daring feats for the spectacle.

They were fearless. Even as Arawn watched, one spear-woman was thrown from a horse during her acrobatics; it had bolted from a raucous group of female spectators. But the spear-woman never lost her stride; she hit the ground in a tight ball and within a heartbeat she was standing again, flinging herself into the saddle of an approaching horse so she could leap back to her own chariot. Three blinks of an eye and it was over, but not before Arawn saw the deep gash which sliced the warrior's calf, swelling blood.

Cheering girls frenzied by the excitement dashed after the chariots, heedless of the danger from pounding hooves as they wove in and out, brandishing their wooden swords or branches which they held like spears. This was not a tribe, to Arawn's mind, who despised the notion of bonding with the Cantiaci.

And there was yet more.

"Papa, look!" Arawn pulled hard on his father's arm in his excitement. "It's Rosmerta Warrior-Princess!"

Emlyn's mouth dropped open. "None of the stories was false then," he said. "About her or her mother."

In stark contrast to their warriors, Rosmerta and her mother rode their chariots gently so they could smile upon the crowds. More striking than this, though, was their likeness to each other. Unlike the charging charioteers, they wore no helmet to protect their head, and their fair hair glinted in the sunset, the glow burnishing their fair skin golden. Mother would disapprove. A real woman, she claimed, had the fiery red hair of a warrior—of Boudica. Gwladus Salt-merchant did, as did her daughter. But fair hair? Such a woman was weaker even than one whose hair was brown. He wondered how hair could affect a person's strength but he'd never once found the courage to question his mother's judgement.

He hadn't realised he was staring, not until Rosmerta offered him the loveliest smile that had ever befallen him. The shock of it rattled his head. From their fourth summer, Atrebates girls were taught the goddess Boudica's words—as *for men, they can live and become slaves*—so all smiles upon the fouler sex ceased. Yet Rosmerta's smile shone through her eyes as though she recognised him. More than that; as though she knew him well and liked him. His body followed the direction of her chariot, but soon all he saw was her golden hair streaming out behind her.

"Can we go to the kaer, Papa? I'd like to see the bonfire."

"I don't see that we have any choice."

People pushed in on all sides, carrying each other towards the towering hill fort where the formidable kaer stood. Epona Warrior-Queen would be waiting to greet her noble Cantiaci guests; and, if he were fortunate, Arawn would lay eyes on Rosmerta once more.

* * *

He sensed the crowd's restlessness when they were subjected to still more of the Druid Gwynfor's writhing and screeching. It had something to do with discerning the dark half of the year's fortunes, or maybe he was hearing the voices of the ancestors… Undoubtedly it was very important, but in truth Arawn just wanted the bonfires lit and the feast started so he could look for Rosmerta. What he would do when he found her he didn't know, but for now he was content to think about looking.

The night was raven black. None of the bonfires across the rolling plains beneath the kaer would be lit until this one was. Scores of Druids throughout the lands were performing similar rites to Gwynfor's, if they hadn't already finished. To them the fort would be invisible—the new moon was ever shrouded in darkness—but soon they would witness the first fire of the new year.

Silence snapped back. Behind Gwynfor, the huge mound of wood which had taken three days to gather suddenly burst into flames. Arawn shut his eyes and shielded his face, turning away from the heat, but he didn't want to miss the first fire of Samhain. Lowering his hands, he yelped in surprise: the Druid stood right in front of him—so close he could have touched his rowan-wood staff. A gaping hole was his mouth and his eyes were as white as his robe. For many heartbeats Gwynfor was still, his mouth working as if he were trying to speak but only a rasp of air left his throat, the dying breath escaping from a fresh corpse.

Arawn sought his father's hand but when the grip wasn't returned he looked up at him. Unblinking, his gaze was fixed on the Druid, his face an orange glow reflecting the growing fire.

"The gods are speaking through him," Emlyn whispered, then shuddered.

Arawn turned back. He'd seen this before, of course, but he'd never understood why it evoked such fear in the onlookers.

"You…have…no…right," rasped Gwynfor. "Forging tribes against their will shall only lead to death. To death!" He screeched the last two words, fell to the ground in a paroxysmal fit, then lay still, silent. Those around Arawn shifted and looked at each other, unsure if the spectacle was over. The only sound in the deepening night was the crack and collapse of burning wood. Then it was eclipsed by a scream of rage.

"The ancestors…" whispered voices around him.

"The gods…" whispered others.

"Boudica!"

So powerful was the voice it commanded instant attention from the watching crowd. Some stepped backwards, others pushed forward, trying to see through the glare of the fire that was so bright now it was difficult to see much except the flames, yet movement caught Arawn's eye. The figure of a woman tall and powerful, burnished hair tumbling towards her waist in a flaming frenzy, stepped forward. Leather and bronze armour shone in the bonfire's light, but her naked arms were streaked with blood, as was her face.

Her face.

Women in the crowd began sinking to their knees whimpering, "Boudica!"

Except Arawn knew that face. Now that his eyes had grown used to the fire he saw scores of spear-women lined up in front of it. They must have been there throughout the ritual, he thought; they could never have crept up that silently and unnoticed.

"Boudica!" cried the powerful voice once more, drawing Arawn back to the apparition before the fire. Though no apparition, she.

She was his Mother.

– 2 –

The moon of Samonios (Seed-fall), 332 C.E.
Kaer Gradawc, near the Stone Circle, Atrebates tribal lands, Brython

"We will not submit!" Mother called above the roar of the flames, and hefted her spear high into the air.

The watching crowd jolted as one from a second night-renting scream. This came not from Arawn's blood-streaked Mother but from behind the spectators; from the kaer itself. Movement rippled amongst the onlookers as those at the back parted, and the scream came again. Wordless rage. Jostled to and fro as the people strained to see the action, Arawn saw nothing save the helmets and spear-heads of many warriors.

A procession reached the opening where the bonfire grew ever more furious, and all the while his Mother's eyes, in a twisted mask of hatred, never left it. When the warriors finally displayed the reason for their entrance, Arawn gasped.

Bound by their wrists and ankles, pushed forward so that they now knelt in front of his mother, were Epona Warrior-Queen of Atrebates, Rosmerta Warrior-Princess and her warrior-queen mother, Sulis of Cantiaci. All three were bruised from battle; Rosmerta's face was bleeding and her fine dress was ripped. She looked to her mother with terrified eyes, and Sulis smiled at her, serene and calm.

Epona's face, on the other hand, held more thunder than a storm-cloud. "You make a grave mistake, Gwladus Salt-merchant," she said.

Mother knocked the warrior-queen's head with the butt of her spear, the crack echoing around the watching crowd, and then turned it so the point was level with her throat. Arawn gasped at the same time as the other hundreds of watchers. Would the ancestors abide such treachery, on this of all nights?

"You dare to pollute our noble tribe with the blood of traitors," said Mother, then spat three times towards the bonfire. "You shame Boudica's name, and there are those amongst us who cannot allow that to happen."

"You have no foresight, Salt-merchant. We defeated the Romans, yes we did. But does that make us safe? We have enemies in our own lands; who's to say what lurks across the oceans?"

Mother spat again. "We defeated the Romans and they slunk back to their pit of corruption."

"Perhaps. And their gods?" Arawn wondered how Epona could speak when she was so close to death. "There are always enemies. You call me traitor for allying our tribe to Cantiaci, but you are willing to sacrifice the lands for which Boudica fought by laying us open to our enemies. You know nothing of ruling, Salt-merchant."

"And you know nothing of honour!" Mother thrust the point of her spear under Epona's chin, and Arawn froze when he saw the rivulet of blood. "You're no better than a man, producing dog sons instead of sacred daughters—you bring shame on us all!"

"And you lack wisdom as well as foresight," said Epona, her voice straining now. "To me!"

Mother, clearly confused by the warrior-queen's command, lowered her spear slightly, but it was all Epona needed; she sprang from the ground, a dagger suddenly in her hand. She slashed the arm of the rebel warrior behind her, who shouted in pain and dropped her spear as she tried to staunch the flow of life-blood. Epona caught it easily and turned to face Mother in one fluid movement.

"Weapons can serve more purpose when they are concealed, Salt-merchant," she said and lunged.

Despite being caught off-guard, Mother still fought fiercely. She parried every spear-thrust, and launched many of her own, her blood-streaked face alive with battle-lust; and though Arawn had witnessed countless mock battles between Mother and his sister, he'd never truly seen the power contained in her body. It made every burst of violence she had inflicted on him over the years seem like nothing but playful teasing. Against a warrior-queen who had given her life to battle, however, she was no match. Epona swung her spear with both hands so that blow after blow rained down upon her foe. Arawn found himself hoping that each one would be the fatal one.

None was. Epona knocked Mother's legs from under her, jabbing the spear down into her hand so she couldn't get back up. Mother screamed and writhed in rage so Epona held her in place by kneeling with one knee on her chest.

It was only when Mother's cries subsided did Arawn realise a battle had taken place around him. Epona's spear-women had fought and captured all the rebels, and the noble family from Cantiaci was protected by a forest of spears. Some of the watching crowd had fled for fear of being skewered like pigs, but many still remained.

"I do not want these women killed," cried Epona to her warriors. "I will not kill my own people. But you," she said now to Mother, "I will execute in the morning, as a warning to all those who might oppose me."

A cry disturbed the captured warriors as someone tried to struggle out of their bonds. After witnessing the battle between Mother and the warrior-queen, Arawn felt no more surprise when he saw it was his little sister, Ffraid. Writhe as she might, she couldn't free herself from the noble spear-women.

"I keep this one with me." Epona pointed to Mother, addressing her warriors, ignoring Ffraid's cry. "Take the rest back to the settlement."

With their leader thwarted, the rebels conceded feebly and the crowd dispersed. The Druid, Gwynfor, slowly rose from the ground near Arawn's feet, his face slack as though he were still in the grip of possession. No heed was paid him, however, so he scurried over to the spear-women who still gripped Ffraid and now led her away from the kaer. Mother was hauled up from the ground by two warriors and dragged away, but despite her humiliation and defeat, she still spat towards the warrior-princess as she passed her.

Hot shame poured through Arawn—how could Mother defile such beauty? Before he realised what he was doing he was in front of Rosmerta on his knees. "I would honour you as my warrior-queen," he said, unable to tear his eyes away from her face.

"Then you are a good man, and kind," she said softly. Her lips parted in that magnificent smile and he barely felt the hands that clasped him under his armpits and dragged him back up to his feet. "Do not be rough with him," said Rosmerta, her eyes still fixed on Arawn's. "He means me no harm."

And then she was gone.

"Let's go, son." He jumped at his father's voice by his ear. "Our family's caused enough trouble for one night. We'll have to tell the boy to pack up our belongings, I don't think we'll be too welcome around here come dawn."

When they reached their roundhouse, however, the boy was nowhere to be seen. Neither was Ffraid, nor Gwynfor. Embers were scattered over the floor by the hearth-fire and two pots were broken.

"They've taken the boy," said Arawn, but his father hadn't even noticed the mess; he was already packing food into a cloak.

"He's run off, more like, and who can blame him? That Druid too, I shouldn't wonder—Arawn?"

* * *

He knew precisely where they'd taken him. The place where all Druid magic was performed. The place where Gwynfor and

Ffraid spent most of their time.

The stone circle.

In the distance and all around he saw the flare of Samhain bonfires, heard the beating of drums, and the singing of songs. All across Atrebates as far as Arawn's eyes could see, rituals were playing out as they were supposed to. He wondered, briefly, if anyone had been aware of the rebellious treason that had taken place on top of the kaer, but he doubted it. By dawn everyone would know, but right now all were welcoming in the new year, and keeping malevolent spirits away.

Everyone, that was, but Ffraid and Gwynfor. Evidently the Druid had used his status to release Ffraid from the spear-women, and the two of them had raced back to the roundhouse to capture the boy.

With his chest screaming for respite, Arawn pushed himself a little farther. There, now, was the stone circle, looming in its blackness. Druids should be here, many Druids on the eve of Samhain, but only two figures danced. Their shadows flickered against the standing stones, thrown by the light of a small bonfire, like tortured souls thrashing in Otherworld.

Only two?

Arawn stopped running, tried to calm himself so that his sister and her Druid wouldn't be alerted to his presence by his harsh breathing, and focused on the centre of the stone circle. The Druid was clearly there; it was hard not to notice his white robes. And that was certainly his sister; no one could mistake that fiery red hair of which Mother was so proud.

But where was the boy?

He crept closer, thankful for the shadows that the massive standing stones poured out; and then he saw him. Bound and naked on the sacrificial stone in the centre. Druid and acolyte chanted, dancing around him, both with daggers in their hands; Gwynfor's appetite for sacrifice surpassed all others. Doubtless it was his idea to offer up a human soul to the goddess Boudica and her goddess daughters to save the soul of Mother. One human soul for another. Yet Boudica was nothing but a dead rebel queen!

Ffraid and Gwynfor stopped suddenly. As still now as the standing stones, Gwynfor slowly chanted magic with words Arawn couldn't understand and raised his hands; one held his powerful rowan staff, the other a silver dagger. Ffraid's eyes were fixed on the blade, oozing lust like pus from an infected wound.

Frantically Arawn searched the ground for a weapon of some kind. The urge to save the boy from his unjust fate was terrible. His scrabbling hands landed on a rock, small enough to fit in his fist. Holding back a scream of rage, he ran into the stone circle. Ffraid looked at him, her whole face a mask of surprise, and as the Druid turned to see what had captured his acolyte's attention, Arawn swung the rock. It connected to the side of Gwynfor's face with a sickening crack. Like a dropped cloak he crumpled to the floor.

For two heartbeats there was silence as brother and sister looked at the fallen Druid, then Ffraid shrieked in rage and plunged her dagger into the boy's chest. He didn't even cry out, only twitched. Ffraid then tugged her dagger out from between his ribs and slit his throat in one deft motion. Blood gushed, subsided; and Arawn drowned in the dead pools of the boy's pale blue eyes.

She looked up at her brother then, and smiled. His rage swelled like blood from a wound, but before he had a chance to move, Ffraid pounced.

He barely managed to stop her from piercing his eye. Older and bigger he may have been, but it was she who had been taught warrior skills; and in the face of her incoherent rage he was all but helpless.

In fact, he was terrified. Of his sister. Of a young girl.

No; of a killer.

With all the force of her body she thrust the blood-soaked dagger at him, each time getting closer. Arawn knew he had to get it out of her grasp, and if he could only knock her to the ground and use his weight to subdue her as Epona had done to Mother then this would all be over.

He gripped, with both hands, onto the arm which held the dagger and tried to move himself close enough to knock her feet from under her, but she scratched at his face and eyes with her free hand, still screeching insensibly. He moved one hand down to her throat, swung them both round and—

Her eyes bulged for a heartbeat as her head connected with the corner of a giant standing stone. He hadn't realised they were so close to the inner circle.

Blood pumped across the face of the stone and Ffraid's eyes no longer saw him. He felt her weight in his hands, then her body started to tumble forwards.

He let go. She hit the earth with a thud, blood pooling around her broken skull.

The shaking started, and Arawn thought it would never stop, but he couldn't take his eyes off his dead sister. In that moment he knew life wouldn't be better without her after all; it was about to get very bad.

– 3 –

The moon of Riuros (Cold-time), 332 C.E.
Dubras, Cantiaci tribal lands, Brython

Rosmerta sighed and looked out of the ancient window to the tiled road leading towards the market square. The grass that grew between the tiles was dusted with frost, giving it the delicate appearance of glass—another secret that had left with the Romans. Yes, her tribe and others besides could still make coloured glass beads for jewellery and adornments, but the great sheets the Romans had put in the palace windows were long since turned to dust. But her mind was wandering.

At this rate they'd never resolve the crisis. Yet the most frustrating aspect of it was that she still wanted to proceed with the bonding. Until there was accordance in the council, however, that would never be.

"The Iceni-Coritani tribe have enjoyed far greater security since they bonded," said Sulis Warrior-Queen. "We should be looking to them for—"

"They were forced into bonding because of the Picts, and because the Parisii are little more than a village now. They didn't unite through choice."

Rosmerta turned her face towards Arch Druid Heddgwyn. There was no smile on his pale face, but she saw one nonetheless.

"And you would see more tribes ended as the Brigantes and Sentanii?" Though outwardly she remained serene, Rosmerta heard the frustration in her mother's voice trying to escape. "We cannot expect the Iceni-Coritani to keep the Picts from the southern lands forever. If we all agree to ally ourselves, to be a single land of Brythoniaid instead of a broken land of many, then we will be stronger. Bonding our daughters to our neighbours is the best way to achieve that."

"I don't doubt the wisdom of your words. But I can't imagine that the tribal leaders will be so willing to relinquish their queenship as you."

"It's not a question of *relinquishing* power, Heddgwyn; I speak of strengthening all tribes against all enemies. We survived invasion by the Romans, but how many other enemies lie across the ocean? More than twenty generations have passed and still we suffer the ignominy of allowing Rome onto our land and I do not want that to be our legacy. I want the Cantii to be a people remembered for uniting the Brythoniaid against the Picts and outlanders to become a…a nation of peace."

"A noble ideal, Warrior-Queen, but it will only work if other queenships agree; the Atrebates didn't."

"Epona Warrior-Queen agreed—my daughter was to be bound to her son."

"Epona may well have, but I said *queenship* not warrior-queen, and I think the Atrebates people made quite clear their desire to disassociate with us."

Rosmerta's hand rose to the side of her face. The pain had long gone, but there remained still a shadow of her beating. And the shadow was a black cloud of fear.

"It was a rebellion of a handful of unofficial spear-women—not even an uprising. It was barely a swell. The people there were happy enough to see us arrive. And Epona is eager to continue with the oath. As am I, as is my daughter."

"Perhaps you should start your noble plan with bonding your daughter to a tribe less opposed to us," said Heddgwyn. "I hear the warrior-queen of the Durotriges tribe has many fine sons."

Her mother smiled. "She also has many fine daughters."

"But if we can convince the Atrebates that other tribes are happy bonding to ours—"

"I intend to bond our tribe with many others. I've been fruitful throughout my reign. But if the other tribes witness the bonding of Cantiaci and Atrebates first despite our ancient animosity, others will be willing to follow. Everyone in this council is of accordance, Arch Druid, save you—will you not concede?"

There was silence in the chamber. This argument had continued ever since Rosmerta and her mother had returned from Atrebates two moons ago, and what worried her was that many of the council members were tiring of it. Soon it would become old news, other events would take place and precedence and the bonding for which her mother had worked so hard would be for naught. Besides, if they knew the Druids didn't consider it important, neither would they; all looked to the Druids for guidance.

"I will need to discuss this with my Fellows," Heddgwyn said eventually. "We must call upon our ancestors for wisdom, and the gods for guidance."

Sulis brought her hand down sharply on the table and Rosmerta winced. "Already you have taken two full cycles of the moon—what else is there left to discuss? And while you talk and chant to find your answers the Picts move ever further from their borders."

"We are safe from them here."

"For now. But what if the Iceni-Coritani should fall? How do we keep a country of ravenous raiders from our door?"

The Arch Druid shrugged, the slightest of movements. "We could build a wall to keep them out."

"From coastline to coastline? You mock me with your flippant remarks. They're people, not beasts; they know how to climb a wall."

"Doubtless you're right. I shall seek guidance from the gods over this matter as well. When the new moon brings Ogronios, call another council. My order will give you its answer then."

He stood to leave, his staff of rowan clunking on the faded tiles before him as he walked, and the rest of the chamber hastily climbed to their feet, heads bowed. Rosmerta peered at her mother from lowered eyelids. Her head was dipped and her face was carefully composed; she'd been Warrior-Queen too long to betray any emotion.

Once the Arch Druid had departed, Sulis Warrior-Queen nodded to the rest of her counsellors and they filed out one by one until only Rosmerta and her mother remained. She rose and walked over to one of the many tapestries adorning the ancient walls, her brightly-coloured dress sweeping the floor.

"You'll speak your mind anyway," she said to her daughter without turning. "You may as well speak it now."

"The majority are in favour, Mother, I don't understand why we must wait until ice-time—that's two moons from now!"

"The Druids haven't bestowed their blessing."

"They've already given it once!"

"That was before the evil omen at Atrebates. You cannot blame them for wanting to reconsider."

"It wasn't an omen, Mother, it was a paltry attempt at stalling a good idea that a handful of people think is a bad one. If we wait too long Epona will bond Dewydd to someone within her own tribe; we can't afford to keep waiting."

Sulis smiled. "The impatience of youth is a wonderful thing. It's a pity it has to fade." She turned to face her daughter, the bands about her neck and arms flaring gold in the morning sun. "You needn't worry about Epona—she's as eager as we are for the bonding, though we would have to wait a little while now, anyhow. To bond during this dead season would only bring more misfortune upon us. Better to wait for Imbolc, when the bellies of the ewes are full and the world is renewed."

"Better to make an oath for the bonding so that the people know our intentions."

"The people know our intentions," said Sulis, her voice deepening a little, turning to look out of the window again, "and tell me that they're good. They're as willing as we are to put our tainted past behind us."

"But are they more willing to follow the Druids?"

"I would have you speak plainly, daughter," said Sulis, stepping a little closer to her. "You're not usually so cryptic."

Rosmerta drew a slow breath, then released it. "I think Heddgwyn is using this salt-merchant's...*rebellion*...as an example for why the order should listen to him. It amazes me they could all so suddenly be against an idea that they'd previously supported."

"It was a—"

"Bad omen; yes, I know, Mother. And the very one I think he was waiting for."

"You mistrust his motives."

"How can I not? How can *you* not? We're now being kept endlessly waiting for something that should have already taken place."

"They will give us our answer soon."

"And what if it's the wrong one?" Rosmerta fought to keep her voice as calm as her mother's, but it didn't help that the warrior-queen was focussed on something outside the window rather than her daughter.

"They will give us the answer we want."

Rosmerta laughed mirthlessly. "You may pine for youth's lost impatience but I crave the certainty of maturity."

"Well, that's something you'll just have to wait for."

"That, unfortunately," said Rosmerta, "is something to which I am becoming accustomed." She stood, suddenly longing to be outside in the crisp air listening to the sound of people carrying on with their lives with no interruptions.

"Don't lose heart, my daughter. Our dream of a united Brython will come to pass."

"I know, Mother; I just hope we're still alive to see it."

Finally Sulis faced her, smiling. "You sensed the tension at Epona's kaer and she was able to prepare for it. I believe we owe you our lives." Rosmerta touched her cheek, but said nothing. "So you know I trust your intuition; but I ask you to trust my experience. Can you do that for your warrior-queen?" She raised a hand to her chest. "For your mother?"

"You know I can."

"Good." She embraced her daughter. "Then I would have you go into the market and see what is drawing such a crowd."

The warrior-princess laughed. Her mother never missed an opportunity to send her out amongst the people. It was good practice, she said, for when she would be in command of the tribe. And, in fact, she was grateful to be outside. Most people had an aversion to this dead part of the new year, but on days like this, Rosmerta loved it. The sun was a distant golden ball, reminding the world that it still watched over them as it rolled across a clear blue sky. Its faint heat could still be felt through the chill air, which cooled her chest each time she breathed in, as soothing as her sister's cold-time healing balm.

She let the noise of the market wash over her as she walked through it. It wasn't as busy now as during the warm season, but locals still came to trade pelts and salt, pigs and cloth with the many Gaulish traders who spent the dark days in Dubras; and, of course, the various weapons and jewels that the warriors so loved to display on themselves were always popular. The shouts and calls, the clank of metal on wood, the indignant cry of animals all helped to make her feel real.

She was on the divine path to deification, like all the warrior-queens before her, back to Boudica herself. Already she was a trained warrior, soon she would be a mother, and when her own mother crossed the bridge to Otherworld she would be a leader. The divine trinity. A living goddess. It was a prospect that terrified her.

"A special apple for the lady?"

Rosmerta turned her head towards the voice. It came from an ancient face swamped in pelts. She couldn't tell if it were male or female.

"All the way from the sacred isle of Ynys Afallach, Lady.

Blessed by the Druids themselves."

Smiling, Rosmerta declined politely.

"No charge, o' course, for the warrior-princess."

"You're most kind, though I couldn't possibly take such precious wares without giving you coin. But they do look delicious; I shall send for some once I've returned to the palace."

The ancient apple-seller grinned until the only feature that was visible was his—or possibly her—mouth. "The lady is too kind."

Nodding, Rosmerta continued her walk to the crowd, reminding herself not to forget the promise. She doubted very much that the apples came from as far away as Ynys Afallach when there were plenty of perfectly good orchards roundabouts, but she felt it her duty to help the local people as much as possible.

She reached the crowd and it parted for her, and she discovered the centre of attention was a man. Or rather, if his chequered cloak and scraped-back hair was anything to go by, a Gaul. A resident in Dubras until windy-time when the shipping lanes re-opened, he doubtless spent most of his moons here entertaining an audience, for Gaulish traders always had interesting tales to tell folk when they landed on their shores. This, by the look of his brooches and bracelets, was a rather wealthy one. Even so, it was unusual that a merchant held the awe of such a large crowd in a market square and not a tavern.

She moved in closer.

" … so the tale goes, and that his son died which means that the gates of Otherworld are open to all."

"Gates?" said someone at the front. "There's no gates, it's a bridge. You die, you cross the bridge to Otherworld. That's the way it's always been."

"Ah, but it hasn't," said the Gaul. "According to this god, Otherworld only opened when his son died and passed through it. And we can only pass through it if we believe in this one god."

There was a mumbling in the crowd and a few derisive laughs. "One single god? Boudica's bosom, what will the Romans think of next?" This earned a few more chuckles, even heartier than before.

"Of what do you speak, good trader?"

The crowd silenced when she spoke, and the Gaul took only a heartbeat to notice her finely embroidered tunic with its jewel-encrusted wrists, and the heavy cloak that was pinned at the shoulder with a weighty but intricately wrought brooch of gold. She smiled her encouragement at him.

"Why, the Romans, fair lady." He grinned at her, clearly needing no such encouragement at all.

"They seek to expand their empire once more?"

"No, my lady—we've not seen a soldier in our lands for generations. But we hear rumours. We trade with our cousins across the mountains and they tell us stories of the Romans."

"One of which you were recounting to my people before I interrupted you."

"You made no interruption, dear lady."

No encouragement at all! She smiled back at him. "But you were speaking of a Roman god?"

"Yes, lady."

"I thought the Romans worshipped many gods."

"They did indeed. Once. But now there are tales of just one. The one true god, they call him, and none other exists."

"How very peculiar."

"Yes, lady. Though my cousins tell me this is no recent change. According to the Romans, the one true god gave his only son to the world some three hundred years past, and that the son sacrificed himself so that he might open the gates to Otherworld. Except that they call it the kingdom of heaven. And only those who believe in the one true god and his son can enter it."

Rosmerta smiled. "What a strange little tale! Tell me; do you believe it?"

"No, lady." His face darkened, and she had the impression he suddenly found the subject uncomfortable. "But the Romans, and others like them, take it very seriously—they kill people if they refuse to believe them, I heard tell."

The warrior-princess raised her eyebrows. Certainly the gods could demand life if it pleased them, but never for a non-believer. The gods had no power over those who didn't believe in them. But then… This was Rome, who tried to take the world by force; such a god made sense for them. And if it was as powerful as it was vengeful, this new god of Rome, then it was a threat her mother should know about.

"All the world must believe in this one true god, they say; otherwise we'll all burn."

"I can't see how that would benefit this god of theirs."

"No, lady. But the Romans are so convinced that they don't even call themselves Romans any more."

The warrior-princess smiled in surprise. "And how have they named themselves instead?"

"They call themselves priests."

Eventually the crowd dispersed; even a good story couldn't halt the necessities of daily life for too long. No doubt her mother would find this information disturbing. The ancient power of Rome was still fresh in everyone's minds, even if it was only because the legend was passed down to every successive generation. That they had marched in their thousands from the other side of the world, sailed across the ocean and landed on the sacred shores of Brython was not a feat to be dismissed. Yes, Boudica and her divine army had beaten them back eventually, but the Romans had still left their mark—she only had to look around the town to see it. And she only had to visit the Atrebates lands to feel it. If they were amassing their forces again…

She looked back over her shoulder to the Gaul, and stopped. He was alone now, save for one young man. He looked as though he had missed several meals and his attire was in dire need of mending but Rosmerta could see that once it must have been of good quality. Despite his dishevelled appearance he was talking to the Gaul with animation.

She cocked her head. Did she recognise him? She was sure he wasn't local but something tugged at the back of her mind. She shook her head. If the memory were important it would come back to her.

* * *

"You've done nothing but chase meat around your platter with bread, Rosmerta. Is something on your mind?"

"Forgive me, Airmed," said the warrior-princess, looking up into the face of her younger sister. She was grinning. "Though it seems you're not offended."

"Oh, I know you too well to be offended by your bad humours," Airmed said, waving a hand. "But I believe the rest of our company were."

Rosmerta looked around. Moments before, she was sure, the great hall had been filled with Druids and wealthy tribes-people as well as Rosmerta's sisters and brothers and the warrior-queen herself. Now it was empty save the two of them and a lot of nearly empty dishes.

"Oh, Rosa!" said Airmed, giggling like a child. "What a face you have! But you needn't worry—everybody was far too busy chattering about everything *but* the Atrebates to notice your inattention. Mother looked over twice or thrice but she seemed contented to let you be. Me, I've just been wondering what plot you've chosen to unseat Heddgwyn."

"Airmed, how can you suggest such a thing?" Rosmerta's cheeks reddened and she pushed away her platter. Was it intuition or sisterhood that gave her such insight?

"Ah. So it's Dewydd then? I should think he'd be heart-glad to hear that."

"You're a very cheeky young girl."

"I've spent more time with Druids than weapons, remember. I've learned a few ways to trick people in revealing themselves."

"I'd rather not talk about the Druids right now."

Airmed's smile was knowing but not unkind. Never unkind. "I'd heard tell Heddgwyn was proving difficult. You needn't look so surprised; it's taken Mother her entire life to conceal her emotions—I'm afraid I can read you as easily as I can the runesticks."

Rosmerta sighed. "He's being deliberately obstructive."

"Indeed? Why should that be?"

"I've yet to uncover his motive, but I'd stake my…my queenship on it."

Airmed's eyes flew open. "What intrigue is this? I should really attend more council meetings rather than tend my herbal garden. What are you going to do about it?"

"That's what I've been pondering. But I don't know."

Airmed tapped her fingers softly on the side of her face for moment; then it lit up like the sun coming out from behind the clouds. "I know! We have a brother who's a Druid."

"He's not a Druid yet, he's an Ovate. And *all* our brothers are Ovates."

She shook her head prettily. "No, Rosa; *we* have a brother who's an *Ovate*. Same father as well as mother. And he loves us best of all. I'm sure if you ask him, he'll happily agree."

"If I ask him what? Airmed, what are you talking about?"

"Ask him to tell you what Heddgwyn is up to. He'd certainly know."

It took several moments for Rosmerta to find any words. "I can't ask our brother to do that—it would break all of the sacred oaths he's taken. Besides, he hasn't passed through all the levels yet; it's doubtful he'd be informed of any decisions Heddgwyn makes."

"Then there's no harm in asking."

"No, Airmed."

"If your concern is for the queenship then it's your duty to."

"No one questions the Druids." No one dared to. It was they who had knowledge of all the histories of all the tribes, they who passed judgement every arbitration-time on those foolish enough to commit crimes against their own, they who knew all the ancient magics and curses of the lands, and they who spoke with the ancestors—and through them, the gods. They had authority to move across tribal borders without challenge, and the power to veto even the will of the warrior-queen. It was the kind of power than could prove fatal should it ever be turned against them, and Rosmerta's soul quailed even as it warned her about it. That she needed to uncover Heddgwyn's motives wasn't in doubt, but she disliked the idea of causing trouble for her brother; the risk was great for him. The penalty of betrayal was death. Could she sacrifice one life for many? She smiled ruefully; this was precisely the kind of impossible choice all warrior-queens must make. It came to her mind once more that she wasn't ready for it.

"No one will question them. Our brother is simply going to give you information. I'll ask him if you don't want to. He's never really forgiven Heddgwyn for forcing Mother to give him to the Druids—he hated studying as much as you did."

"I did not hate studying!"

"If your fears are confirmed then you can do something about it. And if there are no concerns then you've nothing to worry about."

"Except Heddgwyn finding out."

"He won't find out," said Airmed, grinning. "He's hardly going to believe that his novice and only son is spying on him, is he?"

– 4 –

The moon of Riuros (Cold-time), 332 C.E.
Old Dubras, Cantiaci tribal lands, Brython

He knows who they are even before he reaches them. He doesn't want to reach them, but he's unable to stop moving forward. Not walking; moving. He feels neither his feet, nor his body; he's simply moving steadily forward, towards the two figures. One is sitting on his haunches, hunched over, pounding at white stones, except they're bones, turning them into dust so he can add them to the evil-smelling brew that's bubbling in the crucible above the fire.

He can't see the other figure, but she's there. He can feel her. Smell her.

Closer now. The hunched figure lifts up an arm to pour the bone-dust into the crucible, the long arm of his white robe flapping in the heat from the flames.

So hot.

The figure is stirring. Stirring and chanting. The words are foreign to him, nonsensical, madness; but he knows what they mean.

The Dead will find the living. They cannot escape the Dead. The living will be devoured and so become the Dead.

On and on the figure chants. On and on he moves towards him. He cannot stop it, and the sound of the chanting pierces his skull until he wants to scream.

But he can make no sound in this place.

He can only move. He moves past the chanting, cackling figure and the smell of his sister becomes stronger; her sweat, her blood on his hands. He wants to close his eyes, but he can't. He has to look.

Into the crucible.

The chanting stops, and he can't see the figure any more, only the gaping maw of the crucible and the foul-smelling brew it contains. Bubbling.

The bubbles burst slowly, emitting gusts of poisonous stench. Within the brew are swimming strands of red weeds, except they're not weeds. It's hair. Red hair, which slowly, lazily, draws out the fear he feels within, then parts until his sister's face is revealed to him. A dead face, and even though the skin is boiling off the bone he knows it's her. She opens her eyes and her eyeballs burst like the bubbles. Her mouth moves. There's no sound but he knows what she's saying.

Sister-slayer, sister-slayer, sister-slayer.

He steps back from the crucible but he's barred by something behind him. He knows what's there and he doesn't want to turn but he can't help it.

He spins around; glaring down at him is the figure robed in white. The hood has fallen to reveal his bloody head, one side of which is caved in, as though a rock had fallen and crushed his skull.

"The Dead will find the living," the white-robed figure intones. "They cannot escape the Dead. The living will be devoured and so become the Dead."

He wants to scream, drown out the sound of the terrible voice, but he has no breath.

He cannot breathe.

* * *

Arawn grabbed at the blankets around him and struggled to wake. Only, there were no blankets, it was straw. There hadn't been any blankets for two fat moons now and he didn't know when that was likely to change.

With his mind still sweating out the last remnants of his nightmare, he clambered out of the straw-filled pallet and went to the cracked cauldron that hung above the near-dead fire.

"I'm all right," said Arawn. "Just another bad dream." He looked into the cauldron at the thin gruel prepared the night before.

Putting a small log in the horseshoe hearth and coaxing life back into the fire, he said, "I told you; you're not a slave any more. You don't have to keep cooking for me." He dipped a bowl, a rotten treasure from a dead town, into the warming gruel and squatted next to the fire, sipping it, trying to appreciate the meagre warmth. It was the only roundhouse here that still stood, though when he lay down to sleep at night the stars shone down and taunted him; now a bitter breeze and the laughter of crows in the dead thatch did the same. The sun might well send its weak rays through the broken doorway but there was no life here any more; he was a ghost in a skeleton in a town long forgotten.

When his fast was broken he braved the biting wind and walked, passing the grain stores with their broken legs and the graves of roundhouses, to the edge of the ancient hill-fort. North-west beyond the crumbling earthworks, Dubras lay in the land like a polished stone, its name taken from the very hill he stood upon. From his various visits to the marketplace, he'd heard the locals refer to this place as Old Dubras—and old it certainly was. Nothing but a desiccated carcass of a once-proud fort. The very antithesis of new Dubras. Where *she* lived. A jewel within a jewel.

"I have to speak to her this day," Arawn said, and belched. "We can't keep foraging for food like rats. Besides, you're starting to smell." He smiled. "We'll go back to the marketplace. I'm sure we'll see her. I wonder if that trader will be there, what he said was very interesting. Imagine that, Boy—one supreme god to rule all the others! What would Gwynfor say about that?"

An image of chanting and cackling from his nightmare rolled over him like fog and he shivered.

"Anyway. This day will be ours. I'm sure of it. And I'm sure she'll only be too happy to employ us."

* * *

At no point during his sixteen summers did Arawn believe that a woman would be happy to see him. But she was different. This *place* was different. He'd never really thought of his tribal lands as anything other than home. Yes, there was the circle of standing stones—

looming in the firelight, echoing the screams of rage, then fright, then deathly silence

—but there was nothing else that made it special. Perhaps the kaer, but it was nothing more than a hill, when he really thought about it; no better than Old Dubras, just with fresh shit.

But *here*. Here, everything was clean and white and…and built! Now he realised that the Atrebates tribal lands were nothing more than a collection of dirty farmlands salted with squalid roundhouses. Here in the Cantiaci tribal lands the fields looked greener, the wheat looked fatter—but it was the marketplace in Dubras that stole Arawn's breath.

Instead of the muddy earth he had grown up in, any life beaten into submission by years of scuffing feet and trundling chariot wheels; Dubras' marketplace was paved with great white stones, the sides of which touched each other so that the whole place looked clean and flat; in some places great swathes were taken up with intricate patterns and pictures made entirely of tiny stones. Would Mother ever be able to imagine such artistry? People had their stalls arranged in neat rows and their wares sang out to the onlookers—he knew the fruit would be ripe and rich if he sank his teeth into it; the flowers enveloped his head in a perfume that made his nose tingle; and the pottery was the most beautifully crafted he'd ever seen. And this was just a place for common folk!

Around the edge of the marketplace, on the other side of the paved road, were dwellings, only they were like none he'd ever seen before. They were built of stone not wattle and daub; instead of lice-infested thatch they were roofed with a grey stone that reflected the sunlight; and their doorways were made of wood, not hide. The front of each had square holes cut into them for sunlight and these were bordered by prettily painted shutters. Everything was square and neat and clean. No more dirt and scruff and circles, he thought. It was the most wondrous sight and he felt sure he'd never tire of it. Not surprising, then, that Mother never wanted to trade here—undoubtedly she was sick with jealousy. But his purpose wasn't to marvel at his surroundings; his purpose was even now walking through the crowd.

"Should I approach her out here?" he said. "Or perhaps it would be better to speak to her at her home. Maybe she'll even offer us some food." His stomach growled at the idea. "That's what we'll do then. Let's keep our eyes on her."

It wasn't difficult to keep out of sight. The marketplace was packed with people, but there was none of the shouting and pushing that he was used to. Indeed, people were decrying their produce but they made it sound inviting. And those wishing to buy would patiently wait for attention instead of pushing themselves forward to get the best on offer. Even more astonishing to Arawn's young eyes, was that there were *men* working behind the stalls, as though they were the ones who owned the goods and would keep the money for themselves.

He looked up. For a heart-stopping moment he thought he'd lost her, but then he spotted her again talking to a small group of people, nodding her head and smiling that sweet smile of hers. Eventually she moved on, and Arawn made sure his eyes never lost contact with her again.

She headed directly towards the top of the marketplace and mounted an incredible set of steps, wide at the bottom and narrowing towards the top when they reached such an ornate door that Arawn's jaw dropped. Magically, the door opened and in she went, swallowed up by the majestic darkness.

Arawn's eyes swam over the rest of the giant square house and were drowned.

"I don't know if I dare to enter."

* * *

"This will definitely be the day," Arawn said, after another wholly unsatisfying bowl of morning gruel. "This day I will definitely knock, she will answer and accept our offer of servitude."

The now familiar walk from Old Dubras to the marketplace seemed to take only moments instead of half a morning, and as Arawn walked around the outside to the great square house that kept watch over it, his heart raced. As usual.

What if she said no?

But she'd smiled at him… And that wasn't the smile of someone who said no. Even if she was a woman. Only, this woman wasn't like all the others.

And besides, he'd dreamed about this moment; dreams in which she welcomed him with that wonderful smile and sat him down to feast with her. And then she led him to richly furnished chambers where he slept for as long as he wanted. Always Arawn awoke when he fell asleep and it seemed to him at times that his miserable life was the dream and his time with her was reality. Soon it would be so, because what were such dreams if not visions from the ancestors?

The door was in front of him. He took a step back. From behind he felt a slight pressure and knew Boy was urging him forwards.

I'm hungry and exhausted, thought Arawn. *I can't keep foraging on the edge of life.*

He lifted his fist, and pounded twice. It sounded muffled and he wondered how anyone on the other side of it would be able to hear anything at all.

Nothing happened.

He pounded again, this time much harder, and he fancied that the sound carried further.

Still nothing.

He was just about to lift his fist for the third time when he heard scrapings from the other side. He put his ear to the wood and then jumped straight back as the huge door in front of him swung open. After spending so long dreaming of this moment, when he finally saw the girl in front of him his heart sank.

It wasn't her.

"Yes?" she said. Her hair was brown, her face flawed with freckles, and she wasn't smiling. It wasn't her. "What do you want?"

Arawn said nothing. The door closed in his face. He turned and walked down the grand staircase, failure biting his heart.

But then he saw a group of people carrying baskets filled with goods or pushing laden barrows. There was a lot of food there. Arawn's aching stomach growled at the sight of it. He shook his head.

"I can't steal anything from those people, Boy. There's too many of them."

The merchants were streaming down a little alley at the side of the grand building. After spending so long wandering around the environs of the marketplace, Arawn knew there was nothing behind there except the gardens of the square house, farmlands, and beyond much smaller dwellings. But none of those looked wealthy enough to afford all of the merchandise that was passing in front of them.

The copper coin dropped.

"There must be another way in. Let's follow them!"

He bolted across the smooth paving stones and turned into the mouth of the alley. The merchants were almost out of sight, but it didn't take the young man long to catch up with them—not when he had the excitement of possibility giving wings to his heels.

Behind the great square house and protecting its gardens was a sculpted stone wall, a portion of which was given over to a polished wooden gate. Many of the merchants had already passed through by the time Arawn arrived, save those with the heaviest barrows. Up this close, Arawn noticed that their clothes were in better repair than his, and all of them were wearing shoes. If he went too near, someone would surely recognise that he didn't belong to the group. But if he stayed too far behind, the gate would be locked, his entry denied.

Once more he was in an agony of indecision. And once more he felt Boy push him forwards. The last merchant had disappeared with his filled barrow and the gate was slowly creaking shut. His heart beating wildly again, Arawn took to his toes and ran to the gate. He heard nothing from the other side, save the far-off noises of people chattering and laughing. He poked his head around the gate, steeling himself to run if there was an angry warrior-woman waiting on the other side of it.

There wasn't. The only people were the merchants and they were all disappearing through a door that was only slightly less grand than the one at the front of the building. Stretching out from that was the lushest grass, the sweetest flowers, and the most perfect little trees that he'd ever seen. Arawn's heart clenched in anticipation.

"Boudica's bosom," he whispered.

Running down the middle of the garden was a perfectly straight path of tiny pebbles, and on either side of it the soft grass was interrupted at regular intervals by intricate flower beds whose patterns were so straight and true that it seemed to Arawn no mere person could have planted them. Around the outside of the garden were myriad large plants and trees, and it was amongst these that he walked. Taking the path would surely only attract unwanted attention.

Just when Arawn thought he'd be happy enough to hide for the rest of his life among the perfumed flora, he noticed a strange round building made entirely of wood towards the end of the gardens. Quite small, its walls were merely carved posts with an elegant archway facing the path that suggested it was the entrance. The roof was domed, and looked as though several strips of thin wood had been woven to create it, and on top of that, glinting in the weak sun, was something golden, but he couldn't discern it from this distance.

What he could discern, however, was the figure sitting within, on a circular bench that stretched around from one side of the archway to the other. She was shaded from the morning sun but he could clearly see her pale skin and flowing, golden hair. His heart stuttered in his chest, and his feet started walking of their own accord. She was looking out onto the beautiful gardens that lay before her so she didn't notice him until he stood in the archway. The instant she turned her deep blue gaze upon him, Arawn dropped to his knees, a strange mix of pain and excitement boiling within him.

He bowed his head. "Rosmerta Warrior-Princess. My name is Arawn Salt-merchant, and I would honour you as my warrior-queen," he said.

– 5 –

The moon of Riuros (Cold-time), 332 C.E. Dubras, Cantiaci tribal lands, Brython

It wasn't that Emrys was scared… Actually, that was precisely what it was, and he knew it. He just thought that if he told himself the opposite enough times, it would become true.

He loved Rosa dearly and would do anything she asked of him. He never thought she'd ask for something so dangerous though. The problem with Rosa was that she was far too clever; she'd managed to get him to talk himself into this predicament, so he really had no one to blame but himself. He'd be ferociously annoyed at his younger sister if he didn't admire her so much; one day, she would make an excellent warrior-queen.

"Why do you want to become a Druid?" Rosa had asked yesterday when all was still right with the world.

"You know why," he'd replied.

"But are you happy? Even though you didn't choose this path for yourself, are you happy?"

He thought before answering, unaware of her motives. "I was happier when I was a Bard," he said. "I know everyone just sees the white robe and assumes all Bards, Ovates and Druids are the same, but I was happier in the lower orders."

Rosa said nothing, so he continued.

"There's more peace in poetry. It's an honour to study magic, and to speak to the ancestors will be humbling, but it's brought with it a heavy price."

"Oh?"

Emrys nodded. "Fear. Everybody fears magic, they fear the discontent of their ancestors and because that's what the Druids do, they fear the Druids."

Rosa tutted. "Perhaps you mistake respect for fear. Everyone knows the important role you have in society—you know the ancient ways, the ancient histories. You remember who we are even when we've forgotten. There's more to Druids than magic."

"You know that because you've been taught. Most people don't though."

"And this makes you unhappy?"

"A little." He thought about the rituals he'd been involved in recently. "But funnily enough, the more I learn about magic, the less I know about it."

She shifted in her seat a little. "I don't understand."

"There are others more capable than I; it makes no sense why he chose me." He'd stopped then, suddenly aware he was revealing too much about himself. "I just wish he'd left me be as a Bard, that's all."

"You speak of Heddgwyn."

Emrys nodded miserably.

"What a coincidence," said Rosa with a little smile. "It's seems you and I have a common enemy."

But that was yesterday; and at the time Emrys had been quite swayed by his sister's concerns. She'd sworn him to secrecy first, and when she was sure he wouldn't betray her, she'd whispered her belief that Heddgwyn was plotting against their mother, warrior-queen of the Cantiaci.

His first reaction was to laugh—the Arch Druid plotting against the warrior-queen? Impossible. Yet Rosa had remained deadly serious, and when she detailed his behaviours and speeches at the council meetings, somehow it felt true. Countless times during their Druidic meetings Emrys had felt uncomfortable, though he'd never been able to explain the reason to himself. He thought he was having a crisis of faith.

And before he realised what he was doing, he was agreeing to be Rosa's eyes at all the Druid meetings he attended and to report back to her, in secret of course, about all that had taken place.

"You seem distracted, Brother," said Heddgwyn. "I'm sorry, I didn't mean to startle you."

"No, no, you didn't startle me." Emrys kept his voice low. His mind was screaming *He knows! He knows! The ancestors have told him of my coming treachery!* and he didn't want it to escape through his lips. "My thoughts seem uneager to remain still this day, is all."

A smile played around the Arch Druid's mouth. "That I had already ascertained. The brew you are making is no more a potion than a fly is an eagle. Might I suggest you meditate before our Fellows arrive? We'll forgo the teaching today. I need you to be able to concentrate later—we have to summon the ancestors."

Emrys dropped the bowls of useless potion into the fire and it hissed at him.

"It's fortunate they're wooden and not pottery."

Emrys tried to smile. They were going to summon the ancestors? How could Heddgwyn be suspicious already? He'd only spoken to Rosa yesterday.

"Sit yourself against an oak, Emrys; I'll prepare the grove for the meeting. Meditate well—I'll not disturb you until it's time for the summoning."

Pushing himself up from the dry forest floor, Emrys did as he was told, making sure he didn't catch Heddgwyn's eye. It was impossible that the Arch Druid knew already. If Emrys thought about this clearly, if he believed, then he would be able to convince himself. He rested against the trunk of the ancient oak and closed his eyes, forcing his mind not to wander until he felt nothing but the quiet calm of air surrounding him and heard nothing but the steady beating of his heart. This had taken him long years to master but right now he was very grateful that he'd persevered.

Think.

Heddgwyn had summoned the Fellows this day after the council meeting with the warrior-queen. She wanted accordance for the bonding between the Cantiaci and Atrebates. But the minor uprising on the feast of Samhain was a bad omen, according to Heddgwyn, so he would summon the ancestors to see if the bonding should proceed or not.

He breathed slowly. In. And out.

The ancestors will only answer a question that is given to them to answer. Unless Heddgwyn specifically asked if there is a traitor amongst the Fellows, he would never learn of his discussion with Rosa.

In. And out.

But was he truly a traitor? A Druid's task was to protect the land and her warrior-queen, and surely that was what he was doing? Undoubtedly the ancestors would see that he, Emrys, was only acting in the best interests of the tribe. They couldn't be angry at him for that, and Rosa wouldn't have involved him if she weren't certain. As the future warrior-queen of the Cantiaci, how could he refuse her?

In. And—

"Are your thoughts calmer, Emrys?"

Emrys opened his eyes to see Heddgwyn looming over him. "Yes, Arch Druid. My mind is at ease."

"Good. Our Fellows are here. Let us prepare for the summoning."

He didn't yet know the chants well enough not to pay attention, but Emrys was unable to focus his mind during the rituals. He was trying to see if Heddgwyn was doing anything out of the ordinary. So far he wasn't. But then, Emrys didn't really know what constituted out of the ordinary.

Down by the sacred stream the Arch Druid had led the litany as usual, invoking Belisama, the water goddess, to bless them with wisdom. Then he stooped and scooped up water in his hand to put into the cauldron from which all the Fellows would take a sip, and carried it back to the sacred grove.

All in a circle they stood, Emrys next to Heddgwyn, and

listened with solemnity while the Arch Druid offered up their prayers to all the gods and goddesses of the forest. Emrys mumbled his responses with the other Fellows but he barely understood the words he uttered.

Then Heddgwyn took the first sip of sacred water and passed it to his right; to Emrys. The cauldron, though small, always surprised Emrys with its weight, despite having drunk from it several times now. A beautiful object, it was cast all of bronze and gold. Faces of gods and goddesses, symbolising death and resurrection, encircled its mouth. Begirding the middle an endless line of people waiting to be cast into the Cauldron of Rebirth, all walking away from the sun as a symbol of their death. Just above were their reborn, immortal souls. A corpse laid inside the Cauldron would be healed of death and arise from it immortal. Unbidden came the thought that such a thing didn't really exist. Heddgwyn claimed it resided at Ynys Afallach. Convenient. And he always expertly sidestepped the question when asked if he'd ever seen the great artefact. Emrys would have to see the magic be performed before he allowed himself to believe it as true.

But that didn't detract from the beauty of the thing he now held in his hands. Bending his head, he took a sip of the sacred water. It was cool. He didn't feel any wiser but he did feel a little refreshed. He passed it on to the Fellow on his right. Nesta; a fairer maiden he'd never seen. She didn't even look at him as she took the cauldron from his hands.

When the Fellows had finished drinking and the cauldron had been dried and wrapped in cloth by Heddgwyn, he finally looked up and around the circle, holding each gaze for several moments before he spoke.

"Fellows, we are gathered here on matters of great import, matters that affect our tribe. Matters that could affect all the tribes that live in this blessed and sacred island we live on."

Only the birds were chattering, high above their heads in the branches of the oaks. The Fellows remained silent. Their chance to talk would come soon enough.

"Sulis Warrior-Queen still has designs to unite our tribe with the Atrebates, indeed to instigate a union between all Brythoniaid. This you know."

Several of the fellows inclined their heads slightly in agreement.

"My intention this day was to call upon the ancestors to ask their advice on this situation, but during my meditations I had a vision, one given to me by Belenos himself."

It was only a moment, but Emrys felt the circle stiffen. A vision from the father of all gods was no small favour despite the recent preference for Boudica and her goddess daughters.

"In this vision I did, indeed, see a united Brython. She was a green isle and fair, sacred to the gods as she is sacred to us. Sacred because she turned aside the evil of the Romans, and all the gods know they can reside here in peace and safety without being drawn into battle by alien gods. My vision showed all Brythoniaid living side by side with their gods in harmony and joy."

He paused, and Emrys wondered when the Arch Druid had found the time to meditate this day—he'd been teaching him for most of it.

"When my vision cleared, I immediately sacrificed a white bull to Belenos to thank him for his gift. And with the entrails I performed an augury with Fellow Emrys."

He didn't know how he managed to do it, but Emrys kept his head from bolting to the left to look at his father. They'd done nothing of the sort! After their lessons, Heddgwyn had told him to meditate because he was out of sorts. Did he not remember? Unlikely. This, then, would be what constituted out of the ordinary.

"A united Brython is what the gods want," said Heddgwyn, his tone never faltering. "Though it is not the warrior-queens the gods choose for this task. It is us.

"My blessed Fellows—the Druids are to be the rulers of Brython."

* * *

Arawn was still on his knees in front of Rosmerta Warrior-Princess, and for several painful heartbeats she'd said nothing. Arawn wanted to look up but he daren't.

Finally she spoke. "How did you get in here?" she said.

"My lady," said Arawn, fighting tears of shame. "Don't you recall me?"

"Not with your head buried into your chest like that."

Lifting his head and swallowing his heart down his throat, Arawn found the courage to look at the warrior-princess. His memories hadn't done her justice at all; more fair and precious was she than the bejewelled torc that graced her pale neck. She was smiling slightly at the awkward boy in front of her, but it wasn't the same smile.

She blinked, and then her perfect eyebrows drew together. "There is something familiar," she muttered, as though she were speaking to herself. Arawn's heart pounded a tattoo in his ears. "You… You're the boy from the marketplace, aren't you?"

Arawn's mouth dropped open.

"You were talking to that Gaulish trader, I'm sure of it."

Arawn's mind raced. *What Gaulish—?*

Then he remembered the man from across the oceans with news of the Romans' one true god. He felt a simultaneous thrill of excitement that she'd seen him here in Dubras, and an arrow of annoyance that she'd forgotten him from Kaer Gradawc.

He decided to ignore it for the moment. "I've fallen on hard times," said Arawn.

Rosmerta nodded. "But that doesn't explain what you're doing here in my garden."

"Your kindness is renowned, Rosmerta Warrior-Princess. And

I'd hoped you would be willing to accept a servant who is willing to serve you faithfully for all eternity."

Rosmerta blinked again. "Please, sit on the bench," she said, indicating the space opposite her. "Kneeling on wood isn't good for the legs."

He did as he was told and her eyes lingered on him for a few heartbeats; then she lowered her gaze.

"I'm afraid choosing the servants of our household is not my decision," she said. "I cannot offer you service here."

If a great eagle had plucked him from the bench, soared into the air and dropped him from a great height, he could not have felt any different. How could this be so? Had she not *smiled* at him?

"I'm sure, however, that I will be able to get you some food. You do look half-starved. Wait here." She stood and paused, looking at him as though she expected him to say something but no words came. Then she stepped lightly down the steps and walked swiftly down the path of little pebbles.

Arawn shook his head. "No," he said. "She said no. I can't believe it. I had so many dreams… I don't understand."

He sat in silence long enough for the weak sun to shift its position across the garden. Briefly Arawn wandered if she would remain true to her word and come back with food. Taking such charity galled him when he was willing to work, but he couldn't bring himself to stand up and leave. Not if that's what she was expecting—hoping—he would do. He'd sit here forever, if that's what it took, and imprison her in that great square house for breaking her promise.

But soon he heard footsteps, and he saw her hurry along the path carrying a huge bundle. There was someone else behind her carrying a bucket. They came closer and Arawn recognised the bucket-carrier as the rude woman who'd opened and closed the door on him so many days ago. She wore a look on her face that spoke so loudly of disapproval he was suddenly reminded of

Mother.

"Here," said Rosmerta when she reached him. Arawn took the proffered bundle. "There's food enough for a few days and some clothes. Bronwyn here has some warm water for you to wash in."

Arawn looked at her blankly and Bronwyn promptly handed over the bucket of water. Some of it slopped onto his hand. It was, indeed, warm.

"Nobody from the house will see you here so you can stay for a short while, but the gate will be locked before sundown."

She paused again, but still Arawn could think of nothing to say. This wasn't how it supposed to happen.

"I'm sorry I cannot give you more," said Rosmerta, avoiding his eye. "But go and see Trahaearn—he's the town smith. He's always looking for strong boys, young men, to help with his iron-working. Tell him I sent you and I'm sure he'll be happy to accommodate. He mayn't pay you anything, but you'll have a warm place to sleep and food to eat, he'll see to that. He's very kind despite how he looks. We must go now before we arouse any more suspicion. Come, Bronwyn."

And just like that, she was gone.

There were two loaves of fresh bread, a round of fresh cheese, four apples, and several thick slices of pork. His appetite had departed with the warrior-princess, but the smell of the food caused his belly to roar so he picked up a slice of the meat and ripped a huge bite from it.

The pork was well salted, the bread soft and the cheese creamy. "I think this is the best food I've ever eaten," said Arawn with his mouth full. Boy, who had now returned to him, grinned. "I can't pretend I'm not disappointed in her," he continued. "I expected more from such a woman as Rosmerta Warrior-Princess. But I am grateful for this food."

He saved exactly half of it, wanting to keep as much as possible but knowing it would spoil if it wasn't eaten, and wrapped it back up in the cloth in which it arrived.

Then Arawn turned his attention to the clothes. They were very simple—a pair of leggings and a tunic—but they were made of good thick wool; and they'd been wrapped in a good, sturdy cloak. Hoodless, but the wool was of excellent quality and would certainly keep him warm and dry.

"I should think," said Arawn when he was washed and dressed and Boy was admiring him in his new attire, "that these belonged to some of the poorer members of the household. And it just goes to show you how well even the poor people of Cantiaci live. Certainly Mother would never deign to dress me in something so fine as this—if only she could see me now!"

He started to smile, but then he remembered the last time he saw her. Captured by the spear-women of Epona Warrior-Queen. The promise of execution hanging over her head.

The same night he killed his sister.

He shivered. "She's as dead as her daughter by now."

He packed his old rags into the bucket that had carried his washing water. He picked it up and put it on the bench.

"That'll do," he said. "I'm sure she'll send that Bronwyn out at some point to get rid of it for her." He took one last look at the great square house that he wouldn't be working in. "Right, then. Let's go home."

By the time they walked out of the gate at the side of the garden, Arawn had forgotten the trepidation he'd once felt at finally meeting Rosmerta Warrior-Princess. Instead it was replaced with bitter disappointment.

– 6 –

The moon of Anagantios (Stay-home time), 332 C.E
Old Dubras, Cantiaci tribal lands, Brython

Boy did nothing, he simply stood there, but Arawn knew he showed him where the little leveret, a youngling hare, hid from its fate—in the barbed undergrowth that surrounded the dead hill-fort. His brother hadn't fared too well in this hiding place last time thanks to the Boy's keen eyesight, and Arawn had caught him as he jumped out, wringing his neck before he could wriggle out of his grip. His skin and sinews were now covering the hole in his cloak that the last hunting expedition had caused, his strong thigh-bone making excellent material for a needle; but it had been too many days that his stomach had benefitted from his flesh. Even though a new moon had passed, the ground was still too cold for foraging hares to be in abundance, so Arawn had to take his prey whenever he saw it. What would Mother say if she saw him now, hunting the sacred hare of Andraste to fill his belly? He wanted to smile, but he was famished.

Boy was motionless which meant the youngling hare was still in there. He shifted his bone-tipped spear, newly-made and as yet untested, into his right hand ready for the kill, and crept forward. Then a dead branch cracked underneath his foot. Boudica's tits! The little leveret leapt from the thicket, through the Boy and pelted, zigzagging, across the uneven ground. Arawn dashed after him, knowing all the while it was futile—he was too hungry for a sustained chase—and when he disappeared into the frost-laced undergrowth in the distance Arawn threw his spear down with a cry of frustration; then he turned to look back at Boy accusingly, but he just stared with that unchanging mournful expression of his and Arawn held his tongue. He probably wouldn't have even spotted the leveret in the first place if it hadn't been for Boy, and certainly he could slide through the landscape without breaking twigs and scaring off the evening meal, but that just made Arawn even angrier. Snatching up his spear, the head of which had now come loose thanks to its mistreatment and would need mending, Arawn stalked back to the foot of the hill-fort, feeling tears of despair burn his eyes.

He was so hungry! He could steal all the barley and make all the porridge he wanted but it wouldn't fill the iron hole in his stomach. He needed bread and cheese again. And pork! He'd thought he was fed little enough by Mother, especially if she was in one of her particularly hungry moods, but he looked back on those meal-times with a sense of longing now, hating himself for feeling so reliant on her.

Halfway to the plateau of the dead town of Old Dubras, Arawn's legs began to fail him and a cold sweat burst out on his forehead and down his back. He couldn't climb any more. There was nothing in him. He'd wrap himself in his cloak, just for a little while, and sit down until the shaking and sweating passed. Boy was beside him now, his constant companion, looking down with mournful eyes, shaking his head.

"I can't," Arawn whispered. "So tired."

Without shifting his gaze, Boy raised his hand and stretched out a finger until he was pointing down the hill, north-west across the darkening landscape. In the direction of Dubras. Arawn shook his own head and buried it in his cloak, then lay down to rest. He wouldn't go back to that town where the treacherous Rosmerta lived just so he could beg work from a stranger. Old Dubras was his home now. He'd fix the roundhouse. He'd hunt hare. Eat. Sleep.

* * *

He opens his eyes. Boy is gone, so is the wind but it is still cold enough to turn his bones to icicles. Looking around him he sees the landscape is the same, but different. He still clings to the side of the hill-fort, but the brittle grass is now dusty grey, like ash. Beyond, where new Dubras should lie is a lake of fire and ice, burning and freezing the evil souls of Otherworld. Mother is there, he knows it, and so is his sister, Ffraid.

Except Ffraid is in the cauldron. He knows that too.

Startled, he jumps to his feet, his hands sinking slightly in the ash grass—what magic has been worked on him to bring him to this place?

Quickly yet slowly he turns, wanting to run up the hill-fort to Old Dubras and away from the lake where Mother lurks, but he is arrested instantly by a white-robed figure, hoodless, revealing the gory remains of his head. He tries to scream but his breath is stuck in his throat. No…not stuck, for the dead don't breathe…

The Dead will find the living. They cannot escape the Dead. The living will be devoured and so become the Dead.

Gwynfor's voice reaches his head without passing through his ears; without, even, the Druid moving his mouth. But he moves his mouth now, opens it wide like he is ululating a violent, silent scream that screeches the same words, over and over.

The Dead will find the living. They cannot escape the Dead. The living will be devoured and so become the Dead.

Now, the whole Otherworld consists of nothing but that yawning void, and it's coming ever closer, closer, and he knows that he will be devoured. He will be devoured and stay here in Otherworld and become the Dead.

Become the Dead.

The Dead.

* * *

Cold wind sliced his cheek open and the pain woke him. Moving, his cloak crunched and Arawn knew it must have rained a little in the night, only to be frozen by the evil wind that tore through his flesh to his bones. His body was numb except for his stomach which was still as empty and heavy as a cauldron.

He opened his eyes. He was still on the side of the hill. Looking up, he saw Boy hadn't moved in either position or posture; he still pointed at new Dubras. Last night, Arawn thought he had died. He didn't want to beg work from a stranger, but what choice did he have? He was still alive now, but how much longer could probably be counted in sunsets. He had no wish to meet Mother in Otherworld where she would mock him for dying like a starved animal; he wanted to meet her as a person of importance and mock her for dying as a failed rebel.

Looking back up at Boy, he finally nodded. He needn't speak, Boy knew him well enough. And he knew the decision had finally been made so he lowered his arm. With burning fingers of ice Arawn pushed himself up from the frozen ground, beating the wind that fought to keep him down, and looked out again at Dubras. Then he stepped forwards.

* * *

The hammer fell, raising another shower of burning sparks. Just like the first time, Arawn jumped as the metal clanged.

"I'm supposed to ask *him* for work?" he said, his eyes fixed on the hulk of man who was sweating fiercely despite the chillness of the day. Stripped to the waist, the smith's muscles bulged as they worked the metal. And he was covered in iron-grey hair; his head, face, chest and arms. It was no wonder the man felt no cold through all that, not to mention the warmth from the forge. Even from the entrance to the smithy, where he hoped he wouldn't have to say anything to catch the man's attention, the heat emanating from the place made Arawn feel breathless; he could feel his hair curl and crisp.

The hammering ceased, and the smith took up the object he was beating in a huge pair of tongs and plunged it deep into a barrel of water which sat adjacent to him. The steam it threw up almost covered the giant man completely.

"Done," he bellowed, though Arawn assumed he must be talking to himself. "Well, what do you think, lad?"

Arawn's mouth dropped open; the smith guffawed like a donkey.

"There's not many people who just stand at the doorway when there's a lovely fire to warm themselves next to. What do you think?"

He took the metal object in his fist and held it out to Arawn who took it hesitantly. It was surprisingly cool.

"It's a bowl?"

The donkey-laugh came again. "Certainly looks that way, doesn't it? No, lad, what it is, is part of a new suit of armour the warrior-queen has asked me to design for her spear-women. It'll look like fish-scales when it's done, but this particular morsel goes here." The smith held the bowl-shaped metal up to his chest. If he'd been a woman, Arawn realised, it would have fitted comfortably around his left—

The roar of laughter only made his furious blush worse.

"My wife doesn't really approve either. Though I expect she'd think differently if it were her fighting the Picts." He put the piece of armour down and turned to face Arawn. Leaning against the water-barrel and folding his arms he said, "And what is it I can do for you, lad? I'm thinking nothing where you'll be giving me coin afterwards."

Arawn felt himself blush once more. "No, Master Smith."

"Trahaearn's my name. No need to call me Master Smith."

"Trahaearn. Rosmerta Warrior-Princess sent me."

His face glowed as bright as his furnace at the sound of her name. "She mentioned something about sending a boy to me—" he puffed a little as he thought "—must be at least a moon past."

"She said you might give me some work."

The giant smith lifted an iron-grey eyebrow. "She did, and yet it's taken you this long to get here—starved into it, by the looks of you." Arawn said nothing. "Well, then. Ever beaten metal, lad?"

Arawn shook his head. "But I'm used to heavy lifting and hard work."

For several long heartbeats the only sound was the roaring of flames.

"Atrebates, are you? Don't look so surprised, lad, everyone around here knows they're more...hard-working than us. Reckon I can understand why you chose Dubras as your new home as well. Right!" he said, hefting his huge frame from its perch against the water-barrel. "If the lady says I'm to give you work, then I reckon I can find you something. Won't be giving you no coin for it, though—you'll have to make do with food and a bed and I reckon you've not seen much of either lately. That suit you?"

"Yes, Master, thank you!"

"And don't be calling me Master! Trahaearn's my name and it's the only thing I respond to. And what shall I call you?"

"Arawn."

"Right then, lad; let's get some bread inside you, then see what you can do."

It was a long day, and by the end of it Arawn was tired and hot. And truly happy. The work he'd been given wasn't anything more interesting than cleaning the smith's tools, many of which were so thick with soot that cleaning them was near impossible, but Trahaearn was good company. He had many stories to share, not just about himself but of other members of the town too, and he was an excellent story-teller. Arawn didn't notice the sun dip behind the horizon until the smith announced it was time to go home for dinner.

"You'll be meeting my wife and mind you mind your manners. She's as generous as they come, but a bit particular when it comes to manners. Don't know where she gets it from myself, but who's to guess at these things, eh?" Arawn smiled, although this was the moment he'd been dreading—what if she was like Mother?

Their house was at the back of the smithy. A squat, stone affair, but large with several chimneys, and herbs and plants flourished either side of the front door. Despite his nervousness, he was impressed; even common Cantii had wooden front doors in Dubras.

With one fist, Trahaearn pushed open the door and immediately the aroma of baking bread and stewing meat wafted out. Arawn's belly roared.

"I second that, lad," Trahaearn said with a chuckle. "But we'll be feasting well tonight, never you fear."

"You go and wash that grime off you before you come into my kitchen," called a disembodied voice.

"We will, my love, fret not!"

"We?"

The front door opened onto a corridor, wide and paved with colourful tiles swept clean, with rooms off each side and one directly in front of them. It was from there that a woman appeared. Rich brown hair fell in a braid down one shoulder, and her skin was fair and clean, quite the opposite of Trahaearn's at the moment. But unlike most women Arawn had known, this one was tiny. As she walked towards them he noted her fine clothes. Evidently the hard work that the smith did in the town earned good coin.

"I wish you'd tell me when you invite people for dinner," she said. "I'm only a few footsteps away." She stepped up onto her toes as Trahaearn bent down so she could kiss both of his cheeks. Then she cast a glance over Arawn. "And he's as filthy as you are."

"My new worker," said Trahaearn by way of introduction.

"Indeed?"

"This here is Arawn, come all the way from Atrebates."

She raised an eyebrow. "There's a thing, indeed. Well, I'm Nia, seeing as my husband's forgotten his manners and neglected to tell you." She frowned at her husband briefly, then turned her attention back to him. "You'll have to wash up. Can't abide such filth at my dinner table, I'm afraid. And if you need fresh clothes, my husband will have to arrange them for you. Nice to meet you."

And with that, she swivelled on her heel and headed back towards the kitchen.

By way of apology, Trahaearn gave his new apprentice a crooked grin. "Her heart's as big as her mouth," he said. "Go and wash up in there and I'll fetch you something clean to wear."

In there turned out to be a small stone room, clean and scented with fresh rushes and flowers on the floor. In the middle was a stone basin and a prettily decorated jug filled with water. Arawn dipped his fingers into it; cold, but that didn't detract from his astonishment that this family had a separate room where they cleaned themselves. There was even a privy in the corner. Winter ablutions in this house must be quite pleasurable indeed.

The smith came back quickly with a bundle of fresh clothes. "These belonged to our sons," he said. "But they've gone off and found their own wives and families so I don't think they'll be coming back for them any time soon."

"You had no daughters?" asked Arawn, taking his share of the bundle; a pair of green leggings and a red, long-sleeved tunic. The wool was soft with years of wear and washing.

"No, lad. Three strong sons was all we needed. They did their fair share of work for me in the smithy, learned the trade, and then went off to seek their own fortunes. What more could a husband and wife want?"

"No daughters to carry on the family name?" Arawn could scarcely believe it.

"Boudica's bosom, lad!" laughed Trahaearn. "Far be it from

me to judge other tribes on this fair isle of ours; but our family will continue through our children be they sons or daughters. My boys have gone off to be smithies and in that they do me and their mother proud. Any woman'll be lucky to have them. Now, get in them clean clothes and get into the kitchen. Won't do to let our food go cold since Nia's been working so hard over it."

It wasn't until he was confronted by the laden table that Arawn was able to shift his mind from the sacrilegious things Trahaearn had said. But even the unthinkable notion that boys were thought of with pride in this tribe was swept aside when his nose was beset with the bouquet of beef and bean stew, freshly baked bread, bowls of steaming vegetables and platters of succulent fruits and rounds of cheese. Even Mother had never conjured such a banquet—not even for the feast of Samhain. It was as though he'd woken up to his most prized dream.

"My lady," Arawn said, feeling, to his surprise, his throat swell, "I've never seen such a spread. I cannot imagine how I deserve it."

The smith chuckled and Nia tutted, though the slightest smile gave away her pleasure. "Nonsense, lad," she said. "Everyone has to eat. This is simple fare after an honest day's work. And my name's Nia, not lady." She looked at him through slightly narrowed eyes. "What tribe you from again, lad?"

"Atrebates."

She shared a look with her husband before continuing. "I know other tribes sometimes do things differently to us, but are you telling me you never used to eat like this where you came from? Pass me your bowl and I'll fill it with stew while it's hot."

"No, my lady, um, Nia," he said handing over his bowl as he was told, but being served by the lady of the house instead of serving her felt as wrong to him as snow in the moon of bright-time. "We were lucky to get bread and scraps."

"A poor family, then?"

"Not at all. Mother was a salt-merchant. And wealthy enough

to buy a slave, and hire a Druid for my sister."

Stone circle, fire, screams. Blood. Bone breaking against stone.

"Why just bread and scraps, then?"

"What? Oh." Arawn shook his head. "Mother and Ffraid ate first. Papa and I shared whatever was left but Mother was a hungry woman."

"No wonder you're as thin as a poker then," said Trahaearn. "Eat up, lad. I'm a hungry man, and if you want seconds you'll have to beat me to it."

Arawn looked at his bowl of stew, wooden spoon in hand. Even the fat chunks of meat couldn't reignite his hunger—his appetite had been cut down by thoughts of his murderous sister. Nia's brow creased with suspicion so he loaded his wooden spoon and brought it to his mouth.

One spoonful of fresh meat swimming in thick gravy was all his stomach needed to stir back into action. The taste was enough to bring him to tears after so many moons of nothing but porridge, and yet as well as crying out for the goodness of rich food his body also warned him against it. His belly clenched on his second mouthful, and to his wonder he felt nearly full; slowly and carefully was the answer. And the same could be said for the ale that Trahaearn was insistent he drink mightily of. And what ale! The brew that Mother had allowed Papa to buy for himself was dark and bitter, and Arawn had only ever drank it because he didn't want to perish from thirst. This, however, was like drinking sunshine. It was as yellow and sweet as honey and welcomed by his entire body, though already he was feeling very light-headed. It wasn't long before he felt as if his whole being was smiling.

"So, Arawn," said Nia when the meal was nearing its close. "How long do you plan to stay in Dubras?"

"As long as I can, my lady Nia. Life is as sweet as nectar here; truly one can feel blessed by the gods. The old gods, that is. The real ones. Belenos, and all them. Not Boudica and her daughters.

Although, obviously, I pray. To them. Perhaps I can even learn the trade of smithing so I can go off and make my wife and find a fortune." He beamed at Trahaearn who beamed right back.

"I'm sure it'll give my husband great pleasure to teach someone again. Especially someone so willing to learn. But surely you could've learned a trade in Atrebates? Travelling all the way to Cantiaci to learn smithing seems…extreme," she said.

"There was nothing for me to learn in Atrebates. And besides, I had to escape."

"Escape from what?"

"My sister." He scowled.

"I see," she said. "Still. A long journey for a young lad."

Arawn nodded. "But it was easier than staying there," he said. Suddenly his eyes filled with tears and he felt an urgent compulsion to cry.

"I think," said Trahaearn, standing and placing his hands gently on Arawn's shoulders, "it's time the lad made for his bed. He's a long day ahead of him on the morrow. Up you get, Arawn, I'll show you to the stables. There's a loft you'll find warm and comfortable. Up you get."

"Thank you, my lady Nia," said Arawn, swaying ever so slightly, "for such a marvellous meal. And thank you, Trahaearn, for inviting me into your home and smithy."

"You're welcome on all counts, lad. Now let's sleep it off, shall we?"

Arawn nodded, though to what he wasn't quite sure. Smiling again, he followed the smith closely to a door he hadn't noticed before in the kitchen and breathed deeply when the cold night air hit him.

"Here we are, lad," said Trahaearn, handing him a blanket. Arawn took it and looked around him. The room was huge, and barely lit by the taper that Trahaearn was suddenly holding. Everything smelled a bit horsey.

"I'll get you up at dawn and we can start your training."

Clapping a big hand on Arawn's shoulder, the kind smith smiled and walked out of the huge room into the night.

Arawn bent over and vomited up everything inside him, then covered it with straw; and that was the last thing that he remembered.

– 7 –

The moon of Ogronios (Ice time), 332 C.E.
Dubras, Cantiaci tribal lands, Brython

She paced. She knew it made her look frantic, but she couldn't help it. The new moon was dark in the night sky and the council was gathering as Heddgwyn had ordered. Any moment now he would arrive and Rosmerta had heard nothing from Emrys. He'd promised that he'd meet with her before the council, and never in their entire lives had her brother broken an oath to her. Which meant…?

Which meant something had gone terribly wrong and Heddgwyn had discovered their treachery.

Or Emrys had discovered nothing and Heddgwyn was entirely innocent.

Or Emrys had discovered something shattering and was too frightened to tell her.

She pulled her fingers through her hair and concentrated on not screaming. There were any number of plausible explanations for Emrys' absence, and trying to guess at which one was like trying to count the stars; and did she fret at not knowing how many of those there were? No, it was pointless.

Yes, all very well to say that. But unfortunately, the body had a way of acting of its own accord under times of stress, no matter what logical monologues the head offered it. Besides, she couldn't wait in her chambers all night. She was expected at the council. And if she arrived late it would only arouse suspicion.

So much suspicion…

She could only wait a few more moments then she'd have to leave. Emrys was an intelligent man, intelligent enough to become an Ovate, so she would have to trust his actions.

Yes. Trust. That's what she had to do.

There was a soft tap at her door, but she swung around as if she'd heard a crash. She ran to open it.

"Where have you been?" she whispered. "I've had such terrible thoughts!"

"Forgive me," said her brother, just as quietly, looking over each shoulder. "It was difficult for me to get away. And I can't stay long; there's a servant waiting for me at my chamber and if Heddgwyn should discover I didn't go straight there... Shut the door," he said when he was deep inside her chamber. "What I have to say won't take long anyway, but we haven't got time for discussion. I come only as a messenger."

"Quick, then, tell me what news and we can go."

Emrys nodded; then told her of the plans Heddgwyn had revealed to the Fellows at the sacred grove. Plans of a Brython united under the Druids.

If Rosmerta was worried before, it was nothing compared to how she felt when Emrys had finished talking. *Treason*?

And then he just left—as if she didn't have questions as numerous as the stars clamouring for attention!

The main one, of course, being what to do with such knowledge. She certainly wouldn't have time to tell her mother before the council session started; and even if she did, what could she say? It's true because Emrys told me? Then he would be in trouble and she promised that wouldn't happen to him.

Rosmerta clasped her hands to keep them from shaking and concentrated on her breathing. Emrys had left her chamber several moments ago. She really ought to go herself. Standing around in uncertainty wouldn't solve the crisis; she needed to behave like a warrior-princess, not a frightened child.

The corridor was long and cold, the torches lining the walls doing nothing but accentuating the shadows. The palace was always so lovely come Beltane when the sun was stronger and the countryside was blooming. But during these dead months...

Of course, the other tribes hated these buildings whatever the season. Unnatural, they called them, made all of stone and rigid angles. Even though their main door faced east as was proper, the palace was so big, with so many rooms, that the sun couldn't possibly reach in and complete its cycle of life and death as the day wound on. But it didn't mean the Cantii worshipped it any less. It was just that, even though they were barely here for a generation, the Romans left certain things behind them; ways of doing things, administering the people, ideas.

Ideas. Was it so impossible to meld their traditional beliefs with new ideas? The other tribes would say yes, but Rosmerta had travelled across many borders and nowhere had she seen people as happy and well-fed as in her own tribe.

But ideas were also dangerous. Heddgwyn was proving that with traitorous accuracy. And yet, now that she came to think about it, how did his idea differ with that of her mother's? The idea to unite. The very idea the Romans came with those three hundred winters past; unite the tribes under a common leader. But they wanted the tribes to become Roman and were prepared to use deadly force in order to achieve it, whether the Brythoniaid wanted it or not. Her mother, on the other hand, wanted unity through peace, offering a choice to tribes to join or not, and giving them her daughters as a promise of her goodwill. She would not fight them. There would be no violence. She wanted only what benefitted the lands and the people living in them.

There was no hubbub bubbling out from the council chamber's imposing door, but when she stepped through she saw clearly that people were whispering their conversations while they waited for the session to begin. If this were full morning, she thought, I would've heard them from halfway down the corridor. It's funny how deep night can silence the most vivacious of gossipers.

Hush fell across the room like a blanket of snow when Rosmerta sat down. Now that everyone was present, the councillors waited for Heddgwyn to utter the first words to officially start the session. Until then, all must be quiet.

"Thank you all," said Heddgwyn, looking only at Rosmerta, "for attending. The ancestors smile upon you."

Now Sulis Warrior-Queen arose. She looked majestic in a dress of blood-red wool, the golden torcs about her arms and neck shining as bright as her hair in the candlelight. "The moon is black, Arch Druid Heddgwyn, and the council awaits your decision."

Rosmerta scanned the faces for Emrys but he was nowhere to be seen. He didn't normally attend the meetings, of course, though that didn't preclude him. Such meetings were public and anyone could attend if they had a mind to; though at this time of night all would be sleeping. Heddgwyn knew that. Was he somehow responsible for Emrys' absence also?

"A decision has been made, Warrior-Queen," said Heddgwyn, standing, holding his rowan staff of power in front of him for all to see. "Though before I impart it, you must know that it comes from higher minds than mine. Higher, even, than those Druids of sacred Ynys Afallach."

A murmur rippled across the chamber like the disturbed surface of a sleeping lake, and several of the councillors leaned forward. Rosmerta stiffened and looked towards her mother. For a heartbeat uncertainty was in her eyes but she regained her composure. The warrior-princess prayed to Rosmerta, her namesake goddess, the great provider and carer, that the Arch Druid hadn't seen it.

"The council attends you."

Heddgwyn smiled. "There shall, indeed, be unification."

Several approving noises emanated from the councillors, and Rosmerta saw her mother's shoulders sag minutely in relief. *No, Mother. He hasn't yet finished.*

Then he sat down.

"The council thanks you for your decision, Heddgwyn," said Sulis, smiling at him. "Our patience has been rewarded." She looked briefly at Rosmerta and faced her council once more. "Now, I must bring your attention to some information I have received, and I feel it pertinent to discuss it now so that none of our people is needlessly worried."

Rosmerta felt as though someone had walked up to her and slapped her for no good reason. What game was Heddgwyn playing? Where was his announcement that the Druids were to rule the lands as sanctified by the gods themselves? Her thoughts were so muddled that she missed the news her mother imparted.

"That's impossible!" bellowed a voice from the one of the benches, instantly bringing Rosmerta back to attention. It was Trahaearn Smith of course—no one could bellow an opinion quite like him. "If the Picts had come that far south we'd've heard it about long before now. They're not known for their silent trespassing."

"They didn't come over land," said Sulis. "They came by boat."

There was uproar. Rosmerta wished now she'd been paying attention; this was disturbing news.

"The Iceni-Coritani patrol their borders well," said Heddgwyn. "Their spear-women are renowned for their skill and accuracy. Perhaps it was inevitable that the Picts would find another way to steal from us. Building boats and molesting the coastal settlements further south seems like a logical step."

"But the Trinovantes?" said the Smith. "That's just across the shore from us!"

"Which is why the news is so worrying," said Sulis. "We must discuss what should be done."

"Why should we do anything?" came a voice from the back benches. Rosmerta couldn't see her face. "The Trinovantes won't even trade with us, so deep are they in Iceni pockets. Why should we seek to aid those who despise us?"

"Because we can," said Sulis. "We have many boats."

The furore started up again. Boats were expensive, and needed for trading with the Gauls.

"And because I doubt the Picts will stop at the Trinovantes," the warrior-queen continued, raising her hands for silence. "What if they decide to raid our shores? Who will we call upon then to help *us* if we have offered no help to others? We may be a wealthy tribe, but we are small. Once our riches are plundered, our animals and harvest taken, what, then, shall we have?"

Silence crashed back. Rosmerta could well imagine the councillors feeling as wretched and worried as she, though they had the luxury of being able to succumb to it, and the knowledge that it would be dealt with by their warrior-queen. She folded her hand in her lap and clutched at her fingers tightly.

"And," said Sulis, her tone even softer, "what better way is there to start building bridges 'twixt us and our neighbours?" She turned to Heddgwyn and, to Rosmerta's dismay, she smiled warmly at him. He looked like he was about to say something, but the smith interrupted him.

"If you don't mind my asking, lady," he said, "but what do you intend to do? Ride out there and start a war at sea?"

"I don't see why we should do that," said the voice from the back. "Risk our own people when the Trinovantes won't even know who saved their sorry hides? I say we should only help if they ask."

"Though you know very well, Fletcher, that they would rather die than do that," said Sulis. Her mother was always able to recognise the voice even if the face were hidden by shadows.

"Then let them," said Fletcher.

"And we run the risk of being raided next. No; we will have to meet them at sea. I don't know how skilled they are at sea-faring, but if it resembles their battle skills they will be disorganised and lack strategy. I believe a show of strength would scare them off."

"And what if they come back with more boats?" Fletcher was determined to get her point across.

"Then we send out more of our own," said Sulis. "And you

earn more business making more arrows for my warriors. But before you ask any more questions, I think it wise that we now have a constant presence in the water, patrolling our shores and those of our neighbours. They will know it's us from the standard painted on our prows. It may be that we need to build more boats, but we are a wealthy tribe and I'm sure there are many idle hands during these cold months that would be willing to be warmed with honest hard work. Once it is evident that any immediate threat of raiding has passed, I will visit the Trinovantes myself and discuss an alliance."

"If I might ask," said Rosmerta. Sulis nodded. "Would this alliance be a bonding between daughter and son?" Not that she would oppose her mother, but she happened to know that the Trinovantes warrior-queen only had one son, and he was a gibbering fool.

Perhaps Sulis knew what was on her daughter's mind for she smiled, but as she opened her mouth to speak, Heddgwyn interrupted them.

"Bad news comes," he said, and the councillors whispered among themselves. Sulis opened her mouth to question his prediction but the chamber door slammed open, the sound in the deep night causing all to jump and cry out. All save the Arch Druid, who turned his gaze on the royal spear-woman who now stood, framed, before them, chest heaving after running from her post in great speed. Her darting eyes and the deep frown on her forehead betrayed her agitation.

"What is the meaning of this intrusion?" asked Sulis.

"The Atrebates," said the spear-woman. "They were spotted crossing the borders of our lands, led by Epona Warrior-Queen herself, some hundreds. All dressed for battle."

Sulis looked to Heddgwyn, a frown forming on her own brow. "What is the meaning of this?"

The Arch Druid breathed deeply and held her gaze. "The Atrebates are come to war."

– 8 –

The moon of Ogronios (Ice-time), 332 C.E.
Dubras, Cantiaci tribal lands, Brython

Rosmerta hadn't slept since the meeting. Sulis Warrior-Queen had dismissed the councillors once the commotion had died down, eliciting vows from every one of them to tell no one what they had heard that night. It wasn't easy; not one of them could remember the last time Cantiaci had faced open war and the fear surrounding them was as real yet ungraspable as thick fog. Fortunately, the royal women had Trahaearn on their side and he bellowed and ushered them out and to their own homes as well as any hound would herd a flock.

"They will not be able to keep this news to themselves," her mother had said once they were alone. "By tomorrow even the whole town will know and news will be spreading to the outlying settlements."

"You cannot blame them, Mother. A frightened person needs a companion, and why shouldn't she have one?" She looked around the still chamber for the source of the panic. "Where's Heddgwyn?"

"With his Fellows I don't doubt; if ever we needed guidance from our ancestors and the gods, it's now."

Rosmerta didn't doubt it either, but for one who had evidently revelled in the outcry of his prediction—she'd seen the glint in his eye as he'd glanced around the chamber, she was sure of it—he'd certainly made a secret of his exit. Was this merely another strand of his web of usurpation? It seemed too much of a coincidence; the Atrebates arrive for war when he gives his consent for unification at last. A ploy, perhaps, to instil distrust amongst the tribes so that when he took over with his band of treacherous Druids the people would be crying out for their magical protection. But how would he have convinced Epona to march against the tribe with which she'd so recently agreed to bond? None of it made it any sense. And the conundrum was enough to keep her awake every night until dawn.

"You haven't slept again, my child," said Sulis, entering Rosmerta's sleeping chambers as the rising sun failed to penetrate the clouds that cloaked the town.

"No doubt neither have you, Mother."

She offered a wan smile. Rosmerta loved her best when they were alone like this and she revealed her true sentiments. "It is my duty. And will be yours, in time; but until then you shouldn't let yourself become so distracted by such matters. You should sleep while you still can."

"Did you when you were my age?"

The warrior-queen chuckled. "Your tone tells me you know the answer very well." She walked over to where her daughter sat, wrapped in a hide blanket, in front of the dying fire and poked at the embers until there was life once more. Then she fed it until it was crackling merrily. "You're so like me, my child, that sometimes it scares me."

She sat up a little straighter. "Why would that scare you?"

"Ah, despite my best efforts I've made mistakes…" She looked at Rosmerta then, becoming aware of herself and swatting away the last statement with a hand. It still clutched a log and splinters were scattered. "But I wasn't as gifted as you. Always trust your intuition, my child, for it is stronger than even you realise." She rose then and kissed Rosmerta lightly on the forehead.

If ever she was going to admit her fear of her mother's faith in her it was now, this moment, when the warrior-queen was herself, not her role; but if she released the words she feared releasing the tears that would certainly accompany it.

"You have something you wish to say to me, my child?"

Rosmerta hesitated, trying to draw strength from the light touch of her mother's hand on her cheek. "Only that," she breathed deeply, "that I wish to help. There must be something you wish me to do this day?"

Sulis Warrior-Queen smiled down at her. "That isn't why I came here. But I can see your desire to help. Perhaps you would speak with Trahaearn Smith for me about the new armour he's making our spear-women. I should have spoken to him myself when the news first arrived, but I haven't found the time. I had hoped it would be an unnecessary caution against the Picts, but perhaps it will see battle after all. If you could bring him to me when the day is fully begun I shall be very grateful."

And so she found herself outside the smithy, surprised at how yet another eternal morning had passed so quickly after all. She'd barely reached the wide doors of the forge when Trahaearn came ambling out to her, blocking her view of the inside and with it the warmth of the furnace.

"More news?" he whispered. "I've said nothing to Nia."

"I didn't think you would," she said with a smile. "But I'm here on an errand only."

"The armour, is it?"

Rosmerta nodded.

"I'll fetch it for you; I keep it in the house. It's too precious to leave in the smithy overnight. Come in and warm yourself by the fire a moment, there's no mistaking it's ice-time on a morn such as this." He waved her in and disappeared off in the direction of his house.

For the first time since he'd fallen to his knees in the Roman summer house in the garden, Rosmerta laid eyes on the young man called Arawn Salt-merchant. She was pleased that he looked a little less scrawny and haunted than he had done then, but there was still something about him… A sense of hardship, perhaps, that she would never understand. It gave a maturity to his stance and features that was undeniably striking. Suddenly she was aware of the silence between them.

"I see Trahaearn Smith has put you to very good use already,"

Rosmerta said. She smiled, but Arawn seemed not to notice.

"Yes," he said simply, looking at her for several heartbeats longer than was polite. She shifted away from it a little. Finally he bent back to his task of polishing tools.

"I trust the smith is treating you well, however," she said. "He is well-known to me. I knew he would be able to give you work where I could not. I hope that you are able to forgive me for that. In truth I believe that you will be happier here…" She heard her voice and the nonsense she was uttering but she was able to stop. It was as though his eyes were drawing out her very soul.

* * *

Arawn was angry. For so many moons he'd believed that she, Rosmerta, was different to all the other women, but she'd turned out to be no better. Perhaps worse, with her deceptive smile of false friendliness. Yet here she was, reminding him of what she *had* done for him. And he liked Trahaearn, liked working in the smithy with him and sharing his meals. He cared a little less for Nia, always stealing a glance when she thought he wasn't looking, but her food was good and plentiful.

Still, he found it hard to believe that she couldn't have found something for him up in her grand house. Was she not a warrior-princess? Could she not do as she pleased? He looked at her again, and was glad she still looked uncomfortable. No woman had ever felt discomfort in his presence before, only scorn. It pleased him well. Better that than the surge of joy he'd felt when he'd seen her fair face appear at the smithy doors only moments before; that was a sentiment she didn't deserve and he'd have to learn to quash it.

"He treats me very well."

"Then I'm glad," she said. "It may surprise you to learn that things in Cantiaci aren't as in other tribes. I, and not even my mother the warrior-queen, can do as we please."

Arawn looked up from his polishing in shock. Was she reading his thoughts? Mother had always known what he was thinking if ever he'd questioned her wisdom or actions in his mind.

"And for that," she continued. "I believe you will be happier here. You've already seen how our menfolk are treated."

Proving her point, Trahaearn marched in with the unique suit of armour draped over one arm as though it were no heavier than a woollen tunic. Only the bulge in his upper arm gave a clue as to its true weight.

"Quite a creation," said the warrior-princess, her eyes pouring over it. "And you've done well to finish it so timely."

He looked towards Arawn and favoured him with a grin, which Arawn returned.

"Couldn't have done so without my trusted 'prentice. And I've you to thank for him, my lady, and that I certainly do." The smith turned now to Arawn. "I've some business to attend to up at the palace. Be sure and let anyone who needs any smithing done know that I'll be back shortly."

Arawn nodded and smiled. Then he looked at Rosmerta. She said farewell and smiled at him, but it wasn't the same smile. No indeed. Not the same smile at all.

* * *

She didn't understand why it bothered her so much. There were certainly bigger, more worrying, events unfolding, and one boy's opinion of her shouldn't matter, but…

He'd looked so earnest and forlorn that day two moons ago when he'd fallen to his knees and begged for help. Yet when he looked at her today he was…angry? Perhaps. Disappointed seemed more appropriate. Yes, she thought, he was disappointed. In her. As though she had failed him. It was something she'd never come across before. Her mother, her entire family, were well-loved by the Cantii. She knew this to be true, and it was because they never failed anyone. The thought that this one young man who'd needed her help and been refused by her, was disappointed in her, made her uneasy. She wanted to repair it, but didn't know how she could. If she couldn't do it for one, how could she do it for an entire tribe?

"My lady?" Trahaearn was looking at her. "Did you hear any of what I said?"

"My sincerest apologies, Trahaearn; my mind was elsewhere."

"No need to apologise to me, my lady, I know well how matters are standing. Even if I hadn't been at the council that night, the fact that Sulis Warrior-Queen has need to see and discuss this armour would've been clue enough."

"Indeed," she said, glad of the useful conclusion for Trahaearn to jump to. "Of course."

The smith lowered his voice so no passer-by would hear. "Are you sure they're bringing war upon us?"

"I couldn't believe it myself, but our own scouts spotted them early this morn marching towards Dubras. And Heddgwyn seems certain."

The smith looked grave.

"But let us not speak of it out here. I cannot risk panicking the people for the moment. Let us speak of other matters. Your new apprentice, for instance."

"Ah, well! He's a good lad. Hard-working, though I expect he's used to that, coming from Atrebates. You know, we hear tales, but it's hard to believe that men-folk can be so poorly treated just across the borders until you see it for yourself."

"Indeed?"

"Oh, aye. Worse than a slave, that poor lad. And he's got the scars and old bruises to prove it."

Rosmerta raised her hand to her own faded bruise, remembering the fear and pain of unexpected violence. Surely it was no more than a coincidence that the spear-women of Arawn's tribe were descending upon them. A hard life he may have suffered, but he was too insignificant to cause a war. It must be related to the failed bonding in some way.

"I said it to him and I'll say it to you: it's no wonder he wanted to escape. And lucky for me, though I should be shamed to say such, considering all he's suffered. But he's good help. Still has a little trouble with my Nia, though." Trahaearn sighed a little and shook his head. "Think it'll take a bit more than a few good meals to convince him she isn't his mother."

"He speaks of it, then? His past life?"

"Not much. Just enough to show us his happiest moments weren't with his mother. Or his sister, for that matter. I always thought the tales of other tribes following Boudica's words so strictly were just that—tales; but having him with us has certainly opened our eyes. I'd like to say he did well in coming to Cantiaci but if the scouts are right…"

Rosmerta nodded sadly. "Let us just hope that war can be stayed with palaver."

"I don't understand the reason for it; why would they come to fight when four moons ago they were ready to bond?"

"If we knew the answer to that…"

Trahaearn raised an eyebrow, but allowed the thought to go unfinished. The Atrebates were known for their ferocity, beaten only by the Iceni-Coritani. If they were in no mood for palavering then it could very quickly get ugly for Cantiaci's newest guest. Not to mention the rest of her peaceful people.

Just then, Bronwyn, her servant, came flying down the front steps of the palace and ran all the way to meet them though they were still a goodly way off. Rosmerta tensed: Bronwyn never ran. She said it unbecame any lady who wasn't a warrior. A strange notion if ever there was one, but still; the sight of her rushing towards them, skirts lifted, cheeks puffing, sent a tattoo of alarm clanging in Rosmerta's head.

"You're to take that through the merchant's entrance round

the back," said Bronwyn, pointing to Trahaearn's armour. She was breathless and her voice was high. "And you must come at once, my lady, your mother says so."

"What's happened, Bron?"

"The warrior-queen won't risk antagonising them with a show of arms or armour. She won't have anyone saying she started this war."

They were marching back to the palace, and as she climbed the steps Rosmerta's heart sank. The Atrebates had made good time to cross Cantiaci as quickly as they had. She'd hoped she would have more time to prepare herself, but it was not to be.

The Atrebates were already come.

* * *

The hall was many times larger than the council chamber, and infinitely more light and spacious, but when Rosmerta stepped into it she felt her chest constrict.

She'd been brought up as a warrior-princess, and as such she could wield sword and spear as well as any of the women in her family and her army. She was also known for her skill at chariot dancing though she'd not practised for many a long moon. But it had all been for show; tournaments and games to test and showcase skill and dexterity. She'd not yet been tested in battle. She'd never had to be. The thought of it made her legs weak, it always had; and she'd hidden the secret from her mother through her skill. People laughingly said they were surrounded by enemies, but none as yet had had the courage to attack Cantiaci openly. They were strong and wealthy. And they had the friendship of many, many Gaulish tribes thanks to their trade links. And even though the other tribes in this land might not want to admit it, they did rely on Cantiaci for many of their imported goods.

No. Cantiaci had ever been too important to attack openly.

Until this day.

Rosmerta saw no faces. Her mother, she knew, would be seated on the grand throne at the far end of the hall, away from the smoking hearth-fire they'd since built in the middle of the room. How the Romans kept their blood from freezing in the deep of the dark moons was yet another mystery that had fled back with them to their home land. Standing in front of Sulis, obscuring her from Rosmerta's view, were three warriors. With their backs to her she saw shoulders broad and strong, leather and metal armour which gleamed, and red- and black-striped cloaks freshly cleaned. They had dressed up for battle. Not only that, their naked arms bore the blue woad swirls and whorls of ancient warriors; whatever their reason for being here, it was serious enough to invoke the ancient rites of battle.

Only the warrior in the centre had removed her she-bear-crowned helmet, and shining all in silver it marked her out as Epona Warrior-Queen of the Atrebates—for the she-bear was the mark of royalty as it was the mark of Artio the bear goddess herself—come to palaver before battle. The warrior-princess could've wept; they were so close to bonding and now it had degenerated to this. Her first thought was of Heddgwyn and his purposeful delay at the council. Her second thought, which astonished her, was of Arawn.

On either side of her stood a warrior, each holding a spear twice as high as they were, polished wood glowing, sharpened spear-heads glinting. They still bore their leaping-salmon-crowned helmets for they had no need to palaver. That was between the warrior-queens. They stood unmoving, as still as standing stones.

Two hooded Druids stood just to the right of the warriors, facing each other. One was Heddgwyn, Arch Druid of Cantiaci, no doubt; that he was here for such a weighty palaver was obvious. The other Druid was of Atrebates. From her lessons, Rosmerta knew that in ancient days the Druids used to scream and curse and jump and writhe when tribes faced each other, but those days were diminishing. Fearsome spell-casting or talking to the gods could sometimes result in such behaviour, but more often than not the Druids would palaver in their own way while the warrior-queens palavered in theirs. After all was done the Druids then reported to their warrior-queens the minds of their opponents. Learning each other's minds was what the two Druids were doing now.

The journey to her mother was long, the winter sun pouring through each window seemed brighter than it should be as she moved from darkness to light, sunshine and shade, clarity and shadow. No one looked around at her as she walked up the hall, her hard leather shoes gently tapping on the tiles as she walked.

"Let my daughter pass so that she might sit beside me while we conduct our palaver." Her mother's voice was strong and calm, and it soothed Rosmerta to hear it so. Yet only one spear-woman obeyed; she to the right-hand of Epona Warrior-Queen. She to the left remained as stone.

Rosmerta sat. The wooden throne felt cold and hard even through the skirt of her woollen winter dress, but she was glad she was finally there. Her legs felt like a running river and she would never have been able to stand through a discussion of battle. She wasn't ready to go into battle. She didn't believe she had the heart for it. She wanted all the tribes to be as peaceful as hers.

The hall thrummed with silence. This was a palaver between two warrior-queens and so needed no Druid to start proceedings: they waited for Sulis Warrior-Queen. The enemy was in her hall, on her land, so her terms applied. She remained silent, keeping her cool eyes on those of Epona Warrior-Queen until Rosmerta thought she, herself, would start babbling to dash out some of the deafening silence. She wanted to squirm in her seat but she forced herself to remain still. She wanted to look into the faces of the others to see if they felt as uncomfortable as she did, but she forced her gaze to remain fixed on the spear-woman in front of her.

And then she realised what her mother was doing, and had to quash down a little smile. She was drawing out the silence on purpose to make her enemies feel uncomfortable. The need to fill it was so strong that even Rosmerta had almost succumbed.

Finally her mother broke the tension. "Four moons past, you and I agreed to bond our tribes," she said. "Now you march across my lands with spear-women and chariots, and come into my hall bearing weapons and wearing armour. Why?"

Epona Warrior-Queen's gaze never faltered. She looked neither blood-thirsty nor shame-faced. "We are come on a mission of grave import." Her voice carried well in the hall, a strong voice undoubtedly but there were undertones of fatigue. "Since Samhain we have scoured the lands, our own and our neighbours, and now we are come to yours. We did not ask your leave, which is improper, but we have come as a matter of some urgency. I hope that I have not offended you."

If her legs had felt like running water before, Rosmerta now felt as though her body had been swept away beneath her and carried off to open sea, so unexpected was this response. The doomed bonding of their two tribes had failed at Samhain due to a minor rebellion—all present knew that. Why would that cause Epona Warrior-Queen to scour the lands? Had some of the rebels escaped? Slowly and as regally as she could manage, she turned her head towards her mother. Not one flicker of a muscle. Though one eyebrow was a little higher than the other.

"You have not offended me. But you made me think my lands of peace had come to war."

No, thought Rosmerta. Heddgwyn had made her think that. And what purpose did it serve?

"We do not come for war, Sulis, we come for a man."

Rosmerta sat up a little straighter. Arawn's face had flashed up in front of her own again.

"A man," said Sulis.

Epona nodded. "He committed a grave crime against his family and so against me; I would have him found so that he be punished according to our customs."

For the first time, the stone spear-woman moved; she flinched. And even as Rosmerta looked at her she saw her knuckles whiten as she squeezed her spear shaft tighter, stretching an ugly scar on the back of her hand.

"And what did he do, this man whom you search?"

"He slew one of my people. He slew his sister."

"No," said Rosmerta, unaware that she had spoken at all.

"Yes, Warrior-Princess." Epona now turned her gaze towards Rosmerta. "As unimaginable as it may sound, this atrocity did happen. We have a witness."

The Atrebates Druid stepped forward then, lowering his hood as he did so. Rosmerta recoiled. His right eye was blind, nothing but a pearly orb, like the moon, and surrounded by puffy, raw skin that was still trying to heal. But worse than that was the right side of his head. It looked slightly concave, as though something had taken a scoop out of him. He looked monstrous. She wanted nothing more than to shrink behind her mother's skirts until she scared the demon away like she always had done when Rosmerta was a child.

The Druid said nothing, but there was murder in his single remaining eye. The warrior-princess knew then that if these people found Arawn there would be no dawn for him.

"What makes you think," said Sulis, "this sister-slayer would be found in my lands?"

"We've searched far across many lands," said Epona, "but we've yet to find him. I ask your leave now to continue."

"You may search," said Sulis. "What name has he?"

Rosmerta held her breath. She realised she'd jumped to the conclusion that it was the strange young man who'd approached her for help, purely because of the uneasiness she'd felt earlier.

Perhaps it wasn't him at all.

"His name," said Epona, "is Arawn Salt-merchant."

Rosmerta's heart lurched. She cursed her intuition for betraying her, because even though there was a strangeness about him she didn't believe him capable of slaying his sister.

"The name is not known to me," said her mother.

But he was known to Rosmerta. And also Trahaearn. *His happiest moments weren't with his mother. Or his sister, for that matter.*

"Why would he kill her though?" she said. The eyes of everyone in the hall had turned towards her and she felt herself blush.

"The penalty for slaying a woman, especially one who is not yet grown, is punishable regardless of why the deed was carried out," said Epona, her voice tainted with mild surprise. "There is no higher crime. Is that not so?"

No, thought Rosmerta. That is not so. In our tribe slaying anyone, man or woman, is punishable, but we always take into account the cause of the slaying. Her mother knew this too, but neither of them said anything.

And then Rosmerta understood. It was a delicate situation, but if Sulis could help the Atrebates track down this sister-slayer then the Atrebates people would look more favourably on the Cantii. They might even be more willing to support the bonding between the two tribes. As sure as the moon waxes and wanes, Rosmerta knew this was precisely what her mother was thinking.

"Look for Arawn Salt-merchant, you have my leave," said Sulis. "Though I would ask that you leave my people unmolested. If he is hiding amongst them, remember that they do not know of his crime."

Epona nodded. "We start immediately. Some of my women will search the countryside and outlying lands, some the settlements. We ask only that we can carry out task unhindered."

It was Sulis' turn to nod. "I shall see that my spear-women

understand."

Epona turned and marched back along the hall towards the great door, closely followed by her warriors, but not before the stone spear-woman gave Rosmerta a long look. Though impossible to discern from beneath her salmon-crowned helmet, she sensed it offered no friendship.

When the hall was empty Rosmerta turned to her mother and said, "It would be well if we let the townsfolk know what is happening."

"But if the sister-slayer is hiding here he will be alerted instantly and make his escape."

"And if an army of Atrebates spear-women start rampaging through the town they're likely to cause panic. Either way this sis— this boy will be alerted. At least if we explain to our people what is happening they won't be frightened."

Her mother paused and thought for a moment. "I deem you right. I will go out in the square and make an announcement."

Good, thought Rosmerta. And I will go and make my own announcement. To Arawn Salt-merchant.

– 9 –

The moon of Ogronios (Ice-time), 332 C.E.
Dubras, Cantiaci tribal lands, Brython

She couldn't condone the murder of his sister, of course she couldn't. A life was a life. But she couldn't believe it was true. She couldn't believe Arawn was capable of such evil. And hadn't her own mother told her to trust her intuition? Yet they had the word of a Druid; who could argue against that? But her experience of Druids, like Heddgwyn, told her their motives weren't always pure, and the Atrebates Druid had looked less trust-worthy than even Heddgwyn.

Fortunately the market-place was still quite calm. The spear-women had yet to enter in their full force, and she could hear her mother calmly announce that Atrebates spear-women would be arriving to search for an Atrebates criminal. They were not to worry, she was saying, but they should help if they could. Rosmerta prayed to all the old gods that she would have enough time to reach the smithy before the fires of Otherworld were unleashed.

"What's going on?"

Rosmerta was halted by a tug at her arm. "Nia Smith, good day to you." The very person she did not wish to see. "Nothing."

"I saw spear-women enter the palace. And by the looks of them they weren't our own."

"Tribal palaver. Please, go about your business and don't worry." She pulled herself away and walked as quickly as she dared, casting a quick eye over her shoulder to make sure that Nia wasn't on her way back to the smithy. She had an empty basket in her hand and was heading to the market stalls. That was good. But she was also likely to hear her mother's announcement, and that wasn't. It wouldn't take Nia too long to realise that the Atrebates boy currently sharing her food and home was the one they were looking for. Especially since they shared the same name.

When she turned a corner she ran as quickly as she dared, hoping that Trahaearn would still be at the palace. Arawn looked up as she approached, confusion crossing his face when he noticed her demeanour.

"You have to leave," she said at once. He was about to speak but she cut him off. "Epona Warrior-Queen is here with her spear-women and they're looking for you. They'll be here any moment. You must leave right away."

His face drained of all colour. "How…how…?"

"It doesn't matter." She grabbed his arm, hot and slick with sweat. "Just leave. Make for the harbour. Cutios approaches and there'll be plenty of traders readying to leave." Taking off the golden torcs about her neck and arms she continued, "This should be enough for you to find passage. Run as fast as you can and don't stop until you're at the harbour."

He looked dumbly at the gold so she took it from his unresisting hands and stuffed it down his tunic.

"I don't understand," said Arawn.

"They say you slew your sister." She paused. "Is it true?"

The effect of her words was frightening. Arawn's face paled to moonlight, his mouth dropping open while his shoulders tensed in evident fear. But it was his eyes… They stared, unblinking, as though they regarded an aspect so fearsome she would never be able to conjure it even in her darkest nightmares.

"She wanted to kill my friend," he said. "Sacrifice. For Mother. I didn't mean to." He grabbed her shoulders and though Rosmerta cried in shock he didn't notice. "But she would have killed my friend and she would have killed me too!"

She knew it! He'd killed, true; but not in cold blood. At least she could understand. "Then run away and don't let them catch you."

"But how do they know I'm here?"

"There's no more time for talking, you must leave now."

The urgency in her voice wasn't getting through to him so she pushed him out of the smithy. He stumbled into a run, then stopped and look back at her, fear and confusion engraved on his bloodless face.

"Go!" she hissed, and finally he ran.

She turned and her heart sank when she saw Nia Smith walking along the path to her house. Followed closely by two warrior-queens and a troop of spear-women.

* * *

He found the Arch Druid in the hall, wearing what Emrys thought was a rapt expression, but deeper down he noticed the undertone of cunning. He blanched at the thought of ever saying that aloud, though; he'd be sacrificed to the old gods quicker than he could say Boudica's supplanter. That his current facial expression was as a result of the hurried way that the warrior-queens and their spear-women had vacated the hall, Emrys had no doubt. But he wasn't entirely sure what was going on any more. Early this very morning Rosmerta, looking as though she hadn't slept at all, had crept to his chambers (and oh, how he missed the comfort of his old bed here in the palace after so many years of living in the Druid compound!) and announced that Heddgwyn had failed to make his godly declaration of a united Brython ruled by Druids. Instead, he'd made it sound like the Fellows had once again blessed the bonding between Cantiaci and Atrebates.

And by the way, the Atrebates are currently marching across our lands to make war.

Then she'd scuttled off again before any one noticed her.

War? If anyone was to make war surely it should be the Cantiaci for the hideous way that Sulis and Rosmerta had been treated at the feast of Samhain? But Sulis had accepted the outcome philosophically, knowing there would have been some resistance and was content to continue her ideal of a united Brython through peace and goodwill. How could Atrebates possibly turn that into a justified war? And hadn't Epona Warrior-Queen wanted the bonding just as much as Sulis did?

All these questions that Rosmerta didn't answer because she'd already departed. And of course, he hadn't been invited into the hall when Sulis received her visitors, but perhaps, now that they were alone, Heddgwyn would be prepared to answer some questions. He would rather have asked his sister because, in Emrys' experience, the Arch Druid rarely parted with information unless it benefitted him to do so, but Rosmerta had gone hurtling off on her own errands when the hall's door was opened.

Mostly, though, he wanted to see if Heddgwyn would tell him why he hadn't told the council about his apparent vision.

"Do you know," said Heddgwyn when Emrys was halfway towards him, "the history of Boudica's defeat of the Roman plague?"

His steps faltered just for a moment, then he continued walking. "Of course," said Emrys. Everyone did.

"Tell me."

"Camulos, with horse, with heart,
Boudica sent far such foes
As Romans, undone under
Courage fierce that pierced the part
Of their souls so foul, so foetid,
No Goddess would bless with bile.
Lundyn fell, so tell such tales
Of brav'ry; we see with song
Our Goddess bravest, bound in
Loyalty to free, to fire
Corruption. "Nation! None shall
Left alive by my brave might

Be!" she cried, well tried, well tested.
Verlamion she outshone
Next; its end. Come end Coed
Celidon, fight on fellow
Warriors—our shores, our souls
To save; though hallowed hare of
Andraste gave she grave sign.
So Boudica, thee called thy
War host great to wait; to wait.
Darkness came, then fame thee found—
Surrounded, hounded, hunted,
Roman might took flight to flee
From Brython, our home, our heart.
Boudica! Saviour! Saviour!"

It was the childish version that every infant was sung when he was born, and then sung around the hearth-fire with his siblings and playmates. As a Bard, Emrys had learned the fuller accounts of course, but being caught so unaware to recite the history by his father his mind immediately flew to his childhood.

The Arch Druid smiled and nodded his head as though Emrys truly was a young boy reciting his lessons. "A pretty tale, is it not? And so many generations have passed that even the learnèd believe it is true."

"I don't understand."

"You wouldn't, young Emrys; you are yet an Ovate, not a full Druid who has attained full wisdom." He chuckled then, and the sound echoed eerily throughout the deserted hall. "Were you aware that, before Boudica's victory, the Brythoniaid of Camulos and Lundyn were quite contented to be under Roman rule? I see well from your face that you weren't. It will surprise you, then, to learn that those living in Verlamion weren't Roman at all but Brythoniaid playing at being Roman, save for the accident of where they born."

Emrys was stunned. The Arch Druid's words were worse than

blasphemy.

"Ironic, then, don't you think, that only the treachery of Cantiaci has survived while the Trinovantes and Catuvellauni tribes are some of the fiercest supporters of Boudica's legacy."

"How do you know this?"

"Because," said Heddgwyn, passing his gaze across the high windows of the hall, "the Romans, while a plague, did have some interesting ideas. Cantiaci has retained some of them, and for that we are despised despite being a strong, wealthy tribe. Or perhaps because of it. But they also brought with them an obsession of writing everything down. And while some things, like our sacred lore, lose their potency if committed to page instead of memory; some things fare better. So when the Roman plague was ended our ancient Fellows began the task of recording the histories."

"Why?" said Emrys. "And how is this the first I've heard of it?"

"Because all the scrolls are well guarded at Ynys Afallach. And only a few of us throughout the generations have ever been made aware of their existence. Our power, Emrys, comes not through spells or sacrifice, but through knowledge. Our knowledge comes from communing with gods and understanding histories. With such knowledge are we able to advise our warrior-queens and keep our tribes safe from enemy plagues.

"But the Romans understood our power. At first, they feared the men and women of Brython because they were so fear*less*, but they soon learned that they were just men and women, despite their blue-painted skin and piercing war-cries. They learned some could be bought and subdued, though not all, as history as shown us. But they feared we Druids because of our power; power born of our knowledge and our ability to unify the tribes of Brython should we wish it. Of all the tribes in Brython, only the Druids are free to walk where we will, are welcomed in every land, and are heeded by the very highest and lowest. They feared us, the Romans, because if we united Brython, they could never have defeated such a fearsome and numerous host.

"And they had gathered across the Menai to attack Ynys Afallach, to destroy the golden isle and the very seat of the Druids—and they succeeded. Men, women, children; all slaughtered mercilessly in the name of civilisation, but truly through fear."

For several slow heartbeats Emrys did nothing but digest this information. Not only was it a story he'd never heard before, it was also surprising that it be handed to him so freely.

"Did they not fight back? The Druids?" he asked eventually.

"Oh, yes, they fought. They sent forth their strongest magics, chanting and wailing to invoke the old gods, those so many have forgotten now in favour of Boudica and her daughters, and they could see the fear in their enemies' eyes. But the gods had left them that day. Can you imagine it, Emrys; the sound of blade through bone, the smell of an ocean of blood? You can feel it there, even to this day, the spirits of the dead. But all the murdering Romans did was make that isle potent with the souls of the blessed; and after Boudica threw the enemy down the Druids returned to Ynys Afallach, infused now by the spirits of the dead and their collective knowledge, from far and yonder to restore their power. With the Romans gone, the Druids once more became strong."

The young Ovate was unable to speak. Heddgwyn, usually so secretive and hidden, had imparted a wealth of information, freely given. Or was there a cost for such knowledge?

"Why are you telling me this now?" he said.

"Because it is vital you know the importance of uniting Brython against outside enemies. The Picts grow in numbers and confidence day by day, and what else lurks beyond the sea? The Romans may have shrivelled up but there are rumours of other powers growing, new powers with new gods and we must be ready to fight them. The warrior-queens cannot do it, they will squabble about boundaries and pitch their spear-women against each other to ensure no cattle or slaves are stolen. Only the Druids can unite the lands and make them strong as one. Do you understand?"

It made sense, but Emrys hadn't forgotten the lie Heddgwyn had told at the last meeting of Fellows. Only he couldn't risk losing the apparent trust his father was now showing in him.

"Yes," he said.

The Arch Druid smiled. "Good. Then it is time you saw the truth for yourself. Prepare yourself for a journey."

"A journey?"

Another slow nod. "A journey to the truth. A journey to Ynys Afallach."

– 10 –

The moon of Ogronios (Ice-time), 332 C.E.
Dubras, Cantiaci tribal lands, Brython

Fortunately, Nia Smith was so busy talking, not just with her mouth but her entire face and body, that she didn't notice Rosmerta standing in the road a little way down from her house. None of the spear-women noticed her either, so intent were they on listening to what the smith's wife had to say. The warrior-princess ducked into the scratchy shrubbery lining the side of the road and had to stifle a lunatic laugh. What had the world come to that a noble from the highest family was reduced to skulking about in bushes! She knew perfectly well that she didn't have much time. It would take the merest heartbeat for Nia Smith to realise her guest had disappeared. She poked her head up to get a better look at the procession, thankful she wasn't wearing her silver diadem today lest it twinkle in the weak sunlight and betray her position. The vision of herself so bejewelled and hiding in a bush threatened to send her off into mad giggles again.

Nia was in her house, and the four spear-women had just entered with her. Any moment now they would rush back out, raising the alarm that the sister-slayer had escaped and would be on their way. If Rosmerta were to escape her hiding place it was to be now. She scrabbled out, pulling at her skirt which clung desperately to a bramble that lurked at the base of the bushes.

Finally she wrenched it free and ran past the smith's house, the empty smithy, and back towards the market square, slowing herself as she approached it. It was as full of people as it normally was, fuller even, thanks to the number of Atrebates spear-women walking through the crowds, going in or out of the large houses that surrounded the square. Her mother was nowhere to be seen now, nor was Epona, and the warrior-princess gathered that they had returned to the palace to discuss strategies for finding Arawn. The podium in the centre of the square though, despite having been vacated by Sulis, was now occupied by a Cantii spear-woman, and surrounding her were several townsfolk.

"No doubt telling everyone to continue as usual," she said to herself.

"I beg pardon, my lady?"

Rosmerta spun, startled at hearing a voice so close to her ear. When she laid her eyes on the speaker she took an involuntary step back. Peering down at her was the frightful face of the Atrebates Druid. His one good eye glared at her with malicious amusement while the other glistened blindly with pus or infection.

"I did not intend to startle you," he said, his voice and words belying his expression. "I only meant that I hadn't heard what it was you said."

"Perhaps that is because I had not spoken to you." She frowned, not just at his statement but also at herself for being frightened by him.

"Then I beg forgiveness," he said, spreading his hands wide. "You stopped so suddenly by my side I thought you must have been."

What nonsense, Rosmerta thought, but she said nothing and started to turn away.

"They won't find him at the smith's house," he said. "But then I expect you know that already."

She paused. "I know not of what you speak."

"Come now. The whole town is alight with the news of the Atrebates sister-slayer, and you yourself were one of the first to hear it said. You *were* present at the great hall, were you not? I'm sure I remember seeing you address Epona Warrior-Queen. Although…" He fluttered a hand around his dead eye and looked at her apologetically.

"Of course I was in the great hall. But you know perfectly well that I was talking about your allusion to the smith's house, not my mother's halls."

The Druid opened his mouth in a silent *ah!* of realisation and nodded. He looked behind him to where the little road leading down to the smithy joined the main square and turned his head back towards the warrior-princess. "Then for a second time I must beg your forgiveness. I thought I had seen you run from that little road there, just moments after the spear-women were led there by the smith's wife. Unwittingly she had harboured the sister-slayer. Fed him, clothed him even. Poor woman; she's terrified of getting punished."

"Why would Nia Smith be punished?" said Rosmerta and winced—very well she heard the panic in her own voice.

"She may have harboured him unwittingly, but she also let him escape. Or perhaps it was her husband. I understand he'd grown quite fond of his new apprentice."

Rosmerta's mouth dropped open. Just what was he planning to do? For so long she'd had her suspicions about Heddgwyn, but this Druid in front of her made the Arch Druid of Cantiaci look like the mildest of lambs.

Abruptly he stopped smiling and affected an expression of confusion and concern, and looked her over carefully. "You seem to be missing your beautiful jewellery, my lady," he said. "My eye sometimes plays tricks on me, I know; but I remember thinking how magnificently all those golden torcs that adorned your arms and lovely neck matched your hair so well. I do so hope some miscreant didn't take it upon himself to relieve you of them. Certainly your torn dress and scuffed slippers would add weight to that claim."

Her stomach, as cold as the Solstice moon, started spreading its frost throughout her limbs so that she could feel herself start to shake. *He knows!* her mind screamed, and it was all she could do to keep her face from contorting with fear. His eye burned so brightly, and burrowed so deeply into her soul that she thought she'd never be able to look away from it. She had to fight the urge to tell him he was right, that everything he'd said was all true, but she was losing the battle and her will was failing. If telling him the truth was the only way she could stop him from penetrating her with that stare then she would tell the truth.

"Gwynfor!"

The call came from behind, a fair distance, but strong and clear.

"To me!" came the voice again. I must be mad, thought Rosmerta. I would swear that voice is familiar to me.

The thought passed in a moment, the same time it took for the Druid in front of her to scowl and then take his evil glare from her.

She sagged and all her breath rushed out of her in a heavy cloud. The Druid—Gwynfor; she would remember that name forever—glided towards the spear-woman who had called him, the very same who'd stood as still as stone in her mother's hall. She couldn't hear their discussion, but she assumed he was being told that Arawn was no longer at the smith's house. Poor Nia stood close by, looking like a butterfly trapped under a jar, wringing her hands. Then fear swelled her heart and she wondered if Gwynfor would mention the suspicion he held of Rosmerta herself.

She fled to the palace while his back and evil eye were turned.

* * *

"Epona Warrior-Queen, my lady," said the stone spear-woman. "The longer we spend palavering the further the sister-slayer runs."

"The smith and his wife may give us valuable information that may help in our search," said Epona with quiet calm. "We question them first, then take our leave. Have patience."

Again her scarred fist tightened against the shaft of her spear. Rosmerta noticed that both of her own hands could easily be crushed in one of the stone spear-woman's solid fists. She looked away quickly.

Once it had become common knowledge that Arawn was no longer at the smith's home, they had reconvened in the great hall. Rosmerta had tried desperately to find Trahaearn when she arrived back at the palace, but to no avail. But she'd had time to change from her torn and dirty clothes into a fresh dress, for what good it would do. Gwynfor was sure to notice; for a man half-blinded he was frighteningly observant. She'd entered the great hall with her heart hammering against her ribs and head and ears, feeling for all the world like a doe that knows the trap it's walking into will only lead to its demise but is powerless to do anything about it.

"A beautiful dress, my lady," whispered Gwynfor as she'd made her way to her throne. He kept just a few steps behind her so no one would think them talking. "Certainly more becoming than the ragged thing I last saw you in. Fear not, though; I'm sure greater minds than ours are taken up with the pressing affair of murder than what you're wearing."

She'd felt him move away then, and it allowed her to breathe a little easier, but not much. He did know. Or rather, he strongly suspected. And should he decide to tell her mother and Epona Warrior-Queen of his suspicions then she didn't know what she would do.

How had this happened? A few days ago she believed herself nervous at the thought of having Emrys spy on Heddgwyn for her, even more so by the thought of impending war. But it was nothing compared to this, she thought grimly. She knew now what true fear felt like.

Emrys! She'd all but forgotten about him until now. Their minor conspiracy seemed like a thousand generations ago. But even though her own problems had increased exponentially, it wouldn't mean that he would cease to fret about his own task. As soon as she was able, she promised herself, she would seek him out and speak with him. She wouldn't put it past Heddgwyn to use this new crisis in his usurping favour. She wouldn't put it past him at all.

"Trahaearn Smith, you are not under suspicion here. We simply want to ask you some questions."

Rosmerta looked up at the soft sound of her mother's voice, and was surprised to see Trahaearn standing not five paces in front of her. He looked concerned, though not afeared, and that was good. She'd been so caught up in her own thoughts, however, that she hadn't even realised he'd been called and brought forward. Let's just hope that none of Epona's warriors saw him with his new armour, she thought. Any more distrust could be deadly.

"I understand, my lady," said Trahaearn. His voice was steady. "Ask me your questions and I'll give you my answers."

"I fail to see why he should be talking when his wife is here with us," said the stone spear-woman from under her helmet; the one brave enough to call out for a Druid as though he were nothing more than her messenger. "Bring her forward so she can speak for him."

For the slightest moment there was shocked silence amongst the Cantii gathered in the hall. Trahaearn was about to speak when Sulis held up her hand to silence him.

"It is my opinion, spear-woman, that the smith will have more to say on the matter," said Sulis Warrior-Queen of Cantiaci. "It was he who apprenticed Arawn, is that not so?" Trahaearn nodded, his frowning gaze on the stone spear-woman still. "Thus, it is he who can give me the answers I seek. When it is time to speak with his wife, I will call her forward."

Silence. How, thought Rosmerta, could two tribes live so close to one another yet have such distant values?

Sulis Warrior-Queen spoke again. "Tell me about Arawn, Trahaearn."

"Not much to tell. He came to me looking for work because he needed food and shelter, and since my lads have left the smithy I was short a pair of hands, so I hired him. He looked half-starved so I suppose you could say I pitied him somewhat. But as it turns out, he's a good, strong worker and I was glad to have him."

"Despite the fact he slew a woman?" said the stone spear-woman. A brief flash of annoyance flickered across Sulis' face but she said nothing.

"That was something I had no knowledge of."

"This *man* does not even address his betters properly!" the spear-woman suddenly roared, banging her spear down on the tiled floor with a crash. "How can we believe what he says?"

"I should remind you that we are guests of another tribe," said Epona, "and that not all live as we do. Perhaps you should leave the questions for the warrior-queens."

The helmeted head of the spear-woman turned towards her warrior-queen, the graven bronze salmon atop it flashing in the slanting sunlight, as though it really were leaping from a river in Otherworld into this one. Though her face was covered, Rosmerta had no doubt that it was full of rage and scorn.

"It's not like I opened my door to him without asking who he was and where he came from," said Trahaearn, addressing Epona. "Course I did. He told me he came from Atrebates, and that I would've guessed anyway from the way he spoke. I asked why he came to Dubras, and he said it was because he was unhappy in his own lands, begging your pardon, my lady Epona, and I'm not one to judge how others live their lives. But he said he was treated poorly, no more than a slave, and wanted to escape. I believed him. As I said, he was half-starved and looked sore in need of food and ale and thread. It was pity more than anything that let him in. I didn't think to ask if he was escaping because he'd killed someone—it's not something that springs to mind. And if he did kill someone it's not something I think he'd've been shouting about. So I apologise for harbouring this sister-slayer, as you call him; but I was unaware. Can't see as how I did any wrong though."

"Were you aware he ran away this day?" asked Epona.

"No, my lady. He was at the smithy all morning, best of my knowledge. I left only for a short while because I had business elsewhere to attend to. Didn't realised he'd gone until, well, just now."

"To what business were you attending?"

"Charcoal, my lady. Smithy has to have charcoal, and a lot of it. Go out near every day to get me more charcoal, and old Blacky makes a tidy sum because of it. I get my charcoal from him, you see. He's the only one that can do it proper."

"And he can vouch for you, this Blacky?"

"Yes, my lady."

There was another short burst of silence. Rosmerta dared not look at her mother, but she knew well that she must be feeling surprised relief that Trahaearn hadn't mentioned that he'd been at the palace on armoury business. How calmly the man lied! If only she were blessed with such a gift, she would swap it with her intuition in a heartbeat.

"I believe you speak the truth," said Sulis.

"As do I," said Epona. "And you shall not be forfeited for your actions."

Trahaearn nodded at both warrior-queens and was just about to turn away when Gwynfor, the one-eyed Druid spoke up.

"And he came to you of his own accord, this killer?" he said.

Rosmerta felt her muscles clench. She held her breath.

"I beg pardon?" said Trahaearn.

Though she herself had no knowledge of Arawn's actions when he first came to her, she wouldn't put it past this Druid to concoct some fanciful notion based on the suspicions he already had about her if the smith admitted he accepted Arawn because of her word. She prayed wildly to her namesake goddess that Trahaearn wouldn't turn and look at her; even more wildly that he wouldn't say anything.

"The sister-slayer," said Gwynfor in silken tones. "You say he came to you looking for work. It would interest me to know how he came to such an idea."

"Because there's always work in a smithy. And even if there weren't he could've sat awhile and warmed his skinny limbs. Either way would've done him good. Just so happened I could give him both."

"Indeed," said Gwynfor, and seemed to shrink back into the shadows.

Forcing herself not to look at the Druid, Rosmerta kept her eyes on Trahaearn, hoping that her face showed only concerned interest with the proceedings and not leg-bowing relief that she hadn't been named. When all this was over she would have to find some way to thank him. And an entirely other way of apologising for bringing all this upon him.

The only time the smith's eyes caught Rosmerta's was when he was dismissed, and that was only because he was polite enough to acknowledge all the noble ladies present.

Nia Smith was called forward next. Much to Rosmerta's dismay, the poor woman was wringing her hands and looking from face to face at all those assembled in front of her in the great hall. She was scared half-witless, of that there was no doubt. But it also, Rosmerta's churning mind thought, made her look guilty. Pray that it was simply her own guilty conscience that made her see that...

The same questions were put to her.

"What happens in the smithy isn't my concern, my ladies, Trahaearn does as he pleases. It's my job to make sure he has good food and a hot fire waiting for him when he comes home. He's always inviting people to dinner without so much as a begging-your-pardon, and it rattles me sometimes but it doesn't stop me from feeding them or giving them a bed, though there ain't much in the way of beds in our house; we had to sleep the boy in the barn, though I can't say as I was disappointed about that. Was I suspicious? Well, I can't say as I enjoyed his company, but then we're not very popular outside our tribe, are we? And I wondered why a lad would be wanting to run to a tribe that's so hated by others but my husband seemed happy enough with him in his smithy and who am I to argue about such things as that? But if I'd thought there were something amiss I would've come straight here, my lady, and told you—"

The disdainful tut of the stone spear-woman was so loud it stopped Nia in her vocal tracks. She looked at her, shocked. When Epona spoke next Nia's head whipped around to face her.

"It was you who told my spear-woman that the sister-slayer was biding at your house?"

Nia looked like she would cry. "Yes, my lady. I only came to the market to buy some more barley and then I heard the announcement. I had no notion of his evil actions, I swear to Boudica and her daughters I hadn't. If I'd've—"

"When was the last time you saw him?"

"Well, I suppose it must've been when I came out to buy the grain, though I'm not sure because I didn't actually look in the smithy, you see, it's always so hot and smoky and blacks up my clean frocks, and I knew the men would be in for lunch soon enough, so I—"

"I understand," said Epona quietly, "but I would just like you to tell me the last time you actually saw him."

Nia worried at her hands and lips for an interminable amount of time. "Fast-breaking. That was the last time I laid my eyes on him. Fast-breaking."

"So you didn't know he was gone until you arrived at the smith with my spear-women?"

"No, my lady. And I'd swear that he was still there because up until that moment I'd had no reason to think that he'd had any reason to run away. I swear that—"

"I believe you," said Epona. "And I thank you for coming forward when you did. You've helped us greatly."

"I can go?"

"You may go."

"Thank you, my lady. My ladies. Thank you." She mumbled and bowed her way out of the hall—walking backwards, Rosmerta noticed, as though she were afraid they might change their minds and suddenly pounce on her from behind.

Silence poured back in.

"So all that remains," came Gwynfor's smooth tones, "is for us to divine when and where the killer ran."

She felt his eye on her but she would not meet it.

"Epona Warrior-Queen, enough time has been wasted at palavering," said the spear-woman. "We know he was here, we know he's running now. It's likely he started running when he saw us arrive. We should leave now. We're not that far behind him."

"But where would he go? Where would he go, I wonder?" said Gwynfor.

His taunting made Rosmerta's skin itch. If she could've jumped up, grabbed the spear-woman's weapon and shoved it into his remaining eye she would've done so gladly.

"He probably made for the sea," she said. The look of shock on Gwynfor's face was gratifying, but she kept her composure. "We're close enough to the sea here, and there are any number of ports. And where else would he go when he finally runs out of land? I think you should look to the harbour for your killer."

That she was surprised by her announcement was an understatement. She hadn't meant to speak at all, but Gwynfor's tacit suggestion that she was hiding something meant she had to do something. She needed to convince him she was innocent, only then would she be able to help Arawn. And what better way of protesting her innocence than telling them where he had gone? All she had to do now was think of another way to warn Arawn they were coming. Again.

Gwynfor looked at her slyly, and she surprised herself further by keeping his regard without flinching. "A sensible idea, my lady," he said. Then his expression changed as if he had just thought of something. "And perhaps that is what the sister-slayer wants us to believe. What if he's hiding here, right under our very noses, just waiting for us to make our move so he can sneak off in the opposite direction?" The question was put to Epona, but his eyes very quickly slid back to the warrior-princess.

She raised an eyebrow and nodded her head thoughtfully as if to say, *Could be, could be...*

"Yet we continue to waste time palavering about it," shouted the stone spear-woman.

"Ready the warriors then," said Epona, "and we'll leave as soon as we are ready."

"Let us send some women with you," said Sulis. "Surely you will need more if you intend to send some of your warriors to the coast and keep some of them searching here?"

"Pah! We don't need your help," said the spear-woman with shocking venom.

"You are a guest," said Epona, "of Sulis Warrior-Queen and here by her leave. You would do well to remember that. Further, you are only here at all by *my* leave. You would do well to remember that too."

This quietened the spear-woman instantly, and Rosmerta was intrigued as to what her last statement alluded. It sounded like a threat. Not unlike her own mother, there seemed to be a hidden store of ferocity underneath the calm exterior of Epona Warrior-Queen.

Turning to Sulis, Epona said, "I would gladly accept your warriors with thanks. The sooner this dreadful business is finished the better. We have many things left which should be discussed."

The bonding, thought Rosmerta. Both warrior-queens were going to use this false accusation of sister-slaying to their political advantage—Epona to illustrate to her people that the Cantiaci are a tribe to be trusted, and her mother to win Atrebates approval. And all at the cost of young man's life...

Because Arawn was innocent, she was sure of it. That his sister was dead, she had no doubt. But she also didn't doubt it was an accident; she had seen the way the Atrebates women treated their menfolk, and she remembered well that frightful woman who tried and almost succeeded in starting an uprising. What young man wouldn't defend himself with violence if violence were being visited upon him?

She shivered. And yet... Was she really going to try and thwart her mother's plans? If she found some other way of aiding Arawn that was what she would be doing. And going against the warrior-queen was treason. She would be no better than Heddgwyn.

But a life was at stake. An innocent life. Which was worse, treason or murder?

She made her excuses and left the great hall when everyone else had departed. Her mind wasn't yet decided but she knew she must go to Trahaearn and thank him for protecting both her and her mother.

Outside it was dark. Not the dark of night, but the dark of a late afternoon not yet free from winter's hold. The kind of dark that was somehow more frightening. The sun should still be in the sky, yet it wasn't; and it only served to remind that there were greater forces than those of even the strongest warrior-queen and her spear-women. It served to remind how fragile woman and her kin really were.

And because of the early dark the marketplace was empty.

A sudden gust of wind and Rosmerta realised that she'd stepped out in nothing but her dress. Woollen and warm it may be, but only within the confines of a fire-lit room. The smithy wasn't that far, but in this cold she would do herself no good. Walking back later, it would be even colder.

The wind gusted stronger still and she turned on her heel, meaning to go back to the palace; but as well as the cold the wind also brought with it voices. And she recognised one as the cunning, one-eyed Druid.

Quickly, she moved behind one of the now empty market stalls. This was her land, but she had no wish to be seen by Gwynfor and whomsoever he was talking to. A thought stopped her: the band of spear-women were camped outside the the town, and if Epona had left to ready them for moving out, what was Gwynfor still doing here?

She only heard their voices when the wind gusted in the right direction, so she moved slowly, keeping the market stalls between herself and the main square to avoid detection. How fortunate that the dress she'd changed into earlier was of deep blue wool and that she'd decided against adorning herself with more jewellery.

The voices were soon louder, closer, and she stopped in surprise tinged with fear.

"...trust them either, Gwynfor, but what choice do we have?"

That voice was unmistakeable. It was the angry rasp of the stone spear-woman. A tiny part of Rosmerta's mind found it surprising that she would be so close to the tribe's Druid.

"We know that the slayer was here," she continued. "It's the closest we've been since we discovered the body of my precious daughter. We must do everything we can to catch him."

Rosmerta's mouth dropped open. If she's hunting a sister-slayer, and the slain was her daughter... The spear-woman was here hunting her son!

She risked moving forward even more, hoping to be able to catch a glimpse of this woman's face; the woman who had treated her son so badly and raised a daughter to believe she could kill another person, slave or not, without any retribution. Though of course, the sister hadn't escaped retribution, had she?

"But he's here," Gwynfor was saying. "I feel his presence like a canker."

Then that's what it must be, thought Rosmerta, because Arawn's not here—and hasn't been all day. The knowledge that the Druid was entirely unaware of this gave her strength.

"He's not that smart. He's no better than a dog. And dogs always run when they're chased."

There! She could see them. The Druid's hood was drawn up, much to Rosmerta's relief, hiding his evil blind eye from her. All she could see of the spear-woman, however, was her red hair, flaring up like a bonfire as the wind gusted at it. She'd taken off her helmet, but Rosmerta still couldn't see her face, for her back was turned.

"We must go back," said the spear-woman. "Stay here if you must, but I ride to the coast."

Then she turned around. And Rosmerta knew that face.

Though it was now lit by moonlight, Rosmerta remembered it well lit by firelight as women around them screamed and fell to their knees thinking it was Boudica come back from the dead. She remembered it denouncing her mother, and spitting into her very own face. She knew that face well.

Now she knew it was the face of Arawn's mother.

* * *

"It's not that I worry for your safety, Rosmerta; I've seen your battle-practice enough times to know you're a formidable warrior." Sulis drew in a deep breath. "I see no reason for you to go. I've given enough warriors to Epona, and Boudica knows she has enough of her own."

"You don't think it politic to send a member of our family along with our women? Usually the warrior-queens support their warriors, but I notice both you and Epona are staying behind." She felt a little cruel forcing her mother's hand like this, but she wanted to see if the warrior-queen would admit her motives to her daughter. She'd yet to tell Sulis about all she'd heard between Gwynfor and Arawn's mother, but she would use it well if her mother failed to see her point of view.

"Though the crime is a serious one," said Sulis, "it's not as though Pictish raids are being carried out. Neither tribe is going to war, we're simply hunting a criminal. Warrior-queens have more important tasks than that." She paused. Then looked away as she continued. "You've attended the council meetings, you know our neighbours are being harried by Picts. I'm needed here."

She's lying to me, thought Rosmerta, incredulous. "And Epona? Why does she stay?"

"She'll be leaving soon enough, Rosmerta, and I had believed the interrogations were over."

"You intend to carry out the bonding ceremony while she's here. While her troops are otherwise occupied."

She should've known better than to surprise her mother. Instead of the shock she'd anticipated on her mother's face at the accurate conclusion she'd drawn, she was simply angry.

"The responsibilities of queenship require the ability to make difficult decisions," she said, her voice controlled but firm. It was her blazing blue eyes that indicated the depth of her anger. "As you will discover for yourself soon enough. I cannot be distracted by smaller matters when the future fate of our tribe, of all these lands, are at stake. Any decision I make is for the good of the tribe. You of all people should know this well."

"I do, Mother. But what about Epona's decisions? Has she told you who the leader of her warrior-band is?"

Sulis was gifted at not betraying her emotions. But sometimes there was a flash in her eyes that anyone looking, anyone who knew her well enough, could see. There was such a flash now, and it was of uncertainty. It was all Rosmerta needed.

"Gwladus Salt-merchant," Rosmerta said. "The spear-woman who has accompanied Epona to every meeting we've held in our hall. The spear-woman who is leading the warrior-band. The spear-woman who rose up against her own warrior-queen when we were to bond with the Atrebates at Samhain. Have you forgotten how she treated us?"

"I've forgotten nothing." Her mother's voice was small and tight, and again she couldn't meet her daughter's eyes. "Though I should have recognised that name… Arawn Salt-merchant they called the sister-slayer but I did not connect the two. Boudica curse me and my stupidity!"

"It wasn't your place to question, Mother; Epona should have been open with you."

For a heartbeat she feared her mother's wrath, but as she spoke her face softened. "She should have. And would have, if I'd have questioned. I think she fears the delicacy of our situation as much as I do."

"Gwladus Salt-merchant should be dead."

"So she should. But her daughter was slain by her son, so no doubt she was given a reprieve. Perhaps it is their way that the mothers of the slain have the right to seek their killers."

"Perhaps. But, Mother, I distrust that spear-woman, and I distrust the Druid Gwynfor." Sulis looked scandalised by this last; but she continued. "I saw them talking in secret together. I didn't hear much of what was said, though that was when the spear-woman's identity was revealed to me. But why would they need to carry out secret palavers away from their band? My intuition warns me strongly, Mother."

There was silence for several moments while Sulis regarded her daughter gravely.

"Several times you have sensed things when I have not…" Her eyes clouded with the memories of years for moment, then she came back. "It will make you a strong warrior-queen. Better, even, than me."

Hope was swelling like ripening wheat in Rosmerta's chest; she needed to do this for herself as much as Arawn. "Then trust me now, Mother. Let me go with them. I would see true justice be done."

"I would too, but this bonding is too important," said Sulis, and Rosmerta's hope was harvested before it was fully grown. "For the Trinovantes to trust us enough to accept aid against the sea-bound Picts, they must see we are trusted enough by the Atrebates to accept a bonding. And we must do it quickly. More reports of boats spotted beyond the eastern shore arrive every day and soon the attacks will start. You must stay here for the bonding ceremony, Rosmerta; it is your duty."

Frustration threatened to escape as a cry until an idea came to her so suddenly she sat up straighter. "Airmed," she said. "Perform the ceremony with Airmed."

"This is *your* duty, Rosmerta, not your sister's. I gave my oath to Epona that her son would bond with the future warrior-queen of Cantiaci and I will not break my oath."

"You don't have to. Airmed will stand in my stead for the ceremony in all but name. When I return I'll claim the husband who is already bound to me. The people of Atrebates just need to see the official ceremony, but how many of them will remember what I look like? They will remember fair hair of which Airmed has plenty, and when the ceremony is performed here you can explain to our people that she is simply taking my place until I return. They'll understand—they want the bonding as much as we do."

Sulis shook her head slightly. "I don't think Epona will agree to this."

"Then you must convince her she has no choice. That, if she'd been honest with us from the very start, it wouldn't have come to this."

"Your cunning should worry me greatly," she said, trying to

force back the smile from her lips. "But it pleases me that, this time, I can heed your intuition. Go then, with my blessing, and see that true justice is done. I will wait for you in our newly bonded tribal lands."

– 11 –

The moon of Cutios (Windy-time), 332 C.E.
Dubras, Cantiaci tribal lands, Brython

Now that the new moon of windy-time floated invisibly in the sky the night was impossibly dark, no doubt filled with beasts and spirits that would happily tear Arawn limb from limb and swallow those pieces whole. And yet, instead of hiding under the safety of warm blankets in a sturdy barn, he was once more running for his life. The unjustness of it all made him want to weep with frustration. He missed the town and its clean, paved streets. He missed the certainty of meal times. But most of all he missed Trahaearn and his willingness to treat him as an equal. As a son. But a son treated by his father with love. He knew, as well as he knew the dawn would bring a new life of hardship, that he would miss Cantiaci and Trahaearn with all his heart for all the days that followed.

He stopped, not wanting to look back on the leagues he'd covered, but turned anyway. Nothing could be seen in the gloom but firelight—precisely the reason why he hadn't lit one. Yet on the horizon there was plenty. Enough to guide a whole warrior-band over the fields and meadows, through the woods and forests, and all the way to the coast. Arawn felt the deep urge to cry again.

"They couldn't wait for the dawn to start their search for one cursed boy, then." He peered as well as he could, trying to see if the firelight was that of marching torches or static cook-fires. At least the latter would mean he'd have a few more hours to try and outrun his enemies. But it was impossible to discern. The lights were points of brightness in a sea of black, and at times it seemed as though they advanced, at times it seemed as though they stayed where they were. Arawn wiped his eyes.

"I need to keep moving," he said. "I don't want to die wondering if I could have escaped if only I hadn't stopped to rest."

He turned from the sight of the lights and started his blind run again.

* * *

As the red claws of dawn scratched across the horizon the first screech shattered the silence, bringing Arawn to his knees in terror.

It was answered by another screech, this one further away, praise Boudica; but before long the whole sky was filled with it. And birds. Giant white birds that wheeled, wheeled and screeched their horrible song. Arawn had seen or heard nothing like it before and for that he was glad. What a wretched way to start the day.

On he walked, easier now with the new day's weak light, but above the evil birds the sky promised to be sunless, for thick clouds stretched all across the horizon like a heavy grey shroud. If it didn't rain soon it'd be a wonder, he thought.

"Go to the coast, she said, but where is it? I've been running all night. My feet hurt, my legs are sore and my chest feels like it's been sat upon by an ox." In truth, he hadn't been running for a long while, but nor had he rested since the night before the Atrebates spear-women turned up, trampling Arawn's delicate hope of happiness under their marching feet. He watched his own trudge up the grassy slopes of yet another field or meadow or plain because he didn't have the strength left to lift his head.

"What if I just stopped? I know I'd be killed but at least it'd be sooner rather than later. They'll catch up at some point and I just can't run any more." He sank to his knees, the urge to lie down and sleep grabbing him as strongly as Mother's hands used to.

Keep moving.

Boy was back. His absence at the smithy had been difficult, but unfortunately Arawn was too foot-sore and heavy of heart now to be glad. "Why?"

You'll see.

"What will I see?" he said, pushing himself up from his knees, forcing each foot in front of the other.

The sea.

It was vast. They were still a long walk from the beach, but the sea in its hugeness was unmissable. It spread far on both sides and out, out until it reached the sky, looking as hard and unfriendly and uninviting as writhing metal.

And he could hear it. In fact, he realised he'd been hearing it for a while now but had not registered the sound because it had been distant and his mind hadn't known what it was. But looking at it, he heard it, shouting at the shore and smashing it into submission.

Salt. He smelt it clearly, blowing in on the wind that was fiercer now that he'd crested the slope. He'd been smelling that, too, for a while but had ignored it because of what it recalled to him. A small part of him was surprised—he knew where salt came from. It came from the sea. One evening, while Mother and his dead sister were outside at battle-practice, his father had explained how the people from whom they bought their salt to trade would use their secret ways to draw it from the sea. And they must have been magical ways, he thought now, to get something so small and hard and dry from something so vast and fluid and wet.

But he and his father had never been allowed to go into any settlements while the trading took place because she was ashamed of them. They had to wait in the woods until the women were finished, and they would hear the wheels of the laden cart, pulled by Boy, telling them to be ready to leave. So neither of them ever saw the sea because, Boudica forbid, they never defied Mother.

He hadn't known the whole sea would stink of salt.

It was despicable, yet he had made it as far as the sea. The coast. And despite there being only a stretch of stony shore ahead of them, it still meant the port couldn't be that far away.

He had made it. Something ignited inside him and suddenly Arawn decided he wasn't ready for death just yet.

"Come on," he said. "If they didn't sleep through the night either, they're not that far behind." Boy nodded, his face paler and his clothes noticeably more worn than before.

The wind ripped through Arawn's clothes, his skin even, and he ran more to keep warm than for fear of being caught. He marvelled at how the thick woollen leggings and trousers and heavy woollen tunic did nothing to keep the cold from biting him. In his mind he cursed bitterly at having to leave in such a rush, with no time to collect the fine cloak that Trahaearn had gifted him with. Then he cursed his mind for making him think of the smithy with its bright hot fire and dry, warm air.

Running along the shifting pebbles proved a difficult task. He felt as though he were exerting twice the amount of effort for less than half the intended outcome as his feet skittered and slid underneath him. And all the time the sea crashed and smashed to his left. It made him feel small. Just like Mother used to when she was screaming evidence of his uselessness and raining blows down upon him as quick and painful as hailstones until he was cowering on the floor, head between his knees and arms wrapped over it in a pathetic attempt to protect himself.

No. He did not like feeling small.

Fortunately, his thoughts were stopped by the sight in front of him—the port. Arawn whooped, all the tiredness swept aside in the swell of hope. Along the beach he raced.

* * *

The screaming white sea-birds were more numerous at the port, circling closer towards the ground and even landing on the boats. And what boats! Arawn had never seen the like before in his young life. He'd become accustomed to the size of the stone buildings of Cantiaci after a fashion, even though Epona's wooden hall atop the hill-fort in far Atrebates was dwarfed by many of them. But even the wealthiest of roundhouses in his old settlement would have been dwarfed by these floating giants. And how could they even stay afloat? There was clearly some magic being used, and any magic that could conquer the beast of the sea Arawn was keen to learn about. Long they were, longer than Arawn could count, and wide in the middle where he saw goods or hounds or slaves were being stowed. But at the front and back they narrowed coming to a high point, and he thought this was how the magic was conducted. For weren't Druid staffs made of wood so they could draw the power of the land? And so much wood as he saw here must surely draw the power of the sea. Standing tall in the centre of the vessels, all draped with ropes and cloth so heavy and vast that it hung down as though the sailors had tethered a portion of the cloud-blanketed sky, was the biggest staff Arawn had ever seen. Four, five times the height of a man, he guessed, perhaps more. If he rode one of these, he was sure, against the roaring, punching wrath of the water he would be invincible.

But what struck him to the core was the lack of women. There were a few, and by the way they behaved he thought them to be the sweethearts of the traders. Always they stayed on the dry side of the wooden platforms to which the boats were tied.

On board the boats was a different matter. That was the province of men. Many of them were stripped to the waist as they loaded the heavy bales of wool or hide, crates that clinked dully from the metal that was within; others cracked whips and fists as they loaded packs of vicious dogs which fought against their capture and manhandling, or slaves who didn't. Not all the boats were having their bellies filled, however, and Arawn was amazed by the variety of goods being unloaded onto the wooden platforms; huge jugs of exotic shape, crates of strange food and swathes of material he could put no name to.

There was so much activity. Men threw ropes thicker than Arawn's arm to one another, tying this, untying that; and still others who scraped the dirt of long journeys from the wood with wide blades, and a variety of other inexplicable tasks. It was as if he'd stumbled into another land. As he watched he realised that these men all understood the role they had to play and they undertook it with a confidence that made the complicated process of loading a ship and readying for sea look like a simple dance. And all without a woman standing above them barking out orders.

That wasn't to say there weren't any commands being given. With each ship he passed Arawn soon thought he knew which man was the ship's leader. Apart from giving the commands, he was recognisable from the arrogance in his stance, the surety in his expression, thought Arawn. Just like every woman he'd grown up around.

Yet, somehow, it didn't irk him. It felt more natural to have a hard-working team of men lead by a strong man. The sea might be detestable, but certainly Arawn felt he could be comfortable with life on a ship.

Now, though, wasn't the time to think of such things. He needed to find someone who would be willing to carry him across the violent water and deliver him into safer lands, away from the Atrebates warrior-women. And away from Rosmerta.

Rosmerta.

Had he thought wrongly of her after all? If it hadn't been for her warning he'd never have been able to flee the Atrebates. He should be dead by now. Clutching a hand to his chest he felt the treasures she'd given him, assuring himself that they were still tucked safely inside his tunic. If not for her, he'd not be able to pay for his passage.

"Get moving, you worthless piles of dung, or I'll have the one true god strike you down!" The voice, carried by the wind, caught Arawn's attention at once. As did the bellow of laughter that followed the threat. There in the middle of the heaving boat stood a stocky man, his hair pulled back into a queue and tied at his neck, his checkered cloak flapping as fiercely in the gale as the sheets tied to the boat's central staff. "Only Jesus can keep the tide from parting and he ain't here, so let's get moving!"

It was the Gaulish trader he'd spoken to at Cantiaci, he was sure of it. How many other people knew about the Roman's new one true god? Some of the people in the marketplace had been politely interested, others had openly mocked the idea, but no one had heard it before. It must be him!

He looked at Boy then and saw he had raised his arm and extended a bony finger so he was pointing at the very same ship which had caught Arawn's attention. "Let's buy my passage before it has a chance to leave," he said with a grin.

Despite his desire to ride and conquer, approaching the boat made his stomach flip. Though it was tied firmly to one of the wooden platforms, it pulled and heaved at its bonds like a beast eager for its freedom. There was a power here, more than he'd ever felt around the Druids who lived amongst the wealthy families and taught their daughters the sacred rites of the land. He feared it more than he had ever feared Gwynfor, but he wanted it. He wanted that power so he could rise above the women and Druids who had tortured his youth and be free of them.

"We're not trading in slaves, boy, no matter how willingly you offer yourself to us."

There was another burst of laughter at this and Arawn found himself looking up into the face of the Gaulish trader.

"I'm no slave," he said, quelling his urge to flee. "I seek passage."

"Oh, passage!" The trader stood up straighter, placed his

hands on his hips and looked around to his men. "The boy wants passage!"

Arawn knew he was being mocked, but he liked the wide, brown face of the trader with his easy smile. He knew that the mockery wasn't malicious, so he said nothing. He clutched at the treasure in his shirt.

"And what would you be offering for this passage? Can you sail?"

"No," said Arawn, smiling. Partly because the trader was, and partly because his hand had closed around the largest gold torc that Rosmerta had given him. "But I can give you this."

The trader's smile widened, so did his eyes, as the torc glinted before him, rich and heavy and shining despite the lack of sunshine. Arawn heard the whoops of approval from the crew behind the trader and was pleased. He would've gladly produced the smaller bracelets to bribe the trader, but he was thankful he didn't have to. They may well prove useful later on in his travels. Men, it seemed, liked gold as much as women did.

"Then don't waste my time by standing there, boy; climb on board so I can finally cut these ropes and set Nehalennia loose upon the sea."

He clambered up the wooden steps that one of the crew had slipped over the side and scrambled on board the boat.

The trader welcomed him on board by clapping him on the shoulder with one hand and relieving him of the torc with the other.

He whistled low through his teeth and said, "This is a fine piece of craftsmanship."

It was the first time Arawn had looked at it properly, but now he saw that the torc was indeed fine. The gold was thick and pure, and etched all over it were exquisite patterns that wound and curled, dove and dipped. An unlikely item that one seeking passage on a trader's boat was likely to carry.

"So fine, in fact," said the trader, "that I'd warrant a high-born lady owned it before you did."

"True," said Arawn. "Though it was given to me as a gift. A parting gift. I had to leave with some haste."

The trader roared with laughter. "Had to leave a high-born lady with haste! And with a gift such as this I can imagine well what caused such an abrupt departure!"

His crew laughed uproariously, and though Arawn joined in, he wasn't entirely sure why.

"Then we will take you away from the lady's shame, and don't you worry—your secret is safe with us." He waved the torc a little. "You've paid well for it. You can wait back there for now," he said, indicating the rear of the boat, "and wait 'til we're out on the open sea. You'll only get in our way." He clapped Arawn on the back again as he walked past, and he settled himself amongst hide blankets.

The trader started bellowing commands, using words that Arawn neither recognised nor understood; but the ropes tying them to the land were cut, and the vast piece of material that was bound to the staff suddenly flared and the boat moved away from the shore, rocking and dipping as the magic of the boat fought against the might of the sea.

The crew were laughing again and Arawn looked towards them, in time to see the trader leaping across the deck towards him.

"Look over there, boy," he said, pointing across the ship. At first, Arawn saw only the vast, white cliffs that marked the dramatic end of the Cantiaci territory; but the shore had suddenly become dark with horses and spear-women, their weapons winking cruelly in the daylight. "Looks like we just managed to outrun the wrath of the high-born lady's family, eh?" He winked at him, clapped his shoulder, and then bound back across the deck, shouting orders as he went.

An entire army was gathered there. He recognised easily the red- and black-striped cloaks of the Atrebates, flapping furiously in the sea-blown wind. Yet other cloaks were amongst them, green, blue and silver-striped cloaks he'd come to recognise just as easily, and had even come to love—those of Cantiaci. That love suddenly soured.

Though that was nothing compared to the feeling that spiked him when he saw a horse break from that army and trot towards the port. It was a fine horse, a stallion of a high-born lady. Astride it, her golden hair flaring out behind her as impressively as her fur-lined cloak was the woman who had led that army straight to him, had no doubt told him where to run so the hunt would be all the easier. And he recognised that figure, for it the figure of a deceiver.

It was Rosmerta Warrior-Princess.

– 12 –

The moon of Cutios (Windy-time), 332 C.E.
Dubras, Cantiaci tribal lands, Brython

"The journey will be long," said Heddgwyn, "so don't laden yourself with unnecessary items. We'll find food and shelter along the way easily enough. Just ensure you have plenty of votives, our route passes through the territories of many gods."

Emrys nodded. "I don't understand why we're leaving so soon," he said. "Especially now that the bonding between our tribe and the Atrebates is soon to take place." He sounded sullen even to his own ears, but he couldn't help it. Rosmerta had ridden off without even saying goodbye and he'd yet to have a private audience with Sulis, his mother, to find out why this was. Sending her off to hunt for a criminal seemed senseless, especially as uniting these two tribes had been Sulis' sole ambition in recent years.

"It always strikes me how something good can come from a disaster, yes," said Heddgwyn with a faint smile. "But it's merely a ceremony for show. We'll be back for the true one."

"How long will this journey take?"

"Long enough. Longer if you don't hurry. I want to be riding as the sun is rising."

"Can I at least say goodbye to my mother and sister?"

Heddgwyn scowled a little. "There's no time for that. Besides, I doubt either of them will be awake yet."

It irked him, but Emrys knew Heddgwyn was right. Not long after Rosmerta had led her small army out of the town, Sulis Warrior-Queen of the Cantiaci and Epona Warrior-Queen of the Atrebates had announced the bonding of the two tribes, with his young sister, Airmed, to stand in Rosmerta's stead until she returned. There had been a great feast to mark the occasion, but

Heddgwyn had pulled him away before the musicians and dancers had even begun so they could have a few hours' sleep before their journey. If the Arch Druid had told him they were to leave at dawn he could have made his goodbyes during the feast. Now they were sneaking off before the palace even awoke and that made him uneasy.

"We're free to come and go as we please," said Heddgwyn suddenly, as though he'd just read Emrys' last thought. "And Druids should undertake pilgrimages, many and often; it's the only way to learn. You've been idle in this place long enough. Now you must see all the lands the gods gave us, and perhaps that will convince you of the justness of our cause. And bring your second cloak too; it will be bitter riding this day."

Our cause, thought Emrys as they walked to the stables. The air was as cold and still as glass. Their cause to treason. He might be following him willingly but it was only because Heddgwyn scared him. Would all the tribes comply so readily to his idea of the land of the gods ruled as one by the Druids? Would the warrior-queens? They might fear the power of the Druids but Heddgwyn was only one. He couldn't hope to bring them all under his will...not without bloodshed. And that possibility scared him even more than the Arch Druid did.

The horses were ready for them in the stable. Emrys tied his sack to the saddle then climbed up. It was a pity; he should be excited about taking his first pilgrimage—and to Ynys Afallach of all places! But as his horse followed Heddgwyn's out into the pre-dawn dark, their hooves deafening in the silence, his heart was heavy.

* * *

"Our course will take us west through Atrebates," said Heddgwyn, "then north as we travel through Dobunni. From there we'll strike north-west into the tribal lands of Cornovii and

Deceangli. The western passes through the mountains will be difficult and treacherous, even though the warmer season will be on us by then, but after that final trial we'll see the golden isle of Ynys Afallach shining up at us from the water." He was in fine spirits.

"You've made this journey before?" The day was bleak, and even though Emrys had since wrapped his second cloak around him, he was still cold.

"Indeed. Every Druid must. But only the wisest are permitted to live there, the very highest of our order. My hope is to, one day, be accepted."

Emrys said nothing. Though the sun had been up for hours, hidden as it was by heavy clouds that promised rain, he still recognised every inch of landscape. And would do for many days, he didn't wonder. The enormity of the journey was just hitting him, and already his backside was sore from sitting in the saddle for this long.

Then the clouds burst and rain started to pour.

* * *

"There now," said Heddgwyn on the seventh day of their travel. "The sun rises clear on the horizon. This day will prove much better for travelling."

"I hope so," said Emrys. "My cloaks are barely dry, despite hanging above a fire all night." They'd stopped in a hamlet of five huts the last night, and one family had offered their home to the pilgrims while they stayed with a neighbour. It was more through fear than generosity, Emrys noted. Eyes shouldn't grow so wide and faces shouldn't pale so when helping people in need. "I wonder if this pilgrimage of yours has more to do with punishment than returning the lands to the gods."

To his astonishment, the Arch Druid laughed, a rich, deep sound that resonated with genuine pleasure; and as pleased as

Emrys was to hear it, it also saddened him that he hadn't heard it more often. "Travelling seems to please you," he said.

"There's nothing more pleasant for the soul, Emrys."

They made better time that day. Though the ground was still soggy from the soaking it had received during the previous days, the strengthening sunshine held all day and the two pilgrims were able to speed their steeds across the wide stretches of countryside that marked the borders of Cantiaci. They stopped briefly by a brook while the sun was at its zenith to lunch on hard cheese and stale bread; then, after leaving a votive in the water to Belisama, they continued their goodly pace until the sun descended towards the horizon again.

"By nightfall we'll be at the borderlands of Atrebates," said the Druid. "And if my memory serves, there is a small village that will offer us food and bed for the night."

The sky had darkened and true night fallen, though it wasn't yet late, and still they had come across no village.

"I think your memory has failed you, Heddgwyn." They were riding side by side, surrounded by soft landscape, and Emrys felt they were more companionable then they'd ever been. More like his father than his Arch Druid and teacher. He was happy and that surprised him.

"Pity," said Heddgwyn. "I was hoping not to camp under the stars this night."

Emrys looked up. "It's a clear night. With a fire it could be quite pleasant, if a little cold."

"Could be, could be. Though it's not the cold that bothers me." He paused, then dropped his voice. "We're being followed."

"What?" He sat bolt upright, instinctively looking around him, though the darkness thwarted him.

"Since we crossed the border. It's only one man, but it concerns me that he's been on our trail for so long."

"An outlaw?"

"Possibly. Likely."

"What shall we do?"

The Arch Druid was silent for a moment. "We can't keep our horses walking in gloom. The last thing I want is for one of the beasts to break a leg in a fall."

"We can't stop!" Emrys hissed. "What if he slits our throats while we're sleeping?"

"His reticence to attack is clear or he would have done so by now. If we build a big enough fire and take turns keeping watch through the night we should be safe enough."

He stopped his horse suddenly, jumped down, and took a rush light out from underneath his saddle bags. Of course, all Emrys heard was rustling in the gloom; it wasn't until light flared and blinded him momentarily did he realise what Heddgwyn had been doing.

"Where did you get that?"

"Same place as I got this one." Light flared again and this time Emrys almost managed to close his eyes in time. "I left the family a few copper coins for them, don't worry. I haven't turned to thievery."

"You took them from the hut we stayed in last night?" Emrys said when he'd jumped down from his own horse.

"And fortunately I did. We'd not see past our own hands to unpack our dinner, let alone build a fire and tether our horses. And the copper coins more than pay for them so take that look of horror off your face."

There was no possible way the Arch Druid could have seen his face, busy as he was with fixing the rush lights into the ground. Perhaps he knows me better than I think, thought Emrys.

They were close to a small grove, which meant they could tether their horses close by and collect plenty of firewood without straying too far from one another.

"Fortuitous," said Emrys.

"You think I stopped here by accident?"

The village peasants had gifted them with salted pork, oatcakes and apples as well as a flagon of ale, which they shared in front of the fire they'd built between the two rush-lights. By the time Emrys was full he was pleased to see there was still a generous amount of food left. Breakfast, then, wouldn't be mean.

"I'll take the first watch," said Heddgwyn. "Sleep while you can. I'll wake you when the moon has fully risen."

He did as he was told, and was glad for he was exhausted. Spending the entire day out in the cold and riding a horse was tiring work. He lay on one cloak and wrapped the other about him (both, thankfully, were completely dry now after a day of airing in the sun), and lay down with his back to the fire. Aside from the pop and hiss as the wood burned, the night was quiet and he slipped quickly into slumber.

It wasn't Heddgwyn who woke him, though; it was the dawn. He sat up with a start and looked around their makeshift camp. The Arch Druid was nowhere to be seen. His whispered words from last night of their unwanted follower rang through his head.

"Heddgwyn!" he called in alarm. The two horses, which were tethered close by cropping the grass, raised their heads and looked towards him. They lost interest quickly and went back to their breakfast. "Heddgwyn!"

He ran around the fire which was still burning brightly and looked back down the mud road they had followed the previous day. He scanned the fields rolling out in front of him, but a dawn fog obscured his view. A shiver of panic clenched his stomach. "Heddgwyn!"

"Ah, you're up."

Emrys spun around. Strolling out of the woods was the Arch Druid.

"I thought you'd..." He stopped, not really knowing what he'd thought, except that he'd feared the worst.

"Thought I'd been murdered by our follower?" He walked

back to the fire and held out his hands. Emrys joined him and did the same. "Remarkable how such an outlaw would leave our belongings untouched, leave you untouched, and keep the fire nice and hot for you just to murder me."

He said nothing for a while. Then, "You didn't wake me."

"No. But you are unused to travel and needed sleep more than I. Besides, I wanted to keep an eye open for our follower."

"Did you see him?"

"Not once."

"Then he's gone?"

"Doubtful, or I would have seen him pass. He's watching and waiting, I think."

"Is he dangerous?"

Heddgwyn shrugged. "Most outlaws are."

Emrys looked out across the landscape, still fighting against the very last clutches of winter. I'm on an adventure, he thought glumly. Then he remembered something. "What were you doing in the forest?"

The Druid raised an eyebrow. "There are some things you can't do at the camp site. And I suggest you take a stroll to yonder grove before we leave. It's safe. I imagine stopping at the side of the road to answer nature is just the kind of opportunity our follower is waiting for."

By the time Emrys came back from the grove, the camp site was no more. The fire was put out, the spare cloaks put back into saddle bags, and Heddgwyn waited patiently, holding the reins of the two horses. "Let's go, pilgrim," he said.

The morning passed well, but as the sun passed its zenith clouds spilled in from the west.

"I'm almost certain we'll be at this village before the rain starts," said Heddgwyn.

"Almost?" said Emrys, then a flare of white pain lanced through his head and he slipped from his saddle. His blurry eyes could just make out the shape of a tattered figure inching towards him. But even though he was ragged, the point of his spear glinted brightly. He pushed himself up and tried to call out for Heddgwyn, but the Arch Druid was already beside him, heavy rowan staff in his hand.

"Don't be foolish," he called out. "We're two and you're only one. And we're Druids, no less. If you come any closer I'll turn you into a toad where you stand."

"Can you do that?" whispered Emrys.

"So long as he stands there for a fortnight while I prepare the potion, then allows me to administer it to him. But somehow I don't think he will."

"You won't turn me into a toad," the ragged man called back. His voice rasped, as though it hadn't been used for a long while.

"No?"

"No. It would take too long. You'll be dead before the potion's made."

Heddgwyn stood up straighter, but he looked more curious then afraid. "You seem well-versed in Druid lore for a vagabond."

The ragged man just nodded, inching closer, his eyes moving hungrily between the horses and the bags they carried. But, Emrys was pleased to note, they did turn a little fearful when Heddgwyn spoke, despite his show of bravery and knowledge.

"In that case," said the Druid, "I'll just strike you down with my staff and have done with it."

The ragged man looked uncertain now. He was closer, close enough so that Emrys could see each rip in his filthy leggings, and that his tunic had been inexpertly mended with scraps of animal hide. His beard was matted with dirt and grease, and his rusty brown hair was a knotted trail down his back. Despite looking like a broken man, however, he suddenly raised his spear and opened his mouth with a roaring cry and sped towards them. In truth, Emrys knew he was heading only for him while he still struggled to regain his balance; picking off the weaker one to even out the odds for himself.

With a speed that surprised Emrys as much as it surprised the ragged man, Heddgwyn leapt forward, swiping his staff low at the man's ankles and the brute went crashing to the floor with a bellow of rage. Heddgwyn bounded over him, graceful as any dancer from Sulis Warrior-Queen's hall, and kicked the spear far out of reach. Then he bopped him on the head with the end of his staff. Not hard enough to cause any damage, just enough to quieten him and stop him from getting to his feet. He looked as dazed as Emrys felt.

"Never rob a Druid," said Heddgwyn, walking around to face their attacker. "For that is dangerous. Attacking two? That's nothing more than suicide. Tell me why I should let you live."

The ragged man looked up at him. Anger was still in his eyes, but it was quickly being replaced with reproach. "I'm cold. I just wanted his cloak."

"Badly enough to kill? If you'd asked nicely, I'm sure Emrys would have given you one. He's got two, you know. Did you not think about asking nicely instead of throwing a rock at him?"

The ragged man's reaction was so unexpected that the two pilgrims could only look at one another, mouths hanging open; he'd started bawling like a small child. There was pain and loss in that cry, Emrys thought; and despite the pain in his head he pitied him.

"I was wealthy," he wailed. "I worked hard for my coin but I was wealthy! How have I come to this?"

Heddgwyn turned to the saddle bag on Emrys' horse and rooted around for a moment, then approached the ragged man with a fistful of salted pork. When he offered it to him, the ragged man just looked at him dumbly.

"You would feed me after I attacked you?"

"There was no real harm done. My son is alive, as am I."

Emrys looked at Heddgwyn in wonder—he'd never called him his son before.

"I had a son once," said the ragged man with a rueful smile. "But he's gone. They're all gone. Thank you," he said, accepting the food. It vanished into his mouth with remarkable speed.

"You seem strong and brave," said Heddgwyn. "How did you lose your family?"

The ragged man only looked into his lap and shook his head slowly.

"Your story is a long and sad one, I think," said the Arch Druid, "and fate has been less than generous to you. But perhaps it is fate that has made our paths cross this day. You can join us for a short while as our bodyguard, and I'll compensate with you food and coin when we've found a settlement that will welcome us. Outlawry will only get you killed."

The ragged man looked up at the Arch Druid in confusion and surprise, as did Emrys. For so long he'd known him as a bad-tempered teacher who liked no other company except that of other Druids; and suddenly here he was offering this vagabond food and employment.

He clambered to his feet, helped Emrys to his, all the while thanking the Arch Druid profusely for his change in fortune and promising to keep them safe on the dangerous roads. Heddgwyn merely smiled as he climbed into his saddle again. Emrys did the same, and with the ragged man walking just ahead of them, they started their journey again.

"What's your name, outlaw?" said Heddgwyn. "I confess I'm not comfortable calling you such."

"Emlyn ap Anwyn," he said.

Emrys looked at him for a moment. "I though you said you had a family?" he said, and the ragged man nodded. "Then why ap Anwyn? Were you not bonded?"

For a moment Emrys thought he saw a scowl, but the ragged man turned his head forward again.

"I was bonded," he said. "But no longer."

"You'll fare better," said Heddgwyn, "if you used your

bonded name. People trust a man who's been chosen by a woman more than an outlaw who hasn't." The ragged man grunted. "So what was your bonded name?"

It seemed as though the ragged man wouldn't answer. But finally he said, "Salt-merchant. My name was Emlyn Salt-merchant, and my wife was hanged for treason and my children are dead."

The moon of Cutios (Windy-time), 332 C.E.
Ocean

No matter how hard he fought against it, Arawn couldn't stop the shaking that had crept into his body, seized it, and refused to let go. His teeth knocked against one another until he thought he would go mad from the sound, and his limbs were beyond his control. He'd wrapped so many hides about himself that he was sure he was wearing an entire herd of cattle by now, but it didn't do him any good; the sea rain kept falling on him, driven by the wind across the boat, onto the hides and into his bones.

Yet despite his physical coldness, his core burned with fury.

She had betrayed him! And in such a cunning way, and with such cunning conviction that he'd started to believe she cared after all, so that even the most wicked of all the blasted demons that crawled across the lands at night weren't as evil as her.

"You have to leave," she had said, making her eyes big so she looked scared. "They'll be here any moment. You must leave right away."

And he had run because he'd believed her. All so she could lead the army straight to him, and no doubt be rewarded richly for her services.

"This your first time sailing?"

Arawn raised his eyes and saw the trader standing, grinning, above him.

"I can tell because you're not enjoying yourself. People who ride the ocean often don't sit huddled in a corner of the ship looking like they're trying to count every drop of water."

Arawn still said nothing.

"Because of the mighty big frown you're wearing. Makes you look like you're concentrating on something impossible to understand."

"I suppose I am."

"There! The lad speaks at last. It's not a horse and cart, I know, and it's apt to be a little chilly at this time of year, but when you get used it, you'll love sailing as much as the rest of my crew. Aching to get back on a boat once you've stepped off this one, you will."

"I can't imagine there's much truth in that."

The trader barked a laugh, then squatted down so his face was level with Arawn's. "I know what's wrong," he said. Arawn blinked at him. "It's because we're still in sight of the shore." He motioned to the right with his eyes and Arawn looked out. Sure enough, in the distance was a grey smudge along the horizon. "You're still caught up in whatever problems you had there. But soon we'll be out in the open sea and you'll be able to let go of all of them."

Arawn looked back, eyes wide. "Really?"

The trader grinned. "Of course! Why do you think so many men love sailing? Leave all their troubles in distant lands!" he laughed heartily at his own joke, and it was that more than the joke that brought the smallest of smiles to Arawn's lips.

"That would be good," he said.

"And it is. Now tell me, my fine young lad; you've spent the night with me and my crew and not one of us knows your name yet. You'd only been on board a few minutes before you fell asleep!"

"I hadn't slept at all the previous night," said Arawn. "I was very tired." And that was true, he had been tired; but he hadn't fallen asleep instantly, he'd just pretended he had. He didn't want to explain why he was so furious at the young woman they'd all seen coming towards the port on her proud horse.

But when he did fall asleep he was tortured by the dreams again; dreams that had all but disappeared when he was in Cantiaci in the comforting company of Trahaearn. Dreams of his dead sister and the dead Druid who, even from Otherworld, were concocting dark magics against him. Or so his dreams would have him believe. And what were dreams if not the words of the gods? He detested the idea of Boudica and the fact that she'd risen above the ranks of all the old gods in power and status. But how powerful could the old gods really have been if they'd been swept aside by one woman and her daughters? So he doubted the magic of the gods, perhaps he had all his life; just like he doubted the magic of the Druids. He was afraid of them, yes, though he couldn't say why. He didn't believe in their magic—all that seemed to consist of, from his experience, was whispering into the ears of women and convincing them they were better than men.

But was he not, this very moment, witnessing magic in the way the traders controlled the sea? So when he had these dreams, these visions, of the wretched Gwynfor bent over his cauldron and using the head of his sister to perform powerful magic, it always seemed so real at night. And that fear kept him awake throughout, and left him feeling sour in the morning. If the old gods had lost their power, what now could he turn to in order to defeat the sorcery that was being used against him?

"That's as may be," said the trader, looking at him with amusement. "I can accept you were too tired to tell me your name yesterday. But you're not too tired today, are you?"

Arawn shook his head at that. "Arawn," he said. "Arawn…ap Emlyn."

"Ap Emlyn? Sounds unlike any woman's name I've heard before."

"It's my father's name."

The trader looked surprised. "You have no mother?"

"No."

A look of pity ran across the trader's face. "She died in childbirth?"

Arawn shrugged. He had no desire to continue with this line of questioning. The trader probably knew as well as he did that, even if the mother died in childbirth, the child still carried her name.

"Well, then. You can call me Thrax. So! Arawn of Emlyn, the newest member of my crew, and happy I am to welcome such an intriguing lad." He clapped him on the shoulder again, and Arawn smiled his first genuine smile.

"Tell me of your country," he said. "Will I like it there?"

Thrax laughed. "I can't answer that question for you, Arawn ap Emlyn," he said, "because that depends on how much you love your own lands. There are certainly more memories of the Romans in my lands, for they had longer to worm their way into the soil."

"Really?"

The trader nodded. "Brython may have endured them a few score years, but Gaul suffered them for centuries. If only Boudica had been born a Gaul—none of us would've had to suffer the Romans!"

Arawn wasn't entirely sure he agreed with this sentiment, but he said nothing. Certainly the memories of them he'd seen in Cantiaci were impressive enough. The thrill of seeing more in Gaul was much better at warming him than his earlier fury.

"But her victory was felt across the sea nonetheless."

"It was?" said Arawn.

"Indeed. Not only did they suffer defeat, they suffered humiliation as well. We came to learn that they had no great respect for women. As mothers, and slaves to their husbands, that was fine. But as warriors and leaders? It was the reason why they hated the Gauls so much, and all the tribes outside of their empire. It was why they believed we were savages to be civilised."

"Because of the women?"

"Because of the women," Thrax agreed. "Nothing scared a Roman more than fearful, fighting warrior women." He laughed with delight. "So when the Romans fled Brython to recover their wounds, we rose up against them. They'd lost much of their spirit by then, and we outnumbered them by so many that the fight was won before it ever really started. They retreated back to Rome and left us alone ever since. And of course, we keep our fiercest-looking women patrolling the boundaries which always keeps them in check." He laughed again.

"Where is Rome?" asked Arawn.

"Beyond the mountains to the south east of Gaul. Once, Rome covered all the world. Now it's nothing more than ruined settlements inhabited by priests who live in their own shit and whip themselves for having lost their power and might to a woman. What a sight that would be!"

Arawn laughed dutifully, then said, "What's priests? Is that what the Romans call themselves now?"

Thrax smiled. "Only the men. Women are slaves, I think...and bearers of more priests. And if too many girl babies are born, the priests burn them, and the mothers that bore them." He shivered.

"So the priests are the leaders?"

"Yes. If you can really call them that. They've lost all their stomach for battle, and they spend all their time talking to their one true god who tells them to do nonsense things like build churches and burn women, as well as forbidding all those things that make life worth living—drinking, fucking and fighting!" he added when he saw Arawn's look of incomprehension, then rocked with laughter at his childish look of shock.

"Their one true god..." Arawn echoed. "You told me a little about him when you were in Cantiaci."

The trader looked startled for a moment, and looked hard at Arawn's face. Then it creased into his bright smile. "That's right!

I thought I recognised your face, wouldn't have let you on my boat if I hadn't! But there was something familiar about you that spoke to me, and that's what it was, our chance meeting at the marketplace. See how fate deigned to give you passage on my boat?"

"Fate, and the gold," said Arawn. The trader roared with laughter and clapped him on the shoulder.

"You're a good lad, Arawn ap Emlyn."

"I would hear more about the one true god, if you've a mind to tell me?"

Thrax nodded, as Arawn knew he would. He saw well that the trader enjoyed telling his stories of the lands he knew, even if those stories were based on rumour instead of experience. But if Arawn's face had spoken to the trader, then something about this one true god spoke to Arawn; and the fact that he ordered the priests of Rome to enslave and burn women, he knew, was surely a great part of it.

But before the trader could take up his tale again, one of the crew bellowed for his attention. It was almost hoarse, and when Arawn looked to him as the trader did, he could see the fear clearly in his widened eyes.

The trader leapt up as the crew member shouted words that Arawn couldn't quite understand. But from the sudden frenetic energy enveloping the ship, he understood plainly that danger was close at hand.

While the trader stood in the centre of the ship bawling his orders, the sails were unfurled as far as they would go, and he saw that the rudder-man was turning the ship back towards the smudge that had been the horizon of Brython. The smudge had gone now, but it would appear soon enough if the ship continued its new course. Fear swelled in Arawn's chest like a wave.

"What's happening?" he cried out to Thrax.

"Go down into the hold. Hide yourself as well as you can and don't come back out until the fighting is over."

"Fighting?" It came out almost as a squeak.

"Traders aren't the only people to sail these waters. Now go! The deck will be no place for lads soon enough!"

Rushing towards them with incredible speed—one minute it was sliding across the horizon, the next it was close enough to see the figures of men crowding the decks—was another ship, though this one had a long row of oars sticking out of each side which pushed it faster than a lone sail could.

If they try to outrun them, they'll never make it! It was Arawn's last thought before fear finally closed over and swallowed him.

– 13 –

The moon of Cutios (Windy-time), 332 C.E.
Ocean

A terrifying crash, and Arawn pissed himself. He felt it warm against his crotch and down his leg and a distant part of himself wanted to feel anger and disgust but he was too busy drowning in fear. He'd buried himself under bales of wool, but the shock of the other ship smashing into them rattled the very bones in his body.

He was curled in a ball, shaking as though in the midst of a fever, trying to calm his breath in order to stop inhaling the greasy stench of fleece. He had no desire to add vomiting to his list of shameful reactions.

Heartbeats after the enemy vessel crashed into their hull, the boat tipped and swayed as countless foes boarded her; then came the ringing sound of metal on metal. It had struck him as odd that all the crew had been armed with short swords at their sides, as well as the spears that littered the deck, but now he understood. It wasn't the first time they'd been attacked at sea. This realisation made him simultaneously relieved and angered. The first because it meant they knew how to fight, the second because no one, not even the friendly trader, Thrax, had warned him of the dangers.

The battle seemed to stretch out for aeons, the entire world becoming nothing but screams of rage, screams of pain, and that metallic crash that sliced through Arawn's head and froze his blood.

And then somebody was down in the hold. Arawn nearly jumped out of his hiding place, believing it to be the trader coming to look for him and tell him he was safe; but his brain warned him that still the sound of battle came from above. When the intruder began shouting Arawn knew he would be killed instantly if he revealed himself. His words were even more foreign than the dialect of the crew; it was harsh and guttural, offensive to Arawn's ears but frightening in its vehemence.

Then he heard it. The grunting and cursing that came with heaving arm-loads of heavy goods out of an enclosed space. He'd hidden himself at the far end of the hold; but if the traders were accustomed to fighting battles at sea it was because these men were accustomed to robbing them. It might not take them very long at all to discover his hiding place, and then Arawn would finally understand what life as a slave was like.

If they even let him live.

He pissed himself again.

The voices were nearer now, and he could feel the bales of wool around him shift and move. Above, the battle still raged though it seemed the screams were fewer; and either the crew hadn't realised that there were enemies down here, or they were dead.

The choking stench of wool lifted, and Arawn found himself looking at a monster of a man. He was at least twice the width of a normal man and half as tall again, and his entire frame was covered with animal hides. He had a sword at his hip, bloody to the hilt, which matched the spatters of blood covering his clothes and face.

And his face was terrible. Wide and sunburnt it was, with cold blue eyes, a broken nose and a big mouth, which opened wide into a feral grin when he saw Arawn cowering before him. He said something in his own tongue, then smiled even wider, revealing two rows of broken, brown teeth. He leaned forward so Arawn was assaulted with the twin stenches of his rancid breath and the rotting animal hides that covered him. As he moved, thick swathes of dirty yellow hair like hay in an oxen pen fell forward and framed his face. He brushed at it distractedly with one giant hand.

He reached out and grabbed Arawn by the collar and he could feel himself start to gibber. The material of his tunic cut into his neck terribly, but he knew this was the very least of his problems. Those cold eyes were boring into him intently, and he was almost whispering in his ugly tongue; then he suddenly he looked at Arawn with such a look of reproachful shock it was almost comical.

A second later both of them tumbled to the floor, and Arawn scrambled away from the huge hand that had clutched him. Beneath the yellow-haired monster, a growing pool of blood was forming.

"You all right, lad?"

He looked up. Thrax stood there, bloody and battered, in his hand a stubby sword dripping with gore.

Arawn nodded.

"Got the bastard," said Thrax, looking down at the corpse.

Arawn nodded again.

"They're leaving," he said, reaching his hand out towards Arawn. "They've taken their plunder and more dead than they bargained for. But I could do with some help cleaning up and taking care of the wounded. Are you all right?"

"Who were those men?"

"Pirates." He spat on the dead body by his feet.

"That's the name of their tribe?"

Thrax barked a humourless laugh. "You could say that. They're raiders of the sea. They come from a land far to the east of Gaul, but it must be a land of nothing but goat-shit because they spend most of their time plundering trade ships." He pulled Arawn up out of his hiding place, stepped gingerly over the huge corpse then turned to look down at him. "They're called Angles," said Thrax when he'd helped Arawn to his feet. "And they're vicious bastards, the lot of them."

* * *

Still trembling, Arawn allowed Thrax to lead him out of the hold onto the deck. Fear was replaced with horror as Arawn took in the human destruction in front of him. The crew had already starting hauling the dead bodies overboard—kicking the Angles with a fury that was only slightly tempered by the grief with which they respectfully sent their companions the same way. Few bodies were whole as they were swallowed by the hungry waters. Here was a hand, there an ear. Many heads. Coupled with the blood that slicked the wood and made the air stink of copper, Arawn couldn't stop himself from adding to the chaos with his own vomit.

When the deck was cleared of the grisly battle remains, the crew huddled together, and Thrax spoke to them in their own language. They were praying, Arawn thought. Perhaps to Belisama, the goddess of water, to watch over them for the rest of their journey; perhaps to Cernunnos and all the other gods of Otherworld to keep the souls of their fallen. Perhaps, even, praying for vengeance on those that had visited this evil on them. The Angles. He couldn't hear all that they said for his head still rang from the battle and the wind whipped about them, but he thought he heard Thrax say, "Dibu e debu." The words seemed almost familiar… "Dibu e debu," echoed the crew, sprinkling the surface of the water with votives of their own bracelets or torcs, and the silver arm-bands harvested from Angle corpses to whichever gods they had chosen.

"What will we do now?" Arawn said when the blood had been washed from the deck and Thrax was back beside the steering oar.

It was a long time before he spoke. "We've no choice but to return home. Good men died today and their families need to be told." He paused again. "Brython is closer, and part of me wants to return. The open waters are ahead of us, several days of sailing without a proper crew and nothing to plunder. If we're attacked again we won't survive." He looked at Arawn, and what he saw there frightened him more than a little. "We were lucky today. The Angles won much plunder but they also lost as many men as we did. If we hadn't been carrying weapons they would have slaughtered us all and destroyed my boat. As it is..." He sighed. "But I have nothing to trade in Brython, no coin to buy more wares, and a reduced crew. My only choice is to go back home."

In spite of himself and all that had happened, Arawn was relieved. His desire to go back to the lands where women ruled and fought was as dead as the traders now sinking to the bottom of the ocean. He'd been caught up in the middle of a nightmare during the battle, that was true; but one thing was very clear: not only did the tribes across the sea in Gaul, and other more dangerous lands, allow solely men to take charge of boats, they also formed raiding and hunting parties.

And they were fearsome. An image of the giant Angle swamped in his animal hides and covered in blood flashed in his mind, and he shivered. Yet one thing couldn't be denied; he was more terrifying to behold than the most fearsome warrior-woman he'd seen in his own lands. Perhaps he could find his own band of warrior-men and learn how to fight. How sweet it would be to return home with an army of warrior-men and frighten the women who had so frightened him throughout his childhood.

Then another memory surfaced, one where Mother failed in her attempt to rise against Epona Warrior-Queen and was promised death for her troubles. Mother and his sister were already walking through the black and cold wastes of Otherworld, but there was one woman who needed to be taught that treachery against Arawn ap Emlyn wasn't wise: Rosmerta Warrior-Princess. How he would love to lead a frightful band of warrior-men into her lands and swipe that treacherous head clean off her body.

"Are you all right, Arawn?" said Thrax. "You're shaking."

He nodded, startled.

"A battle is no place for a lad."

"Certainly not one who can't even use a sword," said Arawn bitterly. "I'm sixteen summers, I should be a man, but instead I'll die like a beast because my people don't allow men to wield weapons."

Thrax reached out and put an arm over his shoulders. At first Arawn flinched at the touch, but when he realised it was given in friendship he relaxed. Even when his father was at his most companionable there had never been any contact between them.

"Anyone can be taught to wield a weapon," said Thrax, "and I'd be happy to teach you what little I know."

Arawn smiled. "Then perhaps, one day, I can save your life like you saved mine."

"Perhaps you will, and grateful I'd be." He returned the smile. "But we won't start your lessons just yet. Let's put some distance between us and the enemy first, eh?"

Arawn nodded. He knew well that Thrax spoke of the Angle pirates, but in his mind's eye he saw Rosmerta Warrior-Princess, and all the warrior-queens of Brython.

That night sleep came quickly, for fear is an exhausting emotion that drains even the hardiest of men, and Arawn was a frightened boy sailing across the sea to unknown lands.

* * *

Again the dream comes, of Gwynfor huddled over his crucible, and the vacant eyes of his dead sister staring out of it. But then a huge wave erupts out of it bringing with it blood-stained, yellow-haired warrior-men and Arawn finds himself surrounded by enemies who will kill him by magic or by sword.

But then thunder clashes overhead and spears of lightning strike at them, piercing them through the heart and killing them instantly. It frightens him as much as it pleases him.

"How?" he screams up at the boiling sky. "How?"

The one true god, the thunder rumbles. *The one true god will defeat all enemies. The one true god...*

On it rumbles, and Arawn is comforted by it.

* * *

"But that's not fair!" wailed Arawn; Thrax had managed to swipe his legs out from underneath him again. "I lost my balance!"

"Course you did," said Thrax with a wide grin. "That's why fighting on a boat is so difficult. Everything is unpredictable, even the floor under your feet. And if you don't learn how to use that to your advantage, an Angle will have your head. Up you get," he said, holding out his hand. "Let's try again."

They were practising with wooden poles, and Arawn felt clumsy and uncoordinated, despite Thrax's assurances that he'd make a good fighter once he'd practised for long enough. He had strength, certainly—he'd spent his childhood and adolescence chopping firewood with a heavy axe, drawing heavy carts of salt pots, and building and fixing the family roundhouses; but there was no skill in that. With each leap Thrax performed to avoid a blow, Arawn was astounded by his agility. And even while he was still moving he was able to parry. Not once had Arawn managed to land a single hit on the trader; yet Arawn was now the proud owner of several bright bruises. His arms and shoulders ached with the constant motion, but it was a good ache; he knew it would benefit him greatly and he would become strong. But he was also dismayed because he felt it would be a long time before he was as skilled as his opponent.

"Keep your legs bent," said Thrax, "and don't keep your body so rigid. You need to be as fluid as the sea you're fighting on. Feel the motion of the boat and move with her."

Arawn nodded. "And then when I face my first fight on land I'll look like I've spent hours draining ale pots."

Thrax roared a laugh. "You'll not get into scrapes on land, lad.

Strictly on-board fighting, especially if you're part of my crew."

Arawn stood up straight and his arm fell to the side. "You'd let me join your crew?"

"If you prove yourself," he said, then threw him a wink and attacked.

He managed to duck out of the way, keeping his legs this time, and was swinging around with his weapon raised, when a chorus of shouts caught his and Thrax's attention. The trader ran to the front of his boat, and after a few heartbeats he whooped with joy, raising both hands above his head.

"Almost home, Arawn ap Emlyn!" he shouted over his shoulder.

Arawn raised his own fists in the air, the right one still clutching his makeshift weapon, and whooped with joy as well.

They sailed along the coast for a while, then turned east into a headland which, Thrax informed him, would lead them onto the Sequana river which they would then follow all the way to Lutetia, their town. Their home. The names were strange to Arawn, and Thrax smiled when he stumbled over their pronunciation at first.

"Some of the words are still Roman," he explained. "Sequana, for instance."

"Why would you keep words of the enemy in your land?"

Thrax shrugged a shoulder. "The Romans were in Gaul for a lot longer than they were in Brython, remember. Generations had passed, and words got passed along with them. Old words are forgotten soon enough. Just another scar to remind us that we weren't always a free people."

The river wound ever deeper into Gaul, and part of Arawn was surprised that it wasn't so different to the country he'd left behind. There were still vast fields of crops, and great swathes of forest. They sailed past settlements that were home to communities which raised animals for food and hide, and fields of cattle for milk and cheese. But even though folk looked similar to his own he knew if they spoke he'd likely have as much difficulty understanding their dialect as he did with the crew.

While they sailed, Thrax told Arawn the names of the tribes whose lands they were passing through; the Caleti, the Veliocasses. But when he said they would soon pass through the lands of the Parisii Arawn was almost speechless.

"But," he said, brow furrowing, "they're a Brythonic tribe."

Thrax grinned. "And after that it's the Catuvellauni." He laughed at the expression on Arawn's face. "Have you visited the Parisii or Catuvellauni in Brython?"

"Several times," said Arawn. "We traded salt there."

"Then one day I'll take you to visit the Catuvellauni here in Gaul to compare the two. As for the Parisii," he smiled across to Arawn, "you'll be meeting them shortly. Lutetia is the main town in these tribal lands, as well as my home."

"But..." He shook his head, unable to comprehend.

"The Romans did more than rename our towns and rivers," said Thrax. "They drove our people from their homes. There were those who thought that trying to fight the invaders was fruitless so they took everything they owned and sailed away from them—and Brython was the land they came to. I imagine when the first Romans landed on your shores the descendants of those Parisii and Catuvellauni must've thought they'd never be rid of them. But you had Boudica." He looked wistful for a moment, respectful, and Arawn had a sudden urge to slap that look right off his face. He held himself in check, and changed the subject instead.

"Why did they not return to their own lands over here when the Romans left?"

"Because by then the lands of Brython *were* their own lands. Once you've farmed some land, and had some children, it's amazing how quickly your roots have sunk into the soil."

Arawn didn't really understand what he said, but he nodded anyway. "Do you have children?" he said.

It earned him another bout of laughter. "I should do, I suppose. Maybe I have! But I'm bonded to the sea, Arawn ap Emlyn. And while the comforts of women are welcome, nothing is as strong as the call of the sea."

Arawn's eyes widened with wonder. "You're not bonded? Not owned by a woman at all?"

"Arawn ap Emlyn!" roared Thrax, clapping him on the shoulder. Now that they were in Gaul, the sombreness that had surrounded him after the Angle attack had nearly vanished. "Well do I know the workings of your tribes, for I've been trading between mine and yours for longer than you've been breathing. And as strange as it might sound to you, my lad, your tribes moved on after Boudica's victory. Tales tell of many courageous men before her who used to be kings in your lands, but you must have heard of those?"

He just stared, mouth open.

"I'll take that as no," Thrax chuckled. "But here you'll find we've mostly stuck to the old ways. As much as we could, anyway." A brief frown eclipsed his smile like a cloud passing in front of the sun. "Though one thing is certain; men are their own masters over here."

"Men are their own masters."

"That's right, lad. Now look over there." He pointed across the boat and Arawn followed his finger.

When his eyes landed on the sight, his jaw slackened again. Running along the side of the river for quite a distance was an enormous stone building, much bigger than the one the treacherous Rosmerta had lived in. This one, however, was in decay. The roof had collapsed and vines were growing up all along its ancient walls, but it didn't make it any less impressive. Even from the ship he could see the gardens that surrounded it, wild now, but there was still the whisper of the paths that ran through it, straight-edged, dividing the gardens up into pleasing patterns. There were other things that he couldn't quite recognise because they were too over-grown with flora. If it had been any later in the warm season Arawn reckoned he wouldn't have been able to see anything but leaves.

"What are those?" he asked Thrax, indicating the objects.

"Some of them are statues."

"Statues?"

"People made of stone."

Arawn gasped in shock and horror.

"Well, not real people," said the trader, waving his hands as though trying to find the right words. "More like, images of people. Likenesses of people. Important people usually, like goddesses, or the emperor."

Arawn didn't know what the last word was but he pounced on the other one. "I thought the Romans believed in the one true god?"

"They do *now*," said Thrax. "But that came after their defeat in Brython. Much, much later. Before that they believed in as many gods and goddesses as we do. Some of them were quite similar to our own, I believe. Why they decided to cast them all aside for only one is beyond my ability to understand. How can *one* god hope to defeat all of ours?" He chuckled, but Arawn didn't want to get drawn into this conversation. He remembered his dream where the one true god killed all his enemies with lightning and believed he had an idea of his power, but he kept quiet for now.

He turned his attention back to the statues. They were certainly taller, much taller than even the monstrous Angles. "The Romans must have been giants, to build such things," he said in a whisper.

"So the legends say. You'll even find people who still believe that."

"You don't?"

"Unless Boudica and her army were all giants too," he said with a raised eyebrow. "But I've traded with the Iceni-Coritani, and I haven't seen one giant in that land yet."

Arawn thought for a while. "Maybe only ancient people were giants. The Atrebates, my homelands once, have a great stone circle. The Druids use it and say it's a place of power." *Druid and acolyte chanted, dancing around him, both with daggers in their hands.* He shuddered. "And so it is, I think." He looked up at Thrax. "But these stones are thrice the hight of any man, more even, and the circle is a hundred paces across! The Druids say that giants built that place under command from the gods themselves!"

"And perhaps they did," said Thrax, looking impressed. "And more likely than giant Romans, I shouldn't wonder. But they have left behind things we don't understand now. You see that, in between those two statues?"

Again Arawn followed his finger. They were moving away from the wondrous building now, but he could just make out what looked like a vast stone bowl, as covered with the wood-like stalks of vines as everything else. "A stone bowl?"

Thrax grinned. "They called it a fountain. I've heard stories which tell that water would rain upwards from the centre of them, to be caught in the bowl at the bottom, only to rain upwards again."

"Rain *upwards*?"

Thrax nodded, pleased with himself.

"But that's impossible!"

"Yet the Romans had these fountains everywhere."

Arawn whistled through his teeth. "All these incredible things…"

"And in the end it was a woman who defeated them," said Thrax with a grin.

"It was a woman who defeated them," Arawn echoed. A woman who had denied Brython the wonders of the Romans, and Arawn was sure that stone houses with gardens and statues and fountains that rained upwards were only the tiniest part of it. What else had they lost? *The one true god,* came a voice at the back of his mind, the part where all the dreams came from. Yes, indeed. The one true god had been lost to them as well.

He was stunned into silence at the enormous calamity that Boudica had inflicted on the lands of Brython by daring to defy the Romans; so he just watched the ancient monument as they glided past it, mourning the future that had been lost for the wretched era he had been born into.

He thought he saw movement. First, in one of the empty windows that glared out over the river as if in baleful reproach; and then in the garden, deeper than where the marvellous fountain stood with its two statue sentries. He peered, but whatever it was, was gone. Looking at Thrax it was evident he'd noticed nothing for his gaze was now turned ahead of them, a look of anticipation on his face. Wild animals, Arawn thought. Stirred by the ship moving past their territory. Nothing but wild animals. Later, he would discover just how right and wrong he had been.

* * *

They reached Lutetia towards noon. Arawn tried to work out how long he and his companions had been travelling—it felt like many moons—but was unable to. After the leisurely sail down the Sequana river, the Angle attack on the open sea felt like a distant memory. His time in Cantiaci now felt like a past life.

They'd sailed almost non-stop. At night they would moor up to rest but they would never go ashore. Finding food and lodgings would undoubtedly cost coin and the traders had none to spare. Thrax still had the heavy gold torc that Arawn had given him, tucked safely in his shirt and spared the plundering Angles; but that, he explained, would be sliced up and shared amongst his remaining crew and the families of the crew members he lost. It was poor pay indeed, but there was nothing else he could do. Fortunately, he had gold and silver hidden at his home with which he could buy goods, and he would be able to make the return journey to Brython.

"A trader," he said to Arawn, "can live very well. But only if he has a well-hidden hoard."

A strange energy filled the ship as it drew into port in Lutetia. For the time being, the crew knew they were safe and they would soon be back amongst their families and friends, recounting the adventures of their journey and praising the gods for their safe return. Yet doing so without profit, and the deaths of good men on their minds, would sour the occasion.

Not so for Arawn. Here was a place of wonder, a breathing memory of the Romans, and as far as the eye could see! True, Cantiaci boasted a Roman market square, but it was minuscule in comparison, and still surrounded by the thatched, wattle-and-daub roundhouses of the Brythoniaid. But *here*…

It brought to mind the jewel he'd seen on Rosmerta's torc the first time he laid eyes on her. He hated to think of her now, but of what his mind thought he had no control. That torc, he remembered, was twisted bands of silver that entwined round and round themselves to make one; and in the centre, at the base of her throat, was the jewel, bright and blue and captivating. The torc was the river Sequana and the jewel was the island which came to meet them. To Arawn's eyes it seemed to shine, even in the weak Imbolc sun it shone, because there was so much stone. And why shouldn't stones shine? What were jewels anyway if they weren't stones?

"An impressive sight, eh?" Thrax had come up behind him without Arawn even noticing.

He was unable to articulate a response so he simply nodded.

"Better from afar than close up." When Arawn looked at him questioningly he added, "When the Romans started their retreat from my country there were those who wanted to destroy all trace of them. Attacking the buildings was a favourite sport for a while."

"Impossible," said Arawn. "I see them with my own eyes."

"You do, indeed. Some buildings escaped the vandalism—they'd been used for too many generations and people became accustomed to their usefulness, I suppose. I know the chiefs of the Parisii wanted to keep the palaces for themselves."

"Palac*es*?"

"Oh yes. Those Romans didn't waste any time in ensuring the comforts of Rome were right at their bloody fingertips. But over the generations, whatever wasn't destroyed by wrath and fire when the Romans left was reused elsewhere when folk decided they'd like a house of stone instead of wood. Those with gold and silver—the nobility and warriors—were able to protect their new grand residences; but the Romans took with them their knowledge, and so even those buildings that were left unscathed have been slowly eaten away by time."

"That's terrible."

"Is it?"

"Of course! They left you all these magnificent places with statues and fountains that rain upwards and you let them fall to ruin. They left you a great gift and you don't even realise it."

"One man's great gift is another's loss of freedom and identity," said Thrax with a shrug of his shoulder. His tone and behaviour didn't match his words and Arawn felt it difficult to judge if he meant them. Or even believed them. "The Romans didn't come here so they could build us pretty new homes, they came to conquer. Each building you see was built on the slaughtered corpses of men and women who tried to defend their land from those who would steal it from them. They didn't want to live in Gaul with its Gaulish people and Gaulish traditions; they wanted to keep on building Rome and fill it with Romans, and those who stood in their way were cut down. I don't think you realise how lucky you are to have had a woman like Boudica who was able to defend your way of life."

Arawn scowled, but turned his face away. He liked Thrax,

and wanted to continue doing so, but he knew this conversation would only anger him. He'd met far too many people who'd preached the virtues of Boudica to him, and they fell apart when he looked on the wonders the Roman had left behind them. How could having the ability to create something wonderful, and wanting to share it with the rest of the world, be considered so foul by everyone?

Thrax clapped him on the shoulder. "But now is not the time for a history lesson," he said. "Now we feast on fresh meat and wine!"

To his dismay, Arawn saw that they were moving away from the island jewel and coming into port on the southern bank of the river. A multitude of other ships waited there, some bigger than Thrax's, some much smaller, and Arawn realised that the majority of people likely lived on the mainland, Thrax included.

"Don't look so disappointed," the trader said with a grin. "You can go to the island any time you want, you only have to cross that bridge there."

It was a wonder Arawn hadn't noticed the huge construct before. The dark wood leapt across the river, joining the mainland to the island, and even from this distance Arawn could see there was a fair amount of traffic using it.

"Did the Romans build that too?"

Thrax shrugged. "They only did what we'd already done before. They invented many things, but bridges weren't one of them."

He leapt across the deck and spoke to his remaining crew in their own dialect. They'd already unloaded the meagre few bales of Brythonic wool—all that remained after the plundering Angles paid them a visit—and now they were eager to go ashore. Thrax dismissed them, and beckoned Arawn over to him.

"You can stay with me," he said. "But if I bestow on you this kindness," he said, grinning, "I expect your oath that you'll join my crew. I need more hands and it seems pointless letting a strong, young lad like you go to waste. What do you say?"

Unable to find words enough to convey his thanks, he leaned across and impulsively embraced the grinning man. This earned Arawn a roaring guffaw and a clap on the shoulder from both hands.

"I'll take that as yes, then," he said; then held his hand out in front of him so that Arawn could disembark first.

* * *

"Public privvies?" said Arawn with disbelief.

"Public privvies," said Thrax. "A long line of them. And people would do their business, right there in the street, sitting next to a complete stranger, passing the time of day as well as their water."

Arawn laughed. "I don't believe you."

"You can see them, they're still there. I'll take you to them."

He scrunched up his face. "I'm not sure I'd like that."

"They're not used *now*," said Thrax. "We don't know how they piped the water underneath to carry away their shit so they've long since fallen into disuse. But they're still there, for all of Gaul to see. Ah! Here we are—home at last."

Home was a fairly small affair for Thrax, not far from the river and the port. It was rectangular, like the houses Arawn remembered surrounding the marketplace at Cantiaci, and made of stone; it was roofed with thatch, though it looked in good repair and relatively fresh. He wondered, absently, where Thrax would obtain such material, but he supposed there would be fields and farmlands nearby; there had to be, otherwise the people of this incredible city wouldn't be able to eat. He also noticed that, when they reached the porch of the front entrance, it was facing east. Some of the old customs were creeping back indeed.

"Did you build this yourself?" he asked.

"With my own two hands," said the trader, with a grin. "And

a good job I did of it, too. Come in, come in," he said, moving to open the wooden door. "A warm fire is what I need after such a journey."

Before he had time to open it, however, the door swung inwards and framed a strikingly pretty girl. She was short and thin, with sun-browned skin and the blackest hair that fell in torrents down her back. Her brown eyes were wide with pleasure and her smile lifted and lightened her face like a rising sun. Lower down, her tunic was cut so that Arawn saw her breasts heave when she inhaled to speak. Cushioned between them was a skilfully crafted pendant of amber.

"Thrax, you sneaky swine, you're home early!" she said and flung herself at him.

The trader caught her, laughing all the time, and buried his face in her hair; then he held her out at arms' length, looking at her as though she were a haunch of venison and he hadn't eaten for a month, then kissed her passionately. Blood rushed to Arawn's face instantly and he looked away.

After the interminable amount of time kissing was spent, Thrax turned the woman around and pushed her back into the house, slapping her behind as she moved away from him, causing her to squeal like a piglet. Thrax chuckled heartily.

"I thought you said you weren't bonded," said Arawn.

"I'm not," he said, not taking his eyes off the parting behind. "But a man needs someone at home to keep his hearth and bed warm. And also to buy gifts for." He threw Arawn a wink. "Now in you go, there's food and warmth to be found inside that we'll not find without."

Arawn did as he was told, but to say he was disappointed was like saying he didn't like Mother.

Glancing around, Arawn saw that, though not as big as the roundhouse in which he'd wintered amongst the Atrebates tribe, it was spacious enough to fit the three of them easily enough, and certainly big enough for just two occupants. To the left of the door there was a weaving loom currently boasting a half-finished cloak of blood-red dyed wool, and several pots which likely stored their food. To the right of the doorway was a spacious sleeping area, though the two straw pallets were pushed up right next to each other; and on them was a neatly folded pile of blankets. Right in the centre was a hearth. A fire crackled merrily away, and was overhung with a crucible that gave off the unmistakeable aroma of stew. Pork, Arawn thought, and his stomach grumbled.

The woman giggled. "Your guest is hungry, my love; you'd better introduce him to me so I can feed a friend instead of a stranger."

Arawn felt embarrassed by this, and dropped his eyes so that they fell on the exquisite amber pendant that hung between her breasts. One of the many gifts his friend Thrax had given her, no doubt.

"May I present Arawn ap Emlyn. And this," he said, sweeping an arm around the smiling woman, "is Sirom, my woman; maker of stew, tender of fire, and guardian of the hoard." He grinned broadly, while Sirom swiped ineffectually at him, presumably for saddling her with such grand yet ridiculous titles.

"Well met, Arawn ap Emlyn," she said, embracing him. Arawn forced himself not to recoil at her touch. "And now that is done we can sit and eat, and you can tell me all of your adventures—including why you're back before time." Thrax's face darkened for a moment and Sirom's hands fled to her cheeks, and she looked stricken. "You were plundered, weren't you? Those detestable Angles?" A faint nod from Thrax. "Oh, my love. How many men did you lose?"

"Eleven. Eleven good men lost to the bastard Angles and given to Nehalennia." His voice was hoarse.

"Dibu e debu," said Sirom, with her head bowed.

"Dibu e debu," Thrax agreed.

It was the same thing that the crew said after the attack, when Arawn thought they might be praying. Now that the battle wasn't ringing in his ears and there was no wind to snatch the words away, he thought he recognised them. They weren't exactly the same as the words they used in his tribe, but they were similar. "To the gods and goddesses," they'd said. "To the gods and goddesses."

– 14 –

The moon of Cutios (Windy-time), 332 C.E.
Ocean

"I will not allow any of my women to turn back," thundered Gwladus. "Half of them stayed behind to search the lands around Cantiaci as it is, I'll not lose more because of a swollen corpse."

"I would remind you," said Rosmerta, keeping her voice level as her mother always did, "that you are under my command. If these yellow-haired warriors are sailing the waters plundering trading ships, how long before they start landing on the shores of Brython to see what they can plunder there? I would warn Sulis Warrior-Queen of this new threat, and you should want word to reach Epona. Anything less is treason."

There was silence on board the trading vessel they had sequestered to hunt for Arawn; at least, no one was talking. About them the sea roared and wind thrashed at the sails so that it reminded Rosmerta of distant claps of thunder.

It had been a cause of much relief to the young warrior-princess, when they reached the nearest port to her town, that Arawn hadn't been seen. None of the traders they'd asked had recognised his description. But before she was able to turn the army around, an ancient trader with a beard as grey and knotted as his hair told them that a Gaulish trader vessel known as the Nehalennia, named after their sea goddess, had left port just as the army had arrived. Unfortunately, Gwladus heard this exchange, and she was convinced that her sister-slaying son was on board. She gave the trader a small pouch of silver for his information, then bellowed profusely until Rosmerta started to feel quite shamed by her behaviour, and was almost glad when the hateful Druid Gwynfor said the intuition of a Mother shouldn't be ignored. There was no feasible way that she could disregard such a pronouncement, and thus the warrior-princess had no alternative but to commandeer enough trading vessels to take the army across the sea towards Gaul. Even with the silver she offered the crew, their discontented grumbling was well audible.

And then they came across the body. Evidently a warrior because, even though the gashes across his face and chest had been cleaned of blood by the sea, it was clear he'd died in battle. But while Rosmerta and the spear-women were confused about finding such a body in the middle of the ocean, the traders had quietened and turned pale.

"You recognise this man?" she'd asked the trader.

"Yes and no," was his response. "I know his tribe lies to the north-east of Gaul. I know they've taken to plundering the waters between my homeland and yours. And now I know they've attacked here recently." He nodded his head towards the body that floated past their ship and towards the vessels that followed them. Crew and spear-women were already craning forward so they could see it properly. "But I don't know *him*. Although they all look the same with that yellow hair of theirs."

"You know a lot for someone who claims to know little," said Gwladus, looking at the trader with suspicion. But then, she looked at everyone with suspicion if they weren't her spear-women or her Druid.

"I didn't claim anything," said the trader. "But spending your life on the sea means you have to become wise to its dangers, be they natural or unnatural." He looked back towards the corpse though it was already passed.

"What tribe is he from, do you know that?" Rosmerta asked.

The trader nodded his head. "The Angles," he said. "Vicious bastards. Wasn't so long ago that no one knew they existed. Now traders crossing these waters are always on the look out for them. We've taken to carrying weapons, but we're traders, not warriors.

We even started trading earlier in the year than normal, for it was only the moons of late Imbolc and Beltane that saw plundering. But the bastards have grown wise to that too."

"If you know where they live," said Gwladus, disdain clear in every word. "Why do you not attack?"

"Because it's not the Angles on land we have a problem with."

Rosmerta had sensed the anger in the air then and intervened, which only served to cause the current row about sending one of the boats back to Brython. But there were several reasons why she wanted word to get back to Brython. That her mother needed to know of the potential danger went without saying. Yet she also wanted to help this man, this trader who did nothing more threatening than carry goods between her own lands and his, but was now caught in a battle he was unprepared for. At the moment, such help consisted only of allowing one vessel from their fleet to return to Brython to warn the other traders of the recent attack, but it was the least she could do. They had, after all, taken his ship and forced him to leave his goods behind so that he could carry her and the spear-women—complete with horses, shields and weaponry—across the water to Gaul.

But there was one other reason too. It was an ignoble reason and Rosmerta didn't want to admit it, but it was still there. The warrior-princess of Cantiaci was still smarting from being overruled by Gwladus' intuition and the binding words of her Druid. That her intuition was correct was beside the point. Rosmerta now felt that it was time to reassert her noble authority. If she failed to instil it in the spear-woman before they found Arawn she might not be able to help him at all, and wasn't that the very reason for her joining the expedition in the first place?

"Anything less is treason," she repeated. "And you of all women should know what the penalty for treason is. You may have escaped it once, but I doubt even the slaying of your daughter will soften Epona's heart to allow it for a second time." A perverse sense of joy filled her at the clear look of shock that slackened the woman's face. "I know who you are," said Rosmerta. "I know it very well. And I have not forgotten what you did to me and my mother."

She turned away from the woman and focussed once more on the trader. "Have one of the boats turn around, on my order. They are to warn those waiting at the port what we have seen out here."

"And you," she turned back to Gwladus, whose face had become a stone-like mask. "Tell those spear-women that the moment their feet touch dry ground, they are to ride directly to Sulis Warrior-Queen. And may Boudica save your soul if that is not done."

She turned and walked towards the front of the ship, keeping her eyes on the distant horizon where sky met sea, both as grey as the other. The bustle of orders being carried out behind her was pleasing, but she needed a few moments alone to bring herself under control. She was shaking. Anger was part of it, for she disliked Gwladus and any conversation with the woman was apt to bring her to anger. But that anger was borne mostly of fear, and she knew *that* well also. The flame-haired woman burned with hatred and looked like she would rather be cutting people down than listening to them. Even the fact that Rosmerta hadn't bonded with Dewydd, son of Epona Warrior-Queen, hadn't softened Gwladus' opinion of her.

And yet she didn't regret what she had said. It might well work in her favour if Gwladus understood that Rosmerta knew precisely who she was. It could be the very thing that she needed to exert her authority over her.

If… Could be…

It was those uncertainties that made Rosmerta shake. For it was entirely possible that she'd just turned a formidable spear-woman into a formidable enemy.

The moon of Giamonios (Shoots-show time), 332 C.E.
Cantiaci-Trinovantes Borderlands, Brython

"He smells like onions," said Airmed, then giggled when she saw the expression of mock horror on her mother's face.

"Princess you may be, though no one would know it to hear you speak," said Sulis.

"And he was dull. He kept talking about all the things the Druids taught him, which is fine, but it's not exactly exciting, is it? And then, when I started talking about swordplay he had the audacity to look bored! Poor Rosmerta. I know she has her duty to fulfil, and fill it to the full she will, I'm sure. But… I think she's going to find Dewydd boring."

This time Sulis laughed. "What did I do to deserve such honest daughters as you and your sister? Besides, you're also more interested in healing sorcery than swordplay."

Airmed shrugged and smiled. In truth, she'd actually enjoyed the bonding ceremony even though it wasn't really hers and despite the dull conversation with the son offered by Epona Warrior-Queen. Oh, he was handsome enough; he'd inherited his mother's dark hair and eyes, and he was respectably tall. But his wan skin needed more time in the open air and his mind needed more noisy metal and less soft poetry. Her mother spoke true, she *did* prefer herbs and healing to fighting, but there was something about the persistent way he had to show off his knowledge that made her want to knock his feet from under him. Probably better if she didn't indulge that impulse though, just in case people got offended.

"I'm sure Rosmerta will understand him better than I," said Airmed.

"Undoubtedly. Your sister is a fully-grown woman of sixteen summers now; you've still got a few years left to go."

Airmed rolled her eyes theatrically. "And she's in command of a whole army of spear-women travelling to Gaul, I *know*."

"She is, and I pray that she's safe." For a moment, her good humour vanished and Airmed cursed herself for causing it. Before she had a chance to say anything, however, her mother spoke again, pushing aside her sadness as quickly as it had come. "But when it's time for your bonding, I'll be sure to pick someone with less lore."

"So long as he's able to weed and dig my gardens I'll be happy."

"I hear the Trinovantes make for good gardeners," said Sulis with a sly smile.

Airmed's mouth dropped open. "Don't tell me this is actually a secret mission to find my bonding partner?"

Once more her mother laughed, and Airmed was glad; the warrior-queen fretted over her daughter terribly. For her safe return, she said, but Airmed knew as well as her mother that Rosmerta's quiet exterior belied deadly sword skill. It was the bonding that worried her, and her need to unite all the tribes as one. They were so close to bonding their tribe to the Atrebates, but without Rosmerta it would come to nothing.

She sensed also her mother's anxiety over the audience with the warrior-queen of the Trinovantes to which they were riding. With the threat of the Picts literally on the horizon, their need was dire; but they distrusted the Cantiaci greatly. She'd been counting on the formal bonding between Rosmerta and Dewydd to help convince their neighbours of their intentions but it was always snatched away at the last moment. First the uprising, then Heddgwyn now the hunt for a sister-slayer. Intuition told her that nothing her mother planned to do for the future of the tribe, not to mention her dream of a united Brython, would come easily. But with all those omens, if omens they be, only a fool would think otherwise.

She looked across at her mother standing tall in her chariot, looking so undeterred, and every inch a warrior-queen. Her otter-skin cloak billowed out magnificently behind her in the wind of their passage, revealing the sword that had passed down through generations of warrior-queens, and would one day belong to Rosmerta. It was a thing of beauty that sword, hanging at her side in a well-oiled but worn leather scabbard that was a perfect disguise for the fury that lay within it.

Underneath her cloak she wore only simple leather armour, for a truce of sorts existed between Cantiaci and Trinovantes. Certainly Cantiaci would never attack its neighbours, it would risk too much and ignite the old hatreds borne of their ancient and alleged alliance with the Romans. Airmed was certain the stories had been exaggerated over the generations but no one could really know for sure. So there would be no fighting today for Trinovantes was expecting Sulis and her caravan, and though mail was not required, it was only courtesy to meet a warrior-queen dressed for battle. There would also be the customary chariot acrobatics of the visiting tribe (which Airmed was most looking forward to—she'd not done any public acrobatics as yet), though how long they would be allowed to perform was entirely up to the Trinovantes. Airmed supposed it wouldn't be for very long. Despite the universal hatred for their tribe, most people did grudgingly admit that Cantiaci had the best chariot dancers, and not many tribes enjoyed being out-performed by their adversaries.

As it turned out, there would be none of those things. The chariot that Airmed and her mother rode passed the boundaries of their lands and crossed into the Trinovantes' and they clearly saw the warrior-queen waiting for them with a band of spear-women standing in a wall behind her.

"She hasn't even done us the courtesy of wearing armour," Airmed exclaimed as they drew closer.

Sulis acknowledged her daughter's statement but said nothing. When they were only a few score paces away, she slowed the horses to a stop and disembarked from the chariot. Airmed quickly followed suit, unknowing of what the protocol was for such a strange meeting. Her mother had been at great pains to explain how she should comport herself once in the court of Sirona Warrior-Queen of Trinovantes, but meeting in the boundary lands hadn't been covered.

"I would say, well met, Sirona Warrior-Queen," said Sulis when she'd closed the gap between them, "but it would be untrue. I feel I am dishonoured by your refusal to let me pass into your lands."

"You are not welcome here, Sulis of Cantiaci. I would have you turn and leave the way you came. As for dishonour—be grateful I came myself to tell you this. I was of a mind to send spear-women to escort you from my lands, but my Druids convinced me a personal meeting would cause less blood-shed."

To the right of Sirona was a large of group of Druids, at least ten, but Airmed couldn't count them properly for they were huddled tightly together, talking amongst themselves. It seemed an unusually large number; even at court there would only be a handful of Druids from each tribe. A couple had looked up when their warrior-queen mentioned their group, but it was only a passing glance. Whatever their conversation was about, it seemed to carry more importance than the meeting of neighbouring warrior-queens. The shock of such rudeness left Airmed unable to identify precisely how she felt about it.

"Blood-shed?" said Sulis. "You truly think I would have slaughtered your women in order to force an audience with you? Evidently you have much to learn of your neighbour."

"I know enough that you seek to usurp the queenships of those around you to increase your own power." She stepped forward defiantly as she spoke, her bear-fur cloak revealing a dress of deepest blue which was clutched to her waist with a belt of leather. Adorning this was a clasp of wrought gold which matched the one fastening her cloak. Indeed, the clothes and adornments were queenly, as was the powerful body that displayed them. But the face was less so. She must have been stricken with a disease when she was younger, Airmed thought, for her face was all pocked with ugly scars; and her eyes were an ice blue that may have been striking in a beautiful face, but in Sirona's they were chilling and unfriendly. Fortunately, her face was surrounded by a luxurious swathe of auburn hair that flowed like exotic material across her shoulders and reached almost to her belted waist. She was renowned for having birthed an incredibly large brood—eleven, mostly girls—and Airmed found herself hoping for their sakes that they hadn't inherited the scarring malady that had inflicted their mother.

But then her own mother spoke up, shattering the silence that Sirona's last statement had caused. "You think I would steal a sister's land like a common thief? I grieve for you, Sirona Warrior-Queen, if you believe that such a treacherous act could take place when we have more serious matters affecting us."

Sirona looked confused for the merest moment, but she recovered quickly. "Your words are pretty and well-composed, but you cannot deter me from the truth so easily."

"I came here to offer—"

"To offer me one of your whelps for one of my few sons?" Sirona interrupted with a nod of her head towards Airmed. "As you did with the warrior-queen of the Atrebates?" She smiled and it was not pleasing. "Perhaps she was foolish enough to be blinded by your pretty words, or even your acrobatics," now her hand swept across the chariots that were stationed behind them, "but I am not so easily swayed. You intend to bond your whelps to other tribes in the pretence of peace, but in truth you seek to gain control over their lands so you can be the sole warrior-queen of this isle. Is that not so?"

Sulis said nothing. And for the first time in Airmed's life she saw the public mask, so carefully composed to show nothing but regal dignity, slip from her mother's face. Underneath it was an expression of shock and hurt.

"Your silence is your admission of guilt, Sulis Warrior-

Queen."

"I came here to offer my aid," said Sulis, speaking slowly. "The Picts have been sighted off your coasts and I would help you defend your lands against them. We have boats—"

"You have many things, but my friendship is not one of them. I do not need aid to defend my own country." Sirona was angry now. "I am perfectly aware of the threat to my coastal lands and I have spear-women patrolling them even as we speak. Any Pict stupid enough to land on my shores will taste wrath and steel before he is sent off to his barbarian Otherworld where he'll rot with his predecessors. You offend me with your assumption that I cannot battle against such a paltry enemy."

"You know as well as I that many lands to the north have been lost to the Picts, entire tribes of Brythoniaid wiped out. I do not think we should take their new strategy of conquest so lightly."

"You are not welcome here, Sulis, and I have nothing further to say to you. I request you remove your women and chariots from my lands and go back to where you belong."

And to Airmed's horror, she actually turned her back on them in a contemptuous expression of their inability to induce fear, and walked towards the parting wall of the grey and crimson-cloaked Trinovantes spear-women with their wolf-crowned helmets.

For an age, Sulis stood there, eyes fixed on the departing backs of the Trinovantes royal court. The only people who remained motionless were the Druids.

"Mother?"

Sulis shook herself. "That didn't go as I intended," she said.

"I'm sorry."

"I knew it was never going to be simple," she said with a sad smile, and turned back the chariot. Expertly crafted from oak and gilded with swirling patterns all in gold, it was magnificent. "But I'll freely admit I hadn't expected such outright animosity."

"How did she know about your plan to unite Brython?"

"Rumour spreads like a mould, Airmed, poisoning all it touches; and unfortunately there is no antidote for it. But people consume it ravenously. And when the poison comes into contact with something as powerful as hate or distrust, it is made all the more potent." She sighed. "It was never my intent to keep my ideals secret, but I'd hoped to have Rosa's bonding secured before every tribe learned of them."

Rumour, thought Airmed, climbing into the chariot beside her mother. It had spread quickly considering Mother's ambition of uniting Brython had been confined to the counsel chambers. The councillors surely wouldn't be discussing such important matters with people in the marketplace as though they were exchanging opinions on the filling ewes this Imbolc, would they? Granted, Epona Warrior-Queen is privy to the idea, but...

She jolted as a thought struck her.

"Airmed? Are you well?" Her mother looked concerned, reins stilled in her hands.

"I'm well," she said. "I'm very well."

Her mother nodded, unconvinced, but she flicked the reins anyway, spurring the two grey mares which pulled the chariot into motion.

Airmed was thinking only of the councillors, one of whom was the Arch Druid Heddgwyn; and hadn't Rosa expressed worry about him? She'd never fully explained what that worry was, but Airmed herself had given her the idea of enlisting Emrys as her spy. Unfortunately, no sooner had Rosmerta gone off on the hunt for the sister-slayer, Emrys and Heddgwyn had disappeared too. Normally there was nothing unusual in that—sometimes the Druids hid themselves away for days on end in their sacred groves to make their secret magic.

And now she thought of it, the fact that Heddgwyn Arch Druid of the Cantiaci tribe hadn't been at the bonding ceremony was a little strange. Then to be confronted by a neighbouring tribe who accused her mother of wanting to usurp all the queenships of Brython and take them all for herself… There was treason happening somewhere, she was sure of it. She just wasn't precisely sure how or why.

And perhaps if she'd been paying more attention to what was going on around her, she would have noticed that the handful of Cantiaci Druids who had accompanied them didn't join the end of her mother's caravan when they passed. Instead, they rode towards the group of Trinovantes Druids who had barely moved from the spot where Airmed had last seen them.

As it was, she was too busy assembling her own thoughts and wondering how she should broach the conversation with her mother. Accusing the Arch Druid of deliberately spreading the rumour wouldn't be well received by Sulis. Besides, Airmed couldn't quite understand why he would want to do such a thing.

"What's this?" said her mother. The question wasn't directed at Airmed, for her mother was frowning into the distance. When Airmed followed her line of sight she saw a score of spear-women bearing down on them, galloping their horses as fast as they could.

For a terrible moment she thought it might be an ambush from a band of Trinovantes spear-women, but Airmed realised they were well within the boundaries of their own lands. And now that she looked closer, she realised they were wearing the red- and black-striped cloaks of the Atrebates.

Sulis whipped the reins hard on to the flanks of the mares in order to speed up their meeting.

"What is it?" said the warrior-queen, when they'd reached the riders. "Have you found the sister-slayer?"

"No, my lady," said one of the spear-women. "We were sent back to bring you news of a possible threat from beyond the ocean."

"Then speak, woman," ordered the warrior-queen.

And thus did Airmed, Princess of the Cantiaci, learn of the plundering tribe of sea raiders called the Angles.

– 15 –

The moon of Giamonios (Shoots-show time), 332 C.E.
Deep in the Atrebates tribal lands, Brython

"I know that name."

Emrys looked across to Heddgwyn, surprised that the Arch Druid had spoken. He'd been silent for most of the morning and he'd not distracted him by starting a conversation. He knew well enough when his father was inclined to meditate.

"What name?" said Emrys, then followed the Arch Druid's line of sight. He was staring at the wild man. The very man who'd tried to brain him and then was promptly invited to join their pilgrimage. He'd called himself Emlyn Salt-merchant, though he claimed his wife was hanged for treason. He'd also claimed his daughter and son were dead, though so far neither Heddgwyn nor Emrys had been able to uncover any more of his story. "You know *his* name? How?"

The Arch Druid shook his head, then turned his head towards Emrys with a frown. "Oh, it just sounds familiar." He shifted in his saddle. "I hadn't realised I'd spoken aloud."

"Well, you did. So how does the Arch Druid of the Cantiaci know the name of a humble salt-merchant?"

"I travel a lot."

Emrys waited, but he said nothing else. It was one of his more annoying characteristics. It was well-known that Heddgwyn Arch Druid was one of the most learnèd men in the lands; he had to be or he wouldn't have attained his high status. But instead of sharing or revealing what knowledge he had, he'd keep it all to himself and force those around him to guess at what he was thinking. It probably, thought Emrys, gave him great pleasure knowing that he would be driven to distraction divining the reason behind his enigmatic statement.

He knows that name, indeed, the Ovate thought. Well I shan't give him the pleasure of admitting my ignorance this time. I'll drive him insane instead by not playing.

"It could be," said Emrys, "that his name sounds so similar to mine. Although it's amusing that while Em*rys* means immortal, Em*lyn* means work. Language is quite fascinating, isn't it?"

He looked across to the Arch Druid, who was still gazing at Emlyn the wild man, but all he received for his troubles was an indistinct hum of accordance. Emrys doubted that he'd even heard a word he'd said. Whatever game he might be playing, it was very uninteresting.

As uninteresting as the wild man, in fact. Certainly, he was excellent at hunting deer, and the fresh meat they ate for dinner every day had yet to lose its pleasure. But every day he walked in front of their horses, looking out across the mud roads they followed, never saying a word unless responding to an order from Heddgwyn. At meal times he said nothing, only joined in the conversation by watching his two saviours as they spoke. He never questioned them about their pilgrimage, and he never spoke about his life before he met them.

And yet, when Emrys had questioned his father as to why they continued to keep him, especially after he'd started their relationship by attacking them, all the Arch Druid had said was, "The Fates put him in our path. To ignore him would mean failure."

Obviously, when pushed to explain such a statement, Heddgwyn preferred to lapse into his irritating silence. Truth be told, Emrys was a little jealous, and he knew it very well. Heddgwyn had been revealing a far more enjoyable personality before the arrival of this wild man. But now he'd reverted back to his secretive, thoughtful self. The last several days had been dull, and the thought of enduring the entire pilgrimage in this fashion didn't appeal to Emrys at all.

Fortunately the season of Imbolc had well arrived, and while it was still cold, and rained more often than not, he could comfort himself with the knowledge that the ewes were filling out, as were many other animals he didn't wonder, and soon the sun would get stronger and beat the rain clouds away and make the journey seem less of a punishment.

They were still deep in the lands of the Atrebates, though Heddgwyn said soon they would be turning north; and it seemed that the wild man was doing all he could to keep them away from the larger settlements. They only ever came across tiny hamlets, if they came across anything at all. Certainly Emlyn knew the tracks well, and Emrys supposed this was because he'd been married to a salt-merchant and so knew all the routes through his own lands; but why avoid the larger settlements anyway? It was intriguing, but the last thing Emrys wanted to do was play into their game of secrets and mysteries, so he kept all his questions to himself.

Besides, the hamlets were welcoming enough. Two Druids would always be welcome to share a hearth-fire, whether or not they had a wild man with them. Though he was looking a little less like a wild man, thanks to Heddgwyn. In one such hamlet, he'd purchased leggings, a tunic, soft leather shoes and a cloak from a man who'd been careless enough to answer Heddgwyn's question as to how many of such items he possessed. Despite the gold coin that Heddgwyn offered, he seemed reluctant to part with his spare items of clothing, it was still cold and wet after all, and making new clothes would mean trapping enough animals, curing their hides and stitching them together. All time-consuming activities. But his wife leapt up at the sight of the gold and snatched it out of Heddgwyn's fingers before the man could say anything. Like the good husband he was, he accepted his wife's decision without fuss. Interestingly enough though, the wild man did seem almost apologetic about taking the man's clothes.

"With that gold," Emrys had said, mostly in amusement, "our

hosts can buy a whole new set of clothes tomorrow to replace the ones we have bought."

"Is that your proclamation, Druid?" the wild man had said, almost pouncing on him. "Is that your proclamation for spending the gold?"

"Well," Emrys said, with a sigh. Common folk had never understood the difference between Bard, Ovate and Druid. He looked at Heddgwyn, but he was only gazing at the wild man in that way that was to become so familiar. "Yes. Why not. Can't have a man freezing to death on our consciences, can we?"

The wild man looked triumphant, but he remained still. The wife was looking at Emrys with barely concealed hatred as she clutched the gold coin closer to her chest.

"And be warned, good wife," said Heddgwyn then, "that if you spend that coin on anything other than attire for your kind husband, it will be cursed and you will be cursed. Such is the price of Druid gold."

Despite his amazement, Emrys said nothing. That gold coin was exactly the same as any other coin traded in Cantiaci, but the look of hatred slipped from the woman's face like snow falling from a bough, and was replaced with the all too familiar fear.

Both of them had been generous with the food and ale after that, and a better example of bonded bliss Emrys had never seen before or since. But even in his new clothes, Emrys couldn't help but think of Emlyn as the wild man.

Life in such hamlets, Emrys noted, was markedly different to the life he knew so well in town. He knew that women from the Atrebates and all other tribes considered themselves superior to their menfolk—it was the norm rather than the exception, Emrys had to keep reminding himself. Cantiaci's justness was the only exception that proved this rule. But apart from the incident with the gold coin, he noticed that men and women shared their workloads, both inside the roundhouse and out. During the day they would work the fields or see to their livestock while the children were busy with such tasks as grinding wheat from the stores, spinning wool, and making butter or cheese from the milk that had been collected that morning.

The evenings in the roundhouse would be loud with the noise of the husband weaving on the loom while the wife cooked, and then the family would while away dark hours after dinner by asking riddles or telling stories around the hearth-fire.

Emrys found such evenings comforting and was always happy when they came across a hamlet in which to pass the night, instead of under the stars.

Of course, the land and livestock they worked didn't always belong to them. The hamlet where the gold coin incident occurred was such a place. The lands belonged to a wealthy noble who lived in the town, and the hamlet had sprung up because the workers and their families needed to live close by. They weren't slaves, not really. The warrior-queens had stopped the taking of slaves from rival tribes several generations ago, Emrys knew; but those that the Gauls brought over were always popular, as were captured Picts. Foreign slaves were acceptable, past warrior-queens had deigned. But stealing people, even if they weren't from their own tribe, was not. Land needed to be farmed or there would be precious little to trade.

So the people in the worker hamlets were free folk, but their earnings came not in coin or gold, but from the lands they worked. The majority of the produce belonged to the nobles to trade or consume as they would, but the surplus belonged to the workers. Thus, when Heddgwyn held up that gold coin, avarice had been ignited.

Yet for the most part, Emrys noticed a form of equality amongst the simple country folk. And it pleased him well that there was a hamlet not too far ahead of them; he could see smoke rising in the distance from hearth-fires that were being stoked high for the cooking of the evening meal. And because it was early evening and the sun was already nearing the horizon, he knew that Heddgwyn would decide to stop there for the night.

But when they reached the hamlet, Emrys learned that his notion of country-folk equality was entirely incorrect.

* * *

The first sound that came to them was of screeching women. They were still some distance away, but there was no doubt that women were making the high-pitched, ululating uproar. It prompted Heddgwyn out of his day-long reverie and he kicked his horse to a canter. Emrys followed suit, and to his surprise, the wild man was able to keep up with them.

Just before they came to the first of the roundhouses, Emrys heard the cracking of a whip. It cracked through the screeching like thunder drowns the sound of torrential rain.

The roundhouses were built in a rough circle in the corner of a field, all their entrances facing east and the rising sun. The central space had clearly been designed for communal activities, and as the sun was setting on this day, strengthening Imbolc's hold on the world, the communal activity taking place was a flogging.

A wooden, cross-shaped frame had been erected, and tied to each arm of it was the wrist of a man. A middle-aged man, Emrys thought him, likely in his middle thirties. He was stripped naked and so it was clear to see he was well-muscled and strong, but his legs sagged underneath him and his face was stretched in a mask of pain. The ground around him was spattered with his blood, and Emrys was glad that he couldn't see his back.

Even as they approached, a woman of the same age cracked the whip against the man's back again, accompanied by the screeching of the female watchers. They were all gleefully watching the punishment, and the young girls of the community joined in by hurling stones at the prone man; the men of the community huddled together, not saying a word, but looking upon the man with pity.

"Forgive our intrusion, but I would know what happens here." Heddgwyn's voice, deep and powerful, cut through the screams of delight and silence descended like nightfall. But the flogging woman had already unleashed her whip, and the sound of it hitting the man's naked back in the silence made Emrys' stomach turn.

For a single heartbeat the woman looked frightened to be addressed by a Druid, two if Emrys counted himself, but then her defiance returned.

"He raised a hand to me," shouted the woman, pointing at the bound man with her whip. It was viciously simple, merely a club of wood that had several thin thongs of hide attached to it. But judging from the blood, and the expression on the man's face, it achieved its purpose.

"He raised his hand to me," the woman repeated, "and he is being punished."

Now Emrys looked at the woman and clearly saw the bruise that was fresh on her cheek and the blood that was drying on her nose.

At her statement, the gathered women called their agreement, but the sight of the Druids had somewhat suppressed their enthusiasm.

Heddgwyn nodded and dismounted. Emrys remained seated on his own horse. If he should follow, the Arch Druid would give him a sign. As it was, he kept his eyes on the woman and Heddgwyn walked over to the man. If he were aware that the flogging had stopped, he didn't show it for his eyes were still shut tight and his face remained fixed in its grimace of pain.

Heddgwyn walked on until he stood next to the woman, and for a long time he regarded her work without saying anything. Even the expression on his face didn't change.

The woman, on the other hand, was clearly unsettled by his proximity and silence. She started fidgeting with her whip, and looked back at her fellow women, but they were as staring and silent as the moon.

"A man dursn't raise a hand to a woman," she said eventually, quietly. "And he's punished if he does. He's bonded to me and it's my right to give punishment."

Again Heddgwyn nodded. Then he said, "I think, good wife, that you've given punishment enough. Don't you?" He looked at her when he asked the question, and the defiance in her eyes vanished as she flinched away from him.

"Mayhap," she said.

"Emrys," said the Druid, though his eyes stayed with the woman. "You and Emlyn will release this man and tend his wounds while this good wife prepares our evening meal. And the rest of you," he said, raising his voice now, sending the little girls with unthrown stones clenched in their tiny fists scurrying amongst their mothers' skirts. "The rest of you will return to your homes. And while you have Druids gracing your community there will be peace."

The crowd of women dispersed, though with slow uncertainty, like children who have just had their favourite toy snatched away for no reason by an angry parent, yet they were unable to voice their discontent because that parent was still behind them.

The men-folk, though, gathered around their fallen comrade and whispered in anger and horror about the cruelties inflicted on one of their own. Emrys was not looking forward to seeing the man's injuries. The wild man had already joined them and was helping unbind the man's wrists while others supported his weight.

Dropping down from his saddle, Emrys thought about what he had brought and what he would need for the task at hand. Heddgwyn had a pestle and mortar in his bags, he knew, because he'd already used them when making a concoction for the few wounds that the wild man bore when he'd met them. They also had plenty of yarrow and bee balm left, as well as vinegar, though whether it would be enough for this man's wounds, Emrys was unsure. There were other things he needed, but he had to hope the locals could provide them.

The group of men had moved from the flogging frame, and judging by the cluster of them standing outside one of the roundhouses—the other side of the hamlet to where his wife had gone—Emrys guessed they'd taken the injured man inside.

And so they had. Laid on his stomach on a pallet by the hearth-fire, Emrys managed to strangle the cry of disgust before it escaped his throat. What used to be the man's back was nothing now but a bloody mess of lacerated skin and flesh. There were a few welts across his buttocks and thighs, no more than imprints of the whip, though they looked painful enough. Compared to the destruction above them however, they were very much the least of the man's troubles.

"What's your name?" said Emrys, kneeling next to him. His breathing was harsh and fast.

"He's called Celyddon," said one of the men in the room. He'd moved so he was opposite Emrys on the other side of the prone body. "I'm Gethin, and he's my brother. Can you help him?"

He looked into Gethin's large eyes, as black as his hair, and nodded. "I can, but I'll need you to help me."

Gethin nodded.

"Collect as much butter dock as you can find, the bigger the leaves the better, and bring them to me. I'll also need some hide thongs, as long as possible."

There were questions in Gethin's eyes, especially after the last request, but he said nothing. He pulled at two of the other men watching Emrys and they went out of the roundhouse.

"This water's boiling," said the wild man, and Emrys turned to see him standing over a cauldron hanging above the hearth-fire with a square of cloth in his fist. "And this rag looks clean."

"Good. You can clean up some of this blood with that while I make the tincture."

The wild man nodded and got about his business. Celyddon hissed as the hot rag touched his raw back, but he didn't complain.

"This tincture I'm making," Emrys said, hoping his talking would take Celyddon's mind off the pain a little, "won't be very strong because it won't have had time to stew. But when it's ready, I'll spread it over your back, then bind the dock leaves to it to help the healing process. I must warn you though, it will sting."

There was more hissing from Celyddon, and when Emrys looked at him, he realised he was laughing. "Not as much," he whispered, "as that bloody whip did."

"No," said Emrys. "Probably not."

He put some dried yarrow flowers into the mortar with a little vinegar and started grinding. Immediately his nostrils were filled with its sharp aroma. "This will stop the bleeding," he said, "and should keep the wounds from becoming inflamed." He added another handful of the flowers and ground them.

Next, he pulled out the bee balm. The little green leaves smelled of mint, and was fresh and welcome in this little round-house which now smelt of blood and sweat. And there was another aroma in the air, coming from the sweat of Celyddon himself; ale. The man must have drunk a lot of it prior to his beating if it now seeped from his skin.

"The bee balm will stop your wounds from becoming infected, and it should ease the pain a little." He pounded it into the yarrow with some more vinegar.

"Thank you," said Celyddon.

Emrys shrugged. "Why did you strike her? You'd have saved yourself a beating if you hadn't."

Celyddon remained silent for a while, and the wild man threw Emrys a look of annoyance while he gently wiped at the blood on the man's back.

"She was beating my son," said quietly.

"I see," said Emrys. And then, "Did he deserve his beating?" It was curious to him that such violence could happen, but from the sullen silence around him, the men of the community evidently didn't appreciate his curiosity.

"He beat his baby sister," said Celyddon then. "Because of her squalling."

"He beat her so she beat him, then you beat her so she beat you," he said sadly, and shook his head. "If there's so much anger in your home, perhaps there should be less ale." There was a murmur amongst the men folk clustered around. He gathered they were astonished that he'd known about Celyddon's drinking habits. "It's not magic," he said. "Your sweat reeks of it."

"You'd drink too, if you were bonded to my wife."

"Perhaps." The wild man had cleaned the wounds enough to apply the tincture, and Emrys indicated this with a nod and tight smile. The wild man sat back and put the bloody rag in the bloody water in the cauldron.

"Is Gethin back with the butter dock yet?"

"Here I am, Druid," said Gethin, pushing his way through the crowd to his brother.

"Good. I'm going to apply the tincture across his back in sections. I want you to place the leaves on that section in a straight line. We'll hold them in place with a hide thong."

Gethin nodded his understanding, and the wild man stood up and moved out of the way so Celyddon's brother could take his place.

"It will take several weeks for the wounds to heal properly," said Emrys. Celyddon was hissing again as the tincture touched his raw skin. "And you will have to put fresh leaves on it every few days. I'll leave what tincture is left to you as well."

"Thank you for helping him," said Gethin.

Emrys smiled. "I'm an Ov— a Druid. I can't turn away if

someone needs my help. Besides, healing is one of the easier magics even if it's one of the most important."

"Can you not do something about our women folk?" Gethin's dark eyes were large with pleading. "Mayhap Celyddon shouldn't have struck her, but men have been flogged for far less. And it's not often there's a Druid around with a cure. Old Gofannon was flogged so severely by his wife not that long ago that he died. His wounds went all green, stank up the whole place they did, and then he died. Wasn't the first time that's happened and it won't be the last, I'm sure. Can you not do something?"

Emrys looked into his mortar. The tincture was thick and green and smelled oddly sour and minty. If he added more vinegar to it, it would last. It would be thin, but it would last.

"I have the power to heal," he said. "But I haven't got the power to change the natural order of things, I'm sorry. If you want the floggings to stop then I can only advise you to refrain from giving your women cause to punish you. Not losing your anger to ale would probably be a good start."

The wild man gave him a look of such candid disappointment before he stomped out of the roundhouse that Emrys almost felt guilty. One by one, the men folk who'd come to watch him perform his magic on their comrade slowly turned and went back out into the night.

The hamlet, Emrys realised, was as full of problems as it was people. And yet he'd thought folk living such a simple life were relatively harmonious. Was this the one exception that proved the rule? Or had all the other hamlets they'd visited only appeared so contented because there were Druids visiting? If they'd arrived at this place yesterday instead of today, would his belief of a happy simple life continued unbroken?

He didn't know. But that night, there were no stories or riddles around the hearth-fire, and the meal they shared was a quiet affair tainted with animosity from the women folk and disappointment from the men. When the three pilgrims left early the following dawn, Emrys was saddened by the depth of relief he felt.

– 16 –

The moon of Simivisonios (Bright-time), 332 C.E.
Lutetia, Parisii tribal lands, Northern Gaul

Beltane had passed and Thrax had promised that they would be riding the ship Nehalennia again soon. With regard to his trade, it mattered little that the Angles had stolen all of his goods. A sizeable hoard was hidden in his house, he said, and that had enabled him to buy more swords and daggers and knives to sell in Brython. They were his speciality, and he wielded them as well as he traded them, so it seemed to Arawn, for he continued his lessons on the art of battle. But even though he lived with Thrax and his woman, and even though he taught him how to fight Angles, he wouldn't tell him where the hoard was hidden.

"Sirom's the only one who has that information," Thrax had said, "for it's up to her to bring it to me if I'm ever in any trouble." He winked, and held back on his attack, his dagger hanging limply in one hand, waiting for Arawn to ask the obvious question: where is it?

But he didn't. He was caught on one word.

One name.

Sirom.

She was pleasant enough, maybe even more than that. She was very friendly, and did all she could to make him feel welcome. She shared food without any grudge. She'd even made new clothes for her new guest.

But she shouldn't be there.

Thrax had said he wasn't bonded to any woman, and that had pleased Arawn. But every day he was forced to look upon the woman's beautiful, smiling face and smile back when he talked to her, and thank her for her kindness. But Arawn would wager his soul that she'd happily murder Thrax in his sleep to run off with his silver. Women were treacherous creatures, and he was yet to meet one who could prove him wrong.

But that wouldn't be for much longer. Lughnasadh would soon be upon them, the weather was warm and turning finer by the day; Thrax had a trove of weapons ready for trading, and a new crew to help him do it. No, it wouldn't be long before they were leaving.

So that morning, Thrax told Arawn to take the opportunity to explore Lutetia fully before they left. Nearly two full moons had passed and all he'd really seen was the port; Thrax had needed him to make the ship sea-worthy for their next voyage.

"If you're as keen on the old Roman buildings as I think you are," said Thrax, smiling, "take yourself south and see what you come across in that part of the city. I think you'll be suitably impressed."

"Why?" Arawn asked. "What's down there?"

"I'll not spoil the surprise. But I think you'll appreciate it. And when you come back this evening I'll tell you some stories about them."

Arawn smiled. He loved Thrax's stories. He knew so much about the old Roman ways, about their old gods and their battles, about the way they fought and the clothes they wore, about the food they ate and the way they treated their people. Arawn could listen to his stories all night.

"But what about you?" Arawn had asked. "Won't you need my help on the ship today?"

A huge grin spread across the trader's face and he wrapped his arms about Sirom's slender shoulders where she was sitting quietly, minding the oat cakes on the hearth-fire. "The boat will be fine on its own, and I don't need your help with what I have in mind this day." Sirom looked up at the trader and smiled. "It's only fair you should enjoy yourself too. Off you go."

So off he'd gone.

He knew exactly what they'd be doing while he was out of the way. Fucking. Like the dogs he saw in the street. But unlike the dogs, they'd decided they wanted a little privacy this day. That didn't always stop them, in the middle of the night, when the urge to fuck overcame them. They would always wait until they thought their guest was asleep, but Arawn heard them. Sirom with her soft, musical moans and Thrax with his gruff, animal grunts. And after, while they lay panting and stroking each other's sweaty skin, Arawn would just lie there, trying to ignore the aching throb that seemed to envelop his entire body, but which clearly emanated from one particular point.

So night time brought a new sense of dread with it. He hated hearing them, but there was a part of him that waited for it. Wanting it. And if they slept soundly and deprived him of their restrained grunts and groans, he hated that too.

Every morning Arawn would break his fast with them, pretending he'd heard nothing, but imagining what Sirom's face looked like when she was making those soft noises.

He hated her for it.

Fresh oat cakes, a round of cheese, and an apple were wrapped in a clean cloth for his midday meal, and Thrax had handed over a flagon of wine.

"Be home by sundown for dinner," Sirom had said, rising up to her tiptoes to kiss him on the cheek. She was always doing things like that. Blinding men with little acts of false kindness.

So here he was, walking down the straight road that led south through Lutetia. Once it had been flagged with stones, Arawn saw that clearly from the few which still remained. But now it was all fallen into disrepair; so much so that it was mostly mud. The hardier weeds had managed to cling on through the coldest moons, and now that the warmer seasons were upon them, he had no doubt that this road would resemble many of those he'd left behind in Brython.

It was disappointing.

Nearly everything that was once beautiful was now a ruin.

How could the Gauls be so careless about the monuments the Romans had left behind? Without Thrax accompanying him to point out precisely what the buildings had been before they were vandalised and left to rot, Arawn didn't even know what he was looking at.

But what annoyed him most of all, was seeing the ancient buildings transformed into things of ugliness, with wood or thatch or stone stolen from another building, where dirty groups of people now lived without any consideration for what the building once was or what it represented… He was sure, though, the Romans hadn't meant for them to be places to eat and shit and fuck.

The sun was climbing high and its rays were far-reaching and warm. Arawn was contemplating stopping for his midday meal, when he came across the largest ruin he'd seen yet.

He had no idea what the building was supposed to have been but it was immense. The stone had clearly been hewn and polished into incredible shapes because there was still evidence of that—a broken arch here, a laboriously etched pillar there. There were colours too, as though carving patterns into the stone wasn't enough; blues, reds and golds, and hues in between which Arawn couldn't even name.

Beneath his feet, though, was a creation that Arawn found most extraordinary. It was broken now, a vague shadow of its past splendour thanks to the jealousy and vandalism of marauding Gauls, but there was enough left to steal his breath away. Underfoot were images unlike any he had seen before. These weren't the lifeless scratches of dye on wood that he'd seen in his own lands, or the mindless patterns woven into tunics or pressed into jugs; these were real images made of countless, coloured little stones. Each individual stone, as small as his thumbnail but evenly sided, was laid next to another, then another, and then another until a picture was created, more beautiful than a sunset, more incredible than the birth of an infant.

"What is it?" he whispered. "I can see...people, but who are they? Are they the Romans?" Lacking a guide to tell him the history, he would never know. And with so much of the image-in-stones missing and broken he knew he wouldn't be able guess for himself. His instinct told him he was looking at pictures of the Romans; the Romans with their bright colours and skilful hands and creative minds.

"This was their *floor*," said Arawn, still whispering. "Imagine what the rest of the building was like if something so beautiful was their floor."

He walked over it, uneasily at first, as though he were committing some great blasphemy; but then his curiosity quashed his worry and wandered around the ruined building with wide eyes, mouth wider.

Then he found something that would lead to his eventual destruction.

Amongst the fallen beauty it looked entirely unremarkable, but it was that which attracted Arawn's attention. It looked like a symbol, or a sigil, and had been scratched into a fallen pillar, but roughly, and was clearly not the same hand that had carved all the other wondrous things surrounding him. Although it was small, it was scratched deep into the pillar and the sides were sharp, giving Arawn the idea that this symbol had been made here fairly recently. He didn't know what it meant, and he didn't recognise the shape or pattern of it; yet even though he'd never been taught to read or write (that was solely the province of Druids and women), he felt that the numbers or letters he used to speak surely wouldn't bear any relation to what he was looking at now. It was as if a tribal punishment frame had been laid onto the shape of a stylised axe; X on top of P.

Looking around he caught sight of another one of these strange symbols etched onto a statue lying broken on the floor. He was sure it meant something, that it was something he'd been meant to find, but he couldn't explain why.

Follow it.

Arawn stood up straight. He knew that voice. He'd heard it before. Heard it when he'd suffered the twin fears of his sister and the Angles. It was the voice of the one true god from his dream, the one where he smote all of Arawn's enemies with his blessed lightening.

Feverishly he began searching for other signs. There were no more in the ruin, but to his surprise he found one outside it, exactly where he'd been standing before he'd climbed across the broken masonry—and he'd missed it! This one was positioned differently to those he'd seen inside the Roman relic. There, the rounded tops had pointed straight up towards the sky. This one, dug into the ground and scuffed by countless pairs of feet, had its rounded top facing south, or south-east perhaps, he wasn't entirely sure. Was that relevant? Did it mean something?

It's pointing to a road; look.

Arawn looked.

Follow the sign. Follow the road.

* * *

It occurred to him that, unless people sought out the symbol, they would never notice the little scratches. Some had been scraped into the mud at the side of the broken road; another had been hewn into a small branch no thicker than two of Arawn's fingers, and then buried in the mud so that only the carved part of the limb poked up from the ground. He even came across one which had been woven from reeds and left on the side of the road like an unusual votive offering. His conviction of being led somewhere important filled him with warm joy.

The City of the Dead.

It was a real city, with buildings and monuments, nothing like the barrow mounds where his own vengeful ancestors passed away their eternity in hate and spite, cursing anyone who went near them and coming forth every Samhain to visit the living with fear and damnation.

That Romans had built this city of the dead, Arawn was positive. It was beautiful, and the dead reposed in buildings that, while small, were just as wonderful as the buildings for the living. No vengeful dead would be waiting here to prey on the living. But it was clear that the Gauls residing in Lutetia had been afraid of this place, too afraid to come and steal the stone to build their own inferior homes. All of the constructs were whole, as were the statues, and the only vandalism came from the constant weather of the changing seasons and the persistent passage of time. That strange sign with its rounded top and cruciform foot had led him to this place.

But where to go now that he was here? This dead city was large, and he hadn't seen a symbol anywhere.

You fear no danger?

He laughed. "There's no need to be afraid," he said. "I'm perfectly safe here. In fact, I think this is the safest I've ever been since that night at the stone circle." He shook his head. "No, this is the safest I've been in my whole life. Nothing will harm me here."

Good. Then walk.

He walked deeper into the city.

The trees growing around and amongst the houses of the dead were in bloom, life now obscuring their wooden skeletons which looked pale and brittle in the brightening afternoon sun. The grass beneath his feet was dry and as devoid of flowers as the air was of birdsong. Beltane was past, but it seemed to take longer for the light half of the year to reach this place and the earth had not yet regenerated enough to restore it to its life-giving fullest. Yet, to Arawn such a setting felt right. To have the air full of the perfume of flowers, full of the noise of fat leaves rippling in the breeze and the distracting call of birds over-powering everything wouldn't be right. Now, it was tranquil. Now, it was perfect.

Up ahead was not just a house for the dead but a palace. A staircase led up to the large square building and standing on either side of the vast wooden door were two scalloped pillars, the curlicued tops of which held aloft the eaves of the porch. There were no windows, for what did the dead need windows for when they could see all that was seen and unseen?

"In there," said Arawn, his voice hoarse with awe, "is where I must go."

As though confirming his statement, Arawn saw the symbol when he reached the door, his symbol, carved deep and deep into the wood. Above the door was a tarnished plaque and Arawn gave it a cursory look, but the markings meant nothing to him and were of no importance.

Only the symbol, looking right at him, was important. With no fear or hesitation, he reached out his hand and pushed open the door.

* * *

Dry. Still.

And silent. But not dark. Torches lined the old stone walls—not rush-lights, oil torches. Arawn smelt the difference immediately; and the flame they gave off, straightened now after bending in the rippling air from his arrival, was bright and clean.

Cleanly swept was the stone-flagged floor; no dust collected on the tombs, which marched down both sides of this house for the dead forming a low corridor. Atop each tomb was a likeness carved in marble of the Roman who had died so that he could live here in eternity. The very Romans who had built the ancient city of Gaul with all its wonders before the natives reclaimed it for barbarism. He wondered why the spirits of these Romans didn't rise up and strike the Gauls down for what they had done; but part of his mind told him they were too civilised for that.

"Benedictus qui venit."

Sounding everywhere at once, the voice came so suddenly and so loudly in this still place that Arawn stepped back, and his heart jumped, pounding, into his mouth. Perhaps the spirits of the Romans weren't still after all.

"Blessed is he who comes," said the voice again, and this time Arawn understood the words.

Following the shallow, tomb-made aisle, his footsteps were soundless in his worn leather boots despite walking on stone. The ghosts of the ancient Romans might have awakened, but they spoke his language, called him blessed, so he knew he had nothing to fear from them.

Several paces he walked until he saw a figure sitting on a high marble throne. Where the dead house was clean and clear, this figure was mouldy and desiccated, and his attire was unrecognisable to Arawn.

A threadbare tunic draped over an aged body so thin that Arawn was sure it was a Roman corpse of this house risen to greet him. The tunic was so old that it was more holes than material, and though it might once have been a vibrant red when this Roman was alive, it was now the rufescent colour of dried blood. Below the tunic the Roman wore no leggings, but his feet were partially shod in what looked like nothing more than rotting thongs of animal hide.

Over the tunic, covering his torso and shoulders, was ancient armour, eroded to practically nothing. Holding onto the Roman's head was a helmet just as ancient and just as rusted, but no sacred animal projected from its crown to guide the ancient warrior in battle. Peer as he might, Arawn saw no face under that helmet, only the suggestion of cheekbones and eye sockets.

Still he felt no fear. The Roman spectre had welcomed him, called him blessed.

He continued walking forward until he was only a few paces from the throne. The spectre didn't move once, and he didn't speak again, but Arawn felt no disappointment. He lowered himself to the floor, kneeling on one knee, and bowed his head.

"I followed the signs, lord, and they brought me to you," he said.

"Hah!" bellowed the spectre, with what sounded suspiciously like pleasure. He clapped his hands together, and the sound came as quick and startling as thunder-claps. "The ones at the old temple? And along the road?"

Arawn looked up, confusion clouding his face, but he nodded.

"People don't understand them. You did well. Understand what they mean?"

"No, lord, I—"

"No, no one does." He sighed, and it was a strangely un-dead sound. "I despair, I really do. Abyssus abyssum invocat, you know. Hells call hell. And with all those barbarians running around out there, it's as hellish as can be. I've tried to spread the word of the one true god, but no one listens. No one wants to. The old gods have come back to us, they say, but they're wrong, all of them. Would you like some ale? I've not got much, but what I've got I'm glad to share. It's been so long since I've had company."

"Lord?"

"Call me Dexs. And there's no need for you to kneel on the floor like that. Up you get."

Despite issuing the order to Arawn, Dexs stood up himself, the rusted armour scratching across itself and making a noise like the crushing of dead leaves. With some care he managed to place one rotten-thonged foot in front of the other to climb down the steps from the throne. Arawn pushed himself up from his knees and stood to one side so he could pass. He was tall, this unlikely spectre, taller than Arawn. And as well as the dry smells of rust and old cloth there was the stink of an unwashed body.

"Dexs," said Arawn, testing it and thinking the name

decidedly unRoman. He hadn't heard any Roman names, but he'd heard plenty of Gaulish ones.

"Yes?" said Dexs, spinning around and tottering alarmingly.

"That's your name?"

The helmet nodded.

"You aren't Roman?"

"Hah!" bellowed Dexs again, and clapped his hands. "Unfortunately not, dear boy, unfortunately not. It was my bad luck to be born in this godless land of godless people. But I do what I can to prove my loyalty." He caressed the front of his armour softly and there was humility in his voice. "Except no one listens to an old man any more. I should have stayed in the southern lands, in Lugdunum, but I wanted to spread the word of god. I dream of going back, you know, but I fear I'm long past making such a journey. Ale." He spun around and walked behind the throne, not looking to see if Arawn followed.

For a moment, Arawn was rooted to the spot. He couldn't deny feeling disappointed that Dexs was an old Gaul, not an ancient Roman, and he certainly felt stupid for thinking that in the first place. But here was someone who embraced the Romans as he did so it might be well that he stayed and listened to him for a little while, particularly if he told him more about those southern lands—was it possible that Romans still existed there? He walked behind the marble throne as Dexs had done to find out.

When he stepped around the back of it he saw that the great carved chair had only been about two-thirds of the way down this palace for the dead. The rest was clearly Dexs' living space. In a corner there was a straw pallet with a crumpled blanket thrown carelessly over it, and to Arawn's dismay it moved every now and then. He tried not to think of the rats or mice with which the old man shared his bed.

Behind the throne and central to the living quarters was a table, which was actually an old barrel that gave off the faint, foetid smell of sour ale, but he guessed its purpose by the mismatched pottery that was on top of it—beakers and plates, all of them ancient, and no doubt all of them filthy. Next to the table was a stool whose three legs were close to rotten but the seat on top was shiny from the constant polishing it got from Dexs' backside.

Next to all of this was the old man, wresting the rusted helmet from his head and muttering to himself. When he finally succeeded, he bellowed a victorious "Hah!" as frail, white hair floated down around his skull. It was thin and patchy, and Arawn imagined that his hair had been polished off his scalp from the constant removing and replacing of the old helmet as the stool had been polished by his arse. It made him grin, but it faltered when the old man turned to face him.

He was grinning too, Dexs, pleased to have a visitor, but there were no teeth in his maw, just a festering blackness. His face was both wrinkled beyond belief and stretched tight across his skull. Not an ounce of fat was underneath the old man's skin, just bone and blood, but he was so pale it was hard to believe there was much of the latter. His right eye was a distinctive grey gleaming with intelligence, or perhaps madness; but his left was as white and smooth as a sanded pebble. Arawn tried not to shudder.

"Seat yourself here, boy," said Dexs, indicating the sole stool with an emaciated hand. "I'm happy to stand while we parley, so long I've been sitting in that throne. I can brew some ale if you don't mind waiting 'til I fetch some water. And find some barley to malt. Or I've probably got some wine somewhere." He trailed off and muttered under his breath once more as he looked around the dusty corners. There were many pots and jars stacked on and around each other, all as cracked and broken as the crockery on the barrel-table, and when Arawn looked into one of those broken cups and saw the furry mould that climbed the side of it he decided against refreshment.

"Are you sure?" said Dexs with evident surprise. "I found a

half-full amphora after all." He held the article out as proof, and Arawn marvelled at the delicate beauty of it. An amphora—he'd never seen its like in Brython before. It had a long, graceful neck and a bulbous base decorated with fading images of running warriors. He could see that, once, it had had two ear-like handles joining the neck and base but one had split and broken. Dexs was using the remaining handle to proffer the wine to his guest, but the wonder at the amphora was instantly dispelled by the sharp vinegar stench of the rancid wine it contained.

Arawn's head twitched to the side involuntarily. "No, thank you. But I appreciate your generosity."

Dexs grinned and scooped up one of the mouldy cups from the barrel-table and poured himself a drink without even looking into it. Arawn grimaced as his aged host took a long draught, believing the man would retch then vomit, but he just smacked his lips loudly and grinned toothlessly.

"Afraid I can't offer you anything to eat, boy," he said after a second gulp of olid wine. "Been a long time since I had guests to feed as well as myself."

Arawn refused to think about the kind of fare this old man would willingly put in his mouth, and fortunately he remembered he had with him his bag stuffed full of fresh oatcakes, cheese and apples. He doubted the man could eat an apple, but he might be happy to suck on the cheese and cakes. Judging from the way his face lit up when Arawn brought out the food, his assumption had been right. He only nibbled an oatcake himself; watching the man eat and drink had driven off his appetite.

"Anything else in that sack of yours?" Dexs said, craning his neck.

He pulled out the apple. "Only this," Arawn said.

Dexs looked at it thoughtfully, running his tongue along the soft ridges of his gums. Then he snatched it out of Arawn's hand and stuffed it underneath his armour. "Save it for later," he said.

"Can you tell me about the symbol, Dexs?"

The old man raised the eyebrow over his white eye and nodded slowly. "I can tell you. But first, you tell me why I should."

Arawn thought for a moment, wondering if he was being tested somehow, but one name leapt into his head. "Because of Boudica," he said.

The old man jumped and hissed.

"She's the goddess of my people now. She defeated the Romans and all the old gods, and I hate her." It was the first time he'd ever said such aloud to anyone, and the venom in his voice surprised him. Yet it also felt like he'd released a great poison from his heart.

"Boudica," the old man hissed, looking toward the roof. "That bitch and her bitch daughters." His head snapped back to Arawn. "You're from Brython then? I thought you had a strange accent."

Arawn nodded.

"She ruined everything!" The shriek echoed around the dead walls. "For more than one hundred and fifty years the Romans had been in these lands, not always welcomed by my countrymen, I'm ashamed to say, but eventually we learned the error of our ways and embraced civilisation. There were always those who fought against them, like Vercingetorix —" he spat the name out as though it tasted foul in his mouth, "—but even he was finally subdued."

"Who was Vercing… Who was he?" Arawn asked, unable to get his teeth around the strange name.

"Vercingetorix." Suddenly the old man wailed and buried his skull-like face in his skeletal hands. "He was a Roman-hater and a rebel—and my ancestor! The shame burns me to this day, and I've spent my whole life trying to atone for my sinful history." He pulled his hands away from his face and looked at Arawn, closing his eyes to slits, as though in accusation. "But Boudica was worse," he hissed.

"Yes, she was; but she was no ancestor of mine."

A smile illuminated Dexs' face. "Then you are fortunate indeed! You have no burden to bear."

"I bear a burden," said Arawn, his voice low. "I've borne it all my life, for she left behind her a legacy which raised women up to the heavens as goddesses and kept men bound and low like slaves. Worse than slaves. My own mother would have killed me if she'd had the chance, but then she'd have had no one to carry her salt bricks or cook her meals. When she *did* buy a slave I feared for my life—she beat me more and fed me less." His voice caught as the memories came back.

"But you survived," said Dexs, his tone soft with care. "And you came here."

Arawn nodded, not trusting himself to speak just yet.

"How came you here?"

"My mother was hanged for treason and my sister would have sacrificed their slave, my friend, to Boudica to free her. So I killed my sister and her Druid then ran away."

Dexs' laugh was as frightening as it was long. He clapped his hands together and swayed back and forth on his feet. Suddenly he stopped and focused his grey eye on Arawn, the only mark of his mirth the tear tracks on his cheeks.

"All women are treacherous, so says the one true god." Arawn sat up straighter, and a sly smile crept across the old man's face. "Ah, so you've heard. But how much? Not much, I'd guess because the Romans weren't in Brython for long enough to gain followers."

"They brought with them the one true god?"

"Nay, boy, that came after. When the bitch Boudica turned aside the Romans, the traitors in Gaul rose up again, emboldened by the defeat across the ocean. Very soon my own countrymen had driven the Romans back across the mountains, and those traitors were glad because they believed they'd seen the last of them." Again the sly smile came. "But they hadn't. The one true god came to the Romans through a man called Paul, a great and wise man who'd befriended the man Jesus, the one true god's only son on Earth. He explained that god had punished the Romans by allowing a woman to defeat them."

"Why would the one true god want to punish them?"

"Because they were sinners! Bringers of great civilisation, yes indeed, but also sinners! For had they not worshipped a whole pantheon of gods? Did they not bow to a thousand other idols? And so the one true god punished them for their sins by taking away their empire, but Paul told them they could rebuild it, a stronger empire that would outshine the last, and it would be the empire of the one true god—the Holy Roman Empire!" In his ecstasy the old man's face gleamed with sweat, as though struck by a sudden fever. He looked down at Arawn again. "There they worship the one true god and are rewarded. Women live in their rightful place as child-bearers and home-makers, and those who are not married and commit the sin of carnal pleasure are burned! Those who do not obey the men and priests are burned! Those who are not subservient to the rightful rulers of the Earth under god are burned! Burned! Burned!"

The last word he screamed so loudly Arawn wanted to cover his ears, but he was fixated by what he heard. "Where is it?" he whispered. "Where is the Holy Roman Empire?"

Dexs smiled beatifically. "In the land of milk and honey, across the mountains to the south and east of here. Ah, would that I could go, but I am sworn to spread the word of the one true god in my own barbaric lands. Tell me, boy, will you spread the word of the one true god?"

Arawn nodded, eyes wide.

"Then you shall have a place in the paradise of heaven, but your time here on earth will be hard. This land is riddled with unbelievers and they will kill you. And always women will seek to lead you away from the path with their lust and carnal ways. But the Bagaudas will always be your friends, for they are the people who try to protect the legacy of the Romans that still stand in our lands, and they are believers in the one true god. Their fight, like mine, is to bring the one true god to these evil lands and beyond. Seek out the Bagaudas in the lands to the south in the city called Lugdunum, and when you find them, they will know you're a friend when you say Benedictus qui venit."

"Benedictus qui venit," Arawn echoed.

Dexs smiled and held his hands wide. "Blessed is he who comes."

"You've answered so many questions, Dexs, but there is one more thing I would like to know."

"Then ask, my boy, and I'll see if I can answer it." He grinned at his guest then took another swig from his filthy mug.

"Does the one true god speak to you?"

Dexs choked and spat out his rotten wine, and so alarmed was Arawn that he jumped up from his makeshift seat and over to the venerable Gaul.

"Why do you ask this?" Dexs said, ignoring his discomfort. "Has he spoken to you? Don't be afraid to speak the truth."

Arawn nodded. "At first, it was only in my dreams. But he spoke to me this afternoon and told me to follow the signs to this city of the dead."

First Dexs clasped Arawn's face in his skeletal hands and bent in so closely that he could smell his breath—an eye-watering combination of sour wine and mouldering gums. Then he collapsed to his knees and prostrated himself before the astonished boy.

"Then you are blessed indeed; as am I that Constantine's Chi Rho led you to me," said Dexs, looking up. "The one true god does not speak so to everyone—I have never heard his voice. We may choose to follow him but not all of us are chosen by him. You are a very special young man indeed."

Arawn felt tears sting his eyes. "Truly?"

"Truly. He has marked you out to do his work for him. Are

you willing to spend your life in service to the one true god?"

"I am."

"Then find the Bagaudas. If you listen to his voice, you will be a leader among them and you shall lead them to greatness."

"In the name of the one true god."

"In the name of the one true god," Dexs agreed.

When Arawn finally opened the great door which led out to the late afternoon light, he felt lifted. "All's well. All's very well indeed."

Later that night, after the evening meal was eaten and Thrax asked of his adventures, Arawn said nothing of Dexs and the truths which had been revealed to him. He wanted to find out if Thrax was a sinner, but that was a conversation best left for just the two of them, when his sinning woman wasn't around to breathe her sweet poison into his ear.

But she did spread her poison, when the house was dark and the fire was almost cold. She groaned as her poison was released, contaminating Thrax. And even as Arawn's blood pumped painfully through his body, and even as his hips convulsed in time with her moans, he prayed to the one true god that he could save his friend Thrax.

* * *

"Who was Vercingetorix?"

Thrax looked at Arawn with surprise, but also a smile. "Where did you hear that name?"

He shrugged. "Overheard an old man talking about him yesterday when I was out, but I didn't hear much. Who was he?" Later, Thrax would be meeting someone to purchase a last batch of swords to trade. Now was the only moment he would have to find out if his friend was a sinner.

"Vercingetorix," said Thrax, "was a giant among our people."

Arawn looked at him sharply. "I thought you didn't believe in giants?"

He laughed and slapped Arawn on the shoulder. "And so I don't! But even if Vercingetorix wasn't a giant, he was certainly as powerful as one." His voice took on the sing-song quality it always did when he told a tale. "A warrior so fierce, that no matter how hard the Romans fought, they couldn't defeat him; and so tall that all the warriors of Gaul sheltered under him as they fought against the enemy."

"So he defeated the Romans?" Arawn asked, though he knew it wasn't true.

"Alas, the Romans are like a plague, and no matter how many were brought down, there were always more to take their place. One by one the Gaulish warriors fell, and soon there was only Vercingetorix. And even the mightiest man can be brought down by a plague."

"Then the Romans *did* kill him."

"No, the Romans couldn't kill him, for he was a giant among men and they were merely pests. But they out-numbered him, one against one hundred thousand, and they shackled him and forced him into bondage. They marched him across the world into the Roman heartland, and there they paraded him, the Roman people marvelling and afeared by his size and ferocity. But he was shackled and couldn't fight, so the Romans climbed all over him, pricking him with their short swords and eventually he died of his wounds. So ended the tale of the giant Vercingetorix." He looked at Arawn, and in his normal voice asked, "How did you like that story?"

He is a sinner, and there's only one way to save him.

He nodded and offered a smile which he hoped looked genuine.

When Thrax left him at the ship Nehalennia promising to be back in a few hours so he could share the midday meal with them, Arawn saw his opportunity. None of the other men was paying him any attention, too busy at their tasks of scraping off the last of the lichens or filling the belly of the ship.

Thrax was nowhere to be seen; by now he would be in the city carrying out his business. It didn't take him long to lose himself in the hordes of people milling around the port, and if anyone missed him this early on they'd never be able to pick him out amongst all the bodies bustling around him. When he was back on the road, he broke into a run, knowing that his task had to be fulfilled as quickly as it could. Fortunately he knew this road very well.

It was the road which led to Thrax's house, and to where Sirom had been left all alone.

* * *

When he opened the door, she was bent low over the hearth-fire, roasting meat for the evening meal. She looked up, and an expression of mild confusion crossed her pretty face.

"You're back early," she said. "Are you not having your midday meal on the ship?"

Her breasts, clearly visible over the top of her low-cut tunic and emphasised by her stance, were plump, and as sun-browned as her face. Winking between them was the amber pendant Thrax had gifted her with, displaying it like an expensive reminder to all that she owned him. Arawn's blood boiled at the way she displayed her carnal lust. He slammed the door behind him, causing her to start upright. The smile she'd been wearing vanished, her whole face turning to fright when Arawn crossed the room in a few large steps until he was in front of her.

Before she had time to speak he grabbed hold of her throat and it pleased him to feel her pulse there beating fast and frantic.

"You carnal whore," he hissed in her face. "You live in sin and lust. You should be burned."

From her escaped a frightened, choked sound, and her eyes filled with tears. She tried to shake her head but Arawn's grasp was too strong.

He was so strong! Never before had he realised just how powerful he was, even after he'd killed his sister and that Druid. Knowledge of his past kills pulsed through him, and he threw her to the floor, relishing the noise her head made when it cracked against the stone flooring. She lay dazed for a few heartbeats, but she scrabbled up to her elbows, sobbing now in terror and pain.

She pushed herself away from him, moving backwards, and Arawn laughed at the futility of her gesture. Towering over her, he kicked at one ankle so it flung out to the side, then he kicked the other one. Both times she squealed in pain.

Her gasping sobs sounded so like the noises she made when she fucked his friend Thrax that quickly he became aware of the blood pulsing and throbbing in the front of him, but this time he wouldn't ignore it. The carnal whore would have a vivid reminder of why she was being burned before he set her alight.

Even as he pulled up his tunic, Sirom must have known what his intentions were before he unlaced his leggings for she started wailing. Arawn dealt her a swift kick to her side which knocked all the breath out of her and she sank down from her elbows.

He pushed up her skirts and climbed on top of her. Terror filled her eyes again and she began struggling. Arawn pinned her arms above her head so that he was only inches from her face, and the sensation of her struggling underneath him but powerless to do anything made him roar with pleasure. He was so strong! He moved both of her tiny wrists into one of his fists leaving his other hand free to thrust her skirts up to her waist, allowing him to access the depths of her poison. But she couldn't poison him; he was too strong.

When she started screaming again he slapped her face once, twice, and then hard enough to make blood flow from her nose. It made her look less pretty, but the sight of her blood, the copper smell of it in his nostrils, made his own blood pulse and throb so violently he thought he would explode.

Then, fiercely, he took her. Her screams died away to mewls as he pounded against her, but his grew louder until he was roaring at his own strength and ecstasy.

Finished, he stood and looked down at her bloody, heaving body and spat on her three times. He turned towards the hearth-fire whilst lacing up his leggings, and bent to pick up one of the logs from the edge. One end was burning red; the other wasn't even smoking but it was still hot to touch. He grabbed it and threw it into the corner where the carnal whore lay with his friend. The straw mattresses lit up instantly and Sirom, recovering from the beating and the raping enough to know the danger she was in, scrambled to her feet and tried to run for the door.

Arawn launched himself after her and grabbed her hair as she stumbled past. She must have squealed again, but Arawn's head was full of the sound of his own blood and the flames now climbing up the corner of the house.

Still clasping Sirom's hair, he reached into the fire and pulled out another log, this time throwing it into the corner where the loom was—the wool caught splendidly, the flames dancing yellow, blue and green as the dyes ignited. Arawn laughed.

He kicked at the other logs so that they scattered across the floor, spreading fire as they went. Then he pulled Sirom in front of him. She was struggling less, though he didn't trust her not to run away from her fiery death once he left her. He grabbed hold of the front of her bodice and pounded his fist against her head. There was a lot of blood before her body finally went limp.

He tossed her body onto the flames growing around the hearth-fire and smiled as they leapt greedily across her dress and through her hair.

With the stench of her roasting meat filling his nostrils, he turned and walked out of the door. His body throbbed from the strength he'd discovered within himself and he knew he wouldn't get caught.

He looked back to see the first tendrils of smoke rising from the thatch and smiled.

His friend, Thrax, was saved, and it was he who did it.

– 17 –

The moon of Simivisonios (Bright-time), 332 C.E.
Lutetia, Parisii tribal lands, Northern Gaul

With a heavy heart, Rosmerta climbed into her saddle. The horse was still shaken after its voyage across the ocean and she had to grip it tightly with her knees to keep it from skittering away while she waited for the rest of the spear-women to mount their steeds.

It was the moon of Simivisonios, bright-time, and here in the town called Lutetia a truer name she couldn't have picked. To her untravelled skin the sun felt much stronger here than in her homelands. Several days had passed since she last wore her cloak; now she was beginning to feel uncomfortable in her woollen dress. It was possible, she thought, that these people called their moons by another name though she had no desire to find out. But it wasn't her discomfort in this strange land that made her heart heavy; in fact, she relished it, for it took her mind off the current situation.

"We ride until night-fall," said Gwladus, steering her mount towards Rosmerta's and turning it extravagantly. She was a good horse-woman, and she took great pride in demonstrating it to everyone. "The sister-slayer is many days ahead of us by now and we can't afford to waste any time."

"We know that he stayed here for two moons while we tracked him across the ocean and through all the lands to the north," said Rosmerta. And no doubt they would have him by now, she thought, if Gwynfor hadn't said they should make landfall as soon as the Gaulish coast were spotted. Had he purposely delayed their mission, or was he simply inept at reading his own runesticks? She left her thoughts as her own, however. "That would've closed the gap considerably. We ride, and when we need to stop and rest, we shall."

"Pah! You would risk his causing more death upon these people? Upon these lands?"

"We don't even know if he's guilty of committing the crimes that have been laid upon him here. There were no witnesses."

There was something about the single-minded ferocity of Arawn's mother that drove Rosmerta to constantly contradict her. She didn't know whether it was her fast-waning belief that Arawn was innocent, or simply her noble pride in being ordered about by a traitor who should be hanged and dead, but contradict her she did. It was the only satisfaction she gleaned on this tiring mission.

Because, despite there being no witnesses to the murder of the young woman the traders called Sirom, and no one to witness the burning of the house, there were many at the port who had attested to seeing Arawn leave the port when he should have been there helping to prepare captain Thrax's ship for sail. They'd said he'd looked excited, frantic perhaps, before he ran off eastwards into the city. At the time no one had paid it any mind, for he was young and the captain was away on business. They'd all assumed he'd skived off. But then smoke was seen rising to the east, and all on board that ship knew their captain's house lay in that direction. The fire had spread quickly, and many others were injured whilst trying to extinguish it, but there had only been one death—Sirom. When their captain came running at the news of the fire, they'd said, he'd gone mad; scraping through the ashes and screaming the name of his woman, and then howling at the sky when he came across the charred husk that was her body. He knew it was her because of the amber pendant she wore. It was smothered by the ash of her remains, and when he found it, madness took him again.

All knew that the captain had given Arawn a place to sleep at his house, and though all were horrified by his actions, they couldn't think of anyone else it could be. Sirom was a well-loved person in Lutetia and no harm had ever come to her until Arawn arrived.

Gwladus had all but screeched in triumph after hearing the testimony of the sailing traders, and Rosmerta had to admit it was compelling, but… The young man she'd met in Cantiaci who'd come begging to her for work could no more be capable of burning a woman in her own house as he could of killing his sister in cold blood. He'd admitted that tragic event was an accident, so was it possible this was an accident too?

"I'm coming with you."

The voice was hollow, but not without force. The warrior-princess looked down from her saddle into empty eyes. Not entirely empty; anger flared deep inside, but grief overcame any other emotion for the time being. Once the red rings of tears had dried, however, the fury would begin.

She smiled consolingly at him. "Thrax," she said. "Your grief wounds me, and from the bottom of my heart I'm sorry for your loss. But—"

"He's a trader and we're warriors," Gwladus interrupted. "He'll only slow our search down. I'll not have the hunt stopped just because he's lapsed into a bawling fit over his dead woman."

Rosmerta spun around in her saddle, appalled at the spear-woman's insensitivity. Before she could reprimand her, however, Thrax the trader spoke, soft and slow.

"You are strangers in these lands," he said. "Unwelcome guests, some might consider you. I know the lands around Lutetia as well as I know the city herself. If anyone can lead you to Arawn, I can."

"*Sister-slayer!*" shrieked Gwladus so that the horses shifted anxiously around and underneath them. "You will not call him by any other name than that. And knowledge of the lands you may have, but I am a skilled warrior who needs no dog to sniff out the demon who slew my daughter."

"You're a salt-merchant, Gwladus," said Rosmerta, "and

nothing else." She turned back to the trader just as the woman's eyes widened in shock, and said, "Your help will be invaluable and appreciated. Can you ride?"

Thrax nodded.

"Then take any steed you wish and ride with me. I would hear all about the time you spent with Arawn, and perhaps that will give us insight as to where he is travelling."

The trader had no need to pick a steed for a spear-woman from her mother's guard gave up her own willingly enough, much to the disgust of Gwladus.

"My lady, I won't need to give you insight as to where the lad's going," Thrax said when he was saddled and the army was trotting southwards through the city.

Arawn's mother had retreated to the back where her Druid cast his spells. No doubt she would be urging him to find her son before Thrax did, but Rosmerta was glad to be rid of her for a while.

"Indeed?" she said.

"Indeed. I never thought of it before, I just thought it youthful curiosity for the boy loved my stories." He shook his head, then cleared his throat. "But he was always interested in my stories about the Romans, and *their* stories about their one true god. He always questioned me about it, even from the first day I met him in Cantiaci's marketplace, lady, where I met you for the first time as well."

"Truly?" she said, surprised at this mild revelation. She looked at him intently. "I'd forgotten about that, so much has happened. But, yes…I remember you now."

Thrax smiled, but there was no joy in it. "I remembered Arawn from that day too, and when he came to my ship pleading help I gave it to him. All the gods forgive me, I gave it to him." He turned his face away from Rosmerta and covered his eyes with a big, rough hand. She felt her own eyes fill at his pain but she could think of nothing to say that would offer comfort.

"Many years ago," said Thrax when he'd recovered himself, "there were rumours of house-burning in the lands far to the south. No one this far north took much notice, until the burnings came closer and closer. There were a few here in Lutetia," he looked around at the town that they were slowly passing through, "I was but a lad at that time and didn't understand much. Then people started whispering about a people called the Bagaudas, and for years many were afraid of them. But the attacks disappeared, and because I was so young I didn't think anything else of it. Sirom and the sea became my life and the Bagaudas nothing more than a distant memory."

"Forgive me," said Rosmerta, feeling awkward. "But I don't understand what any of this has to do with Arawn."

The trader looked at her. "The Bagaudas are rebel fighters. Gauls who believe that we were wrong to have expelled the Romans from our lands. They hide in Roman ruins and protect them savagely. I hear they've also taken on the beliefs of the Romans' one true god, and burning is their way of purifying all that has returned to barbarism." He snorted a laugh. "Us. Though how burning people in their homes can be thought of as anything less than barbaric, I don't know."

"You think Arawn has become one of these Bagaudas?"

"It's the only thing that makes sense to me. He told me frankly how he hated your goddess, Boudica." Rosmerta gasped a little at this. "And now I think of it, his interest in the new Roman god was more than passing curiosity. And the Roman god hates women as the Romans themselves do, and I come home to find my shining Sirom burned in our house like the attacks of old. There is nothing else it could be."

Rosmerta nodded, though in truth she was a little overwhelmed by all the information, the strange new words and the ungodly behaviours of a mysterious band of people.

"So if I'm right," said Thrax, "there's only one place Arawn would go."

"And you know of this place?"

"I know of it," he said, nodding. "It's where I'm taking you."

The moon of Simivisonios (Bright-time), 332 C.E.
Dubras, Cantiaci tribal lands, Brython

"But what do we really know of these Angles?" The clamour in the council chambers was loud, but Trahaearn Smith managed to raise his voice above the rest. Airmed looked at him with interest; her sister Rosmerta had always said kind words about him. "So far the only evidence we have of them is one floating body in the sea."

Sulis Warrior-Queen of the Cantiaci looked to the original bearer of this news, the spear-women who had met them in the Trinovantes tribal lands after the failed meeting with the Warrior-Queen Sirona.

The spear-woman waited until the noise died down, then directed her answer to the smith. "The fact that the body was still floating meant the attack was very recent—the traders on the ships we obtained were fortunate in that respect; they knew they'd be spared. They don't know much about these new enemies, but they know their ships are bigger than traders', they're crewed by warriors, and they come from lands to the north and east of Gaul. They also know that raids on the ocean between Brython and Gaul have been very rare, but now the Angles surely know of the rich trading that takes place between our countries. Each trader on the ship that brought me back here had heard of someone who'd been plundered on the sea at the point of an Angle's sword."

"So they're growing more powerful," said Sulis.

The spear-woman nodded. "And the promise of wealth will make them braver."

"And now the traders fear that these once-rare attacks will become more frequent, and that will undoubtedly affect our economical situation. Losing trade from Gaul would be disastrous." She addressed this last to the council meeting in general and Airmed noted the looks of concern passing between members. Cantiaci was a wealthy tribe, such was well-known across the lands. But that wealth relied heavily on overseas trade. The tribes to the north and west of their own ever sought to trade with anyone but the Cantiaci because of the ancient animosity that stood between them.

"If I might add, my lady," said the spear-woman. Sulis nodded. "If the Angle attacks disrupt sea trade so much that it slows or ceases altogether, they might be willing to travel even further to find their plunder."

"The thought had occurred to me too," said Sulis. "Then we'll be faced with the Picts pillaging along the eastern coastline and the Angles sacking from the south."

"It may not take them long to discover where the richest pickings are."

There was hush for a moment, and then the council chamber erupted once more. People stood, shaking their fists, demanding what Sulis intended to do about this new threat, and it surprised Airmed that her mother didn't order them into silence. While her face remained serene, a muscle in her jaw twitched as she clenched and unclenched her teeth, exposing her true sentiment. She's as frightened as they are, Airmed thought with wonder. And she can't call them to order because she doesn't know what to do.The idea shocked her. She didn't want to believe it, but there her mother was, silent and watching, while all around council members grew louder as their questions brought to mind new fears.

"We pay them tribute," her mother said abruptly, and all noise ceased. "Such methods of peace-keeping were employed once between the tribes of these lands. We offer tribute to the Angles to protect our lands and our trading routes."

"Their demands could cripple us!" called a merchant from the back of the chamber.

"How do we know they can even be trusted? They're a tribe of thieves, after all!" called another.

"We don't know that they can be trusted, you are right," said Sulis. "We do not know anything about these people." She turned back to the spear-woman. "I want a ship built," she said. There were murmurs from the back of the chamber about the expense, but for the moment Airmed's mother ignored them. "You will find a captain and crew and fill it with spear-women. Then you will sail the seas until you find either an Angle ship or their lands, and demand palaver."

"That will notify them of our existence," Trahaearn said, eliciting cries of agreement. "Won't that be worse? At least for the moment we're hidden from them."

"I would rather stop a battle before it starts," said Sulis, "than wait in fear for it to arrive at my door."

"Are we to have no say in the matter?"

"The whole council must be in agreement. We will reconvene in a fortnight to discuss, but I still want a ship built." She looked across to the spear-woman who nodded her understanding. "Then if there's nothing further—"

There was sudden and loud banging on the chamber doors. Everyone swung to look at it once, startled.

"Enter," Sulis called.

The door opened to reveal a breathless spear-woman, whose cloak was the grey and crimson of the Trinovantes, and whose helmet bore the wolf. That she'd ridden far was doubtless, that she'd ridden hard was clear in her demeanour. "My lady," she said, stepping over the threshold. "I bring urgent news."

Once again the chambers were shrouded in silence.

"Speak," said Sulis.

"It's the Picts, my lady," she said. "They've sacked Trinovantes. Hundreds of them. Arrived during the night and attacked at dawn."

Sulis stood up slowly, watching the spear-woman intently. "These are bad tidings."

"Yes, my lady, but there's worse." She paused and looked around the room, appearing surprised that it was so full of people.

"Tell me," Sulis prompted.

"Sirona Warrior-Queen of Trinovantes is dead."

* * *

The wind stung her cheeks like a swarm of angry wasps, but it had pushed the clouds aside and the sun shone clearly. Even after Beltane it wasn't unusual for angry winds to escape from the north to harry the southern lands. Airmed had excused herself, with her mother's permission, from the council chambers shortly after the news of Sirona was broken and now she walked through the palace grounds, glad she wore her woollen dress and even gladder she'd thought to bring her cloak.

The news of Sirona's death had provoked a peculiar effect on the councillors. Silence and shuffling. That was it. No cries of dismay or shock; in fact, the silence felt more awkward to Airmed than respectful. She hadn't liked the warrior-queen much on meeting her, but she certainly hadn't wished her dead. More drama should have met news of a warrior-queen's death, but that she fell under the blades of Picts was odd. Yes, there were occasional casualties whenever the Picts raided, but very few deaths. Certainly they never got close to enough to assassinate a warrior-queen during their raids.

Airmed checked herself. Obviously, the southern-most Picts had got close enough to kill warrior-queens because they'd taken the northern-most lands of Brython. The Brigantes and Carvetii existed no more and the Parisii were nothing more than a village, too small and too poor now for the Picts to bother. And the Iceni-Coritani were made up of two tribes; so yes, there had been a time when the Picts were brave enough to kill warrior-queens.

Not for many generations, however, and not with a fleet of boats and certainly not this far south. Even so, Sirona had known about the fleet of ships approaching, had scorned the idea of accepting aid from her Cantiaci neighbours, and now she was dead, as were many of her spear-women. It made no sense, and Airmed was disquieted; it was for that reason she had to leave the council chambers.

Yet she had no one with whom she could talk. Rosmerta had sailed to Gaul on a mission to find a sister-slayer, and her brother Emrys had left on a mysterious pilgrimage with Heddgwyn. Of course, she had other brothers and sisters, but they were even younger than she and would find this situation either too complicated or too dull to talk about. So she wandered the palace grounds, into the gardens where Rosmerta so loved to walk, not knowing where her feet took her, just enjoying the sensation of cold wind and warm sun on her face.

Before long she found herself walking though the edge of the wood that mantled the land behind the palace. She loved the pungent aroma of the wood as the ground, now fully thawed from the fastness of the dark moons, prepared itself for the journey throughout the light ones. She filled her lungs with it and walked in deeper.

Sulis would take her spear-women through here often for hunting, for it was rich with deer and wild boar. Apart from the sport, her mother always said, it was a good way of keeping the household fed. Yet there was one area of this wood through which the hunters were forbidden to roam. It was a small clearing with a fine, clear stream running across it, and this was sacred to the Druids. Not only because the grove was blessed by the goddess Belisama as evinced by the stream, but also because it was surrounded by oak, thorn, and ash trees. Emrys had told her once that, above all other trees, these three were most revered by Druids because of their magical properties. Airmed had accepted this politely, not knowing enough herself about the secrets of the Druids to contradict him, but in her mind she knew that all plants, be they the highest trees or the lowliest herbs, had magical properties. One just had to know how to prepare them.

She'd learned all her herb lore from the Druids, naturally. And there was one in particular, Rhonwen, who was always pleased to spend time with the young princess and teach her about flowers and plants. Airmed thought her a good teacher, kind and calm with a seemingly limitless knowledge. She was older than Airmed by possibly fifteen summers, but her complexion was so fresh from spending her days outside, and free from the ravages of disease because of her knowledge of healing, that it was difficult to tell.

As the dappling light of the sun fell across her eyes, she decided that it was Rhonwen she would visit. Though she had a roundhouse near the palace as many of the Druids did, she was usually found near the sacred grove, collecting herbs or making potions with the sacred waters of Belisama's stream. She might not be able to talk to her as she would Rosmerta, but it was rare that she didn't find comfort from Rhonwen's soft words.

It took longer to find without Emrys leading her; the sun had moved noticeably across the sky so that that the shadows of the trees fell long and to the east. But eventually, using the sound of trickling water to guide her, she came to the clearing.

It was empty.

"Oh," said Airmed, and then wondered what to do.

Undoubtedly the Druids didn't spend all their time here, but she'd never been here without seeing at least one or two of them casting their rune-sticks or chanting over a crucible hanging over the fire. She walked to the centre of the clearing where there was certainly evidence of a fire, but it was long cold. Neither was there a crucible, nor pots, nor tools, nor anything that suggested this was a sacred grove used frequently by the Druids of

Cantiaci. She sighed, and with the stream trickling behind her, she walked back the way she came.

The herb garden! If Rhonwen wasn't in the wood collecting herbs, she'd be in the garden. Airmed had been growing and tending it for years now, and even Rhonwen was impressed by it. Some of the disappointment that she'd felt earlier lifted, and she increased her pace as the edge of the wood and the beginning of the palace gardens drew closer.

But even as she approached it she knew Rhonwen wasn't there. She'd tended the herbs well over the cold moons, and the rosemary, thyme, sage, hyssop and yarrow were growing well. But none were so high-grown that they'd cover a white-robed Druid even if she were crouched upon her hands and knees. Still, she walked over to it, ever optimistic until there was irrefutable proof of her disappointment. She brushed a hand along the soft fronds of a rosemary bush and then held it to her nose, delighting in the perfume, sure now that Rhonwen was nowhere to be seen.

The sun was westering, it was colder and soon it would be dark. The reasonable thing to do would be to go back to the palace, warm herself beside the huge hearth-fire in the dining hall and wait for dinner to arrive. But she wanted to find Rhonwen. She wanted someone to explain why she felt so unsettled, but most of all she didn't want to go home having achieved nothing with her afternoon. The Druids lived in simple thatched structures on the palace grounds, not too far from the main building itself so she decided to go there. Even if Rhonwen wasn't there, she was bound to find someone who knew where she was and that would, at least, be something.

The circular compound had the same empty feeling as the sacred grove. It was most unusual not to see a few Druids milling around over here. Then a thought struck her—she hadn't seen any white-robed figures at the council meeting either. Granted, it was normally Heddgwyn who represented his Fellows at such gatherings, but they would doubtless be aware that he had gone off pilgrimaging. Surely, then, someone else should have taken his seat. Heddgwyn would be angered beyond words if all the events that had taken place since his departure were not recorded by one of his own people. And these weren't mere tribal affairs, but the discovery of a potentially dangerous sea-faring tribe, and the death of a neighbouring warrior-queen at the hands of the Picts. So why hadn't a Druid been in attendance?

Feeling the anger of the noble-born stirring within her, she marched into the compound, headed straight towards Rhonwen's thatched, wattle-and-daub roundhouse, and pulled back the hide door.

Empty.

She marched over to the next one: empty also.

Her anger shifted to confusion as, with each hide door she pulled back, she discovered that all of the roundhouses in the entire Druid compound were empty.

Running back to the palace, she tried to remember the last time she'd actually seen a white-clad figure and found she couldn't recall. But that was ridiculous. They must have been around, she just hadn't noticed them.

She launched herself up the palace steps and pushed against the heavy wooden door with such force it banged against the inside the wall. Her mother, sitting at the hearth-fire, still talking with some of the councillors, looked up at the noise with surprise before her face regained its usual serenity.

"There's still plenty of time until dinner, Airmed," she said. "There's no need to burst in like that."

"Mother," she said, ignoring her comment and marching towards the warrior-queen. "Where have all the Druids gone?"

– 18 –

The moons of Equos (Horse-time) – Elembiuos (Claim-time), 332 C.E.
Cornovii tribal lands, Brython

Their journey through the Dobunni tribal lands had been quite unremarkable, much to Emrys' relief. He found it difficult to forget the violence he'd witnessed at that little settlement so close to his own home. He knew other tribes behaved differently to the Cantiaci, but the events he'd beheld in the Atrebates tribal lands had shocked him greatly. And even though their travels had remained peaceful since then, he couldn't help but wonder what atrocities took place before they arrived or after they left.

Heddgwyn seemed less worried. In fact, the incident hardly seemed to have affected him at all. "This is your first pilgrimage," he'd told Emrys. "Your eyes have a long way to go before they're opened."

He supposed it were true, but he didn't find the Arch Druid's words comforting. However, Heddgwyn had been incredibly interested in the words which had passed between Emrys and Celyddon, the man who had been publicly whipped for beating his wife, and Gethin, Celyddon's brother. More surprisingly, the wild man, Emlyn Salt-merchant, had recounted the story with an enthusiasm that felt almost obscene to the young Ovate.

He couldn't rid himself of the distrust he felt for the wild man. But looking at him now, he barely resembled the downtrodden outcast who had crossed their path more than three moons ago. The new clothes they'd bought from a villager were muddied, certainly, but not yet torn, though the hem of his cloak was worn after being dragged daily across the uneven tracks they followed. He'd untangled his hair and beard and washed most of the dirt out, much to Emrys' secret relief. He now wore his hair, which was as rich a brown as polished chestnuts, tied back at the nape of his neck as Emrys and Heddgwyn did. He'd also trimmed his beard with the Arch Druid's knife, and with many silver strands running through it he looked almost distinguished. Handsome even, though Emrys was loath to admit that. Yet despite his changed appearance, Emrys still couldn't think of him as anything other than the wild man. As always, he walked several paces ahead of the pilgrims' horses. Gone was the half-crouch of fear and wariness that made him look ready to attack at the slightest noise. He was tall, and broad of shoulder; and though Emrys was glad to have his strength on their side, he still didn't trust him. Discovering why that should be kept eluding him for the time being.

"You've been very thoughtful of late, my son."

Emrys started. Not because Heddgwyn had called him his son, that was becoming ever more frequent; but because he hadn't expected conversation. "I was just thinking how Equos was passing quickly and soon it will be Elembiuos and all the tribes will be racing and trading horses in honour of Lugh. Time seems to be passing quickly yet we are still travelling."

"Ah, Elembiuos. Claim-time," said the Arch Druid. "But the very meaning of that won't become apparent to you until we've completed another cycle." He chuckled contentedly, but Emrys was in no mood to guess his riddles. "We've made good time. Pilgrimaging isn't about reaching the end of the journey, it's the journey itself. We travel slowly through the countryside, through the regions special to each of the local gods and pay our tribute to them. It may not seem like it to you, but I've made this journey several times and I promise I speak true."

"I don't doubt your word."

"And it's fortunate indeed because, once we pass the borders of the Deceangli and turn west, the going will become ever more difficult. You've never seen mountains, my son, but they are things of terrifying beauty. Crossing them is a deadly trial, but once we pass them and see the sacred isle of Ynys Afallach, you'll understand why we must endure such. Great rewards come to those who suffer."

Emrys nodded. That last was a favourite phrase of Heddgwyn's, and ever he'd used it to explain the mind-thwarting and oft-times physically uncomfortable teachings of Druidic lore. "The Deceangli," he said thoughtfully. "Their lands border those of the Picts, don't they?"

"You've studied your maps well, my son!" He offered Emrys a bright smile. "And indeed they do, but there's no cause for concern. A mountain range separates the Deceangli from the rampaging Picts so we'll be quite safe from them."

"Another mountain range?"

"Oh yes." Heddgwyn was smiling. He loved demonstrating his knowledge. "While the southern lands of Brython are as soft and undulating and plump as a young woman eager to pick a man with whom to bond, the northern lands are hard and spiky and full of barren mountains. It's why the Picts keep raiding beyond their territories. But even though such lands might be impossible to live in, it doesn't make them any less beautiful."

"You've been to Pictland?"

"Of course; I've spent a lifetime travelling those lands—I've had to. The magic that works for us in Cantiaci doesn't work as well in the lands of Dumnonii even though they're part of the southern lands, and their magic won't work as well in the lands of the Iceni-Coritani. So it goes without saying that the northern magics would also be different. If I didn't go there to find this out I wouldn't be able to protect myself from them. People only fear the magic they know, you see."

"You never told me you went to Pictland," said Emrys.

"I had no cause to. But I'm telling you now. And if those marauding Picts do happen to cross the mountains into Deceangli, I'll be able to keep us safe."

But it wasn't their safety that concerned Emrys. It was the fact that Heddgwyn, the Arch Druid of the Cantiaci and his father, had so many secrets. What other information was he keeping from him?

"Emlyn," called Heddgwyn suddenly, and the wild man turned his head towards him instantly. "The sun is westering and I would have the comfort of a bed this night. There's a village not too far ahead of us, and I ask that you go onwards and prepare them for our visit."

"Yes, my lord," said the wild man, and trotted off without another word.

"My lord," Emrys echoed scornfully. "The man tried to kill us for a cloak and now he calls you his lord."

"Stop." Emrys actually jumped in his saddle, so forcefully did Heddgwyn speak. He looked at his father with surprise. "Emlyn has been an invaluable companion on our journey; and though our first meeting may have been turbulent, it was nonetheless auspicious. The old gods intended for us to meet him and I will not have you asperse his uses."

"What uses? Running ahead of us to tell villagers we're on our way? And why do we need someone to do that suddenly—so that you're saved a repeat of what happened in that Atrebates village?"

To Emrys' shock, Heddgwyn roared. No words; a pure sound of anger. His eyes blazed. "What would you accuse me of, Emrys? Cowardice? I think not. I've traversed through lands, in this world as in the spiritual, more dangerous than your safe mind could possibly imagine. And if you did imagine such you'd be driven mad. So don't call cowardice down upon me because you have no concept of what true danger or fear is."

For a moment they only stared at one another; Emrys, breath held and eyes wide, Heddgwyn with his chest heaving and eyes drawn almost to slits.

"I wasn't accusing you of cowardice," Emrys said finally. "I apologise for my words. I only meant to ask why the wild—" he checked himself, "why Emlyn was so important to you."

"His purpose is not clear to me yet," said Heddgwyn, breaking eye contact and facing forward again. "The old gods have yet to reveal it to me. But purpose he has, as do you, my son. That you must trust. If you're worried that Emlyn's fate has overridden yours, you are mistaken."

Blood rushed to the young Druid's cheeks. "I'm not jealous, if that's what you think."

Heddgwyn chuckled again, and just like that, his humour was restored. "I don't doubt it. Though it may please you to know that, once we've passed through the lands of the Deceangli, the wild man," he said, looking at Emrys with mischief, "will no longer be with us."

"Really? Why?"

"Because that's as far as his path with us leads. Only we are permitted onto the sacred isle of Ynys Afallach. You know that, my son."

Emrys nodded. Of course he did. And Emlyn wasn't a Druid, he was just a bodyguard. A man who had been a salt-merchant's wife until she'd been hanged for treason. A man who was fatherless because his children were dead. He was a man with nothing, and Emrys was an Ovate pilgrimaging to the sacred isle. His spirits rose.

He had nothing to fear from Emlyn. Nothing to fear at all.

– 19 –

Elembiuos (Claim-time), 332 C.E.
Somewhere South of Lutetia, Gaul

He tries to back away from the crucible and its evil stench but someone is behind him, barring his way. He knows who it is because he's had this dream so many times now, and even though he knows it's a dream, he can't halt his terror. Slowly he turns to confront Gwynfor, his dead sister's dead Druid.

"The Dead will find the living," Gwynfor intones. "They cannot escape the Dead. The living will be devoured and so become the Dead."

But he hardly hears the words any more because his eyes are ever drawn to the gory mess that is his head. One eye is mashed to a pulp, while the side of his head is concave, blood oozing from the crack in his skull and running down his neck. The other eye rolls madly while he speaks, but now he starts cackling and the eye finally focusses on a point just behind Arawn's left shoulder.

Panic fills him. Normally he wakes after the Druid has intoned his terrible prophecy, but not this time. The cackling fills his head, and even when Arawn clasps his hands over his ears he still hears it. Gwynfor, however, gazes ever more intently past his shoulder, and dread, like freezing water running down his back, makes it hard to breathe.

Without willing it, he turns back towards the foul stench of the crucible where his dead sister's head is being boiled to make a strong and frightful magic. No longer is the crucible hanging still above the fire, it sways from side to side. Softly at first, but gaining in strength. Arawn wonders what would cause this for he feels no wind. Then he sees.

Fingers creep over the lip of the crucible and slip down to find purchase.

He tries to scream but his throat is shut.

Dead hands push against the edge of the iron vessel and he sees blistered shoulders rise from the depths, and he sees that the head is bent so far down that all the bones of the neck protrude starkly.

He knows it's his sister even before she lifts her head. He doesn't want her to raise her head, doesn't want to look into her dead and boiled eyes, but he can't avoid it. Her head is rising, a head so seethed that only patches of vesicated skin remain, attached to which are strands of deep red hair, the same colour as Mother's. Hair of which she'd been so proud.

He tries to turn his eyes away from the rising head, but she suddenly lifts it with such violence that he hears her neck bones crack. A strangled scream manages to escape his throat as he looks at her. It's his sister, but all that remains of her face is bone and a few strands of clinging skin. The skull grins at him, but incredibly her eyes haven't changed. Still hazel, but more filled with hatred than he's ever seen them. Always they hold him as she pushes herself out from the crucible.

The grinning jaw opens, releasing a guttural noise that loosens Arawn's bowels, and even though there are no words, he understands what she is saying.

Sister-slayer. Sister-slayer. Sister-slayer.

And she's coming for him.

Help me! he thinks frantically because he cannot speak. *Help me escape from this!*

But she is out of the crucible now and lurching towards him, hands clutched up around her boiled and welted body as though she is cold.

Behind him the dead Druid shrieks his insane cackle.

Help me! Oh one true god, help me!

And the world is torn apart by thunder. Nothing exists but that noise, and without even looking, he knows that Gwynfor is destroyed.

But his sister still approaches, anger blazing like hell-fire in her eyes. And there are others there now, other figures that he recognises, come to help his sister destroy him.

Mother. Rosmerta. Sulis. Epona. Sirom. Still more women come, come to aid his dead sister in his destruction, and always that noise emanating from her throat, and he hears it with his bowels not his ears for the thunder is too loud.

She is so close now he smells her rank breath, and her arms creak outwards to grab at him, and all the other women he knows—treacherous, evil whores—descend upon him.

But before he is devoured totally by them the thunder releases a bolt of lightning and fire flares up around them, engulfing them, swallowing them greedily. He feels the fire, its terrible heat, but he knows he is safe from it. This is the fire of the one true god, purifying fire, and those who are already pure need not fear it.

He revels in their screams of pain, in watching their bones blacken and twist, and he laughs. But this is no cackling of an insane Druid, it's the joyful laughter of the righteously sane.

For the one true god is come to save him from the evil that is women.

* * *

Dawn arrived and Arawn woke peacefully with the dry smell of stale straw in his nostrils. For a blessed moment he thought himself back in Trahaearn's barn, but he heard porridge bubbling in a cauldron. Nia would never have allowed porridge to be cooked outside her kitchen. Raising his head he saw a tumble-down hut surrounding the hearth-fire which heated his fast-breaking repast.

He let his head drop back. Not in Cantiaci. Not even in Lutetia any more because of Thrax's deceitful whore. He didn't know where he was, and it was only good fortune that had led him to this dwelling. Good fortune of the one true god.

"I told you, you're not a slave any more," said Arawn, walking over to the hearth-fire. "You're not a slave!" he yelled, kicking the cauldron from its hanging, spilling simmering oats across the floor. "I need to piss." He marched to the east-facing doorway that led out to nothing but fields.

There were peasants in Brython, of course there were, but the squat building that he'd secured gave a whole new meaning to peasantry. Likely it was square once, but the wattle-and-daub from which it was built was so weather-beaten and worn, and so patched-up that its original shape was lost. The thatch was riddled with mice, and doubtless the rain would seep through—except he'd never known the moon of claim-time to be so hot as it was in these southern lands.

Not too far from the hut was a copse of trees, perfect for completing morning ablutions, and doubtless where the owners of the pathetic dwelling chopped their firewood, if the axe was anything to go by. Funny how he hadn't noticed that yester-evening.

The bodies of the ancient couple were more or less where he'd left them, although there was some evidence that they had been investigated during the night by foxes, maybe wolves, or whatever nocturnal dogs prowled these parts of Gaul. He walked past them and relieved himself against the trunk of a tree. It was no wonder their home was in such bad repair, considering the age of the bonded woman and man. Even more surprising that they'd still been alive. At least, until Arawn had arrived.

Astonishment had met his entrance, as he was sure it would, and they'd both gabbled something at him in their peasant tongue which may or may not have been threats and curses. Such nonsense worried him less than their presence did.

The old man, at least in his fifties, fell to the floor motionless after one back-handed swipe; and after shrieking like a storm-gale for a few heartbeats, his ancient wife followed her husband's lifeless footsteps. Her neck broke with a satisfying snap when he struck her and she crumpled to the floor as though all her bones had vanished.

Despite both being head and shoulders shorter than he was, their combined weight had surprised him when he dragged them to the copse close to their house. Not wanting nocturnal scavengers to come rummaging close to the dwelling, he'd pulled them in as far as he could; he was exhausted, he wanted to sleep, and the thought of fighting off a wolf made vicious through hunger hadn't appealed to him. Inside, a fire already burned in the hearth and a cauldron of porridge stewed above it. He'd eaten half of it before collapsing on the straw mattress into his troubled sleep.

Pissing done, laces tied, he walked back to the hut, picking up the axe as he passed it. Old and ugly as it was, it still had a keen edge and was well made. For now, his tiredness had to be ignored so he could keep moving. He wasn't running away any more, and that pleased him. No, he was travelling. Dexs, the aged protector of Rome living in the necropolis in Lutetia, had told him there were others like him who admired the Romans and their one true god. The Bagaudas he'd called them, and Arawn intended to find them.

Except he didn't know where to look. Dexs had said they inhabited a town called Lugdunum in the southern lands of Gaul. But south was big. It was a pity that he'd not had time to go back and visit the old man, ask more questions; yet travelling south by the direction of the sun was not a complicated task for he'd spent his youth journeying, guided by sun and stars, and though the land beneath him was different, the sky above him wasn't.

"Take what you want," he said, stepping back through the dwelling's entrance. "It's time to go." He took all the food that was left in the hut—mostly hard root vegetables and stale oatcakes—and wrapped them in a cloth. He found a small hide sack which had a hole cut out of the top of it, allowing it to be looped over a shoulder. Something the peasant used to carry his midday meal in, perhaps, when he went out to till his fields. He stuffed the cloth-wrapped food into it, and then poked through the knives that the woman used to cut her vegetables and skin her meat. They may not be any good as weapons, but they might prove useful in the wilds. He had to eat, after all. Reaching in to his tunic, he pulled out the remaining gold that the bitch-princess had gifted him with before she betrayed him, and added it to the sack.

"Don't stamp out the fire. I'll use it to send a message in case we have any friends hereabouts." He knew the ancient couple weren't believers in the one true god because he'd found a woven Brigid doll in the hut, left over from Imbolc all those moons ago. Dry as tinder it was, and this he held in the hearth-fire until its head caught alight, and then he threw it onto the straw mattress cot which lay just to the right of the entrance, and kicked at the hearth-fire so that the burning charcoals could feed their flame to the rest of the hut.

By the time he'd walked halfway across the field, the dwelling was burning merrily, snapping and cracking intermittently with a sound like the old woman's breaking neck, and when Arawn turned around to look the thatch collapsed, sending up a shower of sparks; beauty which was wasted in the dawn of a new day.

"For the one true god," he said, and continued on his way.

* * *

"They'll be mighty warriors," said Arawn, "willing to fight and die for the one true god. Although, none of us will die because we are blessed by the one true god. Blessed is he who comes. And we'll be welcome amongst them, for have we not committed ourselves to the one true god?"

Benedictus qui venit. Those who welcome Me into their hearts will be blessed by Me. When you find the Bagaudas you will be blessed.

"They'll welcome us," he continued, "and I won't have to run any longer. We'll have a home where we're welcome, with no women to betray us, and we'll spend our lives carrying out the burning will of the one true god."

You'll be a king among mortals and all will kneel before you, Arawn. Women will quake with terror and men will flock to serve you. When you find the Bagaudas your life serving the one true god will be blessed.

He smiled, feeling pleased. Boy had come back to him after a long absence, and while he was glad to see him, he wished his old friend didn't look quite so rotten. His pale skin clung to his bones too tightly, and his clothes looked as though they'd crumble to dust as soon as they were touched, but it didn't matter. Soon they would be amongst the Bagaudas, he felt sure of it. One fat moon had passed since leaving Lutetia, and the current one was waxing gibbous. How many moons had fattened and died since that fateful Samhain night? Eight, perhaps as many as nine. He couldn't be sure.

"When I travelled with bitch Mother and my cowardly father," he said to Boy and the sky and the hot breeze, "every passing moon would take an age. Now they seem to be turning faster than I can count them. Yet when I think back to … that night, it seems like another lifetime. And perhaps it was," he said, pushing through the tall grass he currently traversed. "That was a life before the one true god. Through death and fire I've been reborn into my new life. One where the moons pass faster."

Finally he came to the end of the tall grass and the sun was well past noon; hunger gnawed at the pit of his belly.

Looking around at the endless landscape he said, "Good a place as any to stop." The noon meal was meagre, and Arawn didn't much like his raw root vegetables, but he had no wish to build a fire and boil water in order to cook. Food was food, and soon there would be as much meat and cheese and hot bread as he could want, but only when they found the Bagaudas. For now, stale oat cakes and raw vegetables would suffice.

The stop was short, and Arawn was on his feet even before he'd finished chewing his last mouthful. He smiled as he stood for Boy had raised his bony arm and was pointing back along the leagues they'd already covered. "Not far to go now, but not that way. The one true god leads me now."

* * *

By the time the sun was setting, and just as Arawn's spirits were dampening at the sight of the flat lands that stretched out ever onwards in front of them, he saw it. Judging the distance was difficult in the unchanging surroundings, but he knew that the building sitting on the horizon was Roman. Thatched wattle-and-daub didn't glow like that in the sunset.

"The one true god truly guides me," he said, throwing a look towards Boy. Would he have seen such a sight if he'd followed his advice? No! There was no going back for Arawn.

The sun was perched now upon the western horizon and the Roman building lay directly to the south. "Perhaps if I run, I'll reach it before night falls, and there the Bagaudas will welcome me with warm fires and hot food."

But full night descended and covered him well before he reached it, much to Arawn's bitter disappointment; he had to slow his pace to a careful walk. Even more galling was the fact that the darkness remained complete. He knew the house lay directly before him—he could see its ghostly shape in the light of the gibbous moon. Surely, though, by now fires would be lit?

"Might as well go in." His voice was brought low by the size of the building looming over him. "Better to sleep in there than amongst wild beasts."

He walked through what clearly had once been a garden,

though now it was so overgrown that Arawn found it difficult to imagine what it must have looked like so many ages ago. In the centre was one of those fountains that Thrax had told him about, a magical device that could make water fall upwards; but it, too, was choked and twisted by vines and weeds.

The moon's light cast silvery-white shadows all across the garden and building, and Arawn noticed, with some surprise, that the entrance to this marvellous building was not too dissimilar to the one the bitch-princess and her spoilt royal family lived in. Precisely centred, a wide staircase swooped up to a terrace whose roof was held aloft by an army of marching pillars. There was a wooden door, all carved with patterns and boasting an impressive metal knob that gleamed faintly in the moonlight. It was a wonder no one had stolen it yet, but the first sign of life was a full day's march away, and that sign was now extinguished. He briefly remembered the dead old couple and smiled before returning his attention to the Roman house. It even had many of its shutters hanging next to the windows, though the wood was clearly rotten and uncared for.

He pushed against the door and, to his surprise, it opened. Ahead was a corridor, several paces long, which he tiptoed along carefully.

And he walked into a cave.

The roof was so far up that he couldn't see it, in fact he couldn't see much of anything because it was dark inside, but the pillars that stood to attention on either side of the cave were impossible to miss. People had built this, men just like him with two hands and two legs; they had created a home so gargantuan that he couldn't even see the roof. The very notion stopped his breath.

The floor beneath him was tiled, and in the gloom he saw that patterns raced across them. He was willing to wager that they were made from the same tiny stones he'd seen in the great ruined building and the house of the dead in Lutetia.

He walked, feeling small and awed, wishing it were daylight so he could see the wondrous things around him.

"I'll sleep in here tonight," he said. "I'm sure there are many other rooms to see, but I don't know what kind of animals have made their homes here over the years. Better to wait until morning to explore. In the meantime, I should build a fire. There's bound to be a hearth here somewhere if this is the main hall."

Promptly his foot fell from beneath him and he clattered to the floor, cursing in surprise and terror, fearing he'd stepped into a trap of some kind; until he saw he'd only fallen into a shallow pit. It was straight-edged and square, tiled as neatly as the rest of the floor despite it being a hand-span lower. He saw a pleasing symmetrical pattern made from tiles light and dark, though the gloom stole any other colour from them. Even the shaft of moonlight couldn't help distinguish the true colours.

Moonlight…

Looking up, he saw that a square hole was cut into the roof, allowing him to see the night sky perfectly. "I think I've found the hearth. And that," he pointed to the open roof, "must be for the smoke. All I need to do is find some firewood. They certainly kept their hearths clean," he added, looking at the shallow tiled pit as he stepped out of it, impressed once more by the ingenuity of the Romans.

Leaving his sack of old food and the ugly axe beside the fire-pit, he went back out through the main entrance and into the front garden to collect the firewood. Plenty of bracken and broken branches from the trees were scattered around, sufficient for one night. In the morning he would explore thoroughly to find a better supply. He hadn't given up his idea of finding the Bagaudas, but he was inclined to stay a while in this magnificent old house, so well-preserved and free of the vandalism that had affected so many of the old Roman buildings in Lutetia.

He gathered a bundle by moonlight and dumped it in the

main entrance, then searched for more. The branches were small and damp, and he wasn't sure how long the fire would last. He had the axe he'd taken from the peasants' hut, but he was reticent to use it. Chopping wood would be deafening in such quiet and he didn't want to awaken any sleeping beasts from their lairs.

From inside the house he heard the wooden clatter of scattered logs. His bowels turned sour. Slowly he laid down his second armload of firewood. His first instinct was to run, but then he remembered leaving his sack inside the house—the food he could live without, but it still contained the rest of Rosmerta's jewellery. As much as he hated that treacherous bitch, he wasn't willing to give up precious gold.

"It's just a dog." One swift stroke from his axe would put paid to its threat, but first he had to retrieve it. That, too, was inside with his sack. "Protect me, one true god," he said, and crept towards the staircase.

The firewood was now strewn all across the corridor, and as he approached the main hall he kept his ears sharp for the sound of snuffling, scratching, or growling; anything that would reveal to him how many beasts he faced. As he walked out of the corridor and into the main hall, his bowels loosened in fear.

Several men stood in a rough semi-circle, and the shafting moonlight betrayed the blades they held in their hands. All of them were looking towards the main doorway; looking straight at Arawn.

No one moved, no one spoke. Arawn saw his sack lying next to the fire pit and he rushed towards it, but the men sprang instantly and before he knew what had happened he found himself pressed against the floor, his head singing in pain, his body winded.

"I don't remember inviting anyone in," said a low voice. The accent was strange, but Arawn knew enough to know it was angry.

Unable to speak for he still had no breath, Arawn tried to

struggle but the weight of several men pinned him down. He managed to move his head, though, in the direction of the voice.

"You're a stranger in these lands. And I don't like uninvited guests. I hope you're ready to die."

Panic filled him; he fought against the weight of the men on top of him but it was useless. Within a heartbeat, a cold blade was pressed against his neck and he imagined it slicing through his pale skin, releasing dark blood. The men restraining him laughed at his lamentable attempt to wriggle free and Arawn screamed in frustration—how could the one true god lead him so far only to have him slaughtered like a pig?

You believe I would have you slaughtered? Blessed is he who comes, Arawn; blessed is he who comes.

Arawn raised his head once more and bellowed in all his fury: "Benedictus qui venit!"

– 20 –

The moon of Elembiuos (Claim-time), 332 C.E.
Dubras, Cantiaci tribal lands, Brython

The spear-woman rapped on the door twice then entered. "We've searched the town, my lady, but found no Druids."

Sulis breathed in and out slowly, her expression sedate. "Did you question the townsfolk?"

"Indeed, but they noticed nothing. Some recall seeing a Fellow here or there a few days ago, but none any more recently than that. They must have left gradually."

"Yes," said Sulis.

"But where did they go?" The two women looked at young Airmed, but neither answered her question.

"Thank you," Sulis said finally to the spear-woman. "You may go."

"My lady." She bowed her head and, closing the door behind her, left Airmed alone with her mother in the council chambers.

The rest of the household would be eating dinner right now, thought Airmed, and the waft of roasted pheasant and pig that came in when the spear-woman had opened the door still lingered in the candle-lit room. It smelled good, but her appetite had disappeared along with the Druids.

"How could this have happened? Before my very eyes... How can no one have noticed anything?" Her mother was walking slowly around the great oak table, which shone as soft as honey in the glow from the candles, with her hands clasped behind her. Airmed knew these questions weren't intended for her; if they were, her mother would be still, looking at her directly. Nonetheless, Airmed did have something to say, something that her sister had mentioned so many moons ago now... *Could this be related to Rosmerta's distrust of Heddgwyn?* But if she spoke up she might implicate Emrys, her beloved brother, for wasn't he even now pilgrimaging with the Arch Druid?

"But it makes no sense," Sulis continued. "Why would our Druids vanish after the news from Trinovantes reached us?" She stopped walking and placed her hands on the table. "What do you make of it, my daughter?"

She pulled her cloak tighter about her. She hadn't had time to take it off after she'd burst into the main hall and told her mother of the Druids' disappearance, and now she was glad of that. Though the shutters hanging from the many windows in the chamber were closed, the night breeze still reached its cold fingers in to chill the air, and no fire had been set because this room hadn't been intended for use this evening.

"I wish Rosa were here," Airmed said.

Her mother's calm mask of office came off instantly and she smiled at her. It wasn't a joyous smile for within there was sadness, but her mother's beautiful face shone all the more.

"These are troubled times," she said softly. "And ones I hadn't foreseen. Perhaps I've been so obsessed with my desire to unite Brython under one ruler that the gods decided to remind me that our fate is in their hands, not our own."

"You think this is the gods' doing?"

"Perhaps." She shrugged her shoulders slightly, then indicated a chair to Airmed. "Let's sit. I would talk with you for a while, my child."

Airmed nodded and pulled a chair out from under the table. Made all of oak, it was as heavy as it was well made. She perched on the side of it, so that her shoulder rested against the back, all carved with figures and creatures from so long ago that people had forgotten what they were. Sulis sat in the grand chair at the head of the table, looking nobler than Airmed had ever seen her, and she felt too young for this. They looked at each other.

"Your sister may not be here," Sulis said, "but you are; and you are my daughter, born of warrior-queens with the same noble blood running through you as it does Rosmerta, as it does me. I would have your counsel and listen very well."

She felt her cheeks heat slightly at such praise but she kept contact with her mother's eyes. She was young, yes, but that didn't mean she knew nothing, didn't mean she was incapable of helping. Wasn't it she who had alerted her mother to the Druids' disappearance after all?

"There is something you should know." Her voice was quiet, but her mother straightened as though she had shouted. "It was something Rosa told me before she left to go on the hunt for the sister-slayer."

"Tell me."

"She swore me to secrecy until she could prove her suspicions, but she's not here, and can neither prove nor disprove anything. In light of all that's happened today, I suppose..."

Sulis said nothing, only kept her gaze fixed on her daughter.

After a deep breath Airmed said, "Rosa doubted Heddgwyn's loyalty."

She expected her mother to slam her hand down on the table for speaking so ill of the Arch Druid, but instead a frown clouded her eyes. "She had broached such to me also. What did she say to you?"

"His refusal to back the bonding between us and the Atrebates after the attempted rebellion led her to distrust his motives. She didn't understand why it was suddenly unacceptable when it hadn't been before. So one day at dinner, I suggested she speak to Emrys to see if he would help her find out."

Sulis raised an eyebrow. "You had your brother observe his father, the Arch Druid, so he could tell your sister what he was doing?"

The flush came back, but stronger this time. "I didn't want to cause any trouble, but Rosa was so concerned, and I just thought Emrys would help ease her mind."

"Go on." To Airmed's relief, her mother was smiling.

"Rosa said that she would, and I don't know what, if anything, passed between them; but a few days later Heddgwyn decided to take Emrys on a pilgrimage, one that wasn't even discussed with you first."

"Druids don't have to ask permission for any of their undertakings, you know that."

"I do, but," she paused. "They do anyway. They might not ask permission, but if any Druid were to leave Cantiaci for any reason, they always tell you that they're going, don't they?"

Sulis thought for a moment, then nodded. "Yes."

"But Emrys didn't even say goodbye to me. Rosa had already left, and I'd barely even seen him at the surrogate bonding feast we held, and the next morning he was gone."

"You think, perhaps, his father knew of his plot with his sister?"

Airmed shrugged. "I don't know. It wasn't really a plot anyway, Rosa just wanted some information, and I'm not even sure that she managed to convince Emrys to help her find it. But it just seems like a lot of coincidences to me; first the Arch Druid leaves without saying anything, then the rest of the Druids are nowhere to be found. It might mean nothing, but Rosa was worried that Heddgwyn was planning treason, and if he were, wouldn't it stand to reason that the rest of the Druids would be involved too?"

Silence while her mother digested all this information. "And no one thought to come to me?"

Airmed winced. "Rosa would have, I'm sure, but she needed certainty. Accusing an Arch Druid of treason is a serious crime, isn't it? Regardless of who makes the claim. But then she left. Perhaps I should have told you sooner, but with the surrogate bonding and the Trinovantes and everything else that's happened… I'm sorry."

"No need. I understand your sister's reticence, and I certainly don't hold you responsible." She smiled again, and Airmed released a breath she hadn't realised she'd been holding. "And it may all just be coincidence, but it's better that we know everything. Is there any thing else you think I should know?"

"No, Mother, that's everything. I swear if I had other news I would tell you."

"Good. But we still haven't solved the mystery of our vanishing Druids," she said. "What are your thoughts on that? With all that you know, I would hear what you think."

But Airmed had no time to answer for the door was rapped upon so loudly that it shook.

Sulis stood up at once, and Airmed followed suit. "Enter," the warrior-queen said.

The aroma of roasted meat wafted in again, this time accompanied by the loud clattering of dishes and chattering of a contented household at dinner. It was a pleasant sound, warming, and Airmed wondered briefly how long such simple pleasures would last, for the spear-woman who stood framed in the doorway looked very concerned. No, more than that; she looked scared. But not as much as the bedraggled woman who stood next to her.

The moment the door opened to reveal the spear-woman and her charge, Sulis, already standing, swept over to them, her heavy woollen dress softly clapping behind her in the wake of her walking.

"You bring me news?" she said.

"Yes, my lady," said the spear-woman. "She came into the hall not moments ago claiming she had news from Trinovantes."

Sulis threw a quick glance to Airmed before turning back. "Thank you," she said to the spear-woman. "You may leave her with me."

"My lady," she said, bowing her head and walking away.

"Please, come in," Sulis said softly to the guest. "You look worn and tired. May I offer you refreshment?"

"No, thank you, my lady," the woman said, and Airmed heard plainly that she was fighting to keep control of her voice.

"Be seated," said Sulis, indicating the chair to the left-hand side of her own, "and tell us what brings you here."

"My name's Mair, my lady, and I'm a member of the royal household in Trinovantes… Was a member," she corrected herself, then looked down at the table for moment. "I would have you know that I tried desperately to persuade Sirona Warrior-Queen to accept your aid—we used to be very close—but she refused to listen. Even accused me of treason for loving the Cantiaci." She shook her head, then covered her eyes with a hand.

"You're among friends here," Sulis said soothingly. "You can tell me your tale. I would aid Trinovantes in any way. I said that to your warrior-queen and I say it to you, too."

Mair was controlling herself admirably, Airmed thought. To have suffered a raid by the Picts and lose her warrior-queen, then make the journey across to Cantiaci alone. If *she'd* had to face the same tribulations she'd be fit to do no more than gibber. She looked at their guest closely. Though she was grubby from travel and her clothes were dishevelled, they were certainly rich and well made. Not a member of the royal family, perhaps, but certainly of the nobility.

"Thank you," said Mair. "And I tell you freely that ever I told Sirona this animosity 'twixt you and us was too ancient to be continued. And of all our neighbours it was only you who pledged aid against the Picts." She breathed deeply before speaking again. "Before, she would listen to me. I don't say that she was changing her mind about befriending you because I don't think my words are pretty enough to be persuasive. But she would listen and smile, and never promise to punish me for treason."

"She accused you of treason?" Airmed asked, incredulous. "Just for talking of us?"

"Only once, but yes. Recently. I would say, perhaps four moons past. We'd heard of the bonding between you and the Atrebates and she became convinced that you would seek to conquer her lands."

"From whom did she hear news of the bonding?" asked Sulis.

"Timan," said Mair. When her two hosts looked at her questioningly she added, "Our Arch Druid."

"No," whispered Airmed on an indrawn breath. "Mother, this means—"

"Airmed." She spoke her daughter's name quietly but the warning was unmistakeable.

"I don't understand," said their guest, looking at each of their faces.

"There is a matter we were discussing prior to your arrival, and it may or may not be linked to your story. I would hear the rest of it first before I draw any conclusions," said Sulis. "How is it that your Arch Druid Timan knew of the bonding between Cantiaci and Atrebates? I had not intended on keeping our union secret, but I knew timing was crucial considering our…reputation…in the world."

Mair looked confused. "Timan heard it from a Fellow, another Druid."

"From your tribe?"

"No, he didn't say where the Druid came from, but he told Timan that you were bonding with the Atrebates and had intentions of growing your queenship."

"Mother, it can only have come from a Druid of our tribe or the Atrebates. No one else knew."

"Perhaps, although there is no secrecy amongst the Druids."

"I know, but on matters of state isn't it in their interest to keep secrets until they're ready to be revealed? Warring tribes are no good for Druids either." She slammed her hand on the table. "Rosa was right!"

"Rosa?" said Mair, looking thoroughly bewildered.

"That is another matter," said Sulis. "Perhaps leaking our news to your Arch Druid was intended, but it doesn't help us with your current situation."

Mair's eyes widened. "It might."

"I speak of the Pictish raid, Mair, and the slaying of your warrior-queen." Sulis spoke slowly, as though she thought Mair hadn't understood her. Or as though she didn't understand herself.

"So do I," Mair whispered. "By Boudica and all the old gods…"

"What?" Alarm was clear in Sulis' voice now. "What is it?"

The woman from Trinovantes looked up at them with wide eyes that were as auburn as her hair. Beautiful and strange, thought Airmed, surprised at how she could be so distracted at this time of crisis.

"The Druids," said Mair. "The Picts left but the Druids stayed." Airmed looked at her mother, but the warrior-queen seemed intent on not interrupting the woman's words. "More and more Druids. I never thought anything of it before, but now—" She shook her head, as though in disbelief of her own words. "When Sirona returned from her meeting with you on the borders of our lands she returned with more Druids than the number she left with, I'm sure of it. And only a few days ago, scores of Druids arrived in Trinovantes." She stopped and tears filled her auburn eyes.

"I don't understand what that has to do with the Pictish raid," Sulis said softly.

"They said," she paused and breathed deeply. "When it was clear that the Pictish boats were here to raid us, the Druids said that they would cast spells to protect our lands. They sent the spear-women away from their posts along the coast so that they could work their magic. That's why I assumed all the new Druids entered our lands; so they could protect it from attack."

"But the Picts defeated them?" Sulis was astounded.

"So we thought, for the Picts arrived early in the morning and half the settlement was ablaze before we realised what was going on. Some women and children were taken, as slaves no doubt, but mostly they were just slaughtered in their beds." Her voice caught. "Though, incredibly, the men escaped. The majority of the Picts stormed Sirona's compound. There were spear-women on duty, of course, but they were outnumbered, and though they killed many Picts, they were overcome. Then the enemy went directly to Sirona's chambers, I saw them—hundreds, wielding axes and spears and screaming in their strange tongue. They ran straight past my chamber to Sirona's, and I heard her scream out our war cry, heard the sounds of battle, but she was one and they were many and too soon her battle cry was stilled." This time her voice crumbled and tears overspilled her eyes.

"Boudica curse the murdering bastards," Sulis whispered.

But Mair didn't hear her. "And I just hid," she continued, her voice a whispered wail. "I hid under my bed in terror as they came back through, screaming their triumph, and I listened to them slaughter the rest of the household."

"You could not have defeated them," Airmed and her mother said in unison.

Mair looked at them and smiled sadly, more tears overspilling her eyes as her cheeks moved. "Perhaps not, but I could have killed two, maybe three or four before they cut me down. I could have fought. But instead I hid like a coward. Like a man."

"Hiding from an enemy that numbers hundreds is not cowardice," said Sulis. "If you were cut down, you couldn't tell us your story; now you're here, and we can help you. So please, finish your story. After all you've faced, you deserve to."

Mair nodded, though she didn't look convinced. "When the noise of battle ceased, I crept out of my hiding place, but I was alone in the settlement. I expected to see all the gold and silver taken, all the plates and goblets, but all was still there. They took nothing from what I could see. I thought about checking Sirona's private chambers because I know she keeps her hoard hidden there, only I couldn't bear the thought of seeing her body. Then I remembered that the Picts had run out of her rooms unencumbered. It made no sense—why would they raid us, slaughter us then take nothing?"

Airmed was captivated by the story.

"Eventually I went in to Sirona. The royal compound was empty, dead, and I couldn't leave her body unprepared for Otherworld, so I made up my mind to take her to the altar of bones, and while she rested there I could take her hoard to the barrow and prepare a place for her with her ancestors."

In understanding, Airmed and her mother both nodded their heads.

"She died well with her sword in hand, and when I wrapped her body in a sheet to take her outside I left her sword with her. The altar of bones is on the far western side of the settlement, and it took me some time to take her there, but eventually I laid her body open to the elements. I prayed to Boudica, her daughters, and all the old gods to take her soul and keep it with them. And that was when the Druids arrived."

Airmed sat up sharply and looked across at her mother. Her eyes had widened but otherwise her face betrayed no other emotion.

"Tell me of the Druids," she said.

"They came as though they were victorious," said Mair, then shook her head. "They weren't singing or drinking like spear-women after winning a battle well fought, but they weren't mourning either. When I escaped and came to you, I saw that the town and many villages across our lands had been burned, and hundreds of bodies of women and children lay slaughtered. And the silence of the settlement would have told the Druids it was utterly defeated. Yet they seemed...unconcerned. They were talking, though I heard not what they said, and some went off with horses from the stables and others stayed in the settlement.

There were no spear-women left, Sirona was dead, but all the Druids who'd said they'd protect our lands from the Picts with their magic were alive and well. And that was when I ran away."

"Because you knew you had been sorely betrayed," said Airmed angrily, thinking of Rhonwen, whom she'd loved as a sister. Had she disappeared with the other Cantiaci Druids to hasten the downfall of Trinovantes?

"Yes," said Mair, her lip trembling anew. "The Druids hadn't saved us from the Picts at all, did they? They let them in to slaughter us."

– 21 –

The moons of Elembiuos (Claim-time) – Edrinios (Arbitration-time), 333 C.E.
Deceangli tribal lands, Brython

"It surprises me that you two find so much to talk about," Emrys said to Heddgwyn who was walking back to the fire. The deeper they'd travelled into Deceangli lands, the rarer settlements became, and for several days the three pilgrims had slept under the stars. "I wonder how a wild man could possibly understand all the things an Arch Druid has to say."

"Oh it's not me who talks, my son," said Heddgwyn, smiling. The closer they drew to Ynys Afallach the higher his spirits rose. "I leave that to Emlyn."

"The wild man?" Emrys' voice was full of scepticism. "By all the gods and goddesses past and present, what he could he tell you that's so interesting?"

The Arch Druid chuckled. "He's a well-travelled man, he has many stories. And he has interesting ideas for the future."

Emrys snorted. "How can a man like that have any ideas for the future?"

"How can any man?" said Heddgwyn, raising an eyebrow.

The young Ovate sighed inwardly. There was no speaking to his father in this mood. He loved his secrets, and he was only content when he knew more than the people around him. Then he would take great pleasure announcing his stored knowledge, revelling in subsequent awed reactions.

Emrys wasn't stupid. He would never become an Arch Druid, but that was through lack of ambition rather than incompetence. He'd mastered the healing magics better than most of his peers, and no doubt he could curse an entire village if they believed strongly enough in his words. Which most people did. He understood that his knowledge was lacking when compared with someone like his father, for instance, but he knew when people were plotting something. And if the Arch Druid wasn't plotting something with the wild man then Emrys had even less wisdom than he thought, and had no right travelling to Ynys Afallach to become a full Druid.

And yet, he couldn't bring himself to ask his father directly. There was always the possibility that he would reveal all to him; but the likeliest outcome was outright refusal. He had to know more than everyone else, that was all.

"When is our guest due to leave our company?" Emrys asked, keeping his voice unconcerned.

"Soon," said Heddgwyn. "And we'll be on the final part of our journey to Ynys Afallach." He beamed at Emrys, then focussed his attention on the dancing flames of the fire.

Soon, thought the young Ovate, there will be no more wild man. But however soon his departure was, it wouldn't be soon enough.

* * *

"Thieving bastard!" Emrys roared. "Heddgwyn! The thieving bastard stole my horse in the night! I told you we couldn't trust him!" He was viciously pleased he'd been proved right at last. He stomped over to the Arch Druid in his pile of blankets and kicked at them, though not too hard. "Heddgwyn? Where are you?"

Rain had woken him early enough that dawn had yet to defeat the twilight. While it wasn't heavy, it was cold, and when it had spattered him into full consciousness he became painfully aware that he needed to relieve himself. He hadn't wanted to move to from his warm cocoon of hide blankets. The fire was nothing more than failing embers as the drizzle set to work hissing it out of existence, and the instant Emrys unwrapped himself he knew he'd be pierced on all sides by the sharp teeth of pre-dawn air. But his bladder had been insistent and he was powerless to do anything else but empty it.

Looking across the dying fire, he'd seen Heddgwyn still wrapped deep in his bundle of blankets and considered waking him. But the shivering started and the call from his bladder became more urgent. He found a boulder close to the camp that he could hide behind and piss against, and the relief gave him some comfort against the cold. Lughnasadh was only a moon behind them and by rights he shouldn't have felt so chilled; but the days, while warmer, were getting shorter and the nights were getting longer and up here in the higher Deceangli lands with the rain falling on him there was no denying the light half of the year was drawing to a close.

His hands, palsied with cold, were incapable of completing even the simplest task, but eventually he managed to tie the laces at the front of both pairs of leggings he wore underneath his robes, not to mention the woollen vest and tunic he'd added to keep the top half of his body warm as they passed the nights in the hills and valleys of the northernmost lands of Deceangli.

Empty and dressed, he'd walked back over to the camp, and that was when he'd noticed one of the horses had disappeared. His horse, in fact; along with the sacks of food he'd been carrying. His cries of "thieving bastard!" came then, but his accusations had gone unheard because the Arch Druid wasn't at their camp either.

"Heddgwyn!" he called out again, but the vast landscape sucked at his voice. With no idea what to do, he stomped over to his makeshift bed, picked up both of the cloaks he'd slept on, and wrapped them around himself. Then he sat down heavily on his pile of blankets.

"Now what?" he said. "Thieving bastard wild man has run off with my horse and all the food, and likely killed Heddgwyn and hidden his body somewhere. I knew he couldn't be trusted! And now, I'm stuck in the middle of freezing wet nowhere, with no idea how to go on or go home." He felt his anger turn to self-pity but he was helpless to fight it while the sun was still hidden by charcoal-grey clouds wringing out heavier rain.

"Better to start the fire before the wood gets completely soaked than sit there and rant at yourself, isn't it?"

Emrys lifted his head from his hands but he didn't have the strength to spin around and glare at the owner of that voice. "If you're going to go off wandering in the pre-dawn twilight, I'd rather you woke me to tell me."

"Duly noted."

"And that thieving bastard stole my horse and all our food."

"No, he didn't."

Emrys sighed. "He didn't? Are you going to tell me that you gave it to him?"

"Yes." The Arch Druid sat by the dark fire and placed a pile of surprisingly dry wood on it. He took his fire striker and tinder-pouch from a pocket in his robe and set fire to it, smiling as the flames spread quickly and easily. "Nothing quite so magical as a fire striker, is there?"

Emrys scowled at him. "And I suppose we're going to magic ourselves some food and me a horse for the remainder of our journey?"

"Don't be ridiculous. Magic is a sacred art." The Arch Druid shifted closer to the now dancing fire and stretched out his hands towards it. "Emlyn hasn't got all of the food; my horse will be carrying what's left of it. And we'll both be walking the last the part of our pilgrimage: mountains and valleys are no places for riding.

"Now," Heddgwyn continued cheerfully. "I suggest you make yourself useful and bring us some dried meat and nuts on which to break our fast. You'll find them in the bags already packed on my steed."

"Will you tell me the reason for Emlyn's not-unwelcome but

rather unexpected departure while we eat?"

The Arch Druid thought for a moment, glancing up at the sinking clouds. "No," he said, and returned his eyes to the flames.

* * *

If Emrys had thought the journey so far was difficult, with his saddle sores and stiff limbs from sleeping on cold hard earth, it paled when compared to the hike through the mountains. Days of climbing ever upwards, with nothing in front of his face but a wall of solid earth, would open up into a valley of singular loveliness, fully green now they were deep into the light half of the year. Each time he believed that their pilgrimage was finally at an end, the valley would slope up into more hills and the task began all over again.

The fat moon of Elembiuos passed, waned gibbous and disappeared into the new moon of Edrinios, arbitration time. If he were in the rich lands of Cantiaci, he had no doubt that already he'd be witnessing the annulment of bondings forged at Imbolc which hadn't pleased the parties involved, or listening to Druids pass judgements on land claims or traders suspecting they had been wronged. But here, in the high tribal lands of the Ordovices none of that was necessary, not even for the renowned Heddgwyn who was the most just arbitrator across the lands, for several nights had passed now with no evidence of a single settlement.

"By the time the fat moon arrives," said Heddgwyn one afternoon as they rested in the wind-breaking arms of a valley, "we'll see Ynys Afallach."

"That's only three nights away," said Emrys.

"Yes. And it pleases me that you'll be laying your eyes on the sacred isles for the first time under the masculinity of the Gort Moon."

"The Ivy Moon," whispered Emrys, recalling his lessons. Though everyone counted passing time with the waxing and waning of the moons, only Druids understood the moon's magical properties. "Under the Ivy Moon is the time for healing and protecting against danger." He looked at his father. "Why would I need protection against the sacred isles?"

Heddgwyn chuckled. "It's also a time for exorcism. Your Ovate soul will be driven out to be replaced by your Druid soul. On Ynys Afallach you'll find more knowledge than you can possibly imagine, and when we leave you'll be much changed by it. A young man you'll be when you arrive, but a wise Druid you'll be when you leave."

Emrys stared at him. He knew well the three levels of Druidry; the Bard, the Ovate, the Druid. Already he was an Ovate, senior to the bards whose poems and songs kept the histories alive for the common folk and ensured their tribal ancestry was never forgotten. Emrys, as an Ovate, had moved into the higher magics of healing, reading the stars and simple divination. But he would soon be lifted to the third level, Druid, where the most learned commanded the ancestors and spoke with the old gods. And here the gift of prophecy was learned. He shivered.

"Am I ready for that?"

"Of course you are," Heddgwyn said simply. "You are my son; and one day you'll be a greater Druid than even I am."

* * *

"Do you see it?" Heddgwyn whispered.

Emrys nodded. "I see it."

The sacred isle of Ynys Afallach.

Even the clouds had understood the importance of this moment and the sky was clear, allowing the Gort Moon to shine brightly down, splashing the isle with silver and coruscating the waters around it, mirroring the stars in the firmament above. All his hurts were forgotten, all his discomforts a distant memory, all his vexations vanished.

It was breathtaking.

They had walked all through the night to reach this point, and Emrys realised that his father had timed it just so, wanting his pupil the Ovate, his son, to see Ynys Afallach at this very moment when the Gort Moon was at his highest.

"And under the Ivy Moon shall my Ovate soul be exorcised," he whispered. Heddgwyn looked at him, and smiled.

The walk down from the outcrop on which they had viewed Ynys Afallach passed like a dream. It was no wonder the Arch Druid had never complained while they struggled through mountains which became valleys, and valleys which became mountains; he knew what awaited him at the end of his trials. Emrys knew he would gladly make that journey a thousand times over if it meant he could look upon the silver-shining isle again, and again, and again. He was walking ahead of his father, eager to reach and cross the waters of the Afon Menai, and feel the power of Ynys Afallach under his feet. No full Druid ever spoke completely of his or her pilgrimage, never revealed the true wonder of the place to those who had not yet made the voyage; for it was a journey that had to be fulfilled alone, experienced by the individual, just as they made the journey from Bard to Ovate to Druid. All knew of the power of Ynys Afallach, but only those who had made the pilgrimage to the sacred isle as an Ovate and returned as a Druid ever understood what that power felt like.

Eager as he was, however, when they reached the thin shore of the Afon Menai that separated the sacred isle from the mainland, Heddgwyn took his arm.

"Wait," he said. "You must remember what happened here. You must feel it."

For a moment, Emrys was confused, but he allowed his father

to turn him towards the isle without questioning him.

"Clear your mind," said the Arch Druid. "And open your soul-eyes."

He obeyed, and staggered under the weight of the force that hit him.

Death. Slaughter. Desecration.

He saw images of long-dead Druids on the shore of Ynys Afallach screaming their curses at the Roman horde who stood where Emrys now was. He saw them chant and hurl and screech their magic, calling for the gods to bring them protection, and strike down the invaders. He saw them all; men, women, and children, all trying to defend their isle with their ancient magic while the Romans stood watching. Emrys turned his head and saw them, the Romans, standing in impossibly straight lines; uniforms gleaming, short swords bristling, shields brightly painted with the sigils of Rome.

And he smelled their fear. Rank it was, like stale sweat; for they had never seen such magic performed, and they feared the gods of this strange land where male and female warriors had blue skin and stiff, white hair and ran naked and screaming into battle like demons, inviting death. The Romans feared the gods that such a people worshipped, and feared those priests who could call upon those gods. They did not want to fight such priests and gods, but they had no choice.

Emrys saw the line, no, the *wall* of Romans step forward, and their step was so definite that he stepped forward too, transfixed by the clarity of the vision. They stepped forward again, and again. Marching now; in time, left-right, swords drawn, left-right, shields high. Not once did that wall falter, their shields touching those on either side, swords poking underneath like a terrible, beautiful, deadly machine. A war machine. Built only to kill.

He watched as they crossed the shallow, low-tide waters, heard the frenzy of the Druids' chants as their enemy drew inexorably closer, heard the panic as the children ran in and out of the legs of the adults.

Massacred, every last man, every last woman, every last child. Swords rose and fell, becoming slicker and blacker after every downward arc. The chanting became screams of fear and pain, which became wails and groans of the dying, which became the eerie silence of the slain. An unnatural quiet, an unwanted calm.

The vision vanished, and Emrys was looking at the distant shore of Ynys Afallach, empty now save for the thick line of trees which fringed the isle. He fell to his knees, gasping.

"Why did the old gods forsake them?" whispered Emrys. Tears filled his eyes. "How could they allow such a thing to happen? The Romans were afraid! One sign from the gods and they could have saved an entire people!"

Slowly Heddgwyn knelt until he was beside his son. "The old Roman gods were stronger that day, and we must never forget that. We come here so we never forget."

* * *

A ferry waited for them. Tide was high and even though the strait was narrow the water was too deep for them to cross on foot. As they approached the shallow craft, a white-robed figure stood to greet them; and once again Emrys was struck by the accuracy with which Heddgwyn had organised this pilgrimage. Only now, at the end of it, was he aware of this.

"Heddgwyn," said the figure with evident pleasure in her voice. "It's good to see you again; and not before time. The distance since your last coming is great indeed."

"Ceinwen," said the Arch Druid. He handed the reins of his horse to Emrys, and stepped onto the ferry to embrace her. "These are busy times, as I'm sure you know." She nodded and smiled, then turned her face towards Emrys. "This is my son."

"Emrys," said he, startled at the fairness of the woman. In the moonlight, her skin was flawless and her eyes as dark as the waters lapping at the ferry. She looked much younger than Emrys' twenty-five summers, and he wondered how one so young could already have attained the highest level of Druidry.

"We're well met," she said, holding out her hand. He took it and climbed onto the ferry, leading the horse, which seemed quite at ease, behind him. "You've seen the vision," she said, looking at him intently. "I see it well in your eyes."

Emrys nodded.

"We must never forget it," said Ceinwen, echoing the words his father had said only moments before. Emrys shivered, but said nothing. When his father pulled gently at his arm, inviting him to sit on the bench next to him, he did so without pause.

The night was calm; the wind that had plagued them during their journey through the mountains had dropped, and the only movement in the Afon Menai was Ceinwen's long ferry-pole as she punted the three of them across to Ynys Afallach.

When they reached the shore, power once again overwhelmed Emrys. The memory of murder was strong here, but it was like a current in deep ocean; while a current can shape and move the ocean, the ocean itself is not made of only that one current. There was more to Ynys Afallach than ancient magic and remembrance of bloodshed; there was growth and new life. Rebirth from death. And that force was so powerful that he felt tears spring to his eyes.

"You will sleep well this night," said Ceinwen gently. "Your rooms have already been prepared for you. And when you wake, you will discover the true greatness of Ynys Afallach, though I see that you have sensed some of it already."

He nodded, then looked across to his father. He had removed the saddle and bridle from his horse, and Emrys went to help him carry his load. The Arch Druid accepted with a smile. Then he stroked the long muzzle of his steed, whispered softly to her, and she walked off into the trees as though she knew precisely where she was going.

"She's happy to be home," said Heddgwyn, looking at her with fondness as she went. "She won't be making the return journey; she's made that journey twice in her life and I think that's more than enough."

"And what about us?" said Emrys. "How long will we stay here?"

The Arch Druid smiled. "Now is not the time for answering questions. Now we let Ceinwen show us to our beds."

* * *

Emrys awoke when his father pulled open the hide door, spilling in the bright dawn light through the east-facing doorway. The sound of gulls filled the roundhouse and Heddgwyn smiled.

"It's been too long," he said. "Come here, Emrys, you must smell the fresh air! No tanner pit stench, no animal shit clogging up the pathways, no rotten refuse thrown to the ground by careless people—just clean air, salty sea and porridge."

"Porridge?"

"Porridge," Heddgwyn agreed. "To break our fast. We've a long day ahead of us, you especially, and we need to eat our fill before we start it."

Now that his father had mentioned it, Emrys realised the roundhouse was indeed filled with the aroma of cooking oats. He clambered up from his straw pallet, throwing his cloak over his shoulders. It was a bright dawn, but it was still chilly.

Heddgwyn handed him a wooden bowl of steaming porridge, generously laced with butter and honey.

"Ceinwen will be here presently," said Heddgwyn. "She'll be taking you to Bard's Island this morning while the tide is still low. Bring an extra cloak with you, just in case you get stuck there."

"Stuck?" Emrys lowered his bowl.

"The sea is capricious." His father was smiling. "Finish your porridge."

"I've had my fill, thank you," he said, quietly. "Where is Bard's Isle?"

Very shortly, he discovered that Bard's Isle lay just to the south-west of Ynys Afallach. Ceinwen accompanied Emrys and his father there, and the young Ovate felt a small sense of regret that he couldn't spend more time amongst the ripening apple trees on Ynys Afallach.

"It's no accident that the island is named after the first level Druidry," said Heddgwyn. "And don't be fooled by its small size. There's more there than you could possibly imagine."

He looked at his father, a hundred questions in his eyes, but the Arch Druid said no more.

"Come," said Ceinwen. "My boat is waiting."

It was a strange-looking isle indeed. The northern end was high and rounded while the southern end levelled out into flat lowlands that seemed to float on top of the sea. The more Emrys looked at it, the more it resembled the head of a great sea-bird that peered out from the water, its long bill just resting above the waters. In such a bright morning with calm waters surrounding it, it looked like a pleasant place. But he could well imagine it looking equally desolate if the weather were cold and ugly.

A blanket of birds circled above them, gulls and chough, razorbills and guillemots, all pierced the air with their calls. As they neared the first rocky outcrops of the island, Emrys saw a colony of grey seals basking in the now late-morning sun, for it had moved a fair distance across the sky while Ceinwen had navigated the boat across the choppy waters.

She beached the vessel on the lowlands, pulling out a sizeable sack as she stepped out of it. Emrys followed her.

"What's in the bag?" he asked.

"Food. You'll be here for a few days at least."

"By myself?"

She smiled, and her face was lovely. "You'll sense no

loneliness." She turned and walked towards the huge hill that dominated the hill's northern end.

"We're not going to climb to the top of that, are we?" said Emrys.

"No," said Ceinwen with a chuckle. "But we can if you wish to see the wonderful view."

"I'm not sure all the food in that sack would prepare me for such a walk."

This time Ceinwen laughed. "You crossed the mountains to reach Ynys Afallach. I'm sure you could manage Bard's Hill."

Emrys smiled. "You seem young for a Druid," he said, eliciting a look of surprise from Ceinwen. "I thought only full Druids could come to Ynys Afallach."

"Full Druids *leave* Ynys Afallach," she said. "You're an Ovate, are you not?"

Emrys nodded, feeling a little ridiculous.

"But I was born in Ynys Afallach," Ceinwen continued. "Some families of Druids stay on the isle to protect it. My ancestors were some of the first Druids to return to Ynys Afallach after the Roman massacre, and our duty has been to protect the isle and its magic ever since. But soon, for the first time in my family's history, we'll be leaving the island."

"Why?"

Her smile faltered a little and she walked a little faster. "What you don't know, you'll soon learn. It's not my place to tell you."

"Doesn't seem to be anybody's," he muttered under his breath, but let the matter drop.

The ground was rising now, and Emrys suddenly noticed that there was more to the hill face than only grass and lavender: there was also a door.

The frame and lintel were thick oak, wider than his forearm and twice his height. Oaken also was the door and studded with iron, with an iron door-knob that had a strange hole underneath it. Ceinwen reached into the front of her robe and pulled out a key so large that both ends poked out of her bunched fist. She inserted the key into the hole and turned it three times, each twist eliciting a sharp crack. Then she turned the door-knob and heaved against the door.

"Welcome to Bard's Isle," she said, and walked into the gloom.

Emrys followed.

Compared with the spacious doorway, the corridor was as narrow as his shoulders and only a hand higher than his head. It had the organic smell of freshly tilled soil; unsurprising, for it tunnelled through the very island itself. Wooden beams, most likely oak as the door and its frame, lined the walls and ceiling of the corridor at regular intervals.

"Close the door behind you," said Ceinwen.

"But we'll see nothing."

She took out a fire striker and wax taper from her bag and lit it. Emrys pushed the door closed. It was incredibly heavy.

The taper's light was barely visible from behind Ceinwen, but he saw her outline and that was enough for him to follow.

"We're approaching a stairway," she said. "Be careful."

"Who built all this?" The stairway was hewn into the living rock, and had been inscribed with runes of powerful magic.

"We did," said Ceinwen. "When Boudica drove the Romans from our shores and my ancestors returned to the isles we needed a place of safety for our knowledge."

"It must have taken generations."

"It did."

The stairway ended and Emrys had a sudden feeling of space reaching upwards and outwards. Ceinwen disappeared from his view, but soon a few spots of light sparked into existence. Wall-torches, Emrys thought. And then all thought ceased.

It was a vast cavern, but unlike anything he'd ever seen. Druids weren't famed for their ability to build, but inside Bard's Hill they had hewn with remarkable grace. The ceiling rose and fell in graceful arches; oak pillars, planted deep in the ground, soared up to meet them, and every one was covered in the same runic etchings he'd seen on the stairs. It was dry in there and cool, and though it smelled strongly of earth and rock, there was another unmistakeable aroma.

"Hide parchment?"

Ceinwen smiled. "Welcome to our library. All the histories of our lands are contained here, even before the time of Belenos, to our current time."

Emrys' mouth gaped open. "You recorded *everything?"*

"Everything but our most sacred lore. Magic would lose its potency if it were imprisoned on parchment, but you know that already." She smiled at him. "Come and see what the Bard of Bard's Island has to tell you."

He followed her through the cavern, and he knew they'd reached the centre of it when he saw a single pillar, thicker than any tree he'd ever seen. The bottom was oak as all the others, but the top half was stone reaching down from the top of the cave itself. The magic runes ran all the way up into the darkness until he couldn't see them any more.

"Behold the Bard," said Ceinwen, indicating the impossibly large pillar. "And here are his histories."

In concentric circles, pooling outwards from the base of the pillar were oaken chests, each one as high as his knee, but stacked on top of one another until they reached the height of his head. There was a gap, about shoulder-width, which led directly to the Bard, and as he walked through this he saw the concentric circles of chests were spaced apart by the same width. Then he realised that the chests weren't exactly chests. They didn't open at the top; that would be pointless for they were stacked on top of one another. The front of each had a clasp along the crest. He tugged one at random and saw that it pulled the fore-end down, revealing inside a neat stack of hide parchment scrolls.

"These are the earliest histories," said Ceinwen, indicating the strange circle of chests closest to the Bard. "The further you go out, the more recent the histories."

Emrys closed the chest door and read the runes engraved on the front of it. "Fearn Moon, 67," he said. "What does this mean?"

"Contained within that chest," said Ceinwen, "are the histories that began at the Fearn Moon, sixty-seven years after the birth of Belenos. Most people calculate the passing years from the time of Boudica's birth, but we calculate it from the birth of our first blessed sovereign in these isles, descendant of the sun god himself."

"The warrior-queens wouldn't accept a male god over the goddess Boudica."

"Indeed not," she said with a wry smile. "But it's our duty to remember all that came before her, and to remember the old gods, the true gods of Brython."

"What about all the histories before the birth of Belenos?"

Ceinwen led him to the Bard where she looked at his inscriptions lovingly for a moment, then bent down to the chest that sat next to the aisle. "This is the very first chest, containing some of our very first histories. Look at the inscription."

He did. "There's no moon, just numbers."

"Yes. One thousand, one hundred."

"What does it mean?"

"The number of years before Belenos was born."

Emrys' eyes grew wide. "Can I look inside?"

Ceinwen stood and moved aside for him to do so. He crouched and opened the clasp. Inside were only a very few scrolls, not of hide parchment but of woven reeds. He took one out and carefully unrolled it. The runes were faded, inscribed in rusty brown, perhaps animal blood; and though he knew they were runes, he couldn't read them. "This was written more than a thousand summers past?"

"Not quite." Ceinwen was smiling again. "But these are the

first scrolls that Druids wrote after they returned to Ynys Afallach after the Roman massacre, and so are hundreds of years old. The language is archaic, so it's no surprise you can't read it. There are only a few who can."

"Can you?"

"Of course."

"What does it say?"

"Only those who have learned the ancient runes can know that."

Emrys sighed. "Does my father know?" he said suddenly.

"Your father knows more than most. Many scrolls in this library were written by him, in fact, after his various journeys."

He raised an eyebrow. He hadn't realised his father was so famous.

"Now you must read and study. I'll be back for you before your food runs out."

"You're leaving?"

She nodded. "Time with the Bard is private. There's a pallet outside the circle of chests for you to sleep on. But when I return, you'll wish you could stay longer."

"Why here?" he said. Ceinwen raised an eyebrow in question. "Why keep all the histories here and not on Ynys Afallach? That's our sacred isle, isn't it?"

"Of course, and all know it. If people learned we had a great store of histories, where do you think they would search for it first?" She smiled at him once more and turned away, walking silently towards the stone staircase that led out to daylight.

He lost all track of time.

He read scrolls of ancient heroes who started the tribes of Brython with their prowess in battle.

He read of the coming of the Romans; how Cartamandua, queen of the Brigantes, a tribe now lost to the Picts, capitulated to Rome by sacrificing her husband. What his father had said was true then; not only the Cantiaci were guilty of welcoming the invaders...

He read how the Romans battled behind a shield wall, and that the blue-painted warriors of Brython would throw themselves against it and be slain by the Romans' short swords.

He read how Boudica, shamed and angered at her public beating and the rape of her two daughters at the hands of Roman legionnaires, started an uprising that would be their downfall. He read of her three successful battles, and how the fourth battle was won because a Druid from Ynys Afallach, who had been absent during the slaughter but had envisioned it, then tracked the Roman army marching under a leader called Suetonius Paulinus, forewarned Boudica that he intended to draw her army into a valley and slaughter them on a shield wall. So she fought to control her army's blood-lust enough that they could outwit them by splitting her army and attacking them from in front and from behind.

He read how Boudica declared that all tribes be led by women who were mothers and warriors as she herself was.

He read how men's worth was diminished after Boudica's deification, rising above all other gods. Many battles were fought and thousands of men slain until they submitted to their women forever.

He read how the first tribal queens would sacrifice their first newborn son to Boudica so she might bless them with girls to continue their bloodlines.

So much knowledge. It flowed like the blood of those slain in order to reach the present. He read like a starving man eats, and when Ceinwen came back he was surprised and a little saddened to see her. He'd barely touched the thousands of scrolls that lay here under the watchful guard of the Bard.

"Can I come back?" he said, surprised at how his throat rasped. But then he hadn't spoken for many days.

"Every time you visit us at Ynys Afallach you can come to visit the Bard," she said, smiling. "But now your presence is requested at the council of Druids."

"Why?"

"Because Heddgwyn would start the rituals of Druidry upon you."

"But I've only been here a handful of nights," said the Ovate. "I'm not ready."

Ceinwen smiled. "The rituals will take several moons and you will stay among us during the darkest ones. But we cannot delay."

"Why not?"

"Because time keeps turning, and war is coming."

– 22 –

The moon of Elembiuos (Claim-time), 332 C.E.
South of Lutetia, Gaul

"Benedictus qui venit!" Arawn cried again, and the pointed pressure at his neck eased a little. The knee in his back stayed firmly put, however.

"Where did you learn that?" The voice came from above him, the owner of the knee. His accent was slightly thicker than Thrax's had been, but Arawn understood him well enough. "Tell me!"

"Dexs," said Arawn. "Dexs of Lutetia."

There was a bark of laughter from nearby, and it echoed around the cavernous room. "Dexs! I thought that old bastard would be supping at the table of the one true god long before now!"

"Well he's not." Arawn's initial fear had subsided and he felt anger boiling in his belly. "And it was he who told me to come south and find the Bagaudas. I would say I had, seeing as how you know the phrase; but if you attack an unarmed man in the depths of the night, then you're not the warriors I thought you to be."

The voice from nearby protested at this, but the knee in his back eased off and Arawn was pulled up by the scruff of his tunic. He swung around to the face the man who'd shamed him. "Who are you?"

The man smiled. "I call myself Ardus," he said. "It means high, and I'm the leader of these warriors who you think so little of."

He stood a head taller than Arawn, and his dark hair, knotted with dirt, hung stiffly at his shoulders. From the moonlight shining in through the smoke-hole he could see his face was as filthy as his hair, what little of it that was visible behind his jagged beard. Despite that, it was difficult to guess his age. Certainly older than himself, Arawn thought, but whether he was twenty summers or forty, he didn't know. That his clothes were that old seemed possible however, as was the likelihood he hadn't washed for most of his life. Arawn decided to breathe through his mouth.

"And who are you?" said Ardus. "You're nothing more than a child; are you sure you should be out by yourself at night?"

The band of men surrounding them cackled and Arawn felt blood rush to his cheeks. His hands clenched into fists by his sides. He wished he had his axe.

"There's dangerous people in the wilds," said another voice, mocking. "Monsters. Bagaudas, they call them, and they'll rip your head off and drink your blood as it spurts from the hole in your neck!"

More crowing.

"My name is Arawn ap Emlyn," he said clearly, cutting through the derision. "And I've travelled from Brython, battling spear-women, pirates and godless folk to find the Bagaudas; and all I've found is a group of men who skulk around an empty house."

"An impressive boast, Arawn ap Emlyn," said Ardus. "But we aren't skulking here, we live here. We watched your progress all day, then you trespassed onto our property. What did you expect us to do? If you hadn't known the Benedictus, you'd be dead by now."

"Where's your friend?" a voice said the darkness. Arawn flinched. "We heard you talking, so where's your friend?"

Arawn looked around at them, allowing his eyes to wander far into the gloam. Boy had vanished again.

"Were you talking to yourself?"

"Enough, Nertos," said Ardus. "Our brother has journeyed long and from afar, and in the dark of night any voice is a comfort, isn't that so, Arawn ap Emlyn?"

"So long as it isn't pressing a knife to my throat."

Ardus laughed so loudly that at first Arawn was startled, but it was a joyous sound and he felt as though he were suddenly back on Nehalennia with Thrax and his sailing traders. "Then let us be well met, Arawn ap Emlyn. Now we know you're a friend you will feast with us. This way! I'm not freezing my balls off in the atrium when there's a fire waiting to be lit." He walked over to one of the darkened doorways to the left of the atrium—Arawn had never heard such a strange word—and ostentatiously pushed open the door and invited him in with a flourish. "Crix, start the fire, and you go and the meat, Tarvos." A shadowy figure walked off in the opposite direction. "And don't forget the wine!"

Moments later a merry fire blazed in the middle of the room, and Arawn saw five of his six captors clearly. But they weren't what interested him. "Why light the fire here and not in the hearth?" A rough circle of stones comprised the hearth in this room, and the ceiling was blackened with seasons of soot. The whole room stank of bonfire.

Ardus grinned, showing a mouth with many missing teeth. Ugly certainly, but friendly. "And where is the hearth, Arawn ap Emlyn?"

"It's not the pit out there then," Arawn said, gesturing towards the atrium with his head. "With the hole in the ceiling for the smoke to escape."

"No, friend, though that makes sense. No Roman house has a hearth."

"It doesn't?" said Arawn. All his previous anger and fear had disappeared now that he was learning more Roman lore. "How did they keep warm?" He thought of the fountains. "Magic?"

Ardus barked a laugh. "Almost. They built their fires underneath the floors," he stamped his foot, as though Arawn didn't know what a floor was. "And it heated the whole room without stinking it up. We haven't worked out how they managed to do it, so I suppose it is a form of magic. A clever secret that our people thoughtlessly expelled from these lands with all the rest of them."

A sullen silence fell over the Bagaudas, but fortunately the man Ardus had called Tarvos returned with a dead pig under one arm, and a pleasingly large vessel of wine under the other. It looked like a larger version of the urn Dexs had offered to him in Lutetia, though the base was more bulbous and the neck longer and thinner. Two little handles stuck out of the top of it like ears, looking barely big enough to carry the weight of such a large container and its contents. Regardless, it was quite beautiful.

"Food and wine!" said Ardus. "Let our guest and new friend drink first!" Wooden cups appeared, wine was poured, and Arawn was served first, an unusual experience for him. He took a draught and was stunned by the richness of its flavour; after such a long day and very little food, he felt instantly light-headed.

"Now you must meet the rest of my warriors," said Ardus when the cups had been refilled. "Nertos and Marka are my second and third in command," he said, pointing to two men across the fire. Both looked like they wouldn't be happy until they were brawling over Arawn's remains. "They're brothers, and as miserable as each other, but I'm glad to have them fighting by side." The brothers lifted their wooden cups to their leader and drained them.

"Pass the amphora here!" called Marka, and the wine vessel was handed to him.

Atrium and *amphora,* thought Arawn.

"Crix is the one trying to spit the meat; his sword skills are better than his cooking skills." The band chuckled, and Crix made a hand gesture that Arawn assumed was rude, but he laughed along with them. His features were as dark as everyone else's, but his hair was a swathe of tight curls that he kept pushing out of his face with a calloused hand.

"Next to him is Tarvos, and that's Boduus. You've got them to thank for your welcome this night, because they're the ones who kept sight of you and told me you were coming. They're my scouts." Only Tarvos nodded at Arawn. He was twice as broad as Boduus, but both had watchful eyes that made Arawn uncomfortable. But where Tarvos' face was friendly and quick to smile, Boduus' was criss-crossed with ugly scars that made him look dangerous.

"Well met," said Arawn, raising his cup. "And thanks to the one true god for leading me to you. Or you to me," he added, looking at the two scouts. Tarvos grinned, Boduus only stared. Ardus laughed, drained his cup and called for more wine.

"So, Arawn ap Emlyn," said the leader, "who's travelled all the way from Brython. You must have an interesting tale. I would hear it while we wait for our meat to cook."

He began his tale with the murder of the Druid Gwynfor and his sister because they tried to sacrifice his friend to the bitch-goddess Boudica. It pleased him to see that Ardus, Crix and Tarvos were already impressed this early on in his telling. Next he told of how he out-witted the spear-women of two tribes to escape onto a Gaulish trading vessel, and saved many crew-members from the hungry blades of Angle pirates. The trader, Thrax, knew many stories about the ancient Romans, Arawn said, and shared them freely. It was also he who told him of the one true god, and how he favoured men and burned disobedient women. This called out especially to Arawn because of the evil he'd been forced to live amongst in the woman-infested tribes of Brython. Then he recounted his meeting with Dexs who confirmed his growing belief in the one true god; how he tested his friend, Thrax, with the tale of Vercingetorix. The band hissed at the mention of his name, but Arawn confessed his sadness that Thrax had been brought low by his woman, and so, to save his friend, he raped and burned her. The band cheered and poured him more wine.

"And then," said Arawn. "I travelled across this peasant-ravaged country to find you. Only to have my throat nearly severed as reward." He smiled at Ardus.

"To have come so far on your own is a remarkable feat," said Ardus. "I hope you can forgive us. The one true god tells us forgiveness is a virtue. So will you forgive us, and join us in our fight against the sinful pagans?"

Arawn regarded him steadily. Now that the threat had dissipated, now that he was being asked to join them, he felt the stirrings of anger again, of humiliation for being caught off-guard and brought low.

"How do you fight the pagans?" he asked.

"Excuse me?" said Ardus, a smile of mild surprise on his face.

"I said, how do you fight the pagans? You're only six men. How can you expect to defeat entire lands of godless people?"

Marka snorted in disgust. "The more we kill, the less there are. Hurry up with that pig, Crix."

"There are other bands of Bagaudas," said Ardus, ignoring his third-in-command, "living all over the lands, controlling pagan populations in the ways we like best. But our bands have to be small otherwise we'll draw attention to ourselves. You say you've been to Lutetia so you should know already; most people don't regret the old decision to expel the Romans. They destroyed their buildings and temples in an effort to rid themselves entirely of them. If we find places like this intact," he raised his arms and gestured the room around them, "we defend them with our lives."

"So you stay where you are and hide?"

There was a growl from the two brothers, but Arawn kept his eyes on Ardus.

"We don't hide," he said, voice low. "We defend. We journey to settlements and villages to spread the word of the one true god, and if no one listens, we burn them to the ground."

Arawn nodded slowly, disappointment mounting.

They're no better than the squabbling tribal warrior-queens of Brython, fighting over territory, and guarding with jealousy what is theirs.

These were not the great warriors he'd anticipated at all. How was the word of the one true god supposed to spread with only a few small bands of men? Yes, he could live a better life here among equals, but what good was that if all the treacherous bitches who had ever betrayed him didn't know it?

I would have My word spread farther and wider so that all women are placed beneath your feet, bowing and scraping and doing as they are told while you live the blessed life of superiority.

"Pig's ready," said Crix, and pulled out a dagger from his belt and began hacking off great chunks.

"This isn't good enough," said Arawn. Crix looked at him, startled; but when he realised the guest wasn't talking to him he returned to his cleaving.

"Then what would you do?" said Ardus, scratching his ragged beard.

"What does it matter?" said Marka. "He's a child. No use to us. We should kill him."

Arawn looked at him, stomach tightening, but managed to keep the fear from his face. "The one true god would be very angry with you if you did that."

Marka looked at his brother, moving only his eyes, and Nertos did the same. "Really?" He didn't sound worried in the least.

"Yes," said Arawn. "He speaks to me." Ardus shifted forward and Arawn turned to face him again. "He wants more than this. Pagans should be punished, but if we kill everyone, who'll be left to worship the one true god?"

Even Crix was listening to him now.

"You know the word of the one true god?" Arawn demanded.

Ardus nodded.

"Then we must find a way to spread it across the lands so people can see it and believe it. If more believe, bands of Bagaudas will become armies of Bagaudas, and we can defeat the pagans entirely." He paused, knowing the one true god would speak through him, give him a sign of what he should say. "Signs!" he said suddenly. "In Lutetia there were signs of the one true god scratched all over the place. Dexs did it as a way to draw people to him. We should do something like that...but more."

"Here," Crix said, holding out a steaming chunk of pork.

Arawn took it, bit into it. Ah, hot meat! It seemed like an age since he'd tasted anything so good.

"What do you mean by more?" Ardus wasn't eating; he was riveted. Good.

"More signs," he said. "More ways of spreading the word of the one true god."

Ardus' shook his head. "There aren't enough of us here. We'd need the all the priests of Rome with us if we wanted to spread the word of the one true god far and wide."

"Priests," said Arawn. He'd heard that word before from Thrax. "That's what the men of Rome call themselves now, isn't it?"

"They used to be soldiers, now they're priests," said Ardus, nodding.

"And all of the men are priests?"

"Yes," said Ardus, though he sounded a little uncertain. "It's how they make their women submit to them. Women can't be priests because they're not god's chosen, so all the men are priests."

"Then we need priests here," said Arawn, excitement tingling his belly.

"Is that so?" said Nertos. "We just go to Rome and ask an army of priests to come here to help us convert all the pagans?" He looked at his brother and they both sniggered.

Rankled, Arawn decided he needed to be rid of them. Wiping

grease from his mouth, he looked at Nertos steadily. "Yes," he said. "That's exactly what we should do."

The moon of Edrinios (Arbitration-time), 332 C.E.
Somewhere South of Lutetia, Gaul

"The trail has gone cold, my lady," said Terrwyn, chief spear-woman of the Cantiaci. "We've been chasing the sister-slayer since Cutios, almost five moons past, and found no sign of him for at least one of those. I don't think our warrior-queen meant for us to be away for so long."

She was right, of course she was; she wouldn't have been elevated to such a high position in the household if she'd lacked intelligence. Rosmerta stepped away from the camp so that Gwladus wouldn't hear—the last thing she wanted this close night was a battle of words—and plucked the linen tunic from her back. Despite having bought local vestments two moons ago now, the fires of the Beltane sun burned like a furnace, drawing out her bodily fluids at an alarming rate and smothering her with a lethargy she'd never before experienced.

"Are you suggesting we quit this mission? Go back to Cantiaci only to tell my mother we failed?"

"My lady, he could be dead for all we know. In fact, it's probably likely. We've felt the clutch of hunger in our bellies despite having coin and trained hunters among us; he was just a boy. If starvation didn't kill him, then a beast probably did. The fact that we've been unable to pick up his trail would certainly prove that. Thrax said he would be at that Roman villa we investigated countless days ago but it was empty."

"Though there were signs of habitation." Terrwyn nodded to show she conceded that point, making the scar on her cheek flash silver for a heart-beat. She didn't seem about to change her stance so Rosmerta continued. "He also said it was likely that Arawn had joined with another group of people, those Bagaudas he's told us about. Isn't it possible that he's moved on with them?"

"Why would a group of people willingly leave shelter and comfort for the wilds in the hottest moons?" Rosmerta couldn't answer that. "Hear me, my lady; our quarry is dead."

"If he were dead his mother would know."

Terrwyn snorted softly and glanced back towards the camp. "His mother is blinded by vengeance. She won't believe him dead until she's killed him herself. Even if we were to come across his chewed remains she wouldn't believe him dead."

Rosmerta allowed herself a small smile. Gwladus had done nothing to endear herself to her fellow travellers, even though all were here to help her find her son. She'd bullied them unnecessarily every day with her foul words into continuing the search; she accepted Rosmerta's authority so grudgingly it bordered on treason; and the contempt with which she held Thrax still had Rosmerta slack-jawed with astonishment. So it was no secret that no one liked her, but just this once, Rosmerta felt she and her nemesis would be in agreement. Rosmerta didn't want to turn back either. It galled her to know she was fighting on behalf of such a wretched woman, but at least she could take a little comfort knowing that her own reasons weren't morally reprehensible.

"I can't authorise the abortion of my mission," she said, holding up her hand to stay Terrwyn's argument, "but perhaps we can come to a compromise."

Terrwyn listened with interest, and to Rosmerta's relief, she agreed. Now all she needed to do was inform the rest of her army.

When they approached the camp, Gwladus threw her a look of suspicion so deep she could have drowned entire tribes.

"Spear-women of Sulis and Epona," Rosmerta called. Gwladus frowned deeply, no doubt suspecting some treachery, but the warrior-princess ignored her. It was of the utmost import that she didn't get drawn in by her. "It cannot have escaped your notice as it has not escaped mine that we have lost the trail of Arawn Salt-merchant—"

"*Sister-slayer*!" hissed Gwladus, but still Rosmerta ignored her.

"—and as the light half of the year turns to dark that trail will only become more difficult to follow."

"What are you saying, Rosmerta?"

"Besides which," she continued, "if we leave it too long to get back to the northern coast there will be no ships willing to take us back across the ocean to Brython."

"You cannot give up!" This time it was Thrax who spoke, leaping to his feet, and the pain she heard in his voice made her heart stutter.

"Fear not," she said, holding her hands up, "I'm as unwilling to give up the search as you are. But it would be irresponsible of me to keep so many good spear-women stranded in Gaul over the dark moons when they could be needed back in Cantiaci and Atrebates. Not only do we have raids from the Picts to worry about, but we have discovered a new enemy in the Angles."

"Pah! They're sea-raiders! Why would they make shore when they can raid as many fat trading ships as they want?"

"Because trading ships don't cross the ocean during the darkest moons, and who's to say the Angles will want to stop raiding?" said Rosmerta, cursing herself for becoming ensnared by Gwladus at last. "But that aside, I can see no further point in keeping so many women on a mission and away from their homes when there's little chance of succeeding."

"So you'd rather fail?"

"To that end, Terrwyn will lead the majority of the army back to Brython while I will stay here with a small numbers of volunteers who wish to stand beside me until this mission is completed."

Gwladus scowled at her and Rosmerta had to hold back a smug grin; in volunteering to stay, she would publicly acknowledge to all the spear-women of Atrebates that she was subordinate to the warrior-princess of the traitor tribe, something that had irked Gwladus mightily ever since this ill-fated mission began.

"I will stay with you until the end, my warrior-princess," said one of the Cantiaci spear-women, rising to her feet and standing proudly, brandishing her spear.

"As will I," said another, rising also.

"Thank you."

"If by serving you," said a warrior standing from the Atrebates camp, "I can serve my tribe and my warrior-queen, then I will."

"You will need my guidance," said Thrax. "And I will not rest until I see the justice visited upon the man who killed my woman."

Rosmerta winced, but she nodded her thanks. "Four warriors and our guide. That will suffice. There are still a few hours of sunlight left, I suggest we go our separate ways now so as not to waste them. For those of you travelling north, I wish you the speed of Boudica's chariot and thank you for your service. May the goddesses protect you on your journey home."

She nodded at Thrax and her volunteers, who stepped nimbly over their still-seated fellow warriors to follow their leader. As desperate as she was to witness the expression of tortured indecision on Gwladus' face, she kept her eyes averted; if the woman wanted to join her hunting party she would have to ask. She would give her no opportunity to sneak her way into the group by catching her eye and mistaking it for invitation.

They hadn't gone more than a few steps when a cry halted them.

"Wait! You think you can find the sister-slayer without his mother?"

Rosmerta turned. "Do you also wish to stand beside me until the mission is completed, Gwladus Salt-merchant?"

Gwladus scowled. Rosmerta raised an eyebrow.

"You know I cannot return until I've had my vengeance," she said, her voice full of hate, stalking over to where Rosmerta's group waited.

"Then I thank you for your dedication and service."

"Gwynfor! To me!" she cried without looking back and stomping to the head of the hunting party.

Rosmerta smiled a little; it was only a little victory but she would take any she could against the frightful woman. Then her smile faltered as Terrwyn held her spear up to her in salute and led the army back the way they had so recently come.

Ten moons, she thought. Ten moons had passed since that fateful Samhain night in Kaer Gradawc when she should have been bonded to Dewydd of Atrebates. Would she have borne her own daughter by now? Would she have already promised her to a warrior-queen of a neighbouring tribe, bonding them to Atrebates and Cantiaci both? Never would she know now. Instead, her path had been disrupted by one family, a family with whom she'd had no connection until that night. And here she was, two moons away from Samhain again, still inextricably tied to that same family. Turning away from the departing army, she faced her small hunting party and held her head high as a warrior-princess should. The path of her destiny may have turned unexpectedly, but she would walk along this new one with pride until it led her back home to her mother and victory.

– 23 –

The moon of Anagantios (Stay-home time), 333 C.E. Forest hills north of Lugdunum, Gaul

The little leveret is hiding, Arawn, but you can find her.

Of course he could, he didn't doubt it. Hadn't it been he who had led the Bagaudas to this pagan-infested village? Hadn't it been he who had told them they were ripe for converting? The one true god spoke to him and Arawn listened, and in their turn the Bagaudas listened to him.

A sound caught his attention. In the cold air of Anagantios it echoed through the silence even though it was as soft as breath. Clutching his axe tighter he moved towards it.

"I know you're there, little leveret," he whispered to the skeleton trees. "Andraste is defeated; you can't hide from Arawn of the one true god."

A copse of dead leaves and twigs suddenly exploded and the little leveret was away, screeching in panic and running blindly through frost-touched woods. Arawn grinned and leapt after her knowing that her escape was futile; he was a creature of the one true god, she wasn't. She would suffer the wrath of her mistakes at his hand.

It needn't have been so, for Arawn had explained that if they submitted to the one true god's word they would be saved, but they were surprisingly resistant, even when Ardus and his second-in-command, Nertos, came into the village with the two female prisoners and slit their throats in front of them. The men attempted to fight back, but with Marka and Crix setting fire to the thatch and Tarvos and Boduus firing arrows from the trees, the rebellion was quelled almost instantly. After all, Arawn had had all dark season to practice his system of conversion and the villagers had been unprepared. Those few men who had surrendered to them were spared, and told to spread the word amongst the other villages in this godforsaken place, but with each new village they came to, the more apparent it became that they weren't fulfilling their sacred duty. It made the one true god angry, and he filled Arawn with a wrath that was almost too painful to bear. With each successive village he found that his patience with these pagans grew less and less and only their blood on his skin had the power to cool him.

The little leveret turned unexpectedly, trying to swerve around and turn back on him—a bold move. Arawn lashed out his hand and grabbed at a handful of hair causing the little leveret to squeal in fear and duck out of the way. It was enough to take her out of Arawn's grasp, but fortunately for him the ground was treacherous with frost and patchy snow and the panicked movements of the little leveret meant she could not keep her feet. She stumbled and rolled, scrabbling to her hands and knees and trying desperately to find purchase again but she didn't have the one true god on her side.

Arawn did.

Looming over her scrabbling form, he reached down and grabbed a handful of sweaty brown hair and pulled her to her feet, the little leveret screaming and kicking as though she were possessed with the very devil himself. And she was, for all who refused to submit to the one true god were vessels for demons, none so much as the females. Her terror made her strong in spite of her youth; but Arawn was easily six or seven summers older than her, had spent the entire dark season hunting in the woods and was filled with the strength of the one true god. Even the most powerful demon was no match for him now.

"This is the last of them," he said when he finally reached the village where his Bagaudas had been busy. The little leveret was tiring now, but the sight of six more righteous men spurred her into panic again. Then she saw the fate of her fellow pagan villagers, the fools who wouldn't submit, and her screaming began anew. It tore through the cold air like a knife, causing the gathering crows to take flight momentarily.

"You think you're frightened now, little leveret," said Arawn to the insensible creature writhing in his grasp, "but it is naught compared to the eternal fires in which you'll soon find yourself." She didn't hear him, of course. And when he snapped her neck she cried and heard no more.

"Put her with the others," he said to Ardus, dumping the body at his feet. He never needed to give an order twice.

You've done well, Arawn of the one true god. Now you must take my Bagaudas to Lugdunum. Greater tasks await you.

The moon of Anagantios (Stay-home time), 333 C.E.
Ynys Afallach, Brython

"But it's treason," said Emrys. "What you're doing, what you're asking me to do, it's treason!"

"Why?" Throughout the entire conversation Heddgwyn had remained perfectly calm, as though he were discussing something rational. It infuriated the new Druid, but more than that; it frightened him. "What right do the warrior-queens have to lay claim to the lands of Brython? Do you think they belong to them? The lands belong to the old gods, my son, and no one else. If you would speak of treason, how foul do you think the treachery is of those who would wrest lands belonging to the gods? It goes beyond treason, Emrys; it is sacrilege. All we are doing is giving the land back to those who created it."

"With war! How many people will be killed in this conquest of yours? How many—"

"It is not a conquest, Emrys. We are uniting the lands under the old gods."

"With weapons? I thought we were supposed to teach the histories, not slaughter the people for forgetting them. How does that make us any different from the Romans—"

The slap came so fast that Emrys was made breathless. He stared wide-eyed at his father, now pacing across the round-house in an effort to control his anger.

"This is all my fault," Heddgwyn said, not looking at his son, as though he were the one who had just been struck. He picked up the poker and jabbed it into the hearth-fire. "I thought you were ready for Druidry, but I can see now I was gravely mistaken. I'll call the council at once; it isn't too late to revoke your status."

"What?" Emrys leapt from his stool. "For contradicting you? For speaking my mind? You can't do that!"

"I can't, no. But the council will not want a Druid amongst us deliberately subverting the will of the old gods."

Emrys stared at him. After everything he'd endured to get here, after all the trials he'd sat through to attain the third level, now his father was just going to take it away from him. A tiny, rebellious part of his mind reminded him that he'd never wanted to be a Druid in the first place, but now that he had it… He had access to all the histories of all the tribes across the lands, the real histories; the truth. Could he simply let it go?

But there was more than that. If he were cast out he would be of no use to anyone. Yes, he might find his way back to Cantiaci in time to warn his mother of the impending war, but the womanly skills of combat had only been taught to his sisters, not him. Besides, how could the spear-women of Cantiaci and one failed Druid hope to beat an army of trained ones? Perhaps he could better serve his mother where he was.

"Please, Father," he said, "you cannot cast me out."

"The final decision will not rest with me."

"Please! There must be something you can do to help me understand the situation better? A visioning, perhaps? Or, or…an invocation?"

Heddgwyn ceased his pacing and looked long and deep into Emrys' eyes, into his very soul. Would he see the truth there?

Emrys certainly hoped not.

"You would fight to stay with us, even though you disagree with our vocation. Why?"

The young Druid slumped back down onto his stool. "I never wanted to be a Druid, Father. I think you've always known that. And for the longest time I found it hard to forgive you for taking me away from my sisters and forcing me into a life that was not of my choosing. But over the years I have learned so much, and I can't deny that I enjoy using my knowledge and powers to help the people of our tribe. Of other tribes as well, as I have during our protracted journey here." He risked looking up at his father; it was unusual for him to let a monologue continue without some form of interjection. Pleasingly, his father remained attentive. "And I can't deny that I've enjoyed forging a relationship with you, as I have on this pilgrimage. Coming here to Ynys Afallach has become more than just an attainment of the third level, it's come to symbolise my search for the father I've always wanted. You've led me to both. I can't let that go now." Unbidden, tears sprang from his eyes. Not for the deception he had woven, but because he wished all he'd said was true.

Heddgwyn nodded slowly at him. "That was well-said, my son."

"And also," said Emrys, wiping a tear from his eye, "I really, really want to go back and visit the Bard."

The old Arch Druid roared with laughter, pulled Emrys up from his stool and clasped his shoulders. "And now we get to the truth of the matter!"

Emrys laughed along with his father for a few heartbeats then made his face serious again. "Is there nothing that can prove my intentions to you and the council? If you truly believe that what you're doing is right and according to the will of the old gods, then teach me, please. I want to believe."

"I believe you do, my son," said Heddgwyn. "And there is one thing that we can do, but it involves the most dangerous magic our people know. In order for it to work, you will have to die. Are you still willing?"

Emrys felt his stomach shrink. They would truly kill him that he might prove his loyalty? Such archaic, not to mention wasteful, notions had been abandoned since before Boudica's time, surely they wouldn't resurrect them now? Then the truth burst into his mind like a blossom opening under the sun.

"Rebirth," he whispered, and Heddgwyn nodded.

"Your death will take you to Otherworld where you can speak with the old gods yourself and hear the truth of their will. And when you are reborn, you will be stronger and wiser than many of us."

"Stronger and wiser than even you?"

Heddgwyn smiled. "One can only become an Arch Druid by passing through death and coming back from it. You won't be wiser than me until you've surpassed me in years."

"Then rebirth will have to suffice."

"You are willing to undertake it?"

Emrys nodded. "I wish to pass through the Cauldron of Rebirth."

* * *

The following three days were filled with an intense purification ritual that left Emrys feeling light of body and mind. For three days he was allowed to consume nothing but the clear waters from the sacred well on Ynys Afallach. While the weak Imbolc sun was in the sky he meditated and was prayed over by the wisest Druids on the Isle, including his father. When night came, preparing the world for a new day, he bathed in the Afon Menai until his body was numb.

On the third day, he was dressed in a robe so white it made his eyes hurt to look at it. He was given a final draught of sacred spring water, and then his father entered the roundhouse looking mightier than Emrys had ever seen him in his layered robes and wooden prayer beads. On his head sat the skull of a mighty hound, the Hound of the Sun God, polished until the ivory shone, and decorated with ivy to represent renewal and rebirth as well as newly grown daffodils to represent faith and honesty.

"You are ready, Emrys, Druid of the Cantiaci, to pass through the Cauldron of Rebirth."

Emrys nodded his head, but it felt leagues above his body. When his father pulled him up by the hand, it felt as though it were in another land. Vaguely he remembered feeling afraid when the ritual started but now that fear had gone, replaced by a comfortable acceptance of his fate. Dimly he recalled that he was undertaking this for his mother, his sisters, his tribe, to save them from war and destruction and death, but such problems seemed distant and trifling now.

He felt his feet move, and each stride covered countries, continents, until his father pulled back the hide door of the roundhouse and led him out into the sunshine which blinded him instantly with its intensity. Truly Belenos was looking down on him this day.

The walk to the gathering place took heartbeats and aeons, and as he approached the oak pillars that heralded the doorway, the sacred carvings hewn upon them were in a starker relief than he had remembered. Great owls, their sight ever keen, swooped around the pillars, ready to guide him through Otherworld; deer, with their swift grace, and horses, ever faithful, walked proudly, ready to deliver messages from the gods; courageous bears added their strength to the pillar and Emrys knew they would also strengthen him on his journey; and singing blackbirds, whose voices knew the deep secrets of Otherworld, heralded his approach from the World Tree. Should he be so fortunate, he would soon see these sacred creatures in the flesh.

Dimness closed over him and he was in the blessed gathering

place. The fire in the centre burned and glowed and gave off a heat as powerful as its counterpart up in the sky, and burning upon it was willow-bark and rowan, mugwort and hemp, all giving off an aroma so pungent it made his eyes water. He breathed deeply of them, knowing they would help him on his journey.

Slowly he was pushed into a sitting position in front of the fire and a wooden beaker was placed in his hands. The contents were warm but smelled very unpleasant. A concoction of eyebright for his soul-eyes, liberty cap to project him into Otherworld, and alder to promote death.

"Drink this, my son," said a voice beyond the moon.

Emrys did as he was told, and other voices joined in, chanting the magical words that would reveal his soul to the old gods. The brew tasted revolting, and more than once Emrys gagged, but his stomach was empty and pure and he was able to control it. Seasons passed, but finally he finished it and the beaker was taken from his hands.

Across the far reaches of time Emrys felt hands gently support him under his arms and he was moved to a standing position, but such notions of movement and position seemed irrelevant now. The gathering place swam past him, the chanting filled his ears and made no sense to him, the impression of robed figures were all around him but he could focus on nothing. Except one thing, and it was in front of that which the supporting hands led him.

The Cauldron of Rebirth.

In the unclear surroundings it shone out like a warning beacon in the darkest of nights. In the firelight it blazed gold like a treasure from Belenos himself. And all over it were markings illustrating the arrival of Belenos to the fair isle of Brython and how he conquered the lands to give them to his chosen people. But no ordinary markings, these; they moved. They wove in and out of each other so that Emrys could see the story unfold in front of his very eyes, they writhed and turned so that Emrys could see each stroke of the sun god's sacred sword of flame, so that he could see the evil spirits fall at his feet, so that he could see his chosen people lifted from the chains of mortality to join the gods. For an eternity he was immersed in the story; feeling the fear of the spirits as he felt the joy of the chosen, smelling the blood of the slain as he smelled the reborn blossoms opening, hearing the cries of the damned as he heard the cheers of the saved. It was as beautiful as it was terrifying, as wonderful as it was horrific, as glorious as it was dreadful. How could he ever have doubted its existence?

Then, from beyond time, his hand was moved to his breast where he felt the slow thumping of his heart.

Thump-thump, thump-thump.

Thump-thump.

Thump.

And then it ceased. His heart beat no more. All was as still and silent in his breast as it was now still and silent in the gathering place. Only the Cauldron called out to him and he longed to be submerged in its fiery-gold depths. From another plane, his knees crumpled underneath him and the supporting hands allowed him to fall gently through time and space and blackness until he was no more.

What is this place?

Otherworld.

I am dead then.

Yes.

To whom do I speak?

Everyone. No one. The living and the dead. The earth and the firmament. The stars and the moon. The Sun.

You are the sun god.

Yes.

Belenos.

Yes.

We are the chosen.

Yes.

Belenos, I would ask something of you, will you answer me?

Yes.

The land of Brython belongs to you, would you have us shed blood for it in your name?

Please, Belenos, I beg an answer from you.

When I swallow the moon, blood will be shed in my name. When an orb of blood hangs in the night sky, blood will be spilled in my name. When you find the truth, blood will be spilled in my name.

Is this your will?

The truth is my will.

* * *

It began with pain. First in his head, as though someone had taken great pleasure in beating him; then he felt it throughout his body, a deep aching as though giants had crushed his bones within his skin. He tried to move, but couldn't. He tried to open his eyes, but couldn't. Or perhaps it was too dark.

Of course it was dark, he was in Otherworld. He was dead. He'd spoken to Belenos. He'd spoken to Belenos and was told that blood would be spilled in his name. His father had been right all along and he hadn't listened. Now it was too late because he was dead.

"Emrys."

It wasn't the voice of Belenos this time. For a start, he would swear it entered through his ears; the sun god's voice had permeated the very bones of his skull. It did, however, sound very familiar.

"Emrys."

He tried to get his throat to work but it was as dry as a midsummer's sky. Then there was light, and he felt some pressure ease from his body. He still couldn't move it, but the pressure was definitely less.

"Emrys."

With great effort and a great deal of pain he managed to push some sound from his throat. "I'm here." He barely heard it himself, but it seemed it was all the familiar voice needed.

"He is come back! He is reborn! Come, help me with him!"

Gentle hands rained down from the light above and he felt his painful body lifted carefully, slowly, but still causing him much hurt. He cried out in his agony, but it only left his mouth as a wheezy rasp.

Then the cold hit him and he began shivering uncontrollably. And the light hit him and he was blinded. He had no idea that death was so traumatic.

"Place him here," said the familiar voice, "and wrap that blanket over him, quickly. Bring broth and wine."

"Am I dead?"

"You were, my son, but you have been reborn!"

Emrys fought the pain and opened his eyes. There was his father, kneeling before him, his face flushed with pride and happiness. "I am reborn?"

"You are, my son!"

He was dead. He'd felt his heart cease beating. He'd travelled to Otherworld and spoken with the father of all gods. Now he was alive once more. It was unbelievable. If he hadn't just experienced it himself, he wouldn't believe it. He tried stretching his legs and winced at the pain.

"Slowly, son; resurrection is a painful process; you must let the healers tend to you."

Emrys nodded. "I saw Belenos." He hadn't been aware of all the movement around him until it stopped. Then he became of aware of the weight of many pairs of eyes.

"The sun god came to you in death?" Heddgwyn's face was a mask of awe; a sight Emrys had never seen during his entire lifetime.

"He did."

"And what did he tell you?"

"You were right, Father; you were right all along, and I was a fool to doubt you. He said blood would be spilled in his name."

"Then it is confirmed," said Heddgwyn, turning to face all the Druids who had come to witness the rebirth. "As soon as the festival of Imbolc is finished, we ride to war."

– 24 –

Ogronios (Ice-time), 333 C.E.
Lugdunum, Bagauda stronghold, south-east Gaul

Always would Arawn think of Lugdunum with fondness. Of course, some of the native population called it Lugodunon, preferring the pre-Roman name, but Arawn and his Bagaudas referred to it as Lugdunum in deference to the great people who had once made it a great town.

"Though we'll have to change the name again when we come back with our army of Roman priests," said Arawn. They were walking south along what he called the Great River, and he could see the old city of Lugdunum rising up ahead of them to the left. It was very impressive.

"Why should we change the name?" said Ardus, scratching his beard. "If the Romans saw fit to call it Lugdunum then who are we to change it?"

Arawn smiled. "Hill-fort of Lugh?" he said. "I should think the one true god would be mightily displeased if we named places after the old gods." He frowned then. "It's strange why they didn't change it when they were here before however."

The Bagauda laughed and clapped him on the shoulder, reminding Arawn painfully of Thrax for a heartbeat. "Because they hadn't found the one true god when they first came here. He'd been waiting for them in Rome until they returned so he could show them the error of their ways."

"Benedictus qui venit."

"Absolutely. But they left something here that I believe will impress you more than anything you've seen so far."

"Truly?"

Ardus grinned. "More truly than you can imagine."

They'd been walking for several days now, and while Arawn

was glad he was accompanied by people who knew the surrounding lands well enough to hunt, and while the terrain was showing the first signs of becoming fat and fertile once more, it would be good to see something that was more than countryside.

Just as the sun passed the meridian—and it was hot for Ogronios; Arawn couldn't recall it ever being this strong even when Mother was trading her salt in the most southern lands of the Dumnonii—Arawn and the Bagaudas reached an old wooden bridge that was sorely in need of repair. They walked east for a short while until they reached a second bridge crossing another smaller river, and Lugdunum loomed up from its banks. While the lower slopes of the hill were covered with trees, blossoming now with the buds of new leaves after Imbolc, the base of it was a desolate wasteland. The earth was scorched, and burned ruins of old dwellings littered the surrounding area. Arawn looked at it with dismay when he stepped off the bridge.

"I can't say I find this particularly impressive," he said.

"That's because you don't understand what it means," Nertos said, and pushed past him. Arawn glared at the departing second-in-command's back as he stomped through the ash and rubbish.

"Pagans used to live here," said Ardus, apparently unaware of his second-in-command's poor behaviour. "And while they weren't ignorant of the one true god, they wouldn't listen to the Bagaudas when they tried to teach them the error of their ancient ways. But they were ignorant of how powerful the Bagaudas were becoming. So the Bagaudas gave them a choice: join the one true faith or burn in hell. I think it's clear which they chose." Ardus smiled, his eyes sparkling.

"But if the pagans lived here," said Arawn, "where did the Bagaudas live?"

Ardus clasped him by the shoulder and pointed to the top of soaring, tree-carpeted hill. "Up there," he said.

The climb was hard on his thighs, but pretty on his eyes. Paths had been made through the belt of trees at the base of the hill from constant walking, by two- and four-legged travellers. But it was steep. Halfway up there was a gap in the foliage and Arawn saw the flat landscape run out and on towards the horizon to the north and west, while to the south it continued its hilly course. It would have been quite splendid had it not been for the ugly scar of burned wastelands. Something else the pagans could be blamed for.

On they continued, Arawn and his Bagaudas, and underneath this hotter sun they sweated like battle horses. And then, with no warning, the trees cleared and Arawn's heart stopped.

Beauty was a concept he thought he'd understood. He thought he'd seen it in Rosmerta Warrior-Princess, but then the bitch had betrayed him and the memory of her face would ever sour his belly. He thought he'd seen it in the clean, paved streets of Cantiaci and its stone houses, but it was nothing but a poor, diminished, distant relative to that which he looked upon now.

An entire Roman city. Square houses of white stone with tiled roofs sat side-by-side along roads of rational straightness, most of which were still paved with white flagstones. Walking through, head swinging from side to side, mouth only just wider than his eyes, Arawn saw that some reparations had been carried out with wattle-and-daub, and he was sure that holes in the roofs had been patched up with thatch, but the buildings were too high for him to see—too high! But perhaps even more astonishing was that some of the windows, even though shutters were clearly visible on either side of them, were filled with a kind of reflective surface that threw the sun back into his eyes.

"Glass," said Ardus, looking at him and grinning wide enough to reveal all his broken teeth. "You'll not find any other Roman buildings in these lands still with their original glass, but here their duty to preserve the Roman city is as strong as their belief in the one true god."

"It's beautiful," said Arawn. Then something else struck him. "But where is everybody?"

"Playing games, I shouldn't wonder," said Ardus. "They already know we're here however. Fortunately they know me and my Bagaudas so we're still breathing. Let's go and watch some fun."

Walking through the empty streets, now Arawn knew they weren't deserted he heard a distant noise that sounded like wind through trees, but there was not even a breeze cooling off his dripping brow. He knew then that it was the sound of a great hoard of people roaring and cheering.

"What kind of games do they play?" he asked Ardus as they turned down another street that perfectly dissected the one they'd been following.

"Games that you'd enjoy, as a believer in the one true god," he replied.

It didn't take long for Arawn to find out. The straight road ended at a vast building which soared up from the ground and reached to the sky, filling all the space with its impossible size. He ran towards it, unaware of his action; but he felt as though the edifice drew him towards it like the earth pulls on the moon.

Finally, he exited the road and the building was before him. Physically he couldn't take it all in; his puny sight couldn't encompass the entire structure and it filled his vision. He had to swing his head from side to side in order to see it all, and it was phenomenal. Unlike all the other ancient Roman buildings he'd seen, this one was circular, but it had nothing in common with the roundhouses of his lands any more than the lice in his clothes had anything to do with the eternal sky.

And its size wasn't all that astounded Arawn and fixed his feet to the ground. Carved people—statues, Thrax had called them—posed and bowed and danced in graceful archways; pillars marched around the structure, more than twice the height of Arawn himself, but dwarfed by the building at which they stood sentry; animals and other creatures unrecognisable to him frolicked and played amongst themselves.

"Welcome to the Colosseum," Ardus whispered in his ear.

Arawn looked round and saw all the Bagaudas were gazing up at it in awe, even Nertos and Marka, the permanently scowling brothers.

"You've been here before?" Arawn whispered back.

"Many times." Yet they were still captivated by it, Arawn thought. And no wonder; how could such a sight of beauty, strength and might not take your breath away every time you witnessed it? "This is where they play their games," Ardus finished.

"They play games in here?"

"The Romans took gaming very seriously. And when we go in you'll see that the games the Bagaudas of Lugdunum play are not for their own pleasure, but for the glory of the one true god."

When they stood outside the Colosseum the roar of the crowd had been loud, but now they were in stone corridors and it was hushed. Arawn thought he would never understand how Ardus could thread his way through such a maze, but he climbed the stairways leading to more corridors leading to more stairways as confidently as if he'd built the magnificent structure himself. Shortly, the end of their current corridor gleamed with light, and as they walked down it the sound of the crowd grew louder and louder until they were back out in the open and Arawn felt his heart stop for a second time that day.

The ground fell away from his feet. The roar of the crowd thundered in his ears. He thought he would swoon.

"Have you ever seen anything like this before?" said Ardus, though his grin suggested he knew full well Arawn hadn't.

"No," he said. "Never."

They were standing at the top of what Arawn realised were benches, rows of circular benches that ran in concentric circles until they funnelled down to the ground, and there at the very bottom was the gaming arena. Not all of the benches were filled, he realised with some surprise. In fact, not even a quarter of the great arena's benches had occupants, but the sound of their cheering was carried up through the funnel and released into the air as a great cacophony.

He dropped his gaze back down to the arena floor and he saw five…no, six men battling against one another. They were naked, though it took Arawn several moments to realise this; their bodies were so streaked with blood it looked like they were fully clothed in outfits of red-dyed wool. Their weapons were nothing but axes and scythes, tools of farming rather than instruments of war. But contending with each other was merely one part of the game. Running amongst the fighters, crazed by the blood-filled air, was a pack of wild dogs, teeth bared in constant snarls, jumping onto their hind legs and snapping at any man who moved into their path.

Not all men, he realised; he also saw two women. One, with her back up against the arena wall, fought viciously against two men. She swung her axe wildly, diagonally from side to side, which held the men at bay for the moment, but Arawn wondered how long she would be able to keep up such a physically exerting defence.

The second woman had just been brought to her knees when a wild dog lunged and bit deeply on her thigh. A second dog lunged for her throat, a spray of blood leaping up from her neck and soaking the animal, and a third joined the massacre, tearing off a breast with one wrench of its thick neck. The watching crowd screamed and roared their approval. Arawn felt his own blood stir as a memory of Sirom flashed into his mind, how he had beaten her and seen the blood rush from her nose. This was vastly more entertaining.

"Who are those people down there?" he asked Ardus.

The leader of the Bagaudas didn't take his eyes of the entertainment while he answered. "Pagans," he said. "Brought here by Bagaudas and taught the error of their godless ways. None of them ever learns though." He jumped up from the bench and cried his approval as one of the men cornering the woman broke through her defence and buried his axe into the side of her head. She fell to the floor like a stoned Druid, her hands flapping spasmodically when the man tugged his axe out of her skull—only to nick his own thigh. The watching crowd burst into laughter. The second man saw his opportunity and used his scythe to open the man's belly. He looked at his opponent with shock while his guts tumbled to the blood-soaked ground, but the look quickly turned to horror as three dogs bounded over and began eating them even as he crumpled to floor.

Leaving the man to his slow and hideous death, the pagan turned to face the last two combatants only to see that one had killed the other, and the last was bravely battling against four dogs. He stalked over to him, felling him quickly with a blow to the head, and the dogs leaped onto his body and feasted. While the animals were so occupied, the victor picked them off one by one, snapping the middle of their backs with a single, heavy blow from his scythe.

Which left only the three dogs eating the guts of the man he'd sliced open once they'd defeated the woman. He crept over to them with almost comical stealth and killed them as easily as he'd done the first four.

The audience leapt to their feet, applauding and cheering as the man, exhausted and finished, threw his bloody tool to the floor and looked up at them defiantly.

From behind him a door opened in the arena and two men came out, dressed in armour and heavily armed. They each grabbed an arm and dragged him back through the door from which they had appeared.

"What happens now?" asked Arawn, disappointed that the spectacle was over so quickly.

"The victor will get a chance to fight again," said Ardus. "And if he continues to please the crowd he might just be allowed to live as a slave in the city."

"Truly? You'd let a pagan live?"

"We're fighters, Arawn ap Emlyn," he said with a grin. "You'd be surprised how many of us can be won over by a brave warrior. But it rarely happens. I've never heard of any pagan who's been able to survive more than three or four of these battles. But the promise of life is what keeps them battling so bravely." He roared with laughter and Arawn joined him. This was precisely the type of sport that Brython needed. But it would be female pagan blood that washed the ground red. "And now you must meet Rix."

As soon as Ardus stood the rest of his band followed, and they made their way closer towards the arena floor, so close that Arawn could smell the stink of blood and shit from the last battle. A troop of naked men and women were currently clearing away the human and animal corpses, the onlookers jeering at the women, making unsubtle remarks about fucking them bloody, and then dissolving into laughter as the females vomited in response to their gruesome task.

Eventually Arawn and his Bagaudas reached an area that was clearly intended for people of high rank. They had no need to condescend to sitting on benches for there were ornate throne-like chairs, and Arawn saw that the current occupants were well-fed, well-dressed and decorated with gold. They laughed and spoke among themselves with the carefree confidence of those safe and comfortable in the highest echelons of their society.

"This was the emperor's box," said Ardus as they approached it. "He'd sit in here and watch the games with his noble family. Now Rix watches the games from here with his favourites."

The box was separated from the audience benches by a stone wall, and Arawn thought the box had been built especially to keep the noble family away from the common people. However there was a door leading into it, and this Ardus now opened. He entered first, pulling Arawn by the shoulder.

All the occupants looked round as they entered the room, and a sunburnt, black-haired man leapt from his throne and flung his arms out. "Ardus, you sneaky bastard," he said. "I wondered how long it would take you to finally come and pay your respects to me."

"I'm only here to show my friend what the bastard child of a whore and goat looks like," said Ardus, pushing Arawn forward a little when he said *friend*. "And now we're here, you can pay your respects to us."

Arawn assumed the man Ardus spoke to was Rix, though he was slightly disconcerted that he spoke to him with such rudeness. Rix was built like an ox, a sight made more fearsome by the pair of short swords strapped to his waist. He looked like he could decapitate the both of them without even breaking a sweat.

A moment of silence stretched out while all the favourites in the box looked back and forth between Rix and the upstart who'd burst into their domain and insulted their leader. Rix threw back his head and bellowed so loudly that Arawn jumped in fear before he realised it was laughter and not a battle cry.

"When are you going to come back to Lugdunum, little brother?" said Rix. "The place is much more amusing with you in it."

"I'll come back when you're nothing more than a patch of red jelly on the ground and I take leadership of this useless crew of fools."

Rix laughed again as did his favourites, though they looked less than happy being referred to as fools. Their leader stomped across the box to where his younger brother stood and embraced him strongly. Arawn noticed their resemblance immediately, and found this almost as surprising as Ardus' omission of his family ties to the leader of the Lugdunum Bagaudas.

"What brings you here, little brother?" Rix stood back and held Ardus by his shoulders. "It's been too long."

"It has. But you know I only like to visit when I have something important to give you."

"And what do you give me this time? I still see no chest of treasure."

Ardus smiled with one corner of his mouth. "You'll get it soon enough. But for now I give you Arawn."

It was the first time Rix had looked at him, and his gaze penetrated so deeply that Arawn shifted under it. But it wasn't only Rix's gaze that made him uncomfortable. What did Ardus mean by *I give you Arawn*?

He heard a soft chuckle behind him and looked round. Nertos was grinning evilly at him.

"New blood, eh?" said Rix thoughtfully. "How very useful. We're running short of pagans right now and I'm enjoying the games too immensely to stop now. How are your battle skills, boy?"

Fear was souring Arawn's bowels. He'd pissed himself when the Angle pirate had discovered his hiding place on Thrax's ship. Now he thought he was going to shit himself.

"What do you mean?" he said, and cursed himself. His voice was cracked and high-pitched. He sounded like a frightened child.

"My little brother has always gifted me with good fighters," said Rix, "and I want to know if you'll be entertaining. You're next to fight in the arena."

– 25 –

The Moon of Ogronios (Ice-time), 333 C.E.
Forest hills north of Lugdunum, Gaul

"Why are we relying on a man to lead us to the sister-slayer? I'm the only person that can track him down!"

Rosmerta tightened her grip on the reins of her steed. It was the only way she could avoid screaming at this question constantly repeated. "Because Thrax knows these lands."

"Pah! He knows these lands as well as we do! I've heard him whisper to his Gaulish gods; the further we travel from Lutetia the less he knows the lands. It's time you left the tracking to me and my Druid. His magic is stronger than the abilities of a mere man."

Her Druid indeed, she thought. May Boudica give me strength, and protect this woman from my wrath. They'd probably have Arawn by now if weren't for *her* Druid. "By all means, Gwladus, allow your Druid to help us on this search." She looked into the fiery glare of the salt-merchant. "For we all seek the same end, and we all seek it together."

With an insolent "Pah!" that had Rosmerta grinding her teeth, the salt-merchant swept her horse's neck around that she might seek the company of her Druid at the back of the group, where he no doubt concocted his magic. Rosmerta tapped the sides of her own steed so that she could catch up with Thrax. Likely he had heard the conversation himself and she didn't want him feeling any worse than he already was.

"I know you have only known me for a handful of moons," he said when she drew level with him, "and you have no reason to trust me; but your spear-woman doesn't speak the truth."

"She's not my spear-woman, she's a salt-merchant. And I've learned to take everything she says with a pinch of her own wares." Thrax smiled a little, and she was glad. "But I would be interested to hear where her truth fails her; your knowledge of these lands or your whispering to your gods."

"What kind of man would I be if I ignored my gods?"

"So you do know these lands?"

"Well enough," the trader said with a shrug. "Although I will confess to you that it's been many seasons since I last came this far south."

"I can't imagine that matters overly; how much is a forest likely to change?" She smiled across at him, but he didn't seem to share her little joke.

"I used to buy wine from the villages around here, the sweetest wine you ever tasted—much more so than anything the Romans squirted out from their vines. I would bring jewellery and dyed wool from your country, Rosmerta, and trade it for jars and jars of wine, which I would then take north again and trade for weapons to trade with your people; for a time it worked very well."

"For a time?"

"That was many seasons ago indeed when I was a youth learning the trade from my father. But soon, the southern lands became infested with Bagaudas, the villagers retreated into the forests and the vine-yards were left to rot."

"Did the villagers not fight back?"

"I don't doubt many of them did, lady. But the Bagaudas spend their lives fighting, just as the Romans did, whereas a farmer spends his life working the soil." He looked her deep in the eye then. "They're a fearsome people, lady, you mustn't underestimate them. Not only do they spend their time fighting, they also fester in fury and hatred. They've never forgiven their ancestors for sending the Romans from our lands. And now they have their one true god."

"Ah yes, I remember you speaking of that in Cantiaci."

"He's a fighting god, fiercer than any the ancient Romans

used to worship. And he despises pagans."

Rosmerta frowned. "Pagans?"

"Anyone who doesn't submit to this one true god of theirs."

"How peculiar."

"Don't think too lightly of it—the Bagaudas punish pagans in the most dreadful manner imaginable. And the further south we go, the more we encroach on their lands."

The warrior-princess sat up a little straighter in her saddle. "While I don't doubt the sincerity of your words, Thrax, I also know that stories grow over time. How much of these stories do you know to be truth and how much of it has been exaggerated in the retelling? We haven't seen any evidence of such practices so far." She could tell by the look on his face that he was disappointed in her unwillingness to believe him, but she couldn't allow herself to be frightened by fire-side stories; she had enough hatred to contend with in Gwladus to add a group of religious zealots as well. "But it's as well to be aware of potential threats. I'll tell the rest of the group. In the meantime, do you think you could lead us to one of the villages you used to know? We're running low on food and I think we could all do with a proper bed this night."

Thrax nodded. "I recall one not too far from here. We should be there by sundown."

"Thank you, Thrax."

"They may even have news of our quarry."

The warrior-princess wasn't so certain but she nodded anyway and turned her horse so that she could talk to the rest of her women.

"Pah!" said Gwladus after Rosmerta had briefed them on the possible threat the Bagaudas posed. "Excuses for his cowardice! There would be none of this if a woman were leading the hunting party!"

"A woman is leading you," said Rosmerta with tight control, "and I'm warning you that a native of these lands is aware of dangers that we aren't. So if you'd like to see the end of this mission, I suggest you keep your wits about you."

She turned away before the salt-merchant could reply and goad her into yet another argument. That woman! For a terrible heartbeat she wished that they would come upon a wild band of Bagaudas just so Thrax could be proved right. And perhaps have the spiteful woman killed in the crossfire. She shook herself. Her mother hadn't raised her to wish death on anyone, not even one so vicious as Gwladus. Her daughter had been slain, after all; her suffering must be grim. She knew full well that her own mother would be distraught beyond words if she ever heard of her daughter's untimely death.

The sudden thought of her mother, so far away now, made her heart ache and her eyes burn with tears. Always she'd been so close at hand to offer her counsel and her wisdom, but now Rosmerta had no one to whom she could turn. A flurry of regret settled around her like a flock of restless birds; she'd been so desperate to prove her worth as the next warrior-queen that she'd put herself on this mission without thinking of the consequences—she wasn't capable of undertaking such a task without her mother's words to guide her. And now she would probably get them all killed by a group of fanatics of a fledgeling religion.

"Rosmerta?"

She jumped a little in her saddle and pushed all of her detrimental thoughts aside. "Yes, Thrax?"

"The village is just past this clearing if my reckoning is correct."

"Thank you."

Life once more! She knew well that forests were sacred to so many gods and goddesses, and she admired trees for their age and beauty, but she couldn't quash her desire to see other people again, to talk and eat with them, to swap stories over a friendly hearth-fire. It would be welcome respite to what, for her, had turned into a gloomy day.

Thrax trotted on ahead in order to inform the villagers that friends were arriving seeking shelter and food, if they could spare such. Alarm enveloped her when she heard him cry out, and a monstrous murder of crows rose up from the trees ahead like a storm cloud. Her stomach turned sour at the omen but she nudged her horse into a trot, only to pull it sharply to a halt when she finally drew level with Thrax.

"Boudica preserve us," whispered Gwladus as she joined Rosmerta on the outskirts of the village. "What happened here?"

"Dibu e debu," the Gaulish trader whispered hoarsely.

Rosmerta couldn't answer her either, and was glad that she couldn't for the sight that had befallen them was too evil to be true.

Hanging from the trees were the inhabitants of the village; men, woman and—Rosmerta choked back a sob of dismay—children. All of them had been stripped naked and carved across their skin were strange markings, but these were only visible on those bodies which had been strung up on the outskirts of the village; those closest to it were scorched and blackened where the flames of their burned dwellings had reached out and grabbed at them. The stink of burned and rotting flesh was unbearable. Jumping out of her saddle, she bent double and vomited until there was nothing left inside her.

"Cut them down!" she cried and the spear-women jumped from their own mounts to obey her. "Gwladus, to me. We need wood for pyres."

She didn't want to look upon the desecrated and crow-pecked bodies, but it couldn't be avoided as she helped to lift them onto the pyres. The images would haunt her for the rest of her life.

When the fires were finally lit and prayers were said to Boudica and the Gaulish gods to guide their souls to Otherworld, Rosmerta turned to Thrax.

"The markings. Have you seen them before?"

He nodded, and the others gathered around him. "One

marking. Repeated several times on each body."

Rosmerta dropped her head and offered her own prayer to her namesake goddess to watch out for the souls of those who had suffered so terribly at the end of their lives.

"What does it mean?" said Gwynfor. "I've never come across it before."

"And nor would you," said Thrax. "It's the mark of Rome's one true god."

"But what does it mean?"

"It means," said Thrax, looking up at each of them, "that the Bagaudas were here. The Bagaudas did this and left them as a sign that they were here to any who came across this village."

Rosmerta felt her heart go cold. Had she done this? Had her wish for proof of their existence been granted to her? She sobbed into her hands once more.

"What can we do?" said Gwladus. "If they have a lair near here then we should hunt them out and seek revenge for the people they've defiled in the name of their false god!"

Thrax shook his head. "The Bagaudas have always taken old Roman villas as their hideouts, it's why I led to you that one south of Lutetia."

"Then let's seek out the nearest Roman villa and rain punishment down upon them! If you're right and the sister-slayer has joined such a band of murderers then we catch him at the same time!" said Gwladus, looking at the other three spear-women for accordance to her plan.

"You don't understand," said Thrax. "When we exit this forest, there is only one place the Bagaudas would go."

"Then we go there too!"

"It's not just a Roman villa," said Thrax, "it's a Bagauda stronghold, an entire town. There could be hundreds of them there; we'd be outnumbered."

"Pah! I'm not frighted by them or their false god!"

"Rosmerta," said Thrax, finally turning to her. She saw the

fear clearly in his eyes. "You've seen what these men are capable of; would you willingly lead your women into such danger?"

No, she wouldn't. But she had an oath to fulfil to her mother. And perhaps to these poor people who were now burning again because of her careless wish. "If you're right and the sister-slayer has joined a group of Bagaudas, how likely is it that he would now be in this stronghold you mention?"

The trader rubbed his face with hands then pulled them through his queued tangle of dark hair. "Very. Most Bagaudas go there eventually. I'd hoped that we'd have found the boy who killed my love before going so far south, but..."

Whatever the end of his sentence was, he clearly couldn't bring himself to say it. "You're not beholden to us in any way, Thrax," Rosmerta said to him then. "You've already done enough. All I ask is that you show us this place you speak of that we might fulfil our duty. Will you do that for us? For me?"

He nodded sombrely. "I will, lady. I'll take you to Lugdunum."

– 26 –

The Moon of Ogronios (Ice-time), 333 C.E.
Dubras, Cantiaci tribal lands; Brython

"Trahaearn said he's made enough suits of armour for your household guard," Airmed told her mother, "and they're waiting in the armoury. But if you want enough for an entire army he'll need many more hands."

"Tell him he can use whomsoever he wishes," said Sulis. Her face was grave, and the flicker of disappointment at hearing that only three hundred suits were ready had not gone unnoticed by Airmed. "If we're going to march on the Druids at Trinovantes then I want at least a thousand armoured warriors."

"A thousand? But, Mother; it's taken him four seasons to build three hundred!"

"I know. I intend to take war to the Druids when this moon has passed and I don't expect Trahaearn to have built seven hundred new suits by then. But if he knows that is what I want, he will work his hardest to try and please me."

"I see. I'll go directly to the smithy."

"Good. Have you heard news of Mair, our Trinovantes guest?"

Airmed had heard a good deal of news for she had become quite friendly with the woman since her arrival. At first she had simply wanted to comfort Mair because she'd been through a terrible ordeal; witnessing the murder of her warrior-queen at the hands of the Picts, only to discover that it had been the Druids who'd betrayed their entire tribe. She'd barely escaped with her life. And despite the ancient animosity that existed between their tribes because the Cantiaci had once welcomed the Romans into their lands more than three hundred summers past, Mair had come to Sulis Warrior-Queen to warn her of the danger they might be facing.

But there was more to their friendship than even that. Mair, instead of collapsing under the weight of her woe, had found strength. She had no intention of letting the Druids get away with the betrayal and murder of her warrior-queen; and every spare moment was spent preparing herself for facing Sirona's killers. Airmed admired her courage, and her stubborn resolve reminded the young princess a lot of her sister, Rosmerta. Thus, she would seek out her company whenever she could. And just like Rosmerta, Mair was only too happy to sit and talk with her.

"She's practising with the spear-women this very moment," Airmed said. "She intends to march to war with you."

"Good," said Sulis, and Airmed saw her mother was impressed. "She will be invaluable to us when we reach the heart of her lands."

Airmed nodded. She hadn't yet found the courage to ask her mother if she would be permitted to ride with them. She wanted to, with every thread of her tender spirit; but she suspected her mother would be more than reticent about sending yet another daughter into battle.

"Take my message to Trahaearn, then," said Sulis. Airmed smiled and turned to walk out of the grand door that separated the great hall from the market square. "Airmed. You've been a source of strength to me during this trying time," said the warrior-queen. "I wanted to tell you that. You've made your mother very proud, and it reassures me to have you bonded to the Atrebates tribe."

She smiled broadly at her mother, blushing slightly at such high praise. "Thank you." She turned and walked towards the door again. Yes; it was going to be very difficult to convince her mother to let her march to war.

The Moon of Ogronios (Ice-time), 333 C.E.
Lugdunum, south-east Gaul

The silence stretched out interminably; Arawn didn't know whether to try and cut down as many people as he could with the axe strapped to his back, or to cry.

"You're next in the arena," Rix said again.

He looked around at Ardus, Rix's younger brother, and was surprised to see an expression of tired annoyance on his face, as though he'd put up with type of thing too many times before. Behind him came a loud guffaw, and soon the crowd in the emperor's box was laughing along with their leader. Arawn felt a blush creep up from his neck. This was the second time the Bagaudas had shamed and humiliated him and he was fed up with it.

When they shame you, they shame me; this should not be tolerated.

Arawn slammed his axe into one of the marble pillars close to Rix's throne. The laughter ceased abruptly.

"As much as we enjoy your jesting," said Ardus, laying a calming hand on Arawn's arm, "we came here for a reason."

"Indeed?" said Rix. His eyes never left Arawn's.

"Our new friend here speaks to the one true god."

The box was once again wreathed in silence. Some mouths dropped open. Rix leaned forward in his throne, mimicking his brother's reaction upon first hearing the news. Arawn felt a surge of pride explode in his chest.

"Is that true?" said Rix.

Arawn nodded. "He tells me that we should be doing more to spread the one true faith throughout these pagan-infested lands."

Now many of the people in the box looked startled. It probably wasn't often, thought Arawn, that someone interrupts their games to tell their leader what to do.

"And how are we supposed to do that?"

"By travelling to Rome," said Arawn, then smiled as the Bagaudas began talking among themselves in incredulous whispers. "We bring the Roman priests through these lands all the way to Brython, and with us the one true faith. With the might of Rome behind us, we'll no longer have to suffer the foulness of pagans and the humiliation of women."

To his delight, a few of the assembled Bagaudas cheered.

"A very ambitious undertaking," said Rix. "Some of our predecessors have tried to reach Rome and failed. There are many more pagans out there than Bagaudas. And Rome is far away. What makes you think we'll be successful?"

"Because I speak to the one true god," said Arawn, "and he tells me this shall be done."

"If we march with a large enough army," said Ardus, "we needn't fear the wrath of pagans. And once we've passed the mountains we're bound to find others who want to join us. Just as there are Bagaudas throughout these lands fighting secretly against the pagans, there will be those like us over the mountains."

"And what if there aren't?" said Nertos suddenly. Arawn knew the second-in-command hated this idea purely because it wasn't he who had been chosen for communion with the one true god, and to Arawn's annoyance there were some in the box who nodded in agreement with him.

He stifled a growl. "If there aren't others like us across the mountains," said Arawn, "it means they will see the wisdom of the one true god when we send them to hell."

Ardus beamed at him and he grinned back.

"With the might of the Roman priests beside us," said Arawn, turning now to Rix, "the pagans won't be able to resist, and the one true god will be lord over all these lands, as he should already be if not for the dead rebel witch-queen of Brython." He spat, not wishing to have even her name in his mouth. "And if we gift the one true god with the lands of Brython then we will be blessed indeed and gifted beyond our wildest dreams. No longer will we suffer warrior-queens, for we will be made into priest-kings and shall rule all the lands in the name of the one true god."

The crowd cheered properly this time, with Rix cheering loudest of all.

"How many men do you have here?" Arawn asked him.

"Close to five thousand live here, including slaves and whores," said Rix. "But no more than three thousand are warriors. I would need to leave at least a thousand here to guard Lugdunum while I'm gone."

Arawn nodded. "Two thousand spears will be enough to convince the Roman priests that we are ready to take the lands in the name of the one true god."

"We shall be the army of the one true god!" called Rix, and his followers cheered.

Arawn turned to Ardus and spoke quietly. "How long do you think it will be before we can leave?"

Ardus shrugged. "He'll have to organise his men, plus all the food and maybe some horses. None of us has ever attempted an expedition such as this so we might be here for several days at least. You should enjoy yourself while you're here; we'll be on the road for a long time once we've left. There's plenty of wine, soft beds, and women we can use."

Arawn nodded. "But we stay here no longer than necessary."

* * *

He left the business of organising to Ardus and Rix. As a speaker to the one true god Arawn was above such things. Instead, he felt a desire to demonstrate his power from the one true god to the pagans. He often thought about how he'd overpowered Sirom in order to save his friend, Thrax, from her evil, and it made him burn. He longed to feel such strength again.

On their first night in Lugdunum, after the evening feast of roast boar and wine, he went to where the pagan slaves were kept. Some would be put to work, some put into the gaming arena, but until that was decided they were all put into wooden cages in an area of the city far enough away from Rix's great hall where he wouldn't be offended by their stink.

The cages were as tall as a man and as narrow, forcing the pagans to stand. Once they were in, they were unable to even turn around. The opening of each cage was held shut by a knotted thong of hide, but the slaves were unable to undo such a simple contraption because their hands were bound behind them.

Arawn walked among the cages, looking into the faces of the pagan slaves, determining which one should experience the power of the one true god. He still wore his axe strapped to his back; the weight of it there comforted him. And tied to his waist was the knife he'd taken from the old couple's hut in which he'd spent the night and burned the next morning before finding his band of Bagaudas.

None of the women appealed to him as Sirom had done. Yes, they were as scared as she was, perhaps more so. But they were already afraid. Sirom hadn't been at first, because she hadn't expected her punishment for defiling his friend, Thrax. Thrax, with his solid shoulders, large blue eyes, and wide mouth always smiling. How he had loved listening to his stories! But he had been defiled by that evil witch woman, and should have been punished with her. He should have beaten Thrax to the floor and forced him to feel the strength within him as Sirom had felt it.

Burning excitement coursed through him again and the urge to take someone filled him violently. Then he saw him: a slave who looked so much like Thrax he could have been his younger brother. He was perhaps only two or three summers older than Arawn himself, but shorter and broader. He looked at Arawn with hatred and defiance, and Arawn smiled. He probably thinks I'm here to take him to the gaming arena, he thought.

"My name is Arawn ap Emlyn," he said. "I've come to take you away."

Slicing through the leather thong, Arawn pulled open the cage door, the wood creaking under the force. The pagan shifted but there was nowhere for him to go. Arawn pulled him by the front of his tunic, glad he didn't have his flailing hands to worry about, and led him roughly away from the rest of the slave cages.

"I won't fight for you," the pagan said, his voice showing no signs of fear. Yet. "The moment you hand me a weapon I'll kill myself. I won't fight for your pleasure."

"I don't expect you to *fight* for my pleasure," said Arawn.

They were in a quiet side-street. Most of the men were making preparations for the coming expedition to Rome; those who weren't were drinking wine and enjoying women. There was nobody around to hear Arawn enjoy the pagan slave.

He pushed him hard against the wall, relishing the sound of his head knocking against the stone. Then he took his knife again and sliced open the front of the slave's already torn tunic. With his hands bound behind him it was unable to fall to the ground, but it didn't matter. Fear was starting to show in the pagan's eyes, so like Thrax's, and Arawn's blood pounded. He ran the knife down his chest—only scratching not drawing blood—but the slave whimpered. When he reached the hide laces of his leggings he ripped them open with a flick of the wrist. The pagan tried to bolt then but Arawn cracked his head so hard against the wall it dazed him, and Arawn lowered him gently to the floor, kicking his legs apart as he had done Sirom's.

He stood above him, slowly untying the laces at the front of his own leggings with his knife still in his hand, aching with anticipation.

"And as you feel my power pouring into you," he said, his voice hoarse, "I'm going to slit your throat and send you to hell."

– 27 –

The Moon of Cutios (Windy-time), 333 C.E.
Deceangli tribal lands, Brython

Thousands of men waited for them. It seemed as though they'd been camped there for many days; fires burned, many of which had piles of wood next to them waiting to be fed to the flames. Some had cauldrons hanging over them, or the carcass of a wild animal. Men were sitting and talking in groups; some were wandering from camp to camp, some were singing. It had the air of a festival, but if it were indeed such, there was something missing from it.

"There are no women and children," said Emrys. He was walking next to Heddgwyn, and the Arch Druid looked at him with surprise.

"Children can't fight, and women are their enemy." He turned back to the hoard of men. "They're hardly going to invite the enemy into their camp, are they? Don't tell me the journey through the mountain passes has stripped your communion with Belenos from your memory?"

"Of course it hasn't, but…all women? I thought we were going to battle the warrior-queens and their spear-women. Us. The Druids. Now we have an army of men, and you're telling me they're willing to kill *all* women? Their mothers, sisters, wives?"

"How many happy households have you seen, son? During the course of our pilgrimage, how many men did you meet that were thankful for their lot in life?"

An image of a man receiving a public flogging for raising a hand to his wife flashed into his mind. Celyddon, he was called, and there were men all over these lands who would be only too happy to take such control away from their wives.

"You're right. If Boudica and her daughters hadn't stolen these lands from the old gods, men wouldn't suffer the injustice they do now."

"Precisely, my son."

Heddgwyn led the Druids towards the camp, and when the men at the outer end of it saw them they began to cheer. It spread through the camp until the sound was deafening; men stood and bellowed their approval, their contentment at finally fighting back, their hope that soon their lives wouldn't be terrorised by the women who lived in them. Some banged swords on shields, others swung leather slingshots around above their heads, others still punched spears high into the air as they roared with happiness, and Emrys wondered how they had got such weapons; such dangerous tools were solely the dominion of warriors and women. Other men had brought with them anything that could be vicious in battle; axes, hoes, scythes, hunting knives. The women they fought would no doubt be more skilled, but he knew these men had the old gods on their side. They were fighting for truth and justice.

"Men of Belenos!" cried Heddgwyn then, raising his arms and gaining instantly the attention of all men around them. Emrys never realised the silence of so many people could be so tangible. "We ride towards a new era. No more will Boudica and her daughters, the greatest usurpers since the Romans, control these lands. No more will you be slaves to your women. These lands belong us. They belong to men!" The rapt crowd roared their approval.

"But more than that, they belong to the old gods." Now Heddgwyn turned to his son and held him out for all to see. "Emrys, Druid of the third level, died and was resurrected through the Cauldron of Rebirth, and during his time in Otherworld he spoke with Belenos himself."

It was as though the world had stopped turning, and all sound had been sucked out of it. Not even a bird dared break the silence which now surrounded them.

"Tell them what the sun god said to you, my son."

Never before had Emrys been the focus of such attention. A small part of him found it alarming, but the greater part of him found it intoxicating, to have so many eager eyes looking at him, holding their breath until he uttered his words. He felt that he wanted to prolong the sensation but if he did so, he knew he would burst.

"The sun god said—" he looked all around at the upturned faces before him "—blood would be spilled in his name!"

The gathered hoard raised the very sky with their uproarious approval. Heddgwyn laughed and pulled his son towards him that he might embrace him.

"That was well said, my son," he said when they parted. "You do me proud."

Emrys felt his chest swell. But all too soon it was deflated.

"Heddgwyn!" A man ran towards him. Tall and broad-shouldered, hair like polished chestnuts tied back with a leather thong. He was dressed head to foot in fur and hide, but despite his changed appearance, Emrys recognised the wild man instantly.

"I thought we were rid of him," he said to his father.

"He has an important role to play in taking back these lands for the old gods." He held up his hands in greeting. "Emlyn! I can't say how good it is to see you again! You've done well here." He looked around the camp with approval.

"Thank you, lord," said Emlyn, the wild man, though there was no pride in his voice. "The Deceangli fell quickly, just as you predicted, but I fear news will spread fast to the Cornovii, if it hasn't reached them already."

"Then time is of the essence."

"Deceangli fell quickly? What do you mean?" said Emrys.

"When Emlyn left us I told him to rally an army and take out the warrior-queen and her spear-women which, as you can see, he's done with great efficiency."

"She's dead?"

The wild man nodded once, his face betraying no emotion. "And all her spear-women. Of course, the Deceangli Druids helped us enter her fort—they had been ready ever since Gwynfor's signal last Samhain." Now he looked at Heddgwyn with admiration. "If I had known my wife's…that the Atrebates rebellion was nothing more than a signal for all this then I wouldn't have hidden in the wild."

"Then I wouldn't have found you," said Heddgwyn, laying a hand on the wild man's shoulder. "And while my Druids have been ready for a long time, I needed you to organise the men. Now tell me, is there any other news of the Deceangli?"

"Some of the female subjects tried to fight for their dead queen, but as our numbers grew the women eventually submitted. Deceangli is ready for Druid rule, but we must move now before Cornovii can prepare for attack. Our numbers may be many, but none of these men has ever been trained as a warrior. We lost some to the Deceangli spear-women, but we were fortunate in that they were unprepared for battle."

Heddgwyn nodded. "Then we move out at once. The Druids of each tribe may not be able to convince their warrior-queens of their loyalty for very much longer."

"I'll rally the men," said the wild man, and walked into the forest of camp fires.

"You look disconcerted, my son, are you well?"

The figure of the wild man had been completely consumed by the horde, but in his wake Emrys saw the men stand and cheer, gather their makeshift weapons and stamp out their hearth-fires now that they were called upon to take the next tribe. Blood would be spilled in his name. Blood had already been spilled in his name; and even though he knew it was as the sun god demanded, deep in his secret heart there was a seed of doubt. Did that make him a traitor? He looked at his father, his face so full of concern, his hand resting lightly on his shoulder to give him comfort. It was a father he'd never known before; it was a father he didn't want to lose.

"I remember," said Emrys, "before I was reborn, I was looking at the Cauldron."

"You saw the carvings move?"

For a moment he forgot his concern in his surprise. "You saw that too?"

"We are father and son in so many ways," said Heddgwyn, clasping both of his shoulders and smiling into his face.

"In the carvings, I saw the sun god conquer the demons with a sword of flame."

"As did I."

"But the people of Brython are not demons, Father; they're flesh and blood. I understand that these lands were usurped by Boudica and her daughters, I understand that they must be reclaimed for the old gods; but must the cost truly be so much death?"

His father smiled at him and pulled him a little closer. All around, the sound of a thousand men readying for war was a dull roar.

"You have a gentle spirit, Emrys, and for that reason alone it will make you one of the greatest Druids these lands have ever seen. And even though you know it to be right, your heart still breaks for those who have angered the old gods and must be punished. Your pain makes me proud, my son, for I feel it too. What kind of men would we be if we didn't suffer to inflict the wrath of the old gods on the damned?

"And they are damned, for not only do the women worship Boudica the usurper, but generations of warrior-queens have believed they become living goddesses once they are crowned. This is gravest sacrilege, Emrys. You must remember that we work for the old gods. We are the chosen ones amongst all the people on this sacred isle of Brython. You yourself have spoken to Belenos and heard his words."

"Blood will be spilled in my name."

"Blood will be spilled in his name, yes." Heddgwyn clasped his son's shoulders a little tighter. "So we mustn't falter from the path."

"We won't, Father."

"Good. That is very good."

Watching his father move through the gathered host as the wild man had done, Emrys strengthened himself as best he could. He had his father on his side. He had the old gods on his side. Now he must march to war.

The Moon of Cutios (Windy-time) 333 C.E.
Cantiaci tribal lands, Brython

She pushed Dawn-chaser as hard as she could but she still wasn't sure if she would reach her mother in time.

This morning, Airmed had been disappointed that her mother had refused her request to march on the Druids in Trinovantes; so disappointed, in fact, that she'd left the palace at dawn, taken her beloved horse, Dawn-chaser, from the stable and ridden out to the white cliffs of Dubras so she wouldn't have to see her mother leave without her. As the beast beneath her pounded the damp downs that stretched on flatly to the cliffs' edge she'd wondered at her feelings. She didn't enjoy warfare. Neither did Rosa, though she believed she hid it from her younger sister, but in that respect the two sisters were twinned. Airmed preferred herb-lore; tending her gardens, and watching things grow. She had no desire to see anything cut down, no matter how traitorous. But Rosmerta had left her, then Emrys, and now her mother. She couldn't bear the thought of being left behind again so she'd taken herself away to avoid the pain.

And now, as Dawn-chaser scudded into the town, hooves clattering across the pave-stones, she realised just how fortunate she'd been. Truly the gods and goddesses had been looking down on her and guiding her thoughts this morning; and she knew that the instant she'd seen the most welcome sight ever to befall her eyes when she stared out across the wind-blown ocean.

Expertly she guided her horse through the streets, avoiding any mortal accidents with any of her subjects, until she was back out on open land and she saw the gleaming, deadly band of warriors who would take back Trinovantes from the Druid traitors. She bent down low in her saddle, clinging to Dawn-chaser's neck, and pushed him on.

"Mother!"

Still she was too far. The wind snatched her voice as soon as she opened her mouth and threw it behind her so that even the last of the spear-women that followed their warrior-queen to battle couldn't hear her.

"Dig deep, Dawn-chaser," she whispered into his ears as she clung to his neck. "I must reach the warrior-queen. I must reach my mother."

The horse obeyed as Airmed knew he would, and she felt him strain and push to reach his brothers and sisters in the war-host.

"Mother!"

This time her cry was heard. A warrior turned at the sound, recognised her in an instant and sent the call along the host until it reached the ears of her mother. Well-trained, the war-host parted so that Airmed had a clear path to the warrior-queen, who looked fearsome in the full battle-armour that Trahaearn had constructed for her; and the chariot in which she stood gleamed from the oil used to ensure suppleness and flexibility in battle.

Not until she was level with her mother did Airmed rein in her mount.

"What are you doing here?" Her mother wasn't angry; she knew her daughter wouldn't disobey her unless there were good reason. But neither was she pleased.

"Boats! I saw boats!"

"Calm yourself and catch your breath, Airmed, then tell me clearly what you mean." But she must have guessed because she was already tugging on the reins of the steeds pulling her chariot.

"Boats coming into harbour, Mother, I saw them! Bearing the flags of Cantiaci and Atrebates! I saw them and came directly to you! It can mean only one thing!"

"Praise Boudica and all the old gods, you're right, my daughter, and I thank you for it," said the warrior-queen with a smile of pure pleasure. "It means our Rosmerta has returned to us at last."

* * *

The war on the Druid traitors would not be delayed, Airmed's mother assured Mair, but the spear-women must ride without their warrior-queen. Rosmerta Warrior-Princess had returned with the sister-slayer of Atrebates and Sulis of Cantiaci needed to be there to meet them. Mair of Trinovantes, in Airmed's young eyes a most capable woman in spite of her ordeal, agreed eagerly to take Sulis' place and lead the Cantiaci warriors through her home lands and seek revenge against those who had slain her leader.

When they reached the town, she saw that the first of the Cantiaci spear-women from the boat had already arrived and she marvelled; they must have pushed their steeds almost to breaking point to have made such time. The thought had Airmed's heart constricting; they didn't race back to bring bad news, did they? Her eyes poured over the handful of warriors in the town square but she couldn't see her sister among them. It meant nothing, she assured herself, only that she'd sent spear-women ahead of her to warn of their arrival. Any heartbeat now she'll arrive victorious on her steed. Any heartbeat now.

"Terrwyn," called her mother as she steered her horse to a stop and leapt from the saddle. Her most trusted spear-woman did the same and they caught each other in the strong embrace of true and life-long friends. "It is so good to see you again! Tell me what news you bring! Tell me what good, good news you bring!"

While Terrwyn's face showed happiness at seeing her warrior-queen again, it didn't match the joy that shone from her mother's. Airmed kissed Dawn-chaser's neck to thank him for working so hard for her, then leapt from the saddle even as her heart leapt into her throat. Why wasn't Terrwyn overjoyed? And why hadn't her sister arrived yet?

"Sulis Warrior-Queen," said Terrwyn, bowing. "I bring you news, but I fear you will not think it good."

"Boudica save me, is it my daughter? Is she—"

"She is alive and well, my Warrior-Queen."

Airmed steadied herself against the strength of her horse.

"Then where is she?" said Airmed's mother.

"Still in Gaul, my lady. The sister-slayer evaded us, I know not how. I believe him dead, but Rosmerta believed that to come back without him would mean her failure." Airmed's heart broke as she saw her mother's eyes fill with tears. "She has good warriors with her still, and a Gaulish guide whom we met in Lutetia. He knows the lands there well for he is a trader and widely travelled."

"I would not have thought her a failure for coming back to me," Sulis whispered. "She has been away too long."

Terrwyn nodded. "It was for that reason she sent me back with the host, my lady. And I can see from your dress you were marching to battle. Is it the Picts? My women will be ready to fight after a good meal."

Airmed's mother waved a hand, brushing away Terrwyn's question; nothing was important compared to her lost daughter. "Tell me, my dear friend, do you think she'll come back to me?"

Now the warrior held the warrior-queen's arms tenderly, one friend to another. "She is wise and skilled beyond her years, you have taught her well. But more than that, she is mightily gifted with intuition. She will succeed where we cannot, and she'll come back to you victorious. She'll come back to you safe."

Sulis nodded. "She is, you're right. She'll come back to me safe. Now you must come back to the palace to rest and eat; and while you do so you can tell me of your adventure in Gaul. And I shall tell you of the sad deeds that have befallen Brython and why I march to war."

The warrior-queen and her favoured spear-woman leapt back up into their saddles and Airmed followed suit, but she didn't share the hope that Terrwyn had bestowed upon her mother. Twinned they were, Airmed and Rosmerta, in that they preferred peace over warfare; but she fervently prayed that they weren't also twinned with intuition.

Because Airmed felt the war-host's return without its leader was a bad omen. A very bad omen indeed.

– 28 –

The Moon of Cutios (Windy-time), 333 C.E.
Near Lugdunum, south-east Gaul

"Pah! It's nothing but a burnt wasteland," said Gwladus. "You can smell it from here. Once the horses are watered and the women are rested we should follow the river south."

"The wasteland you see is where the pagans used to live," said Thrax. "The Bagaudas live in the city on the hill. They call it Lugdunum. And while it may look quiet, be assured that we are being watched."

"We're not even sure if the sister-slayer has taken up with Bagaudas," said Gwladus, squaring up to the trader. She was a head taller than him, and the moons of travelling had been kind to her, Rosmerta realised. She was still well-muscled, but she was leaner now and her skin glowed brown from exposure to the sun. If her face weren't twisted with bitterness she'd probably be beautiful. "You could be leading us farther away rather than towards him."

Thrax had no fear of women, whether they held spears or not. "We followed his trail all the way to the old Roman villa which only looked recently deserted by the time we got there, and only bands of Bagaudas ever occupy such places. If the buildings aren't demolished, or the stones haven't been taken to build other homes, no local tribesman would ever live in it for fear of the Roman ghosts. And would you deny the evidence we saw at that village in the forest?"

Gwladus only glowered at him.

"There are no other settlements in these parts, only that." He pointed to the hill that grew out of the bank of the river. "The largest settlement of Bagaudas in all of Gaul, and I know he's there. No one goes near the place now except other Bagaudas because of the stories."

"What stories?" asked Rosmerta.

"The Bagaudas capture people who don't believe in their one true god and kill them. In that place."

"One true god. Pah!"

"Why would they do that?" said Rosmerta.

"Because they hate us," said Thrax. "They call us pagans and they hate us because the Romans hate us. Because we don't believe in their one true god. And as ridiculous as their god may seem," he said, looking at Gwladus, "he's fierce, and he's made them so."

"If their god is male," said Gwladus, "how could he possibly be powerful?"

"Because he's a god," said Thrax. "Before your goddess Boudica was born there were many male gods, and all of them were very powerful. New gods are as powerful as old gods, and male gods as powerful as goddesses. If you don't accept that then the Bagaudas will kill you before you've even realised you're dead."

"Pah!" Gwladus spat three times and stalked off.

"She is not a pleasant woman."

"She isn't," Rosmerta agreed with a smile. "But she's strong, and if these Bagaudas are as bad as you say they are, we'll need her strength here. Unfortunately." She looked up at the hill called Lugdunum. "You say they already know we're here."

Thrax nodded.

"Then we should wait until nightfall before we climb the hill. It may not give us much of an advantage, but we'll be harder to see in the darkness."

"And we won't be able to see them, either."

"Then let's hope all of our gods, old and new, prove stronger than their one god so we can breach their city."

* * *

At long last the sun sank below the horizon and Rosmerta felt she could breathe again. In truth, the woollen dress she wore, with its long sleeves and long skirt, wasn't as appropriate for this foreign land during Cutios as it was in her own lands during the same moon. At home it was windy-time, and how welcome a strong breeze would be right now to cool the sweat off her brow. But she wasn't at home. She was far away in an alien country where the days were hotter than they should be because, for all she knew, the moon of windy-time didn't even exist here.

She pulled the dagger out from the side of her right boot—her mother believed that all royal women should wear concealed weapons, and so she'd had the boots made especially for that purpose—and, plucking up the sleeve at her left shoulder with her left hand, she cut into the material.

"What are you doing?" Gwladus' tone wasn't one that Rosmerta cared for.

"Precisely what it looks like." She pulled the severed sleeve off her arm, put the dagger in her left hand and started on the opposite side. "Cutting off my sleeves."

"We should leave our horses here," said Thrax. "It's too steep a climb for them. Especially as they're laden."

"Agreed," said Rosmerta, pulling off her right sleeve. "That's much better." She slid the dagger back into the hide straps on the side of her boot. "How many Bagaudas will we be facing once we're inside the city?"

Thrax shrugged. "Rumours say countless thousands. But it's difficult to judge the accuracy of rumours."

"Indeed," said the warrior-princess. "The truth can be so distorted that it becomes a lie. Which some people may use to their advantage." Her eyes flicked to Gwladus. "Perhaps the Bagaudas are responsible for such hearsay. But what do you think?"

Thrax shrugged. "Enough for an army so terrifying it frightened all the local people away."

"It's pointless trying to guess at numbers when nobody has any," said Gwladus. "We are five women. It's probably safe to assume that we're outnumbered."

Thrax looked at Rosmerta and she saw the hopelessness in his eyes.

"But while they might be vicious and numerous," Gwladus continued, oblivious, "we're trained and deadly. They may well be willing to hand the sister-slayer over to us once they see their men die."

"You're women and you're pagans," said Thrax grimly. "They'll fight you until either you're all dead, or they are."

"Then we'll just have to make sure it's them," said Rosmerta. Brave words, and even Gwladus looked faintly impressed. But she didn't feel brave. She'd come on this mission to ensure Gwladus didn't unjustly slay her own son; she hadn't thought she'd be going into battle against armed fanatics. She'd brought her weapons, but no armour. She smiled ruefully. Only moments before she was complaining about wearing too many clothes. Now she wanted more.

"What's there to smile about?" Gwladus demanded.

"Nothing," said Rosmerta. "Absolutely nothing at all."

* * *

It was some time after the sun had disappeared behind the horizon that it was finally dark. The three spear-women who had remained with their warrior-princess were restless having been promised blood, but having to wait to claim it. Gwynfor, Gwladus' pet Druid whom Rosmerta distrusted even more than the salt-merchant, was bent over his rune-sticks and cater-wauling in his strange, magical language. The spear-women gave him a wide berth but she could tell from their countenance that they were comforted by his presence even if they were discomforted by his deformed appearance. They had a Druid, but the Bagaudas, according to Thrax, wouldn't allow such an evil because of their faith in their one true god.

"Build a fire," Rosmerta ordered. "We must look like we're setting up camp for the night." It was a simple ruse, but sometimes it was easier to fool those who believed they were infallible purely because they believed they were.

At least it was cooler when they started their ascent up the hill. Smothered with mud from the river bank so their bronze armour and iron spear tips wouldn't shine in the moonlight, the three spear-women marched snake-like up the hill, in single-file behind Rosmerta and Thrax. Gwladus and Gwynfor came after, and he was still mumbling under his breath and scattering stinking herbs about himself.

"What's he doing?" Thrax whispered to Rosmerta.

"I'm veiling the sky," said Gwynfor, his voice cracked. Rosmerta looked up. It had been a hot, cloudless day, and the night sky was similarly empty. The moon was rising and the first stars were coming out.

"Is that what your rune-sticks told you to do?" asked Thrax.

The Druid tutted. "The rune-sticks told me we would have success, but only if we move unseen."

"These trees will keep us hidden for a while, but when we reach the city gates we'll have to trust to your magic."

Gwynfor didn't grace that statement with a comment.

Under the trees the darkness was almost complete, but there was a well-worn path so finding their way wasn't too difficult. Entering the city would be the problem. The Romans, Thrax had told them, had built a wall around it, as they did with all of their most important cities, and the only entrance was through a city gate. Assuredly this would be guarded now by Bagaudas. And where old city walls had been torn down by local tribes in other cities, the Bagaudas would have kept the walls around Lugdunum in good repair in order to protect their stronghold.

There would be a back way in however, Thrax had certified,

and it would likely be less guarded. He didn't know precisely where this was, so Thrax kept them under the cover of trees until they had walked a fair distance around the other side of the hill.

Rosmerta then ordered two spear-women to creep out of the trees and find the city's back gate. They were gone for such a lengthy time that Rosmerta felt the stirrings of fear deep down in her belly. The Bagaudas had followed their progress the entire time, had killed her two spear-women, and were now waiting for them to reveal themselves so they could all be slaughtered. She was about to face her meagre troop and order them to retreat when she heard soft footsteps through the undergrowth.

"We found the gate, my lady," said one of the spear-women. "It seems to be unguarded. But it was difficult to tell because the moon is hidden by thick cloud now."

Rosmerta looked at Gwynfor who smiled at her smugly.

"Did you see a way in?" she asked the spear-woman.

"Yes. Though the wall is high, the gate is rotten. It shouldn't be difficult to break through. The opening will be narrow, though; we'll have to enter one by one."

"If they're waiting for us on the other side, they'll kill us as soon as we enter."

"What shall we do, my lady?"

"They'll charge as soon as the gate is down," said Gwladus. "We let them come to us."

Rosmerta's instinct to gainsay Gwladus was strong, but she realised just in time that if she did, it would make her look cowardly. They would have to fight. "We make a stand outside the city wall and kill them as soon as they come to us," said Rosmerta. "But as quietly as we can. It's possible they're waiting to ambush us; but it's equally possible they're not there at all. If we have the advantage of surprise I don't want to lose it." She looked across at Gwladus, who nodded. To Rosmerta's intense annoyance, she was pleased by the woman's agreement. Then it was time for the two spear-women to lead everyone to the back gate.

The sky *was* veiled when they came out from the trees, and for the first time Rosmerta was glad to have Gwladus' one-eyed pet Druid accompanying them. Eventually, the gate came into view and she was surprised it was still attached to the wall. Chunks of wood had fallen out, and when she dug her fingers into it, it crumbled between them.

With no visible way to open the gate from this side, she pushed against it. Clearly it was bolted or barred on the other side but the wood bent under her. Breaking through would be easy though conspicuous in such absence of other noise. The sound of cracking wood would peal like thunder in the quiet.

She turned round, waiting for her four spear-women to get into position before she spoke, but heard a shifting behind her. A dry, scratching sound, as of rotten wood against stone. She turned slowly, and saw the gate shifting inwards. It hung limply on one rusty hinge, but standing next to it was stocky, dark-haired man whose eyes had opened so wide in surprise it was almost amusing. He'd obviously heard her push against the gate and had come to inspect it. This meant there was no ambush waiting. They had the element of surprise after all, unless this man with his mouth hanging open raised the alarm.

Without thinking she reached for the sword held at her waist and stepped forward through the archway of the gate. With a back-handed swipe, her blade flew through air and sliced the man's throat, a spray of blood glistening black in the darkness. He fell to his knees, then to his face, and the glistening black pooled out around his head. It was over in a few heartbeats. She walked over to him and grabbed a handful of his tunic, then dragged him out through the gateway. He was heavy and left a trail of black, but it was better that no one came across a dead body just yet.

She dumped the corpse at the foot of the city wall and turned to face her troops. Thrax looked at her in utter shock, Gwladus nodded her approval.

"He was the enemy," the warrior-princess said. "His people were responsible for massacring that village and we must not forget that. We're lucky that they don't yet know we're here," she continued, "but if we all march through their city, they soon will. Gwladus, Thrax and you two spear-women will accompany me to search for Arawn." She turned now to the Druid and the remaining spear-woman. "You both will wait here and hold this gateway—it's our only way out."

They walked through silent, dark streets; and the further they walked into the city the more unnerved Rosmerta became. Instinct had caused her to draw her blade the first time, though the kill hadn't gladdened her. Knowing she was about to go into battle and take lives was a duty that sat as a heavy burden on her shoulders.

"Where are we supposed to find one person among thousands?" Thrax asked.

"By getting someone to tell us," said Gwladus, though the warrior-princess didn't believe it would be as simple as that. Thrax had told them much about the Bagaudas' behaviours, and cooperation with pagans wasn't among them. "Though it would be helpful if we knew where we were going." She looked at Thrax.

"Don't ask me," he said. "This is the first time I've set foot in this city. My only concern is getting back out."

They turned down another street, and Gwladus tripped, dropping her spear which clattered deafeningly across the flagstones, though it wasn't quite loud enough to drown out her curses.

"Boudica's tits," she said, once she'd recovered. "It's a body."

The company stopped. Rosmerta looked down and saw the corpse of young man with his throat slit and a dried puddle of blood haloing out around him. More disturbing, his tunic and leggings were so torn that he was almost naked. Rats had already begun the work of eating his rotting flesh, which was when she noticed the rank smell.

"This has been here for a while," she said.

"There's another one down here," said a spear-woman.

"And here," said Thrax. His voice was tight, as though he were trying hard not to lose his evening meal.

By the time they reached the end of the street Rosmerta had counted nine bodies.

"Are they Bagaudas?" she asked.

Thrax shook his head. "Slaves, I should think. Bagaudas wouldn't murder their own, and if they did they'd hide the bodies rather than dump them in an alley. I would say this is the work of a slave-murdering Bagauda."

"You've seen something like this before?"

"No. But it doesn't surprise me that they've thought up new ways to exterminate us."

The next street they turned onto was wider, evidently a thoroughfare of the city. But it was still empty. "If so many Bagaudas live here," said Rosmerta. "Why have we only seen one?"

Thrax shrugged.

At that moment Rosmerta heard a wailing. At first she thought it was an animal, but then she realised it sounded more like a woman in great distress.

"All Bagaudas are men, is that right?" she said to Thrax, who nodded. "Then there's a woman in trouble. We must help her."

"We're here to find the sister-slayer," Gwladus hissed.

Rosmerta rounded on her. "You'd let a woman suffer at the hands of these barbarians? You, a devout follower of Boudica? You've seen what they do to men, imagine what they'll do to women." Suitably chastened, Gwladus walked past the warrior-princess towards the direction of the wailing woman.

A sharp stench filled the still air, the rank odour of excrement and urine.

"We must be close to the city's middens or tanning pits," said the salt-merchant.

"These are no tanning pits," said Thrax. He was several steps ahead of them, but suddenly he stopped. "These are slave pits."

Rosmerta ran over to him. "Boudica bless and protect me," she whispered.

There must have been hundreds of them. Wooden cages all stacked next to each other, tall enough and wide enough for a man or woman to stand up in, but no more. The wailing had stopped now, but other noises could be heard; weeping, praying, whispering.

"Dibu e debu," said Thrax quietly.

"We must release them," Rosmerta said, shocked to her very core. They had slaves in Brython, of course they did. But they were never kept in such conditions as these, and certainly not because they believed in different gods to their masters.

Thrax needed no more encouragement. He pulled out his dagger from the sheath at his side and cut through the hide thongs that locked the cage. When he swung the door open, the occupant tried pathetically to keep out of reach of his grasp as though he were afraid, but Thrax spoke soothingly to him in a tongue that sounded like Rosmerta's but also sounded different. Eventually the slave allowed himself to be coaxed out of the cage, then Thrax cut off the bonds from his wrist.

"Help us release the others," he said to the slave, who nodded and set to work.

Though the freed slaves could unpick the knotted thongs at the front of the cages, they couldn't untie the wrist bonds, so Rosmerta spent her time slicing through them with the dagger she had pulled from her boot. It was taking a long time, and she felt sure that a band of Bagaudas would pass by at any moment and set to slaughtering them.

One of the slaves she'd freed, a very young woman of no more than fourteen summers, found a sharp stone and stood next to

Rosmerta, helping her slice the bonds of the uncaged slaves.

"Can you understand me?" Rosmerta said to her.

The young woman looked frightened, but nodded.

"What's your name?"

"Aballo."

"That's very pretty. How long have you been here, Aballo?"

The young woman shook her head. "They took me during the last moon."

"And they've kept you here ever since?"

She nodded briskly. "They take the strong men and women first."

"Why?"

She was silent for a moment, then whispered: "To fight in the arena."

"I don't understand."

"They make us fight in the arena, kill each other while they watch. There's wild animals too. We hear the sounds of battle from here." She shuddered and was silent. "But then a man started coming here at night to take a man away."

"Take which man?" said Rosmerta. She was horrified but fascinated.

"Any man," said Aballo. "He'd take a man away who'd never come back. I don't think he freed them. They never free us."

Rosmerta's heart grew cold. "How many men were taken?"

"Eight, perhaps, or nine. But then he stopped coming."

They were the bodies we found in the alley, Rosmerta thought. It wasn't enough for him to watch them kill themselves in this arena of theirs, he wanted to kill for himself.

"Why did he stop coming?"

"I don't know," said Aballo. "He just did."

A slave whose bonds she had just cut turned around. "I know why," he said. "They left. A great host of them. I heard some of them talk about it when they came to collect more of us for the arena."

"Are you sure?"

He nodded. "The man who was talking was angry about being left behind. He wanted to go as well. He talked about the glory of the one true god, but only those who were leaving were going to find it."

That was why the streets were so empty. Most of them had gone away. "Do you know where they went?" she said.

The man shook his head.

"Thank you," she said. "You've been very helpful." She turned to Aballo. "I need to talk to my friends. Can I leave you here for a moment?"

Aballo nodded, and Rosmerta pushed through the stinking crowd of freed men and women until she found Thrax.

"They've gone," she said. "Someone just told me. He said they'd gone to find the glory of the one true god. Do you know what that means?"

Thrax's eyes widened. "The one true god is Roman," he said. "If they've gone to find him…they're going to Rome."

* * *

The two spear-women led the party of freed slaves back through the deserted streets to the back gate of the city. Rosmerta had wanted to tell them to avoid the alley strewn with the dead slaves, but they didn't know their way around this city. She cursed herself for not moving the corpses when they came across them, but there was little she could do about it now.

She waited with Thrax and Gwladus. They would follow the freed slaves just in case any Bagaudas came up behind them.

"We don't know if the sister-slayer went to Rome with these Bagaudas," Gwladus hissed. "I say we stay here and look for him."

"If we do that and he has," said Rosmerta, "Arawn will get further and further away from us."

She saw Gwladus' face twist when she mentioned her son's true name, but before she could screech, a passing slave said, "Arawn? Arawn ap Emlyn?" and looked about himself in terror.

Rosmerta looked at Gwladus with confusion. "Emlyn was the sister-slayer's father," the salt-merchant said. "How do you know that name?"

"He came here," said the slave. "At night. To take men away."

Rosmerta felt her gorge rise. "No," she whispered.

"I was near the last man he took, and he told him his name. I prayed to all the gods and goddesses that he wouldn't come back and take me the next night, and he didn't. He stopped coming when the great host left."

"Thank you," Rosmerta said. "Keep following the others."

"It was *him,*" Gwladus whispered. "He killed those men we found in the alley."

Rosmerta nodded, but she didn't want to believe it. She could believe that his sister's death was an accident. She *had* believed it. And she'd managed to convince herself that Sirom's death was just a terrible coincidence; that Thrax's poor woman had been slain by another just as Arawn had started living with them. Even the deaths of those poor villagers she could lay at the feet of the faceless Bagaudas instead of Arawn's. But not this... This was neither accident nor coincidence.

"I think," said Thrax, his voice tight, "that it's clear Arawn left when the host of Bagaudas did. Which means he's going to Rome."

"Then that's where we'll find him," said Gwladus. "And that's where I'll kill him."

– 29 –

The Moon of Giamonios (Shoots-show) 333 C.E.
Beyond the mountains, Cis-Alpine Gaul

The pagan woman's spear skewered Nertos' shoulder even as Arawn watched and he laughed to see him cry out in pain and anger.

Leaping over the bodies of those he'd already slain, he swung his axe with all his god-strength and felt the lightning shock as the biting edge was buried in the pagan woman's face, then he grabbed her loosened spear and pulled it free from Nertos' shoulder.

"She was mine!" the unbeliever screamed.

"She would have killed you," Arawn replied. "Stuck by a woman and a pagan. The one true god isn't impressed."

"I would have had her if you'd left well alone!"

Turning, Arawn swung his axe and gathered the damned souls of two more pagans before facing Nertos again and grabbing a handful of his leather armour.

"Believe me when I say I would have let you die were the choice mine, but the one true god has a something special planned for you."

"He told you that, did he?"

"Look around you!" cried Arawn above the sound of crashing weapons and squealing pagans. "Did I not warn you of this very battle this morning? I ask you again; what will it take for you to believe?"

* * *

Waking, Arawn smiled and pulled his cloak tighter around him against the pre-dawn chill. It wasn't too long ago that he was terrorised by dreams, night visions of his dead sister and her dead Druid; but these days he awoke with joy in his heart, knowing he was chosen by the one true god and on the path to glory. Ah, if only dead Mother could see him now! Perhaps she could. Perhaps she saw him from her pit of fire in Otherworld and cursed her stupidity for maltreating her special son, for lifting up Ffraid instead of him, for being executed after her failed rebellion in the name of a false bitch goddess. The image made him smile wider.

The camp stirred. No doubt Crix was setting about the fire, coaxing the embers into flame in order to cook one of their trapped hares to break their fast, and Ardus would be making sure there was enough wine to go around. They worked well for him, these Bagaudas to whom the one true god had led him.

Sitting up, painfully aware of his bladder's insistent call, he rubbed his eyes and looked beyond his own camp. They made a magnificent sight. Two thousand men, all ready to do the work of the one true god, ready to convert pagans away from their false gods, ready to punish those who would not submit to their will. The journey thus far had been easy—boring even, if Arawn were so bold. All across the lands of south-east Gaul, following the eastern mountains south until they came to the coast, the only settlements they had come across had been deserted, either purged from earlier Bagauda attacks, or the inhabitants running away before the great host descended upon them. Arawn was annoyed and pleased in equal parts for half of him wanted to show Rix's Bagaudas how the one true god worked through him, but the other half was glad that his journey to Rome wasn't being delayed by pagan-infested villages.

Nor could he delay his bladder any more. Pushing himself up from his makeshift bed and nodding to his Bagaudas, he walked away from the waking host and into a copse of trees suitable for his morning's ablutions.

Empty and satisfied, he meandered back to camp looking

forward to walking through new lands that the one true god promised would be his once they had the Roman priests on their side.

"He thinks he's better than the rest of us. How do we even know he speaks to the one true god? We've only got his word for it."

Interesting, Arawn thought. Nertos will take any opportunity to spit his poison into Ardus' ear. He's far too dangerous to remain second-in-command.

"Be careful what you speak," said Ardus. "We've all seen the one true god work through Arawn, and we know he punishes those who don't believe in him."

Nertos snorted his derision. "He's led us to a few pagan villages and helped us slaughter them. If that's all the evidence you need then we've all had the one true god working through us at one time or another."

Ardus hissed, and even the other four were shocked into stopping what they were doing.

The unbeliever must be proved wrong, Arawn, my chosen one. You must tell them exactly what I say.

There was no doubt that Arawn would comply, he was the chosen one and he did the work of the one true god. He marched back into the camp, relishing the look of hatred that Nertos threw at him and the look of guilt the others shared for having listened to his venomous words.

"Ardus, I have information that your brother will want to hear," said Arawn.

"You've seen something? Enemies?"

The chosen one shook his head. "I've seen nothing. But I've had communion with the one true god." He looked at Nertos and the unbeliever scowled at him. "When the sun passes its meridian this day, when we've marched ten leagues closer to the heartland of Rome, we'll be set upon by pagans. They will be numerous, and they will have female warriors amongst them, but we will be victorious. I say this in the name of the one true god."

Nertos threw his beaker to the ground and stood.

"Where do you think you're going?" said Arawn.

"To get Rix. You said he needed to hear this. I think he does too." The unbeliever stomped off, and Arawn didn't like the look of the sly smile that crept about his mouth like a cunning serpent, but he kept it to himself; if the one true god wanted him to do anything about it he would tell Arawn when the time was right. Fortunately for the host, Rix was as devout as his brother and ordered his army of Bagaudas to stay alerted to enemy attacks. Arawn managed to rein in the smug grin at Nertos' disappointment. It wouldn't do to let the host see the chosen one playing the same childish games as Nertos.

As the sun approached the meridian, Rix sent scouts out into the surrounding countryside to gather information about their waiting enemy. Their host was two thousand men strong and doubtless outnumbered any band of pagans waiting to ambush them in the name of their false gods but, as Ardus told him, his brother never went into battle unprepared.

"And if there is no army of pagans waiting to do battle with us," said Nertos, his hand-shielded gaze fixed towards the movement of the sun, "what of our one true god speaker?"

"That is a pointless question," said Arawn. "The one true god wouldn't lie to us. I'm his chosen one and he speaks through me."

"Oh, I don't doubt it. But what if they're not there?"

"Enough, Nertos," said Ardus finally. "Save your energy for battling pagans, not your own people."

The unbeliever lurched away from their little band, a foul mood settling around him like a stink, but not before Arawn heard him say, "He was never one of my people."

What am I to do about him, god? Arawn prayed. At every turning he seeks to undermine me with his doubts and barbed comments. Surely he is the serpent in paradise come to tempt us away from your will.

Do not worry yourself about Nertos, my chosen one, for I have something special planned for him. He will see the truth in the end. Now you must heed the scouts for they return with important information.

Arawn nodded his head and thanked the one true god for his guidance, then turned to Ardus. "The scouts return. We must listen to what they say."

"Rix! Halt the host! Arawn says the scouts return with news!"

It took a while for such a grand army to come to a complete stop, and Arawn smiled to see Nertos walk with Rix to the head where he waited with Ardus.

"You would see me made a liar," Arawn said to him.

The unbeliever said nothing but moved his gaze back to the sky where the sun hung at the meridian.

"What will it take to make you believe?"

"Oh, I believe in the one true god," said Nertos. "I just don't believe in you."

The men around them shifted and muttered as the scouts finally came into view, running through the scrubby landscape at an impressive pace.

"Then you are a fool," said Arawn, and turned his attention to more important matters.

When the scouts were finally level with the host they addressed their news to Rix. Arawn took no offence for they were his men.

"Arawn was right," said one. "There is an army, about five hundred paces south of here past that hill."

"How many?" said Rix.

"Some hundreds. Four would be my guess."

"Then we shall crush them easily."

The scout looked a little doubtful. "They've got the high ground, Rix. The only way we can continue our journey is through them, and though we might be numerous, I don't think it will be easy. They have proper weapons; they look prepared."

"That's as may be," said Arawn now, "but we have the one true god. The path to paradise is scattered with many enemies," he continued, with a glance at Nertos, "but the chosen shall prevail. The waiting army is nothing more than an obstacle that we must overcome, and overcome it we shall. For the glory of the one true god!"

The host took up the chant, and the clamour sounded as fearful as it did beautiful. No doubt the pagans on their hill heard it and trembled.

Placing a hand on Arawn's shoulder but looking at his brother, Rix said, "You brought me a rare gift in Arawn, Ardus, and I don't think I ever thanked you. Listening to the men now, I don't think there are words enough to say it properly."

Arawn and Ardus grinned at each other, and the chosen one realised that he hadn't felt like he belonged somewhere as much as this since Thrax asked him to join his crew of traders. But this was better, of course, because he wasn't working for personal profit, he was working for the one true god, ridding the lands of the false gods and bringing the Romans back to Brython where they belonged.

Then the Bagaudas were marching again, marching with renewed vigour, marching to battle, and singing the praises of their god as they went.

Before them, and halfway up the steeply sloping landscape, stood an impressive army of pagans. With a brief realisation that brought a smile to his lips, he knew that a few moons ago he would have been terrified by such a sight. He recalled Mother's spear-women and the failed rebellion they brought against Epona, and how the sight of their muscled bodies standing ready to fight, brandishing their weapons with skill and ease, the gleam of death in their eyes accentuated by the Samhain bonfire, had made his legs weak. Now his legs were strong and he brandished his own weapon ready to smite the pagans in the name of the one true god. If only Mother could see him now!

And then they were running. Arawn led the charge from the centre of the great host, leading his men straight to the heart of the waiting pagans. From his peripheral vision, he saw Rix lead a third of the host around to the left as planned, and Ardus a third around to the right, attacking the pagans on three fronts. They had no possibility of surviving.

I don't want to die today, Arawn prayed, even as he pushed himself up the hill and screamed death to the waiting wall of pagans.

You won't die here today. I have something special planned for you. Today, you will be victorious.

Boosted by the promise and protection of the one true god, Arawn dug deeper and forced his legs to work harder, faster, even though they burned, even though his chest burned for more air, even though his shoulders burned from holding his axe to the sky in honour of his god. And then his entire being slammed to a stop as he hit the pagan wall with all his force.

He knew the sound of battle because he'd been leading his band of Bagaudas against the pagans for many moons while they journeyed to Lugdunum; he knew the sound of a woman screaming because his axe had bitten deep into her body; he knew the smell of blood as it poured from the god-given wounds of the pagans; and he knew the stink of shit as the fearful voided their bowels in a final admission of their disgrace and weakness. But every battle before this one had been nothing. A drop of rain in the ocean. A blade of grass in a meadow. A single feather in a flock of migrating birds. Everything that had come before had been intimate, just Arawn and his prey. He could look into their eyes and see their fear as they realised that the one true god's chosen would send them to an Otherworld filled with demons and damnation.

But here... Everything was of such magnitude that it lost all meaning; the sound of clashing weapons and the screams of the dying, the smell of the blood and shit as bellies were torn open. All around. Inescapable. Unrelenting. So much that it meant nothing any more. Arawn was nothing but a vessel for the wrath of the one true god and he swung his axe from left to right, up and down, around and around, not stopping until he had fought through the entire wall of pagans. When he finally broke free he staggered, his axe still swinging but with nothing left to bite into. He turned then, knowing that his work wouldn't be done until every last one of these pagans was bleeding into the grass and the hill ran thick and red with their blood. And then he saw Nertos face his demise.

The pagan woman's spear skewered his shoulder even as Arawn watched and he laughed to see him cry out in pain and anger.

Leaping over the bodies of those he'd already slain, he swung his axe with all his god-strength and felt the lightning shock as the biting edge was buried in the pagan woman's face, then he grabbed her loosened spear and pulled it free from Nertos' shoulder.

"She was mine!" the unbeliever screamed.

"She would have killed you," Arawn replied. "Stuck by a woman and a pagan. The one true god isn't impressed."

"I would have had her if you'd left well alone!"

Turning, Arawn swung his axe and gathered the damned souls of two more pagans before facing Nertos again and grabbing a handful of his leather armour.

"Believe me when I say I would have let you die were the choice mine, but the one true god has a something special planned for you."

"He told you that, did he?"

"Look around you!" cried Arawn above the sound of crashing weapons and squealing pagans. "Did I not warn you of this very battle this morning? I ask you again; what will it take for you to believe?"

A sneer spreading across his bloody face, Nertos pushed Arawn away from him. "Much more than a few lucky guesses, Arawn of Brython. You may have Ardus and Rix in your thrall, but I'm telling you now; I won't be taking my eyes from you."

"Then I may just be the last thing you see before your damned soul is sent to Otherworld." Then Arawn leapt and threw Nertos to the ground so that his axe could sever the neck of a pagan that dared to attack the men of the one true god. As the body crumpled onto the mangled remains of his companions, Arawn turned back to Nertos. "But that won't be this day."

* * *

A great feast was held that night in honour of Arawn and the one true god. The defeated pagan army, all of whom now lay rotting on the ground, had prepared themselves well for battle—Crix found wagon-loads of dried meat, oatcakes, nuts and cheese for the Bagaudas to share, as well flagons of sweet red wine. None of them could guess at how they had come to hear of the approaching host and none much cared as he ate the spoils the defeated had left behind for them. Arawn himself was relishing the glow of a battle well-fought and well-won, but it wasn't just that which kept a large smile fixed on his face.

It won't be long until we are at the gates of Rome, my chosen one, and there you will see your glory before your very eyes. Your name will be remembered throughout all of history as the saviour of your people, and soon it will be time for that history to start.

I am ready, Arawn prayed. I am ready to change history for you.

– 30 –

The Moon of Giamonios (Shoots-show) 333 C.E.
Dobunni tribal lands, Brython

This wasn't his first battle. But with each successive clash Emrys' belief failed him a little more. He watched from the fringes, his father having told him, as usual, to lead the rear guard should it look like they were faltering. Only they never faltered; they slaughtered every woman in their path without mercy. The sound was atrocious. Punctuated by the percussion of striking weapons, the army of Belenos chanted their battle song unceasingly.

Blood in his name! Blood in his name!

But every hateful heartbeat, a soul-tearing screech would permeate it; another life lost in savage agony.

Emrys turned and fought back the treacherous tears that threatened to undo him. This was Belenos' will, it must be done. But if it truly were the sun god's will, why did he feel so wretched? So guilty? So horrified by his fellow Druids?

A hand landed on his shoulder and Ceinwen's voice sounded in his ear. "We'll be at Dobunni's kaer by midday!" she shouted. "Our men are fighting well for the old gods!"

"They are," Emrys responded, swallowing hard and only turning to look at her when he trusted his own voice wouldn't give him away. "And then these tribal lands will be ours as well."

Ceinwen smiled. Not that long ago on the sacred isle of Ynys Afallach she had smiled at him so and he'd thought her beautiful. Not just because of her fair face, but because of her knowledge and wisdom. Now, he looked into her eyes and saw something different there, something hard and cold. It made her fair face ugly. This surely couldn't be the gods' will, this death and destruction, this blood and fear. It certainly had never been the Druids' way. When had it all changed?

What if he'd misunderstood the word of Belenos when he was journeying through Otherworld?

A cold sweat slicked down his back even as his mouth dried of all moisture. Was it possible that this was all his fault? Turning back to stare across the field of battle, facing the carnage that he'd brought upon the lands, he sent his mind back to his journeying, forcing himself to remember the words that had been said to him in his death.

When I swallow the moon, blood will be spilled in my name. When an orb of blood hangs in the sky, blood will be spilled in my name. When you find the truth, blood will be spilled in my name.

The truth is my will.

What did it all mean? He looked to the sky, but all he saw was the sun approaching its zenith, and fat clouds gathering to rain upon the new shoots of Giamonios. He certainly couldn't see the moon, and there was definitely no orb of blood hanging up there. But perhaps that wasn't the most important part of Belenos' message, perhaps the most important part was the truth. Emrys had to find the truth. But what was it? Was this the truth that he was feeling now—that he'd been gravely mistaken in telling his father and all the Druids that blood would be spilled in the sun god's name? If only he'd asked more questions!

"Emrys! Emrys!"

The young Druid shook his head and focussed on the red-robed figure that was running towards him up the hill. No, he wasn't red-robed at all. His robes had been white once. Now they were stained with the blood of countless hundreds of women who had fought to defend their warrior-queens against the Druids who had betrayed them.

"What is it?"

"Arch Druid Heddgwyn asks you bring some of your people down to help us. The battle is nearing its end and victory is ours, praise Belenos, but the men down there are tiring."

Ceinwen grabbed his arm. "Let me come with you, Emrys,"

she said, that ugly glint still in her eye. "I would be there for the last charge against the usurpers."

"You can go in my stead," Emrys said.

"What?"

"I won't be leading the charge."

"Why not?" Both Druids looked at him with confusion. He hadn't thought this far ahead, and he needed to think of something quickly. Something that sounded likely.

"I'm going to the kaer."

"Whatever for? There are only children there, and common women. The fighters are all on the field of battle!"

"So we are led to believe," said Emrys, an idea sparking into his mind thanks to Ceinwen's words. "But what if there isn't? What if they have a rear guard waiting for us there, waiting to ambush us when we are unprepared and drunk with victory? I cannot allow that to happen."

Ceinwen grinned. "You are truly your father's son." Her face became serious then. "It will be my honour to lead the last charge in your name, Emrys."

"If there is danger in the kaer, I will come to the battle field and warn you."

"Praise be to Belenos!" The two Druids chanted, and he nodded at them, leaving the hill quickly before he had the chance to see Ceinwen revel in her chance of bringing death upon innocents.

* * *

The lower settlement of Dobunni was as silent as a barrow mound at midnight. All around was the evidence that the inhabitants had had war thrust upon them with no warning; wagons of precious food were overturned and left on the walkways, pigs and hounds wandered freely without their mistresses to pen them or command them, and no fumes rose from the smoke holes in any of the roundhouses. When had they realised their danger? wondered Emrys. Had they noticed first that their menfolk seemed to have vanished? Or had the treachery of their Druids been perceived? Or perhaps it wasn't until they saw the vast host of raging men pouring down from the horizon.

The biggest structure, as in all settlements, was the roundhouse of the tribe's warrior-queen so Emrys made his way there, unsure of what he would, or could, do if he found any survivors. Like many of the other tribes, they had built their royal compound on top of a kaer to protect the royal family and keep the greater part of their food stores safe from raiders and enemies. Aware that his time was short, Emrys raced up the steep slope, ignoring the pathways that spiralled around it and instead used his hands as well as his feet to push and pull himself into the main compound, his desperation at having caused all the bloodshed giving him never-before experienced strength and speed.

When he finally crested the hill, sweating and panting like a hound at the end of a hunt, he jogged past the stilted grain-house with all its stores littering the ground to the largest roundhouse in the very centre, but soon he slowed to a walk, and that soon slowed to a dazed amble. Bodies were everywhere. Mostly spear-women with their throats or bellies cut open. The stench stung his eyes and made his stomach heave. And when he saw one woman so lacerated and dismembered that she was barely recognisable as a person he finally gave in to his compulsions and disgorged all that he'd eaten over the past few days.

Steadying his legs, mindful that he was here for a reason, he continued on to the roundhouse, and he saw that a few white-robed figures also counted amongst the slain. Evidently, the warrior-queen had become aware of her Druids' treason—that was why there was now a battle taking place outside the settlement walls, of course.

Averting his eyes from the staring corpses, their hands

outstretched as though pleading to him for mercy, he ran into the warrior-queen's roundhouse. It was as upturned as her village below, and there was a disconcerting amount of blood scattered over the floor, but there were no living souls here. Careful so as not to step in any red puddles, he walked across to the north side of the roundhouse to where the sleeping area was and pulled back the rich blankets that separated it from the main gathering space. Nothing. Perhaps they had escaped the village themselves while they still had a chance.

He walked back out into the sunshine, keeping his gaze lifted from the ground, and began a methodical search of all the roundhouses in the compound. Each one showed signs of destruction, and greater or lesser amounts of spilled blood, but none sheltered any survivors. He breathed a sigh of relief. They had escaped. Perhaps they would even make it to Atrebates and warn Epona of the coming war.

Retracing his steps, and walking past the grain-house balanced on stilts to protect the stores inside from rats and mice and insects, Emrys noticed something odd. All the grain had been emptied, littering the floor beneath it. He'd noticed it on his way in but had paid it no mind. Why would the surviving Dobunni do that before evacuating their settlement? Perhaps to deny a food supply to their conquerors, but Emrys wondered… Certainly within it was a big enough space to hide many people.

He walked over to it, his feet crunching in the wheat that was now wasted, and stood underneath the central opening. Unsurprisingly, it was covered with wood. He pushed. It gave a little, then suddenly there was resistance and he could push against it no more.

"My name is Emrys," he said, his voice sounding obscenely loud in the barrow-silent village. "I'm here to help you."

Nothing.

"Please! The battle is almost ended and they'll come here next—please let me help you!"

There was whispering and urgent hushing but the wood covering remained in place.

"You have every reason to distrust me," said Emrys, "but I'm alone, I won't hurt you. I swear by Boudica and all the old gods. But if you don't let me help you the Druids and their army will swarm through here and kill every last one of you; I've seen them do it to many others. Please hear me!"

A roar sounded, distant, but brought to him on the breeze, and he looked back towards to the battlefield, the kaer providing him with an excellent vantage point.

Blood in his name! Blood in his name!

The men were cheering, and even though he couldn't see any individuals from this distance, the frenetic energy that had been visible there not too long ago had vanished, replaced by a casual meandering, as though all the combatants were taking the time to congratulate each other on a battle well fought.

Urgency ran through him like lightning and he banged on the wood covering, heedless that it might frighten those who hid within. "They are coming!" he cried. "The battle is won, and they are coming! You must escape while you can!"

Amidst cries, the wooden covering finally lifted and Emrys looked up into the terrified eyes of scores of women and children.

"He's a Druid!" one of them screeched in her fear. "He'll kill us all!"

Chaos ensued as those hiding inside the grain-house tried to move beyond his reach, shoving each other aside in an effort to move away from the central opening.The weaker women and younger children were pushed to the bottom and trampled by stampeding feet that had nowhere to go in such an enclosed space.

"Stop it! You'll kill each other!"

But no one was listening to him. There was no other choice left to him—he would have to go in and help the younger ones get out. He pulled himself up through the narrow opening until he sat upon the edge, his legs dangling down, ignoring those brave enough to approach him and throw a kick to his head. He deserved such pain and punishment for all he had done.

Lying in front of him, dazed, a growing bruise on her forehead, was a girl-child of no more than five summers. He pulled her towards him and, holding her arms as gently as possible, lowered her to the ground. She stood there, looking around, as though she'd just woken from a dream. Then she looked back up at him and graced him with a smile of heart-breaking beauty.

"Breaca, Breaca," she said, tapping a tiny hand to her tiny chest.

"A beautiful name," he said to her, earning him another smile. He could have looked at that innocent face all day, but there were many more who needed his help.

"Let me help you down," he said calmly to another girl-child who looked at him with green eyes made enormous with fright. "Your friend is out now, let me help you too."

She came to him slowly, arms outstretched, and allowed herself to be lowered out of the grain-house.

"Mama!" she cried up. "You come too!"

Emrys looked around him. The women were quiet now, staring at him with a mixture of terror and hope.

"There's only me here," he said quietly, "for now. But the battle has finished. And unless you let me help you, they will come here and…you don't want them to find you."

"We would have been safe in here if you'd left us alone," said one woman, tears streaming down her face.

"If I managed to find you, I can assure you they would have found you too. Let me help you now so that they won't."

"Mama!" came the voice of the second little girl. "You too!"

The mother could no longer ignore her child's cries and she pushed her way out of the crowd and, keeping her eyes on Emrys the entire time, lowered herself out of the grain-house.

A heart-beat later she called back up. "He's right! The battle has finished and I think they're coming towards the kaer!"

"There's no more time," said Emrys, urgency colouring his voice. "Let's get you all out of here, then I can hold them off while you make your escape."

Thankfully, once the women cooperated, it didn't take too long to get them all out, and soon they were all huddled in a group, six-score women and the village's children, underneath the grain-house.

"You must leave the kaer by the east gate," Emrys said to them, "and don't use the walkways; you must scramble down the slopes as best you can. Then keep going east until you reach Atrebates: you must warn Epona Warrior-Queen of the coming danger. Do you understand me?"

A few of the women nodded.

"Good, then go, now. I'll do what I can to hold up the army so they don't see you in the fields below. And remember not to use the pathways!" he shouted after them once they finally left him.

Breathing deeply for several heartbeats, he prepared himself to face his father, hoping he would believe the lie he told him.

If the approaching army used the walkways to enter the kaer they would enter by the east gate and Emrys knew that the women and children wouldn't have had enough time to escape down the hillside if that came to pass, so he slipped and slid down the west-facing slope in order to meet his father as he came from the battlefield. After the frantic rush to get the women-folk out of the grain-house, and having stood still to watch the last of the survivors exit the gate, his legs were weak and his anxious energy was utterly spent. It took all of his concentration to stop his body from tumbling head-first down the kaer. When he reached the bottom, he had but a few heartbeats in order to gather himself before his father caught sight of him.

"My son!" he cried, and Emrys had to force himself not to

recoil. The man stank of death. His white robes were now red. Even his hair, which had been grey with wisdom, was stained by blood. "We have vanquished the usurpers!"

"Glad tidings indeed, Father."

"Ceinwen tells me you came here to hunt out those who might ambush us? It was well thought! Evidently this tribe was more prepared than the others," he turned to the men swarming around them, "but none can defeat the men of Belenos!"

Blood in his name! Blood in his name!

"I searched the entire village, the lower settlement and the kaer, but I found no one."

"Good!" The Arch Druid stepped forward, but Emrys held his hands out, blocking him, though being careful not to touch his blood-wet robes.

"Would the men not rather rest here awhile before climbing the kaer? They must be exhausted after such a battle."

"Nonsense! There is food, ale and plenty of places to rest up there; better to rest in comfort than not." He took another step forward then stopped again, looking at Emrys strangely. "You're injured."

"I am?"

"Your brow is cut."

The young Druid touched his fingers to his brow and winced at the pain; when he pulled them away again they were sticky with drying blood. His own. From when he had been kicked in the grain-house. "Ah, yes," he said, and tried to look embarrassed. "I…well, I was searching the warrior-queen's roundhouse, and…well, there was a body lying on the floor. I didn't see it. And I tripped."

"A nasty blow that caused."

"I must have knocked it on a stone from the hearth-fire."

"I shall heal it for you when we're settled up there." He turned back to his men. "We climb, men of Belenos, for a well-deserved rest!"

The swarm of men cheered and billowed forwards; Emrys knew he wouldn't be able to stop them now that they were gathering momentum again so he lunged forwards himself and began climbing back up the kaer, avoiding the walkways and heaving himself up the slope as he had done before. To his relief when he looked around, the bloodied, chanting men had followed his lead. Surely, by the time they reached the top, the women and children would have fled far enough away to avoid detection.

By no means was he the first to make it to the top; despite having spent the whole morning battling against innocent women, Heddgwyn's men of Belenos still had enough energy left to race each other to the top of the kaer and swarm through the settlement like drought-starved insects. Panting, Emrys staggered through the village now, smiling weakly should a male warrior (and still it seemed too strange to think of them like that, even though he'd witnessed their fighting for many days now) hail him and offer congratulations on another victory for Belenos. He had to fight every urge to flee to the eastern edge of the settlement and ensure that no women and children could be seen running into the nearby wood. Instead, he did what he could by clearing away the bodies that littered the place, silently saying the words of the death ritual over them so their souls would make it safely to Otherworld. Then he found an empty roundhouse to crawl into and hide. He didn't want anyone to see him shaking.

Hunger pains woke him. He hadn't realised he'd fallen asleep; and for such a long time. The roundhouse was as dark as despair. The sun must have already set. He thought about getting up to find some food, but the noise of the singing, celebrating men outside recalled to him the day's events and his appetite fled as quickly as a startled wren. Would he be able to hide in here until the men left? Would he be able to hide in here until the end of all time and never see the destruction his thoughtless words had caused?

"So this is where you've been biding your time."

Apparently not, then.

"I didn't realise how tired I was. Father," he added as an afterthought.

"The men of Belenos are entitled to their rest," said Heddgwyn, entering and heading straight towards the central hearth-fire, pulling out his fire-striker as he did so. Before long, a merry blaze illuminated the deserted roundhouse and the telltale signs of an abode exited in a hurry. Did this place belong to one of the spear-women now feeding the crows on the battlefield, or one of the women he had helped escape from the grain-house?

"But I said I would heal your wound," continued the Arch Druid, "and so I shall. Let me look at it."

Emrys did as he was told. As he always did. Always had done. And Heddgwyn pulled out a wad of clean linen and a clay phial of ointment that was secreted in his robes. The familiar scent of yarrow reached his nostrils as the wound was tended to, and he closed his eyes against the sting.

"How did you say you got this wound, my son?"

"I fell."

"Against a hearth-fire stone in the warrior-queen's roundhouse."

"Yes," said Emrys.

"Because you tripped over a body."

Emrys stiffened slightly. The Arch Druid's tone was perfectly friendly, but the atmosphere seemed suddenly cold. "Is it really relevant to the healing of the wound?" he said.

"No, not at all," said Heddgwyn with a quick smile, then stoppered his phial. "Except, I've been resting in that very roundhouse, and there were no bodies to be seen."

Emrys' stomach soured. "I removed it," he said weakly.

"And after that, did you remove all the stones from the hearth-fire too? Because I found none."

Emrys said nothing.

"You see," said Heddgwyn, making a show of finding the right pocket in which to put his potion, "it struck me as a little odd. And then, when one of my men came to me and said he'd found a group of women and children hiding in the woods east of here, I thought, it's not possible my son has betrayed me."

"Survivors?" said Emrys, and found he didn't have to pretend surprise. "How many?"

"Two score. Mostly children."

He fought to school his face. Most of them had escaped after all, but oh, those who had been caught! "Did you bring them back here?"

The Arch Druid scoffed. "My man slaughtered them where they hid." Then he laughed. "He wouldn't have found them at all if one of the female younglings hadn't wandered towards him saying her name!"

Breaca! He couldn't stop his head from dropping to his chest. A child of five summers! Cruelly slain because of him!

"You seem distressed, my son. Did you know they were there? Did you help them escape? I would know if my son has betrayed me." His voice remained quietly friendly, making it all the more frightening.

Betrayal? Heddgwyn would speak to him of betrayal! But he hadn't betrayed the Arch Druid, he'd betrayed the land! He'd committed treason against every soul here! Then Emrys remembered with sudden dismay all that Rosmerta had told him about the intentions of their Arch Druid father to commit treason. She hadn't known what form it would take, she merely suspected—and she'd been proved right when Heddgwyn lied at the grove about Emrys having witnessed his meeting with the old gods. How had that memory escaped him? But then she'd been called away to chase a sister-slayer across the land and so had been unable to warn their mother, Sulis Warrior-Queen of Cantiaci. And what had he done about it? He'd gone on a pilgrimage with his traitor father and forgotten all about it! Or had he? Had he, in fact, been so awed by the fact that Heddgwyn had treated him like a son for the first time in their lives that he chose to ignore it? Possibly.

Probably.

And now the Druids had brought war to Brython.

He felt wretched and powerless; ironic considering he'd passed from Ovate to Druid now and was amongst the most powerful people in the lands. He'd sworn to his Fellows that he would protect and serve the old gods, he'd passed through the Cauldron of Rebirth in order that he might save his mother and sisters, but instead he'd taken the words of Belenos and turned them into destruction and death. Wretched and powerless were not words strong enough to describe how he felt; now he truly understood the meaning of despair.

"I haven't betrayed you, Heddgwyn," he whispered finally. "I've betrayed my mother and sisters." He looked at the man who was once his father and saw his face cloud with anger. "I've betrayed all the mothers and sisters across the lands, and the wives, and the nieces and the aunts and the grandmothers. I've betrayed Brython. As have you. As have all the Druids. As have all those who have fought in your name."

The Arch Druid launched himself to his feet. "Blood will be spilled in his name! Those are the words you brought back from Otherworld! Words of the sun god himself! And you call *me* betrayer?"

"Those were his words, yes; but he spoke also of finding the truth, and I think the truth is that we have brought an unjust war upon the people of Brython."

With a wordless sound of rage, Heddgwyn turned to walk out of the roundhouse but Emrys leapt up after him. "Those cavorting men out there were helped in their murderous treason by the Druids; does that mean you knew what was going to happen before your men of Belenos even rose up against the warrior-queens?"

"Of course, my son. This has taken many, many seasons to organise. And we are not committing treason; we are taking back the lands for the old gods. You should be careful what you say amongst a company such as this," he gestured outside the roundhouse where still the horde feasted and caroused in the carcass of the kaer, "or they might wonder where your loyalties lie."

"So you would kill your own son if he stood in the way of your plans for domination?"

"These are not my plans for domination!" Heddgwyn roared. "I do this for the old gods! I do this to return our lands to the sacred place they once were! And you are my son, and I want you to continue this sacred duty long after I have gone."

"You lied," Emrys hissed. "You told our Fellows that you had been visited by the gods, that I had witnessed it, but you lied. And now they're fighting a war for you, are killing innocent people for you, and all for a lie."

"This war was planned before you even called yourself Bard, planned to the day, the very heartbeat! The Cantiaci Fellows needed a little more nudging than the rest, they've grown complacent amongst such wealth; not even the portentous Atrebates rebellion I devised was enough to stir them, hence the need for your participation that day."

The Arch Druid turned, now, and clasped his one-time son by the shoulders, gripping so tightly that Emrys had to clench his jaw to keep from calling out in pain. His eyes shone with anger and when he spoke it was through clenched teeth. "You have until Elembiuos to decide where your loyalties lie," he said. "When the Tinne Moon passes, you can choose to stay with me and work for the glory of the old gods. Or you can choose to die with your mother and sisters." He released his grip with a shove, and Emrys watched, open-mouthed, as Heddgwyn stalked back through the camp site to where his Druids and men waited.

And for the first time in his adult life, he fought back tears of fear.

– 31 –

The Moon of Giamonios (Shoots-show) 333 C.E.
Dubras, Cantiaci tribal lands, Brython

"Airmed!"

The cry came as the young princess stepped off the staircase that glided down into the street. She turned towards the voice, and was startled to see Epona Warrior-Queen of the Atrebates cantering towards her on her warhorse. She had a few riders with her, but not nearly the number expected of travelling royalty; and there was not a chariot in sight. They looked like a small band of people making an escape. When Airmed looked into the face of the warrior-queen and saw the fright in her eyes, the realisation came that perhaps she was right. Her heart flipped.

"Epona Warrior-Queen," she said respectfully. "How can I aid you?"

Epona pulled hard on her horse's reins and jumped out of the saddle even before the steed had fully stopped. Her small war-band halted as well, but remained with the horses while their warrior-queen raced to Airmed.

"Is your mother here?" she said, apparently forgoing graceful conduct.

"Yes, she's in the great hall."

"You must take me to her at once."

"Indeed. Follow me." But Epona ran up the steps ahead of her and was already through the door before Airmed had reached the top step.

She walked in to see the look of surprise on her mother's face. Quickly it became calm again, and the warrior-queen of Cantiaci walked towards the warrior-queen of Atrebates, extending her arms in welcome.

"We were not expecting you," Sulis said, but whatever else

she would say was truncated by Epona.

"You must help us," she said. Fear was in every word and she was visibly shaking. "The Druids are marching on us. Already they have crossed our borders, and it won't be long now before they are at Kaer Gradawc."

"The Druids?" said Sulis. "How can that be? My own spear-women brought battle to the traitors at Trinovantes already, and I have sentries posted along our borders, reporting back on all their movements."

Epona looked confused, her head swinging from Sulis to Airmed. "They didn't come from Trinovantes," she said. "They came from the west, from Dobunni."

"I don't understand," said Airmed. And from the look on her face, neither did her mother.

"Nor do I," said Epona. "Do you mean to tell me the Druids have taken Trinovantes as well?"

Airmed nodded solemnly, and Epona's hand rushed to her mouth in surprise.

"*As well*?" said Sulis.

Epona turned to her. "Three days ago some four score women and children came to Kaer Gradawc from Dobunni; they said they had managed to escape the slaughter. Hundreds of Druids are leading thousands of men to war, they said. Deceangli was the first tribe to fall, then the Cornovii. They marched into Dobunni but the warrior-queen was ready for them, she'd already heard the news from those who'd escaped the battles. But their numbers were too great; these women said there were more than fifty thousand men."

"Fifty *thousand*?" Airmed's knees went weak.

Epona nodded. "The numbers grow with each tribe that falls—the men join the battle while all the women are murdered."

Sulis choked back a sob. "Did the warrior-queens not take back the lands when the army moved on?"

Epona's eyes filled with tears. This frightened Airmed more than her words did. "They kill the warrior-queen and her spear-women first. When the tribe is leaderless the Druids bring the men into battle. I don't understand how this could have happened!" Her tears overspilled. Airmed was aghast, and for a heartbeat so was her mother; then she went to her and laid her hands on Epona's shoulders. When she spoke, her voice was steady and calm, which seemed to give Epona strength.

"I don't understand how this could have happened either," she said. "But it has, and we must fight it. We join our forces and we take the war to them. You will stay here, but you will send messengers back telling all of your warriors to come here, and all women of fighting age. In fact, all women. If it is men who are joining the Druids' army then I think we must assume that no woman is safe."

Epona nodded. "I'll tell my warriors now."

"Go. Then we will discuss where to meet the enemy and how to overcome them."

Epona left, and for a moment mother and daughter watched her go. Then Airmed said: "The Druids must have been organising this for a long time. To have three tribes fall so quickly… Four, including the Trinovantes. Why would they do such a thing? How could they harbour a hatred of the warrior-queens so deeply without us realising?"

"I cannot answer your questions, my daughter. But I understand now why the Arch Druid Heddgwyn opposed the bonding of our tribe with Atrebates."

"He didn't want us to join forces so we'd be easier to conquer."

Sulis nodded.

"Rosa's intuition was right all along."

"And now the enemy is marching towards us from the west, and if my women haven't recaptured Trinovantes, we have enemies lying dormant to the north. If they hear that we intend to fight alongside the Atrebates, I fear they will launch a second attack."

"Can we not call for aid? Surely other tribes have heard the news by now and will be willing to fight."

"The Dumnonii and Durotriges are too far to the west. If they haven't already fallen, I doubt we can get a message to them in time to march to our aid. I will send a message to Damara Warrior-Queen of the Regni, perhaps she will come to our aid."

"You sound uncertain, Mama."

"I have three hundred household warriors, and three thousand trained warriors. There are, perhaps, another two thousand women across my lands who are skilled with spear and sword, but..."

"But we have relied on our wealth and trading power more than our fighting power for too long."

Sulis nodded grimly. "Epona and Damara may have twice as many warriors and fighting women across their lands as we do, but that would still number less than half of the enemy's army. And that's assuming Damara will even answer our call."

Airmed's mouth dropped open. "Surely she would put aside the stupid ancient hatred of us in light of this new threat."

"Sirona was willing to die at the hands of the Picts rather accept aid from us, if you recall. The Regni may well be pleased to see their treacherous neighbour fall."

"But then they will fall next! If the Druids only wanted Cantiaci they would have marched straight to us, but they didn't. They're conquering the tribes as they come!"

"Hatred results in irrational decisions, we've already seen that."

"Then how do we defeat them? How do we defeat the Druids and an army of fifty thousand men?"

"On our own? We can't. If Atrebates falls then we fall next."

"What? Mama..."

Her mother looked at her and Airmed saw fear in her eyes. It terrified her. Mother had always been brave and wise; now she was scared, just as Airmed was scared. She felt as though the world were ending.

"But I will do anything to keep my lands falling into the hands of enemies."

She turned and walked out of the great hall towards her private chambers. Airmed, numb with fear, watched her go.

* * *

She would do anything to keep her lands from falling into the hands of enemies.

And enemies were all around her now. Trinovantes had fallen, Atrebates was under attack. With the Druids as leaders of the enemy army, how could Sulis possibly fight them on her own?

She couldn't. It was as simple as that. But there might be a way. If the Druids had fifty thousand men, then *she* needed fifty thousand men. Undoubtedly, if there was the promise of silver and gold, men would fight, just as her own spear-women did. Of this she was sure.

Her private chambers were small and sparsely furnished, just a writing table and a stool underneath the window. Nothing else was required here. On top of the writing table was a beautiful box of ash wood, carved with intertwining patterns that chased each other along the sides and top of the box with no beginning or end. Inside it was where she kept her stretched-hide parchments and her boiled hawthorn bark ink. She took out the clay pot of precious liquid, and took the top sheet of stiff parchment from the pile. Then she took a fresh goose feather from the bundle on the side of the writing desk and clipped it with a blade. She thought for several moments, head bent, while she ordered the words in her mind before committing them forever onto the parchment. Dipping the quill into the ink, she wrote her letter.

Once finished, she rolled it carefully and bound it with a strip of leather.

Airmed had left the great hall by the time she went back out there, presumably to warn Trahaearn that his workload had just become more urgent. She was glad. As much as she trusted her daughter, she didn't want to have to explain her course of action. As capable as Airmed was, she was much too young to understand just how perilous their situation was, and how her mother was forced to take this last resort.

Thankfully, Terrwyn had returned to her, even though it was without her beloved Rosmerta, but she could entrust this task to no one else. And she knew her most trusted spear-woman would fulfil it quickly, efficiently and with discretion. She couldn't risk anyone finding out until the time was right.

In the practice fields with her troops was where she found Terrwyn now, along with many new faces. Evidently she had taken it upon herself to recruit new women; a necessity, undoubtedly, but even if she recruited every last woman throughout Cantiaci it still wouldn't be enough to go up against their new enemy.

When she approached the field, Terrwyn caught sight of her, ordered her new recruits to keep practising the moves she'd shown them, and jogged over to her warrior-queen. She was tall and well-built, her skin already browning in the warming sun, except for the scar across her cheek which always shone a pale silver. Her skill with sword and spear was renowned, and Sulis trusted Terrwyn with her life. More than that; the lives of all her subjects.

"A pleasure to see you, Sulis," she said, slightly breathless from her morning's exertions. "Have you come to see us practice?"

"It would give me great pleasure, Terrwyn, my dear, but I've come to ask you to perform another task; this one of utmost urgency."

The spear-woman stood to attention and nodded her head. "Anything you wish, my lady."

Sulis held out the bound letter. "Many moons ago I sanctioned the building of new boats in our main port. You must take this letter there and have one take you across the ocean to deliver it. Read it." Terrwyn raised her eyebrows. "I would have you know what is contained in this letter so you understand the importance of it, and the importance of not letting it fall into the wrong hands."

She nodded and took the letter, untying the hide thong with careful grace. As she read, her eyes widened in alarm. "My lady… Is this truly necessary?"

"More necessary than you can imagine. If there were another course of action I would take it. But enemies surround us and we are running out of time. Can I trust you with this task?"

"Yes, my lady. I'll leave at once."

"Good. Tell no one." She laid a hand on Terrwyn's shoulder. "Thank you. May Boudica and all the old gods go with you."

– 32 –

The Moon of Elembiuos (Claim-time), 333 C.E.
Rome

"There," said Ardus. "The walls of Rome. Can you see them?"

Arawn nodded, a smile spreading across his face, and he urged his horse, a victory prize taken from the pagans they had bested some two moons past, into a trot.

Long and arduous the journey to Rome had been. The sun became hotter every day, though sometimes there were incredible storms, the likes of which Arawn had never seen in his native Brython. Ardus told him the thunder was the sound of the one true god punishing the pagans for their blasphemous beliefs, but Arawn knew it was the one true god praising him, Arawn, for leading his army of Bagaudas to Rome to start the conversion of all pagans from here to Brython. After each storm he was invigorated and he would push his army into travelling further and faster through and across the sodden countryside, only stopping when the horses wouldn't walk any more.

Not all of the Bagaudas had horses, and those who travelled on foot would reach the camp much later, tired and worn out, though Arawn barely noticed because he would be holding court near the biggest camp-fire sharing with those around him all that the one true god had revealed to him that day. He spoke of the glory of Rome, and how their might would be restored, and as new priest-kings of the one true god they would be worshipped above all others.

And the Bagaudas believed him and followed him. Of course they did, because they hated the pagans with ferocity. Arawn did too, but he hated women more; and he dreamed of the moment he would face treacherous Rosmerta and her bitch mother with all the might of Rome behind him.

Arawn rode at the front of the army with Rix and his brother Ardus, and Arawn suffered him because of the great horde he'd given to march to Rome. He suffered Ardus also because the Gauls knew the best route to the sacred city. And although they followed the Roman roads, the brothers claimed the ancient warriors had built many across these lands in particular, and only they knew which were the right ones to follow. Their father had been a wealthy trader, bringing wine, weapons and skins from Gaul, trading them across the mountains into the lands beyond and bringing back olives, spices and silks. It was how the two brothers had come to learn so much about the one true god; and it was how the one true god had had their father killed for his pagan ways. The two brothers understood this now, and were grateful to those first Bagaudas for showing them the true way.

Each night, Arawn had watched the night sky and saw the moon pass from Simivisonios to Equos, and from Equos to Elembiuos. It was remarkable. Twelve full moons and nine had passed since he opened his sister's head on the great standing stone near Kaer Gradawc, and how afraid he'd been! How she and her dead Druid had haunted his dreams! Now, here he was, marching with a great army to mighty Rome where the one true god lived, and he would lead them all back to Brython.

"We should set up camp here for the night," said Rix. "Finish our long journey in the light of the morning."

"We go there now," said Arawn.

"My men are tired. It will be well past moonrise when we reach the gates, and—"

"And when we get there we'll have a welcome fit for priest-kings. Plenty of food for our bellies and soft, warm beds to sleep in. You would deny your men that?"

"I don't deny them anything which is why they remain loyal to me. And I won't deny them a night of rest after a hard day's marching." Rix turned to the horde amassing behind them. "Build fires! We make camp here for the night," he called. He turned back towards Arawn as though expecting him to contradict his orders. His face remained expressionless. When Arawn said nothing he turned and walked into the army of men.

Arawn seethed. Now, as well as Nertos, he would have to deal with Rix once he had the power of the priests behind him. He was too important to be humiliated now. Did Rix not realise he was no longer the son of a salt-merchant? He had led the Bagaudas into battle and won! He was the speaker of the one true god!

That night he camped away from the others, away from the fires and away from the noise, looking up into the night sky where the one true god lived. The moon waxed gibbous, tomorrow night it would be fat; and it would be the last thing Rix ever saw.

Hear me well, Arawn son of Emlyn. He sat bolt upright. The voice of the one true god was louder and clearer than it had ever been before. This close to Rome he was closer to god.

"I hear you," he said.

Nertos is not worthy of Me. Rix is not worthy of Me. Ardus is not worthy of Me. You are to lead My army across the lands to bring low the women and destroy the pagans. Anyone who opposes you is not worthy of Me. Their blood must nourish My lands and make Me strong. Do you hear Me?

"I hear you well, one true god. Tomorrow I will lead my army into Rome. And kill all those who oppose me."

* * *

The walls looked impenetrable from a distance, growing more imposing with each step. The river they had seen to the east suddenly looped before returning to its south-easterly course, and when the road turned east as well they were walking towards its watery path; until finally their own was halted by a gate of monstrous proportions. It strengthened Arawn's belief that the ancient Roman warriors must have been giants to have needed a gateway so vast to admit them into their own city. All of stone it was made with a great arch in the centre from which the wooden gate hung, and jutting out from either side were two great towers, the bottom two-thirds of which were precisely square while the top thirds were circular. The archway, by Arawn's reckoning, was ten times higher than he; but it was dwarfed utterly by the monument surrounding it. On top of it all stood a line of sharply pointed turrets, sentries for the sacred city that lay beyond.

"How do we get in?" he heard Ardus ask of his brother.

"I've been chosen by the one true god to lead the Romans back to Brython," said Arawn without turning. "If I push, it will open."

He stepped forward, placed his hand against the ancient wood of the gate, and pushed.

It swung inwards.

The susurrus of the Bagaudas' awe behind him made him smile. Then he walked through, leading his army into the sacred city of the one true god.

The road continued straight and Arawn noted that it was as worn as it was outside the city walls. Several of the stones were broken and grass now grew between the cracks. It looked as though it was a road used very often. It pleased Arawn because he sensed that the Roman priests of the one true god were numerous and evidently spent much of their time travelling outside of the city to convert or punish pagans.

What disconcerted him, though he refused to let his mind dwell on it, was the state of the buildings between which he led his army. They were ancient, obviously; but where the old buildings in Lugdunum retained their grace because the Bagaudas cared for them out of respect for the ancient Romans, the buildings they passed by now looked dishevelled. He caught the flash of a face at a broken window every now and then, but when he looked it was gone. And there was a distinct lack of priestly Romans. He had expected a great welcome, or at least someone stopping to ask who they were. They were a large horde, some two thousand men strong, dressed for battle; not the kind of band which could easily be ignored. He was grateful that the poisonous mouth of Nertos hadn't dared to question him because he wouldn't know how to respond. He listened intently for the voice of the one true god, but he was disconcertingly silent. A sour feeling threatened his stomach but he actively disregarded it; the one true god led him here to fulfil his purpose. He trusted in him to show Arawn the way.

By the time the sun, so high in the sky and beating down with a palpable ferocity, passed the meridian, Arawn came to a crossroads. Still the voice of the one true god was silent.

"Which way do we go?"

Arawn's heart sped at the sound of Rix's voice so close behind him. He wouldn't turn around in case the Lugdunum leader saw the uncertainty in his eyes. "Let me listen," he hissed. "I can't hear his voice if you disrupt me." Nothing. He chose the road that led off to the right.

The sound of the river filled his ears, as did the ugly call of ducks which rode it. Traversing the course was a bridge; a monument that had once been ornate but now had the same dishevelled appearance of the buildings surrounding him. The road then crossed to a small island floating in the river and turned into a second bridge, but this one opened out into a square that brought to Arawn's mind Dubras' market square in Cantiaci where he had spent a short yet happy time with Trahaearn Smith. In fact, there was a market in progress right now but it was considerably less vibrant than the one from his memories. However, there was one marked difference; almost every person he looked upon was female.

His stomach, soured by the silence they had experienced in the empty streets, finally twisted. This sight was all too familiar in his native lands of Brython that it couldn't possibly exist in the sacred city of Rome. For a dizzying moment he felt as though he'd discovered he'd been daydreaming his rise to the one true god's communion, and now reality had crashed back into him.

Hoping that his sense of dislocation would pass, he moved from the fringes of the crowd into the thick of it, unaware of the horde of Bagaudas that still followed him. His erratic movements caught the attention of the women buying and selling their wares in hushed tones and he became aware that their voices were rising. Looking at the army of men coming towards them, passing among them, they started calling out to one another in their strange tongue. The words meant nothing to him but instinctively he knew they were slandering him. Those closest to him pushed through the crowds to escape the market square and reach the crumbling buildings that surrounded it; and as they scrambled their slanderous words grew ever louder and more shrill.

They are running to arm themselves.

"God?" cried Arawn, relief exploding in him so strongly he wanted to weep. "I hear you very well! Tell me what I should do!"

They run to arm themselves. They're no better than the bitch-whores you escaped. They will kill you if you let them. You must kill them. Kill them all.

"Yes!" Arawn shrieked. "Kill them all!"

He reached both hands over his right shoulder to the axe that was tied to his back and wrenched it from its leather thongs. In one fluid movement he swung it round into the head of a screaming woman, spraying blood. Her body dropped like a felled bird; with his axe still buried in her skull the weight of it pulled him forward. He rammed his foot onto her neck so he could pull his weapon free then he pivoted so he faced his army.

"Kill them all!" he cried.

The Bagaudas needed no further invitation. They had been

travelling for a long time and their killing had been sorely limited. There had been no death-games to watch, and when Arawn's axe released that first spray of blood, their blood-lust had ignited quicker than dry thatch. They spread out through the now panicked women, felling all in their paths; they battered the market stalls with axes and short swords to hack at the cowering women who had foolishly attempted to hide; a section of the horde broke off from the main slaughter and chased those who ran down alleys and side-streets in order to escape the fury.

And Arawn felt the one true god fill him, giving strength and accuracy to his weapon, and with each swing he brought down another bitch-whore, and another and another, until finally his divine axe connected with nothing but air.

He was standing on a corpse—the ground was blanketed now in blood-stinking corpses—and surveyed his holy work. No bitch-whore had survived to draw arms against them. He lifted his foot and brought it down hard on the corpse's skull. The crack was as loud as a log popping in a bonfire, and he smiled. He was safe.

The killing done, the Bagaudas raked through the remains of the market stalls, looting for coins and food and anything else that took their fancy. The bodies of the women hid no such treasures, for they were dressed in only the simplest linen robes and wore no jewellery. The spoils of battle were meagre, but it didn't detract from their enjoyment. When there was nothing left to take, Arawn led them away from the carnage.

* * *

If news of the bloodletting travelled through the sacred city, there was no evidence of it. At the very least, Arawn expected the Roman priests to come and thank them for eliminating a very serious threat, but as they wandered through the deserted streets, and as the sun wheeled across the sky, they remained unseen.

The Bagaudas took to looting the houses they passed in the streets. Pathetic female wails emanated from them, as did, to Arawn's surprise, male voices.

"Who was in there?" Arawn said once to Ardus as he came back from one such foray, bloody and grinning.

The Bagauda shrugged a shoulder.

"I thought I heard a man's voice."

"You did."

"Was he a priest?"

Ardus barked a laugh. "Can't have been. He didn't even try to defend his woman or children. And they had very little in the way of loot so they must have been slaves. Only good for killing."

And so the afternoon passed.

The sun was setting when they came across a deserted taverna which they raided for ale and fresh food. There wasn't nearly enough to feed and water the entire Bagauda army but those who were left wanting were happy enough to go in search of other such establishments. By now it was apparent that they would meet no more female resistance in this city.

Arawn was restless. His elation at hearing the voice of the one true god earlier was dissipating now he had gone silent again. And the suspicious glances that Nertos kept sliding over made him feel edgy. Getting up from the table that he, Ardus and Rix occupied, he walked out into the street. The fierce heat of the day had departed with the sun when it sank behind the horizon of the city, but it was still warm.

"Speak to me, oh one true god," he said to the sacred city. "Tell me what to do now. Tell me where I should go."

"Does this mean our one true god speaker doesn't already know?"

Guilt was his first instinct, almost as strong as the urge to turn around at the sound of the voice. But it was one he recognised, and it didn't belong to the one true god.

It belonged to Nertos.

"The one true god is leading me," Arawn said.

"So you *don't* know."

"Do you doubt the one true god?"

"No," said Nertos. "But I've told you before, I doubt you. The others may be content to rape and loot and drink wine for now, but me? I wonder where all the priests are."

"They're here."

"Where? Apart from the women at the market and the people we've found cowering in their houses, we've met no one. Certainly no priests."

Arawn rounded on him. "This is the sacred city, home of the one true god and home to his sacred priests. Did you think this task would be easy? Did you think we wouldn't have to work to achieve our goal?"

"No." Nertos wore a smug grin. "But you said we would be welcomed here, treated like priest-kings and raised high in the glory of the one true god. You lied to us. And it makes me wonder what other lies you've woven; if you truly speak with the one true god."

Arawn bore it no more. He whipped his dagger out from the sheath at his waist and plunged it into Nertos' gut. The shock on his face made Arawn laugh out loud. He pulled the dagger back and his enemy's hands immediately flung in to take its place. He staggered back, still looking at Arawn with bewilderment.

"Murderer," Nertos whispered.

"No!" Arawn shrieked. "Ffraid is the murderer! She would have killed my friend!"

The dying Bagauda's bewilderment was replaced by utter confusion.

"I told you once before that the one true god had something special planned for you," Arawn said now, "and your death at my divine hand is it." He bore down on the staggering Nertos and clasped him by the front of his leather armour and pulled him close. "I also told you that I would be the last thing you saw before your damned soul was sent to Otherworld." Then he raised his dagger and swept it across his enemy's throat. Warm blood drenched him immediately and he threw the corpse to the floor.

One of our enemies is vanquished. You must vanquish all the others. It is time you found our sacred priests.

"But where?" cried Arawn. "I hear you well, one true god, but will you not tell me where I can find them?"

Lead our army to the Colosseum.

"Is that where I will find the sacred priests? At the Colosseum?"

Nothing. Silence. The one true god had spoken his instructions and Arawn had to obey.

All talking and laughter ceased when Arawn entered the taverna. Nertos' blood was still wet and warm on his face and he wondered if it was that which had caused the silence.

"We march now to the Colosseum," he said. "The one true god has spoken to me. The sacred priests await us."

"Where's my brother?"

Arawn's eyes snapped to Marka and he scowled. "Slain by the one true god for questioning us. And he will slay you too, if that is your wish. Then you will be reunited with your brother in the fiery pits of Otherworld. Is this your wish?"

Silence.

Slowly Ardus stood and said, "Lead us to the Colosseum."

Arawn nodded and left the taverna.

* * *

The Colosseum proved none too difficult to find; though the road they were on stretched ahead for at least a hundred paces, it loomed up just as its cousin in Lugdunum did. The very first glimpse had him running, then a feeling of overwhelming joy spread through his body and he sprinted, pleased at the sound of two thousand pairs of feet, less one treacherous pair, running behind him.

He came out into a clearing as the moon rose in the darkened sky above him, and the structure in front of him was even more magnificent that the one he'd seen in Gaul. Undoubtedly it was built by the same hands; but this one was bigger and infinitely more beautiful.

He fell to his knees and lifted up his hands to the heavens. "Here I am, one true god. Bring me now the sacred priests!"

And a great wailing filled the night. Not the wailing of frightened women. The wailing of frightened men.

He pushed himself to his feet and looked around, dazed. The sound hadn't come from the Colosseum. In fact, unlike the one in Lugdunum, the structure in front of him swum in silence.

Another wave of wailing crashed through the night. Arawn turned towards the sound and his eyes fell across a many pillared building with a grand staircase that swept up to an empty porch. The pillars supported a high pointed roof, and the whole structure recalled the villa where he'd found his first Bagaudas. Yet this had an air of greater importance.

The wail sounded a third time.

Arawn dashed over to the pillared building, leaping up the staircase two steps at a time and pounded towards the great door. It was locked. He beat it with his fists, then kicked it, eliciting a thump like thunder and more frantic wailing from within. He struck it again and again, fighting against a surfacing memory of Thrax mockingly recounting the fate of the once-mighty Rome.

Now it's nothing more than ruined settlements inhabited by priests who live in their own shit and whip themselves for having lost their power and might to a woman. What a sight that would be!

"Open the door!" he shrieked. "Benedictus qui venit! Blessed is he who comes! Open the door!"

At his words the wails ceased.

"How come you to speak our tongue?" The voice was distant through the thickness of the door but Arawn heard it well enough. "Benedictus qui venit, words of our tongue. How come you to speak it?"

"Open the door in the name of the one true god!"

A pause stretched out and Arawn fought against beating it again. Soon he could bear it no longer and he raised his fists, but he heard scraping and sliding sounds on the other side so he halted, arms still raised as though in supplication. Slowly, so slowly the door opened inwards.

* * *

The door opened and Arawn stood face to face with an ageing man. The top of his head was shaved of hair, and his robes were simple and white, though Arawn recognised expensive cloth when he saw it. The fear in the watery eyes before him was spread through the man's entire body. He shook like a newborn lamb on a cold day after Imbolc.

"Why do you taunt us, Barbarian?"

Arawn's chin dropped. It was possible this man was even more pathetic than his father. His voice was like the whine of a dog. "Who are you?"

"I'm the scribe," the ageing whimperer said. "They sent me out here because I speak the Barbarian tongue. The Lord save me, your face is covered in blood…"

"Who are *they*?"

"They say they will not try to convert you if you leave them in peace."

"Who are *they*? Speak, man, by the one true god, or I'll kill you where you stand!"

"Oh, please, spare me!" squealed the old man. "I'm only a scribe. I speak on behalf of the priests."

"The sacred priests are inside this building? Get out of my way." He pushed the scribe aside; dramatically he fell to the floor, wailing and flailing his arms about his head.

Once inside, the keening chorus started again. Surrounded by marble walls and underneath a high ceiling it sounded a hundred times louder than before. Arawn clamped his hands over his ears. With astonishment, he saw that many of the robed men before him were lashing themselves with many-thonged whips. "Quiet!" he roared, but the cacophony continued. He roared again, and this time they ceased. "Are you the sacred priests of the one true god?" The sound of his voice echoing around him was pleasing, but no one answered. "Are you the sacred priests of the one true god?"

"Please," the scribe whispered. Arawn turned to see him crawling over on his hands and knees. As well as sounding like a whining dog, he now looked like one freshly beaten by his mistress. "They can't understand you. I'm one of the few who speak Barbarian. But they are all priests of God."

"Who is the chief of your priests?"

"The Bishop of Rome, but—"

"I want to speak to him."

"Please," he cringed. Arawn lunged forward and seized him by the front of his robe and hauled him to his feet. A groan escaped from the watching priests. This was not how he had expected his first meeting with the sacred priests of the one true god to unfold. He was confused and the confusion made him angry.

"Call to this Bishop of Rome and tell him to come forward to speak to me. Otherwise I'll slice your throat open where your stand and end that wretched whimpering of yours."

Instantly, the scribe unleashed a stream of incomprehensible words, but the pleading and squealing in his tone recalled to Arawn the women in the market square. It did not please him.

No one moved.

Holding the scribe out at arm's length, still clutching the front of his robes, Arawn drew his dagger slowly. "Blood will spill if I don't see the Bishop of the Rome."

Again the scribe spoke in his strange tongue.

Finally someone pushed through the crowd. When he broke free, Arawn saw he wasn't as old as the scribe, neither was he that much younger. His robes were infinitely richer; deep red and purple silks were added to the expensive white linen and he was decorated with a lot of gold. His jowls and fat belly were a testament to plentiful meals; and even though there was fear in his eyes, there was also an element of disgust. He spoke in his own tongue, and his tones were deep and rich. It was the voice of someone who expected his words to be obeyed.

"He asks you," said the scribe, a little calmer now that he wasn't the sole focus of Arawn's attention, "why you attacked our city."

"I came here because the one true god speaks to me. He told me to come here to the sacred city of Rome."

The scribe translated this to the Bishop, and when he responded it was relayed to Arawn. "How do you know of our God and why would He tell you to attack our city?"

"I didn't attack your city. I came here with my army of Bagaudas to find the Roman priests."

"You mean to kill us?" At this, groans filled the air and lashes cracked against backs.

"No!" Arawn barked. He dropped the scribe to the floor again. "I was led here by the one true god."

"God despises pagans." The scribe's whine now came from near Arawn's ankles but he didn't move his eyes from those of the Bishop. "He would never lead you here. He keeps us safe from you inside these walls."

"*I* despise pagans, so do my Bagaudas. We came here from Gaul to join with the sacred priests, to lead our armies out across the world, even to Brython and speak the words of the one true god."

At the word Brython, the hall rang with cries of anguish and those with whips cracked them down hard upon themselves.

"We have no army," said the Bishop. "Once, we would send out Missionaries to convert the pagans, sometimes they were successful, oft-times they were not. We would burn the heretics, and for a time that convinced the pagans of the glory of God, but over the years your kind became more numerous and would attack our Missionaries before they reached their villages. Then, one fateful day, they killed our beloved Emperor."

"Constantine!" wailed the priests, lashing themselves once more.

"And while their numbers grow, ours diminish."

"Why?" said Arawn. "If you are sacred to the one true god, why would he let your numbers diminish?"

"Because we are cursed!" wailed the Bishop, and the whole congregation followed suit. "We allowed our great empire to be defeated by that foul woman from Brython" —again, the priests groaned and lashed themselves— "and God has cursed us ever since. We burn every woman who is disobedient, but no matter how many we burn, God still curses us for our great failure. Yet despite their inherent evil, there were some women whom we found worthy of breeding new generations of priests, and those we kept separate from the rest of society. Except God sent you to our city and you slaughtered them all this very day! God has cursed us for an eternity, and all we can do now is pray for our souls!"

These are not sacred Priests. They are vile pretenders, spawn of evil. Kill them all.

"I hear you well, one true god." He turned, leaving the pretenders to their false prayers.

Walking back down the staircase, with the magnificent Colosseum filling his peripheral vision he was pleased to see the mass of Bagaudas waiting for him; Rix and Ardus stood at the bottom of the stairs.

"Well?" said Rix. "Did you find the source of that infernal noise?"

Arawn nodded. "They claimed to be the sacred priests of the one true god." Uproar followed this statement, as he knew it would. No true priest would sound that scared. "They are but vile pretenders. Kill them all."

The horde streamed past Arawn, whooping and hooting their battle song; but it wasn't loud enough to drown the sound of the screaming, violent death they perpetrated. When they finished the work of the one true god, the looting would be more rewarding. Not only were some of the priest pretenders drenched in gold, but their hidey-hole was dripping with it.

For Arawn, his interest wasn't in gold or jewels now. He realised that the one true god had led him here, to Rome, to discover the truth; the sacred priests did not exist. It was up to him to lead the Bagaudas to the woman-infested, pagan lands of Brython and strike the fear of the one true god in their black and treacherous hearts. He looked up at the looming arena in front of him and truly saw it for what it was; a decaying monument to once-proud but now dead people. The time of the Romans was truly over. The era of the Bagaudas was beginning this very night.

He looked up into the night sky and saw the full moon of Elembiuos hanging there, fat and bright. For several moments he watched it, knowing that when it set and the dawn followed in its wake, the world would belong to him.

Then, to his horror, the moon began to disappear, right there in the middle of the sky. At first it was barely noticeable, but the longer he looked the more the moon vanished into blackness, as if some dark and hideous beast were slowly consuming it.

Such was the shock of this vision that Arawn could only stand there, staring; eyes wide, mouth wider. Even when the great orb, as familiar to him in the sky as the sun, finally disappeared entirely he couldn't bring himself to move, or even scream.

An eternity passed, then the moon reappeared, fat and full as before, but no longer shining bright. It was as red as blood. Arawn's bowels turned sour and he felt a warm wetness spread out from the front of his breeches as he pissed himself.

"What is this devilry?" he whispered. "One true god, why do you show me such evil? Have I not done everything you wished?"

A fierce cackling echoed through his skull, bringing him to his knees, making him clutch his hands to his ears. He felt a scream pour through his throat but he couldn't hear it.

One true god? said the voice, mocking. *One true god? You fool, Arawn; you simple fool! How easy it was to trick you! How willingly you chose to corrupt your spirit! Know now that when you come to Otherworld your rotten spirit will belong to me. And for all the evils you've done, you will pay dearly.*

"I don't understand," he gibbered.

The frantic cackling filled his head anew. *You still don't know who I am? The Dead will find the living. They cannot escape the Dead. The living will be devoured and so become the Dead. Tell me, Arawn; do you not recognise the voice of your own sister?*

"No!" Arawn screamed, leaping to his feet, pulling at his hair. "No!" He screamed it over and over at the bleeding moon, blind to the Bagaudas that were exiting the building behind him with their shining treasures.

He ran to and fro, still screaming, like a crazed animal who finds himself caged. Finally he found the road which had led him to the Colosseum, to the priests, to the blood moon. He sprinted down it wildly, whipping his head from side to side as images of his dead sister assaulted his mind.

Dashing her head against the standing stone.

Blood spraying from the wound.

Her limp body crumpling forwards.

Her boiled bones rising from the cauldron.

Lurching towards him, hands clutched up around her seethed

and welted body as though she is cold.

Instinct took control, and though he didn't know his way around this city of evil his legs carried him back through the streets where buildings now housed Bagauda-slain corpses. They carried him through the square where he'd led the massacre of women, and there he stumbled in the crook of a dead arm, or slipped on puddles of guts. Stray dogs, who had been feasting on the unexpected banquet, scattered ahead of his screeching, erratic progress; but soon he was scurrying down the first Roman street he'd set foot upon, the street which led to the gargantuan gate that barred the way into the city but was now his means of escaping it. All the while his shrieks of rage and fear bounced off the crumbling stone walls on either side of him, battering his head and ears, but no matter how loudly he cried, he couldn't block out Ffraid's frightful laughter.

The wooden portal of the great gate still hung open and he sped towards it, laughing now because he believed he would escape his dead sister's curse if only he left the damned city she'd led him to.

The sky was wide and open when he ran through the gate and the blood moon still hung there, mocking him. He howled at it. When all his breath was spent his dropped his head, but the sight in front of him reignited the terror in his bowels.

An army of dead waited for him.

* * *

"So this is Rome? Pah! What's so sacred about crumbling walls of stone?"

Please, Rosmerta thought, closing her eyes and praying to her namesake goddess, please let this be the end of my journey. I can't bear to listen to this frightful woman any longer. Thankfully, dear Thrax answered Gwladus before she got herself caught up in another argument.

"It may look weak from the outside," he said, "but contained within those crumbling walls are thousands of blood-thirsty men, made even more dangerous by reaching their goal. If your son—"

"Sister-slayer! *Sister-slayer!* You will not call him my son!"

"Forgive me," said Thrax, his eyes as wide as the rest of their little group's. Save Gwynfor. "But if the sister-slayer is also in there I don't doubt he will believe himself invincible. We must tread carefully. In fact, it would be better if we were to take him by himself."

"And how do you suppose we'll manage that, man?"

Rosmerta sat up a little straighter in her saddle. She hadn't taken her eyes from the city walls since her prayer, and it seemed it had just been answered. "We let him come to us," she said.

"Pah! How—"

And then, blessedly, her noise stopped, and Rosmerta knew she had seen him too.

Arawn Salt-merchant, sister-slayer, and perhaps slayer of countless others, had just exploded from the wooden gate not two hundred paces before them.

"Gwynfor, you were right!" Gwladus screeched. "The blood moon is an omen of my vengeance! I shall spill his blood and send his spirit to the fiery pits of Otherworld!"

Surprising even herself at her speed, Rosmerta whipped her arm out and caught the salt-merchant before she had time to leap from her saddle. The scarlet orb above them may have signalled revenge to her, but for Rosmerta it portended something more sinister. She felt it, but she couldn't name it. A blood moon could only bring death, but there had been too much death already. Regardless of whichever augury chose to show its red face, she would speak with Arawn first and hear his story. Above all else she had to believe in justice, and a slain son could speak for himself no more than a slain daughter could. She knew Gwladus' face would be an ugly twist of rage and hatred but the warrior-princess didn't see it; she kept her gaze fixed on the boy whose own gaze was, in turn, now fixed on them.

"You will have your moment, Gwladus Salt-merchant," she said. "But as Warrior-Princess of Cantiaci, and on behalf of my mother, Sulis Warrior-Queen of Cantiaci, and your mistress, Epona Warrior-Queen of Atrebates, I will be the first to approach him." Now she raised her voice so that the three spear-women who had chosen to complete this mission with her would know she spoke to them. "If she so much as twitches in her saddle, kill her."

Then she slid from her own saddle and walked slowly towards Arawn.

* * *

The blood moon's glow was dull and red, but it cast enough demon light to shine from bronze armour and helmets, to glint from spear-heads and turn them into single flames, to show him the dead warriors that he had so recently sent to Otherworld. And there was the little leveret from the village in the forest he'd caught, surrounded by all her villagers. And there was the old couple whose necks he'd snapped so he could take their paltry dwelling. And there was Sirom, bloody and burned, aching to take her revenge.

"Bagaudas!" he cried. "To me!" His voice was hollow; he doubted anyone would have heard it, and turning back he saw the road leading into the devil city was empty. He turned back to face the dead army, and saw how they strained to unleash their hell-fury upon him. He gripped his bloody axe and planted his feet, forcing his body to calm in the face of such horror. Fear made the axe seem heavier than ever before but he was determined to die like a warrior. Because he *was* doomed to die. Why else would a blood moon be hanging above him? Why else would his Bagaudas have deserted him? His wretched sister had caused all of this; this was her revenge from Otherworld. But if he could damn others and bring them with him, he would.

For the moment, the dead army was stopped a few hundred paces away from him, but as he looked, one slid from her skeleton steed with supernatural ease. Her long hair glowed red in the light of the demon moon, and she wore no armour; only a sleeveless dress. She walked towards him, her arms, boiled of all their flesh, bore no weapon but she needed no weapon. She was filled with her dead Druid's devilry from Otherworld. And Arawn looked into her face.

His sister, Ffraid.

Did I not tell you I had something special planned for you? she screeched in his head. *Arawn, the chosen one, here is your special end! Your special, special end!*

The fear which existed deep in his bowels now erupted and an inhuman wail rose from his throat. Still she came forward.

"Come with us, Arawn," she said, her skull grinning. "I'll make sure no one harms you."

"It's all your fault, you bitch!"

Her jaw bone dropped, her skeletal step faltered.

"You led them to me! You led every one of them to me!"

"No, Arawn." Her voice was calm. She was only a few steps away from him now, and she waited there. "I came with them to make sure they wouldn't harm you. You've been accused of terrible crimes; I came to ensure you were fairly heard."

"You've brought my doom to my feet!"

Three more riders broke away from the dead army then, galloping their ghostly steeds towards him. One called out to his rotting sister; and though Arawn couldn't make out the words, it was enough to attract Ffraid's attention. This was his chance—he swung his axe high above his shoulder and launched himself towards her, screaming.

She turned just as his axe was on its downwards sweep, and a fierce pleasure swept through him when he saw understanding in her eyes. *Her* doom was upon her, and once more it was he who brought it. His axe blade bit into her boiled neck, jarring his arms momentarily; then her head tumbled to the ground, blood soared up from the hole at the top of her body. So much blood from an already dead body.

A Roman fountain of devil blood, he though wildly, outside the Roman devil city.

For a heartbeat the corpse of Ffraid's corpse teetered where it stood, then fell forward, landing with a dull thud, spraying his feet with warm wetness.

Joy at defeating his sister-enemy was short-lived however; the three riders were upon him now, all of them calling for his death. He recognised one instantly; Thrax! Thrax had betrayed him by joining with this dead army that would be his doom. He looked upon Arawn with such hatred, but it was *he* who ought to show such hatred at such a heinous betrayal.

"Villain! You slew Rosmerta Warrior-Princess!" the pagan roared.

"No, I killed your woman!" he screeched. "I fucked her then burned her! She died the death of a filthy pagan and I dream of it every night!"

Thrax threw himself down from his horse, but the phantom of a filthy pagan spear-woman who had ridden with him did the same, grabbing his arm before Thrax could reach his woman's killer. Throwing his head back, Arawn laughed. No one, it seemed, would have the chance to kill him this night.

The dead spear-woman walked towards him; perhaps she would try to kill him as his sister had, but he would slice off her dead head too. He would slice off as many dead heads as he could before he died. As though hearing his thoughts and eager to comply, the dead warrior-woman raised her hands, one of which clutched a fearsomely long spear, to her salmon-crested helmet and removed it.

Fright shook him so much he fell to his knees.

First his sister… Now Mother…

"You're dead," he croaked. "They hanged you for treason!"

Just then, the third rider came into view; Arawn saw him clearly for the first time and knew him from his nightmares.

He was a Druid. A Druid with one side of his head dented and sunken, as though he had been struck by a rock…

Arawn crumpled forward onto his hands.

The Dead will find the living. They cannot escape the Dead. The living will be devoured and so become the Dead.

The dead had truly come to claim him. Ffraid's frantic laughter started again in his head and he shrieked. He felt a light touch on his shoulder then and his throat closed. Daring to open his eyes, he looked upon a face he hadn't seen for moons, for so many moons. The pale face and pale blue eyes were as familiar to him as a close friend's, and it was indeed a close friend who had finally returned and now looked at him with such a mournful gaze that Arawn felt tears spring to his eyes.

"I did it to save you," he whispered to Boy. "I didn't want her to kill you. I saved you."

Boy, paler now than Arawn had ever seen him, shook his head slowly. So slowly.

"Then what have I done?"

But Boy didn't answer his question. Never could. Never would.

"You have done evil things." Arawn tore his eyes away from his friend. Dead Mother looked upon her gibbering son. "And I will take great pleasure in destroying the one who slew my daughter."

"But you're dead," Arawn said. "You're dead for treason."

"No," said Mother. She levelled her spear at his chest. "But you will die for murder."

He felt the blade pierce his chest, felt Mother push it deep into his body, and was aware of pain but fear had deadened his senses as it had deadened his throat.

The spear was then wrenched out from him and the motion pulled him to the ground. He tasted dirt and blood. He tried to push himself up, but his arms failed him and he fell back. Something poked his shoulder repeatedly, and then he was rolled over, looking up into Mother's face. Nothing showed there; it was emotionless. A mask. She spat on his dying body and moved out his sight.

The bleeding moon hung fat and swollen in the sky as Arawn's bleeding body lay under it. Soon the moon passed into darkness and came out the other side, as white and pure as it had been before; but Arawn's staring eyes didn't see it, and he remained in eternal darkness.

– 33 –

The Moon of Elembiuos (Claim-time), 333 C.E.
Atrebates-Cantiaci borderlands

"It matters not that Epona escaped," said Heddgwyn with indifference, waving a hand. "Her lands have fallen to us now."

"They fell because her army retreated," said the wild man Emlyn. "Don't you find that suspicious? All the other tribes fought until they died—no one retreated, except the Atrebates."

"And why does that make you suspicious?"

"Judging by the trail we've been following all the way to Cantiaci, I'd say they've fallen back to Dubras." He sounded, for the first time, exasperated at his master, as though the Arch Druid should have thought of this himself already. "They're regrouping with Sulis Warrior-Queen's army: we could be facing a real battle this time. I think our luck is running out."

Heddgwyn frowned. "Luck has nothing to do with it, Emlyn, once Salt-merchant, husband to a hanged wife, father to dead children; we fight for the sun god. It just means we'll have them all in one place for our final battle. Where can they fall back to in Dubras? We'll be in front of them, the sea will be behind them. And even if they have their full complement of spear-women, their numbers will be no match for us. No matter how furiously they fight, they'll be no match for us."

Emrys, newly-officiated Druid, son of Heddgwyn Arch Druid and Sulis Warrior-Queen of Cantiaci, looked at the two men with open dismay. Heddgwyn was right; no tribe had stood a chance against them. Why? Because the Druids, in their quest for knowledge, had committed to parchment the tactics the Roman soldiers had used to conquer all the lands that made up their once-worldwide empire. They fought in shield-walls, an impenetrable barrier against which the enemy would only dash themselves to death. They knew how they'd used their short-swords to stab and slay their enemy from behind the safety of the shield-wall, and how they also used their shields as weapons to beat back the enemies before them.

They even knew that the Romans had fought in units consisting of five thousand men, and these men were divided into ten cohorts, each cohort comprising four hundred and eighty men. Five cohorts would make up the front lines, five the rear; and that's how Heddgwyn organised his army of three-score thousand men. When the enemy came at them throwing their spears and launching clay missiles in their leather slings then Heddgwyn's army would march in a tortoise formation, the soldiers holding their shields above them to protect themselves. When the enemy stood in front of them, Heddgwyn would order a wedge formation so his soldiers broke their lines. Such organised tactics were alien to the spear-women who relied on speed, ferocity and sheer numbers to defeat their enemies who, over the generations, had been other tribal warriors who fought the same way. But even their numbers couldn't save them against Heddgwyn's army. Nearly all the men from each tribe that had fallen had joined the army. They weren't skilled fighters like the women, but they were strong and brave and angry. And numerous. They obeyed Heddgwyn's commands without question because he promised them a united Brython where men would be the rulers of women, no longer subject to their cruel whims, no longer treated as slaves, able to build a life for themselves without having to bond to a woman in order to secure a livelihood.

And Emrys, in misunderstanding the words of Belenos, had stood by and watched it happen.

Their camp that night was on the borderlands of Cantiaci. The men knew they wouldn't be molested by Sulis Warrior-Queen's spear-women so they drank plenty of ale while they ate, and when the roasted meat was finished they sang songs and laughed heartily. Emrys had no appetite, but he waited until the meal had finished before he approached Heddgwyn.

"May I speak to you?" he said.

The Arch Druid looked mildly surprised, perhaps at the formality of the question, perhaps because the young Druid's standing pose indicated he wanted to speak away from those Druids who hadn't been left behind in the newly conquered tribal lands; but he rose nonetheless.

"I would ask you to spare my mother's life."

Heddgwyn looked affronted. "All lives would be spared if the women had submitted to Belenos."

"I can't recall you giving them much of a choice before you marched your army of men upon them."

Now Heddgwyn looked angry. "Boudica may have saved these lands from the Romans but she usurped the old gods, and since that time half the nation has become slaves while the other lives in praise and blasphemous deification. These lands were once just and equal, and because we neglected our true gods they have neglected us. I didn't want to start a war, but I wasn't so naïve to think the change would come without bloodshed."

"This was never a war!" Emrys hissed. "You massacred those tribes! None knew your intentions and they had no chance to defend themselves."

"Defend themselves?" Heddgwyn grabbed his son's elbow and pulled him closer. "You would have them fight *against* us? Against the old gods? Think carefully about your next words, Emrys, because they could turn you into a betrayer."

"Stop saying that!" he said. "I've already betrayed everyone in these lands, which is why I cannot betray my mother or my sisters any more. Let me go to her. Her only ambition was to unite the lands of Brython—perhaps I can make her see that that's precisely what you are trying to do. Under the old gods. She was never as susceptible to Boudica anyway, thanks to the enmity of neighbouring tribes. I may be able to convince her to submit to the old ways."

"She'll never relinquish her queenship."

"Perhaps not," said Emrys. "Or perhaps news of the other fallen tribes has made her realise that opposition is futile."

Heddgwyn's manner changed suddenly. He released his grip on Emrys' arm and smiled slightly. "There is a magnificent symmetry to all this, don't you think?"

He didn't, but he nodded anyway. A placated Heddgwyn was more likely to be amenable to his request than an angered one.

"Here we are," the Arch Druid continued, "on the eve of our fourth battle, one that has the potential to change the very history of these lands. If wealthy Cantiaci falls, hated Cantiaci, Roman-welcoming Cantiaci, then the remaining tribes to the south-west will be more willing to submit to those who defeated their treacherous neighbour."

Emrys thought that no warrior-queen would be willing to hand over her lands so easily, but he said nothing.

"And the tribes to the north of us will be so harried by the barbarous Picts that they will not be able to defend themselves against them and us. Reclaiming the old gods will seem the fairer choice than submitting to the northern barbarians. And so our fate comes down to this fourth battle."

Emrys finally saw to what his father was alluding. "Boudica and the Romans."

The Arch Druid beamed. "This must have been what she felt like on the eve before her great, decisive battle. She fought for the lands, for the old gods, to keep the Romans from eradicating our own ways and replacing them with theirs. What we do now is no different to what Boudica did then—we're fighting for our old gods and our old ways. And when the gods reward us for embracing them once more, the histories told of this very moment will hail us as heroes as Boudica was. But our greatest achievement will be uniting these lands under our gods, and that is something no warrior-queen, no matter how great, has ever achieved."

"So who are we; Boudica? Or the Romans?"

Heddgwyn smiled, and all the old slyness Emrys remembered from before their pilgrimage came rushing back to him. "We are Druids," was all he said.

Emrys nodded. It felt safer to agree with him. "So will you let me speak to my mother? She might well be persuaded by your arguments as I have been."

Heddgwyn looked at him as though he'd just asked a silly question, one to which he should already know the answer. "This is the fourth and final battle, Emrys. We must fight it. So, no; you can't speak with Sulis Warrior-Queen."

The young Druid inclined his head and walked away. Heddgwyn had always been obsessed with the old gods and the old ways, he knew that. But that obsession had turned to madness. Unfortunately, Emrys thought, he had fed that madness after he was reborn.

"A Druid saved a warrior-queen more than three hundred summers past," he said to himself, remembering the histories he'd read at Bard's Island. "Perhaps history can repeat itself in that respect too."

* * *

They marched all the following day, and when the sun was setting the fields gave to way to villages, all of which were emptied of people; and Dubras, home to Sulis Warrior-Queen and the seat of power in Cantiaci, was close enough almost to touch. But their way was very much barred.

A wall of spear-women stood in front of them, stretching from horizon to horizon, bearing the salmon on red and black standard of Atrebates and the boar on green, blue and silver standard of Cantiaci. Emrys' heart sank. They were all ready for battle and Heddgwyn would be only too willing to accept the invitation. He would never be able to reach his mother in time before the carnage started. She was likely even waiting in the front lines herself, perhaps with his sister, Rosa, victoriously returned from her mission to find the sister-slayer and in time to help their mother save their tribe.

He suddenly thought of the conversation he'd had with her, all those moons ago when the world was still dark and cold and almost eight seasons younger. She had suspected Heddgwyn of treachery but had she anticipated that it would come on such a scale as this? Turning all the menfolk against the womenfolk in the name of the old gods? Most likely not. Still, she'd distrusted the Arch Druid enough to come to him and ask him to report his intentions to her so that she might save her tribe, her queenship. And what had Emrys done? He'd pilgrimaged to Ynys Afallach and become so seduced by Heddgwyn's attentions, by the idea of rising to full Druid status, that he'd forgotten all of his sister's fears. Forgotten them, or purposely ignored them. And it had led him here, to a battle with his own tribe, his own warrior-queen. His own family.

Heddgwyn brought his army to a halt, and in the warm glow of the setting sun, the two armies faced one another. The spear-women stood straight and tall. Perhaps if he were closer Emrys might have seen fear in their eyes, but from this distance they looked strong and professional even though they must have been waiting there all day. They kept their eyes fixed forward, looking unperturbed, like an army that had never been defeated. And for so many generations that had been true.

By contrast, Heddgwyn's vast of army of men were boisterous, calling out taunts and insults to the women who had suppressed them for so long. They banged their weapons against their shields, waved them high in the air, dared each other to go further and further from the front lines to throw their curses. Emrys had read, deep inside Bard's Island, that the Roman armies were organised, composed, well behaved; but

Heddgwyn's army was anything but. The men were filled with the confidence of three battles already fought and won. Easily, at that. The army of spear-women they faced may well be larger and more prepared than any they'd yet encountered, but it didn't perturb them.

For they had a secret weapon—knowledge. None of the three armies they'd already defeated had ever witnessed the tactics used against them: how could they? The Romans had left Brython in disgrace, remaining only as a bad memory, and passed down to each generation as a story of how the Brythons, under the might of Boudica, had defeated an army that had once terrorised the whole world. All knowledge of their methods and tactics was buried in a secret cave that only the Druids of Ynys Afallach knew of, and those Druids had passed it on to the sections of the army for which they were responsible. Emrys doubted that Heddgwyn's men of Belenos could have defeated the Roman army if they suddenly appeared, but they were alien enough to confuse the spear-women, and in such confusion Heddgwyn's vast numbers had easily overrun them. The men knew all of this, and they weren't afraid to boast about it.

Belenos, thought Emrys, looking up to the sky and spying the fat moon as it rose from the horizon. *Is this what you intended for us? That we should fight amongst ourselves until the lands are red from the blood of our own people? Why were your words to me so veiled?*

Eventually the men grew tired of taunting the spear-women and fires were lit. The smell of roasting meat filled the still night air as the bright moon moved ever higher in the sky.

"See how afraid they are!" said Heddgwyn, riding towards him on his steed. "Even though my men have turned their backs on them and are feasting and drinking, they dare not attack us."

"They're facing an enemy they haven't yet encountered," said Emrys hollowly, "and they've no Druids to start the proceedings. I doubt they'll start fighting until they're forced into it by your attack."

Heddgwyn grinned. "And they'll be defenceless against us."

Emrys nodded, then looked back up to the sky. The stars were out and the sky was clear save for a few wisps of clouds made luminescent by the fat moon.

But... By the fiery strength of Belenos, what was happening to the moon? It looked as though it were disappearing, but surely that wasn't possible...

"Heddgwyn," he whispered, unable to tear his eyes away from the unbelievable sight.

The Arch Druid laughed. *This* strange reaction was enough to draw Emrys' gaze down from the firmament. His father's face was filled with glee, his eyes bright and shiny. "It's beginning!" he cried. "The new era is beginning!"

He yanked on his horse's reins, snapping the poor beast's neck around so far that Emrys winced for it, and then kicked it until he was back among his army of men.

"Men of Belenos!" he cried, still pushing his mount through the crush of men. "Men of Belenos!" Eventually their carousing and laughter subsided and they sat still to listen. In the stillness of the warm Elembiuos air his voice carried far. No doubt the spear-women could hear him as well, Emrys thought. Would they also be able to hear the manic pitch to his tone?

"Men of Belenos, we are come here on the eve of a new era. Look you now to the sky!" He threw his arms and head upwards, and a shiver of fear rippled through the scores of thousands of men assembled around him as they saw the ever diminishing moon. Glancing towards the spear-women Emrys saw they had indeed heard the Arch Druid's proclamation, and for the first time their straight lines faltered.

"For more than a generation, the Druids at Ynys Afallach have planned this union of Brython with the guidance of the old gods. For too long they have been ignored since the usurper Boudica took their place."

A roar of anger and resentment rose from the assembled horde. It was deafening.

"But Belenos, greatest and strongest of all the old gods promised us the day would come when all the true gods would be restored to Brython, and we would be the ones to restore them—a great horde of Druids and men! And to the Druids of Ynys Afallach he promised a sign when the Tinne Moon, the Holly Moon, was at her fattest. Look to the sky!"

The army did as it was told, as did Emrys; despite the Arch Druid's madness he was powerless to resist his powerful words.

"The Tinne Moon is feminine, a moon of encirclement; but Belenos told us he would consume this moon, break her circle, and give us in her stead a red moon, a blood moon, and that would be our sign. Our sign to shed the blood of those who ignored the old gods and raised a usurper to godly glory. Men of Belenos, you see the mightiest of gods doing his work before your very eyes! You see him consume the Tinne Moon! When she is fully eaten you will see the blood moon of battle!"

Silence. Not even the dull clink of ale jar against wooden cup could be heard, so fixed on the firmament was every eye. Thousands of eyes on the ground reflecting the thousands of stars in the sky, and the light of the Tinne Moon was diminishing. Fear gripped Emrys' heart with its icy talons.

When I swallow the moon, blood will be spilled in my name.

And the Tinne Moon vanished, and was replaced by an orb of blood.

When an orb of blood hangs hangs in the sky, blood will be spilled in my name.

Astonished gasps fluttered through the silence like moths. Emrys' fear clutched his heart so tightly now that he felt pain in his chest. Was this really what the sun god wanted? Was Brython doomed to war after all?

"Belenos speaks to us!" Heddgwyn shrieked suddenly in the silence, startling Emrys so violently he nearly fell from his saddle. "Dawn will bring us a new era—an era that belongs to us! Under the blood moon of Claim-time we shall claim the lands once more! A united Brython where men are no longer the slaves of women! A united Brython under the reign of the old gods once more! Lift up your voices now, and let Belenos know you have seen his sign!"

The landscape erupted into cheers and shouts; men leapt from their positions near their fires and danced around and over them; Druids raised their voices in magical chants to draw the power of Belenos that was so evident in the sky onto their army. And in spite of the evidence hanging redly above, Emrys refused to believe death was the will of the sun god, he who gave life to all living things. He'd also spoken to Emrys of truth, and there was time, there must be time, yet to find it.

He kicked the sides of his steed, urging him straight into a gallop.

To the enemy lines he deserted.

* * *

The blood moon hung above him, fat and swollen and huge. From the field where the men of Belenos were camped, the line of spear-women looked strong and undeterred; up close they were much less fearsome. As he came nearer he realised how pitifully few their numbers were. And they stank of fear. All of them gibbered up at the blood moon, clearly believing Heddgwyn's portentous words, and now mortally feared their own deaths. There would be no welcome for them in Otherworld if the old gods were as displeased with them as the Arch Druid of Cantiaci proclaimed. If they stayed here at this place of battle, they would face their gods' displeasure sooner than they could have ever imagined for they would never defeat the army that Heddgwyn had raised. Emrys knew this as surely as he knew his own name.

"Retreat!" he screamed as he galloped past the unravelling

lines. "Retreat! Fall back to Old Dubras! They'll slaughter you where you stand! Retreat!"

They wouldn't be able to stop the battle just by retreating, and there were certainly no defences in Dubras, but there was an ancient hill-fort not far from where the Romans had started to build their more modern town which the Cantii had reclaimed after they left, renaming it Dubras. But at least the hill-fort would offer them some protection; the men of Belenos would be forced to charge uphill, for the Cantii spear-women would have the advantage of height. It surprised him that his mother hadn't already thought of that, but likely Heddgwyn would lead his army through the newer town, demolishing and killing, before realising the warrior-queen and her army were waiting for them at the hill fort. By then, all her people would be dead. And so, Emrys realised, she'd sent her warriors to defend the town's border instead. A wise move, if the army they faced didn't outnumber them ten to one.

"Sulis Warrior-Queen!" he cried out. It might be a pathetic army by comparison, but searching for one helmeted face amongst five thousand was going to be frustratingly difficult. "Sulis Warrior-Queen! Mother!" He lashed his steed along the team of charioteers who waited at the end of the lines of warriors. There would be another such team at the other end, he knew; and it would be just his luck that his mother was waiting at that one.

"Where is Sulis Warrior-Queen?" he screamed at the faces which now turned to him instead of the blood moon. "Have you seen my mother?"

Ah, it was no good! He would have to cross to the other team, but the spear-women were starting to panic now, both from the evil omen in the sky and the vast army of men which had suddenly become more blood-thirsty than before. Emrys heard them baying at the blood moon like monstrous wolves. Soon chaos would be amongst them, and if he hadn't found his mother by then...

He pulled hard to the left and start galloping back along the lines of warriors to where the second team of charioteers was waiting.

"Emrys!"

It took a while for him to realise that someone from behind had called his name. Hope swelled his heart, forcing fear to relinquish its grip just a little, and he halted his horse so he could turn around and face his mother.

A bronze helmet covered her face, but he recognised the charging stag on top of it. All of Sulis' spear-women boasted charging boars on their helmets to represent their fighting spirit; but his mother had wanted charging stags on the helmets of the royal warriors to represent their swiftness—they were all of them charioteers.

He urged his horse forward again so he could meet the oncoming chariot, and he saw how slight his mother was. Clad all in armour that looked like fish-scales, and though it must offer much more protection than the leather and bronze she had previously worn, it made her look tiny.

"Emrys, you traitor, what are you doing here?" The words stung, but he knew he deserved much more than words. She pulled off her helmet, and he cried out in grief. It wasn't his mother at all, here on the massacre-grounds of Belenos; it was his little sister.

"Airmed! You cannot be here! Heddgwyn's army will slaughter you all!"

"No thanks to you!" She halted her chariot with practised ease and drew her sword. "I should kill you right now for betraying us!"

"You should," he said. "But we haven't got time. I must find Mother!"

"So you can take the glory of slaughtering her and giving our lands to Heddgwyn the deceiver? I think not!"

Another chariot was racing towards them; a warrior had finally seen sense enough to come and protect the young warrior-princess.

"I don't want to kill her, I want to protect her. You can't defeat Heddgwyn's army. The Druids have collected information on the ancient Roman fighting tactics and no tribe has been able to overcome them."

Airmed spat on the ground. "The Romans were defeated by Boudica's army; their tactics were no match for hers."

Emrys roared in frustration. "Boudica had vast numbers and the will of the old gods on her side. You haven't! Heddgwyn has got over sixty thousand men to your five, and battle techniques you've never seen before. And he's called on the power of Belenos!" He flung out his hand and pointed up at the blood moon. Finally, fear flickered through the hatred on Airmed's face. "Please," he pleaded now. "Take me to our mother so I can try to save her and our people."

The charioteer reached them. She leaned across to Airmed and said: "Is all well, lady?"

"Airmed; please. I swear by all the ancestors that I only want to save our mother. Tell me where she is, then lead your army to Old Dubras. From there you'll be able to survive Heddgwyn's army." He didn't know if that were true, but it was more likely than facing it out here in the open.

"Lady?"

"Retreat to Old Dubras," Airmed said to the charioteer; "I'm taking my brother to the warrior-queen." She whipped her long reins and her horse bounded away.

Relief so strong flooded through Emrys that he thought he might cry; but he was a little confused by the direction in which his sister headed. They were moving away from the army altogether. He pushed his steed so he drew level with his sister in her chariot of wood and bronze. "Why are we going this way?" he said.

"Because Mother is waiting," said Airmed, "in Dubras."

* * *

He had expected her to be waiting in the palace perhaps, but Airmed led him through distressingly deserted streets. It seemed the news of the impending battle brought into their comfortable lives by the Arch Druid's army of men had forced the residents of Dubras into hiding. Mayhap some were already in old Dubras, and that thought cheered him. But it was a cold cheer and dull because no one would have had to run anywhere if only he had remained true to Rosmerta.

On they rode, through the town and out. The blood moon, while still lingering, was starting to disappear. He wanted to feel relieved, but Heddgwyn's assertion that it indicated a new era frightened him. What would happen when Belenos' omen finally passed?

The truth is my will.

And so strongly did Emrys believe that. But the truth wasn't in Heddgwyn and his men of Belenos and their slaughter of all women who refused to submit to them. It wasn't even in his mother and her plan to unite Brython under one queen, for still men would remain subordinate to them. The truth was equality. The truth was peace. And the sacred lands of Brython needed both if she were to survive.

Is this the truth, Belenos? he screamed inside his head even as his horse thundered forwards. Is this the truth you seek? Equality and peace—is this your will?

Yes. This is the truth. This is my will.

Emrys was so startled by the voice he nearly fell from his steed. And instantly he knew: that blood would be spilled in Belenos' name was never meant as a command. It was meant as warning. And Emrys had missed it! But he didn't have time to think about it now, for Airmed abruptly reined in her horse, swinging her chariot around to look across the distance they had ridden. Her brow was deeply furrowed and her mouth was nothing but a thin line.

"What is it?" Emrys said, slowing his horse until he was level with her.

"Listen."

He did as he was told, and heard a distant rumble, like that of a storm far on the horizon. But it wasn't a storm.

"The battle has started," he said, and his heart plummeted.

Airmed only nodded, then whipped her reins and took off.

They continued riding until he knew they would soon run out of land. From this part of their tribal lands the ground ended in a sheer drop to the ocean, and the cliffs in between were an astonishing white. He wondered madly if Airmed planned to run them both off to their deaths in hopelessness after seeing the extent of her traitor brother and traitor father's betrayal. Then it occurred to him that perhaps she only wanted to run *him* off the cliff as punishment. Then a more horrific thought struck him: perhaps Airmed was taking him to the place where their mother had ended her own life. Would his mother truly abandon her tribe upon learning of the advancing army? And likely it was Epona Warrior-Queen who had given her such news of inexorable doom; she had, after all, escaped the raging men of Belenos. The wild man had been all too conscious of that fact and had fretted to Heddgwyn about the repercussions. But the wild man had thought of resistance. Emrys could think of nothing but his mother's dead body, dashed against the white rocks in the furious sea after she threw herself to her death.

The Tinne Moon glowed white again. It was still half-consumed, but it was no longer a terrifying shade of blood. And it was under that light that Emrys was able to see the figure of a woman, standing tall and proud at the edge of the cliff, looking out at the night-black ocean, her fair hair streaming in the wind that blew in from the vast space before her.

Sulis Warrior-Queen was still alive.

* * *

She felt like a coward. All of her warriors, including her youngest daughter, by Boudica and all the old gods, were waiting for battle on the border of Dubras; but here she was, looking out across the ocean. She'd been here for so long now, looking, that she could barely see any more.

She hadn't wanted Airmed to go. In fact, she'd riled at her usually pacific daughter not to, but something primeval had woken in her young child's spirit and she would not be swayed. She claimed their warriors would need her medical attention, and certainly her chariot had been loaded with herbs and cloth and tinctures to heal wounds, but Airmed's anger at Heddgwyn had been nothing short of terrifying, and she knew full well that her daughter would draw blood if she had the chance.

At that moment, she had regretted sending Terrwyn, chief of her spear-women and most trusted battle-partner, away on the mission to deliver the letter. She smiled ruefully to herself, knowing no one was around to see it. She'd sent Terrwyn to accompany Rosmerta in the hunt for the sister-slayer, only to have her return on her own. Now she'd sent her away again where she couldn't protect her youngest daughter on the battle-field.

Because a battle there would be. She'd hoped, so hard that her chest hurt, that Terrwyn would be back in time after successfully delivering the message, bringing back with her the means to dissuade Heddgwyn's army of men. But she hadn't. And then the moon disappeared only to be reborn as a great orb of blood that hung evilly in the sky above her. She knew that moon portended vast and bloody death, and such death could only come from battle.

Yet still she remained here, staring out out at the ocean,

breathing in the salty air instead of the salty tang of battle-sweat; hearing the wind cry in her ears instead of the cries of her warriors; seeing undulating waves on their relentless march towards the shore instead of a field of her spear-women on their relentless march to their ruin.

And for that she was a coward.

"Mother!"

The word cut through her thoughts like a blade through flesh, and it was no less painful for knowing it was Airmed. Only the worst news would have drawn her away from the battlefield. Sulis Warrior-Queen turned slowly, composing her face in preparation for receiving the worst tidings.

Airmed had abandoned her chariot, not wanting to frighten her steed by bringing him to the cliff's edge, and was now running towards her. Her child's face showed all the emotion that Sulis had spent her queenship masking. Following closely behind her was someone she had never expected to see again.

"Emrys," she said when they reached her, pleased her voice remained neutral. She thought anger might flare, hatred, because of his treachery; but there was only a sharp sadness. "Do you bring me tidings, or death?"

To her astonishment, he dropped to her knees. "Forgive me, Mother."

Sulis looked to Airmed, and her youngest daughter nodded. Evidently sufficient words had passed between the siblings that Airmed felt comfortable enough to bring him to her. She turned back to her son.

"You are your father's son," she said, "and you have served him well. But in so doing you betrayed me, your sisters, and your lands. I do not believe I can forgive you for that."

He turned his face up towards her and she saw naked grief in his eyes. Pity stirred in her heart but she kept her face still.

"It was never my intention. I'm so sorry." He buried his face in his hands and wept. Airmed turned away and Sulis knew she wept too. Rosmerta may have hidden her feelings but Airmed was like a mirror; any emotion shown by another was reflected back from her. Such empathy was what made her a natural healer.

Emrys' hands found hers and she looked back at him. "I didn't come here to explain my actions," he said, "because it's too late for that. I came to tell you that Heddgwyn is mad. He won't stop until all the lands are united under the old gods. He believes that we must fight to draw them to us again because we've turned them too far away through our worship of Boudica. He said the blood moon was a sign from Belenos himself."

A jolt of fright shook her. Belenos was the most powerful of all the old gods. If any god could consume the moon and turn it to blood, it was he. They both looked up into the night sky. The Tinne Moon was white again, and almost whole. If she were just looking up to the heavens for the first time this night she could have believed it were waxing gibbous. But the image of the bloody orb was seared onto her spirit now. She would never forget it.

"Is that what you believe?" she said.

Emrys' mouth worked as he fought to reply. "I believe—I know—Belenos wants us to live in peace as equals...but I'm frightened."

Her hands were still clasped in his and she pulled him to his feet. She didn't truly understand all his words, but there was no time now for riddles. "As am I. But you didn't come here to tell me you're scared."

He shook his head. "The battle is already begun, but even though he's mad for blood, I think Heddgwyn will spare your life and the lives of your warriors if you agree to unite with him under the old gods."

"I never stopped believing in the old gods."

"So you'll agree to unite with him?" he smiled faintly, hopefully, through his tears.

"No," said Sulis Warrior-Queen. "These are my lands. Heddgwyn does not want to unite Brython under the old gods, he wants to unite Brython under himself. Before his army commenced their march across the lands, toppling each tribe, he ensured that the Druids of Cantiaci joined forces with the Druids of Trinovantes, and they cleared the pathway for the Picts to pour in and murder Sirona Warrior-Queen and all of her spear-women."

Emrys winced at this news, but he didn't look astonished.

"You knew of this?" she asked.

He looked at her beseechingly. "During our pilgrimage Heddgwyn told me he'd had dealings with the Picts. He said he'd travelled through their lands to learn their barbarian magic. I thought nothing of it at the time, just took it for another of his stories. I was so glad that he was finally speaking to me as a son instead of a disappointing pupil that I only felt admiration at his pursuit of knowledge. Now I wonder if it was truly pursuit of knowledge or gaining of allies. Druids have always been able to pass unhindered through all the tribes of Brython, even in the barbarian north."

"His treachery runs deep," Sulis said, sighing. She looked back out to sea.

"Deeper than you know; he's planned this war for more than a generation. All the Druids have."

"And he pulled you in with him because you are his eldest son."

Emrys nodded. "I was made a full Druid at Ynys Afallach, I learned all the secrets. I passed through the Cauldron of Rebirth and was resurrected. I spoke to Belenos."

She swung her head back to him. "What did he say?"

"He said blood would be spilled in his name, and that truth was his will. I wrongly believed that he wanted this war, but he was warning me against it. Mother, please listen; the truth is peace and equality. This is the will of the sun god."

"I fear we are beyond that now," she said with a sigh. "And I cannot deny my responsibility in this. I gave you to him to become a Druid."

"He commanded you to, as Arch Druid."

She waved her hand, dismissing the excuse. "And then I bent my ambitions on uniting the tribes under one warrior-queen. I fear I forced his hand in bringing war upon us."

"He would have made this war regardless of your ambitions. He's been organising this since before Airmed was born." He looked across at his sister who still kept her distance. "Since before Rosa was born, even."

The mention of her eldest daughter made her sigh again. "What have I left for my heir to come home to? A land of war and fear."

Emrys reached out and touched her arm. "Not necessarily. If we speak to Heddgwyn, just tell him you agree to his terms so he'll call off his army, Rosa can come back to a land of peace. Then we can change the laws so all people here are equal."

"No," she said, looking deep into his eyes. "I will never submit my lands to a traitor. And I would not use trickery to save my own skin." She looked back out to the ocean, and once more she smiled ruefully. "I won't have to. I've done what Sirona Warrior-Queen was too proud to do when the Picts attacked from the sea. I've called for aid."

Her son followed her gaze. He stepped back and his hand fell from hers. She knew he'd seen the multitude of ships on the horizon. "You sought aid from the Picts?" He faced her again, his face so pale in the growing moon. "But they've ever been enemies to these lands…"

"Those ships don't belong to the Picts. I sought out a tribe that I knew would be willing to fight for me for wealth. I would do anything to save my tribe."

"If not the Picts, then who?"

With tears in her eyes she looked at her son again. For better or worse, she knew her decision, born of a desperate attempt to save her tribe, would irrevocably change it. "The Angles," she said. "The Angles are come to Brython."

TOP HAT
BOOKS

Historical fiction that lives.

We publish fiction that captures the contrasts, the achievements, the optimism and the radicalism of ordinary and extraordinary times across the world.

We're open to all time periods and we strive to go beyond the narrow, foggy slums of Victorian London. Where are the tales of the people of fifteenth century Australasia? The stories of eighth century India? The voices from Africa, Arabia, cities and forests, deserts and towns? Our books thrill, excite, delight and inspire.

The genres will be broad but clear. Whether we're publishing romance, thrillers, crime, or something else entirely, the unifying themes are timescale and enthusiasm. These books will be a celebration of the chaotic power of the human spirit in difficult times. The reader, when they finish, will snap the book closed with a satisfied smile.